# H.R.H.

www.booksattransworld.co.uk

## *Also by Danielle Steel*

*Published outside the UK under the title PASSION'S PROMISE

# DANIELLE STEEL

## H.R.H.

BANTAM PRESS

LONDON · TORONTO · SYDNEY · AUCKLAND · JOHANNESBURG

TRANSWORLD PUBLISHERS
61–63 Uxbridge Road, London W5 5SA
a division of The Random House Group Ltd

RANDOM HOUSE AUSTRALIA (PTY) LTD
20 Alfred Street, Milsons Point, Sydney,
New South Wales 2061, Australia

RANDOM HOUSE NEW ZEALAND LTD
18 Poland Road, Glenfield, Auckland 10, New Zealand

RANDOM HOUSE SOUTH AFRICA (PTY) LTD
Isle of Houghton, Corner of Boundary Road and Carse O'Gowrie,
Houghton 2198, South Africa

Published 2006 by Bantam Press
a division of Transworld Publishers

A catalogue record for this book is available from the British Library.
ISBN 9780593053317 (cased) (from Jan 07)
ISBN 0593053311 (cased)
ISBN 9780593053393 (tpb) (from Jan 07)
ISBN 0593053397 (tpb)

Typeset in Charter

Printed and bound in Great Britain
by Mackays of Chatham Ltd, Chatham, Kent

1 3 5 7 9 10 8 6 4 2

Papers used by Transworld Publishers are natural, recyclable products
made from wood grown in sustainable forests. The manufacturing processes
conform to the environmental regulations of the country of origin.

To my beloved children,
Beatrix, Trevor, Todd, Nick, Samantha,
Victoria, Vanessa, Maxx, Zara,
with all my thanks and love for the
wonderful people you are,
with deep gratitude for how good you are
to me, how kind, how loving, how generous
with your hearts and time.
May your lives unfold with ease and grace,
May you find joy, serenity, and love,
and may all the opportunities you dream of be yours.
I wish you happy endings, happily ever afters,
friends, companions, and spouses who treasure you and
treat you with tenderness, love, and respect,
and children as exceptionally wonderful as you are.
If you have children like mine, you will indeed be blessed.

With all my love,
Mom/d.s.

# H.R.H.

# Chapter 1

Christianna stood at her bedroom window, looking down at the hillside in the pouring rain. She was watching a large white dog, soaking wet with matted hair, digging excitedly in the mud. Every now and then he would look up at her and wag his tail, and then return to digging again. He was the Great Pyrenees her father had given her eight years before. His name was Charles, and in many ways he was her best friend. She laughed as she watched him chase a rabbit that eluded him and promptly disappeared. Charles barked frantically and then splashed happily through the mud again, looking for something else to pursue. He was having a great time, as Christianna was, watching him. It was the last of summer and the weather was still warm. She had returned to Vaduz in June, after four years of college in Berkeley. Coming home had been something of a shock, and so far the best thing about her homecoming was Charles. Other than her cousins in England and Germany, and acquaintances throughout Europe, her only friend was Charles. She led a sheltered and isolated life, and always had. It seemed unlikely she would see her Berkeley friends again.

As she watched the dog disappear toward the stables, Christianna hurried out of her room, intent on going outside and following him. She grabbed her riding slicker and a pair of rubber boots she used to muck out her horse's stall, and ran down the back stairs. She was grateful that no one noticed her, and a moment later she was outside, sliding through the mud and running after the big white dog. She called his name, and in an instant he bounded up to her, nearly knocking her down. He wagged his tail, splashing water everywhere, put a muddy paw on her, and when she bent to stroke him, he reached up and licked her face, and then ran away again as she laughed. Together, they ran side by side along the bridle path. It was too wet today to ride.

When the dog strayed from the path, she called his name, he hesitated only for an instant, and then came back to her each time. He was normally well behaved, but the rain excited him, as he ran and barked. Christianna was having as much fun as the dog. After nearly an hour, slightly out of breath, she stopped, the dog panting heavily beside her. She took a shortcut then, and half an hour later, they were once again back where they began. It had been a wonderful outing for both mistress and dog, and each looked as disreputable and disheveled as the other. Christianna's long, almost white-blond hair was matted to her head, her face was wet, and even her eyelashes were stuck together. She never wore makeup, unless she had to go out or was likely to be photographed, and she was wearing the jeans she had brought back from Berkeley. They were a souvenir of her lost life. She had loved every moment of her four years at UC Berkeley. She had fought hard to be allowed to go. Her brother had gone to Oxford, and her father had suggested the Sorbonne for her. Christianna had been adamant about going to college in the States, and her father had finally relented, though reluctantly. Going that far from home spelled freedom to her, and she had reveled in each day she was there, and had hated to come home when she graduated in June. She had made friends she missed sorely now, they were part of another life she missed so much. She had come home to face her responsibilities, and do what was expected of her. To Christianna, it felt like a heavy burden, lightened only by moments such as these, running through the woods with her dog. The rest of the time since coming home, she had felt as though she were in prison, serving a life sentence. There was no one she could have said that to, and doing so would have made her sound ungrateful for all she had. Her father was extremely kind to her. He had sensed, more than seen, her sadness since returning from the States. But there was nothing he could do about it. Christianna knew as well as he did that her childhood, and the freedom she had enjoyed in California, had come to an end.

Charles looked up at his mistress questioningly as they reached the end of the bridle path, as though asking her if they really had to go back.

"I know," Christianna said softly, patting him, "I don't want to either." The rain felt gentle on her face, and she didn't mind getting soaked, or her long blond mane getting wet, any more than the dog did. The slicker protected her, and her boots were caked with mud. She laughed as she looked at him, thinking it was hard to believe that this muddy brown dog was really white.

She needed the exercise, as did the dog. He wagged his tail as he looked at her, and then with a slightly more decorous step, they walked home. She was hoping to slip in the back door, but getting Charles into the house, in his disreputable condition, would be a greater challenge. He was too filthy to take upstairs, and she knew she would have to take him in through the kitchen. He was in desperate need of a bath after their muddy walk.

She opened the kitchen door quietly, hoping to escape attention for as long as possible, but as soon as she opened it, the enormous muddy dog bounded past her, dashed into the middle of the room, and barked with excitement. So much for a quiet entrance, Christianna smiled ruefully, and glanced apologetically at the familiar faces around her. The people who worked in her father's kitchen were always kind to her, and sometimes she wished that she could still sit among them, enjoying their company and the friendly atmosphere, as she had as a child. But those days were over for her as well. They no longer treated her as they had when she and her brother Friedrich were children. Friedrich was ten years older than she, and was traveling in Asia for the next six months. Christianna had turned twenty-three that summer.

Charles was still barking and, shaking the water off enthusiastically, had splattered nearly everyone around him with mud, as Christianna tried vainly to subdue him.

"I'm so sorry," she said as Tilda, the cook, wiped her face with her apron, shook her head, and smiled good-naturedly at the young woman she had known since birth. She signaled quickly to a young man, who rushed to lead the dog away. "I'm afraid he got awfully dirty," Christianna said with a smile to the young man, wishing she could bathe the dog herself. She liked doing it, but she knew it was unlikely they would let her. Charles yelped unhappily as he was led away. "I don't mind bathing him . . . ," Christianna said, but the dog was already gone.

"Of course not, ma'am," Tilda said, frowning at her, and then used a clean towel to wipe Christianna's face as well. If Christianna had still been a child, she would have scolded her and told her that she looked worse than the dog. "Would you like some lunch?" Christianna hadn't even thought of it, and shook her head. "Your father is still in the dining room. He just finished his soup. I could send something up for you." Christianna hesitated, and then nodded.

She hadn't seen him all day, and she enjoyed the quiet moments they shared when he wasn't working, and had a few minutes to himself, which was rare. He was usually surrounded by assorted members of his staff, and was in a rush to get to meetings. It was a treat for him to enjoy a meal alone, especially with her. She cherished the time they spent together. The only reason she had willingly come home from Berkeley was for him. There had been no other choice, although she would have loved to go on to graduate school just so she could stay in the States. She didn't dare ask. She knew the answer would have been no. Her father wanted her at home. She knew she had to be doubly responsible because her brother wasn't at all. If Friedrich had been willing to shoulder his responsibilities, it would have lightened the burden on her. But there was no hope of that.

She left her slicker hanging on a peg outside the kitchen, and took off her boots. They were noticeably smaller than any other pair there. She had tiny feet, and was so small she was almost a miniature. In flat shoes, her brother often teased her that she looked like a little girl, particularly with her long blond hair, which was still hanging wet down her back. She had small delicate hands, a perfect figure nothing like a child's, although she was very slight and always just a little bit too thin, and a face like a cameo. People said she looked like her mother, and somewhat like her father, who was as fair as she was, although both he and her brother were very tall, well over six feet. Christianna's mother had been as small as she was and had died when Christianna was five, and Friedrich was fifteen. Their father had never remarried. Christianna was the lady of the house, and was often her father's hostess now at important dinners or events. It was one of the responsibilities expected of her, and although she didn't enjoy it, it was a duty she performed lovingly for him. She and her father had always been extremely close. He had always been sensitive to the fact that it had been hard for her growing up without a mother. And in spite of his many duties, he had made every effort to be both father and mother to her, not always an easy task.

Christianna bounded up the back stairs in jeans, sweater, and stocking feet. She arrived in the pantry slightly breathless, nodded at the people there, and slipped quietly into the dining room. Her father was sitting at the dining table alone, poring over a stack of papers, wearing his glasses, with a serious look on his face. He didn't hear Christianna come in. He glanced up and smiled as she slipped silently into the chair beside him. He was obviously pleased to see his daughter, he always was.

"What have you been up to, Cricky?" He had called her that since she was a little girl. He gently patted her head as she leaned over to kiss him, and he noticed her wet hair. "You've been out in the rain. Were you riding in this weather?" He worried about her, more than he did about Freddy. Christianna had always been so small and seemed so fragile to him. Ever since losing his wife to cancer eighteen years before, he had treated their daughter like the priceless gift she had been to them when she was born. She looked so much like her mother. His late wife had been exactly the age Christianna was now when he married her. She was French, half Orléans and half Bourbon, the two royal families of France, who had been the ruling monarchy before the French Revolution. Christianna was descended from royal families on all sides. Her father's ancestors were mostly German, with cousins in England. Her father's native tongue was German, though he and Christianna's mother had always spoken French, as she did with her children. Once she was gone, in her memory, Christianna's father had continued speaking to his children in French. It was still the language in which Christianna was most comfortable, and which she preferred, although she spoke German, Italian, Spanish, and English as well. Her English had improved immeasurably during her years in college in California, and she was totally fluent now.

"You shouldn't go out riding in the rain," he scolded her gently. "You'll catch a cold, or worse." He always feared her getting ill, excessively so, he acknowledged, since the death of his wife.

"I wasn't riding," she explained. "I just went for a run with the dog." As she said it, a footman set her soup down in front of her, in delicate two-hundred-year-old gold-rimmed Limoges. The set had been her French grandmother's, and Christianna knew there were many equally handsome services of china from her father's ancestors as well. "Are you very busy today, Papa?" Christianna asked quietly, as he nodded, and pushed his papers away with a sigh.

"No more than usual. So many problems in the world, so many things that can't be solved. Human problems are so complicated these days. Nothing is simple anymore." Her father was well known for his humanitarian concerns. It was one of the many things she admired about him. He was a man worthy of respect, and was regarded with great affection by all who knew him. He was a man of compassion, integrity, and courage, and had set a powerful example for her and her brother to follow. Christianna learned from his example and listened to what he said. Freddy was far more self-indulgent, and paid no attention to his father's edicts, wisdom, or requests. Freddy's indifference to what was expected of him made her feel as though she had to attend to duties and uphold traditions for them both. She knew how disappointed her father was in his son, and she felt she had to make it up to him somehow. And in fact, Christianna was much more like her father, and was always interested in his projects, particularly those involving indigent people in underdeveloped countries. She had done volunteer work several times, in poor areas in Europe, and had never been happier than when she did.

He explained his latest endeavors to her as she listened to him with interest and commented from time to time. Her ideas on the subject were intelligent and well thought out, he had always had a deep respect for her mind. He only wished his son had her brains and drive. And he knew only too well that she felt she had been wasting her time ever since she got home. He had recently suggested that she consider studying law or political science in Paris. It was a way of keeping her busy and challenging her mind, and Paris was close enough to home. She had many relatives there, on her mother's side, could stay with them, and come home to see him often. Although she would have liked it, even at her age, there wasn't even the remotest possibility of her staying in an apartment on her own. She was still mulling over his plan, but she was more interested in doing something useful that would make a difference to other people, than in going back to school. At his father's insistence, Freddy had graduated from Oxford, and had a master's degree in business from Harvard, which was of no use to him, given the life he led. Her father would have allowed Christianna to study something more esoteric, if she chose to, though she was an excellent student and a very serious girl, which was why he thought law or political science would suit her well.

His assistant entered the dining room apologetically as they finished coffee, and smiled at Christianna. He was almost like an uncle to her, and had worked for her father during her entire life. Most of the people around them had worked for him for years.

"I'm sorry to interrupt, Your Highness," the older man said cautiously. "You have an appointment with the finance minister in twenty minutes, and we have some new reports on Swiss currency that I thought you might want to read before you speak with him. And our ambassador to the United Nations will be here to see you at three-thirty." Christianna knew her father would be busy until dinner, and more than likely his presence would be required at either a state or official event. Sometimes she went with him, if he asked her to. Otherwise she stayed home, or appeared briefly at similar events herself. In Vaduz, there were no casual evenings for her with friends, as there had been in Berkeley. Now there was only duty, responsibility, and work.

"Thank you, Wilhelm. I'll be downstairs in a few minutes," her father said quietly.

His assistant bowed discreetly to both of them, and silently left the room, as Christianna looked at him and sighed, her chin in her hands. She looked younger than ever, and somewhat troubled, as her father looked at her and smiled. She was so pretty, and a very good girl. He knew her official duties had weighed on her since she got back, just as he had feared they would. The responsibilities and burden they carried were not easy for a girl of twenty-three. The inevitable restrictions she had to live with were bound to chafe, just as they had him at her age. They would weigh heavily on Freddy too when he got back in the spring, although Freddy was far more artful about dodging his responsibilities than either his father or his sister. Fun was Freddy's only job now, a full-time career for him. Since leaving Harvard, he had indulged himself constantly. It was all he did, and he had no desire to grow up or change.

"Don't you get tired of what you do, Papa? It exhausts me just watching all you squeeze into every day." His hours were seemingly endless, though he never complained. His sense of obligation was part of who he was.

"I enjoy it," he said honestly, "but I didn't at your age." He was always truthful with her. "I hated it at first. I think I told my father I felt like I was in prison, and he was horrified. One grows into it in time. You will too, my dear." There was no alternate course for either of them, except the one that had been set for them at their birth and for centuries before. Like her father, Christianna accepted it as her lot in life.

Christianna's father, Prince Hans Josef, was the reigning Prince of Liechtenstein, a principality of 160 square kilometers, with thirty-three thousand inhabitants, bordered by Austria on one side and Switzerland on the other. It was entirely independent and had been neutral since the Second World War. Its neutrality set the stage for the prince's humanitarian interest in oppressed and suffering people around the world. Of all the things her father did, his humanitarian pursuits were what interested Christianna most. World politics were of less interest to her, and more her father's passion, out of necessity. Freddy had no interest in either, although he was the crown prince of the principality, and would step into his father's shoes as ruler one day. Although Christianna would have been third in line to the throne in other European countries, in Liechtenstein women were not allowed to reign, so even if her brother did not take his place as reigning prince, Christianna would never rule her country, and had no desire to do so, although her father liked to say proudly that she would have been capable of it, more so than her brother. Christianna did not envy her brother the role he would inherit from their father one day. She had enough trouble accepting her own. She knew that from the day she returned from college in California her life would be here now forever, carrying on her duties, and doing what was expected of her. There was no question and no choice. She was like a fine Thoroughbred racehorse with only a single course to run, that of supporting her father, in the small unimportant ways she could. More often than not, the work she did seemed utterly meaningless to her. She felt as though she was wasting her life in Vaduz.

"I hate what I do sometimes," she said honestly, but she wasn't telling her father anything he didn't already know. He didn't have much time to reassure her, since he had the meeting with the finance minister in a few minutes, but the anguished look in his daughter's eyes touched him to the core. "I feel so useless here, Papa. As you said, with all the troubles in the world, why am I here, visiting orphanages and opening hospitals, when I could be somewhere else, doing something important?" She sounded plaintive and sad, as he gently touched her hand.

"What you're doing is important. You're helping me. I don't have time to do what you do for me. It means a great deal to our people to see you in their midst. It's exactly what your mother would have done, if she were still alive."

"She did it by choice," Christianna argued with him. "She knew when she married you that that would be her life. She wanted to do it. I always feel like I'm just passing time." They both knew that if she followed her father's wishes, eventually she would marry someone of similarly high birth, and if he was a reigning prince like her father, or a crown prince like her brother, this was preparing her for that life. There was always the remote possibility that she would marry someone of lesser rank, but as a Royal Highness on one side, and a Serene one on the other, it was less than likely that she would marry anyone not of royal birth. Her father would never have allowed it. The Bourbons and Orléans were all Royal Highnesses on her mother's side. Her father's mother had been a Royal Highness as well. The reigning prince of Liechtenstein was a Serene Highness. By birth, Christianna was both, but her official title was "Serene." They were related to the Windsors in England, the queen of England was their second cousin, Prince Hans Josef's family were Habsburgs, Hohenlohe, and Thurn und Taxis. The principality itself was closely allied to Austria and Switzerland, although there were no ruling families there. But every single one of Prince Hans Josef's and Christianna's and Freddy's relatives, and their ancestors before them, were of royal birth. Her father had told her since she was a little girl, that when she married, she was to stay within the confines of her world. It didn't oc-cur to her to do otherwise.

The only time in Christianna's life when she had not been affected by their royal status on a daily basis was when she was away at col-lege in California, where she lived in an apartment in Berkeley with a male and female bodyguard. She only confessed the truth to her two closest friends, who kept her secret religiously, as did the administra-tion of the university, who were aware of it as well. Most of the people she had known there had had no idea who she was, and she loved it that way. She had blossomed in the rare anonymity, freed from the re-strictions and obligations she had found so oppressive since her youth. In California, she was "almost" just another college girl. Al-most. With two bodyguards, and a father who was a reigning prince. She was always vague when people asked her what kind of work her father did. Eventually, she learned to say he was in human rights, or public relations, sometimes politics, which were all essentially cor-rect. She never used her own title while there. Few people she met seemed to know where Liechtenstein was anyway, or that it had its own language. She never told people that her family home was a royal palace in Vaduz, which had been built in the fourteenth century, and rebuilt in the sixteenth. Christianna had loved the independence and anonymity of her college years. Now everything had changed. In

Vaduz, she was the Serene Highness again, and had to endure all that went with it. To her, being a princess felt like a curse.

"Would you like to join me at the meeting with our ambassador to the UN today?" her father offered, to try and cheer her up. She sighed and shook her head, as he stood up from the dining table, and she followed suit.

"I can't. I have to cut a ribbon at a hospital. I have no idea why we have so many hospitals." She smiled ruefully. "I feel as though I cut one of those ribbons every day." It was an exaggeration of course, but sometimes she felt that way.

"I'm sure it means a lot to them to have you there," he said, and she knew it did. She just wished that there was something more useful for her to do, working with people, helping them, making their lives better in a concrete way, rather than wearing a pretty hat, a Chanel suit, and her late mother's jewels, or others from the official state vaults. Her mother's crown from her father's coronation was still there. Her father always said that Christianna would wear it on her wedding day. And she herself had been startled to discover how agonizingly heavy it was, when she tried it on, just like the responsibilities that went with it. "Would you like to join me at a dinner for the ambassador tonight?" Prince Hans Josef offered as he gathered up his papers. He didn't want to rush her, in her obvious misery, but he was late by then.

"Do you need me there?" Christianna asked politely, always respectful of him. She would have gone without complaint if he said yes.

"Not really. Only if you'd enjoy it. He's an interesting man."

"I'm sure he is, Papa, but if you don't need me, I'd rather stay in jeans and go upstairs to read."

"Or play on your computer," he teased. She loved e-mailing her friends in the States, and still communicated with them often, although she knew that, inevitably, eventually the friendships would fade. Her life was just too different from theirs. She was a thoroughly modern princess, and a spirited young woman, and sometimes she felt the weight of who she was and what was expected of her like a ball and chain. She knew Freddy did as well. He had been something of a playboy for the past fifteen years, often in the tabloids, allied with actresses and models all over Europe, and the occasional young royal. It was why he was currently in Asia, to get away from being constantly in the public eye and in the press. His father had encouraged him to take a break for a while. The time was approaching for him to settle down. The prince expected less of his daughter, since she was not going to inherit the throne. But he also knew how bored she was, which was why he wanted her to go to the Sorbonne in Paris. Even he knew that she needed more to do than cutting ribbons to open hospitals. Liechtenstein was a small country, and its capital, Vaduz, a tiny town. He had recently suggested that she go to London to visit her cousins and friends. Now that she had finished school and was not yet married, there was too little to occupy her time.

"I'll see you before dinner," her father said as he kissed the top of her head. Her hair was still damp, and she looked up at him with her enormous blue eyes. The sadness in them tore at his heart.

"Papa, I want something else to do. Why can't I go away like Freddy?" She sounded plaintive, like any girl her age who wanted a big concession from her father, or permission to do something of which he was unlikely to approve.

"Because I want you here with me. I would miss you far too much, if you went away for six months." There was suddenly a spark of mischief in her father's eyes. He had been at his best when her mother was alive, and had led a life of responsibility and family ever since.

There was no woman in his life, and hadn't been since Christianna's mother died, though many had tried. He had devoted himself entirely to his family and his work. His was truly a life of sacrifice, infinitely more than hers. But she also knew that he expected as much from her. "In your brother's case"—he smiled at his daughter—"it's a great relief at times to have him away. You know how outrageous he is." Christianna laughed out loud. Freddy had a way of getting into mischief, and then being caught by the press. Their press attaché had had a full-time job covering for him since Freddy's Oxford days. At thirty-three, he had been a hot item in the press for the past fifteen years. Christianna only appeared in the press at state occasions with her father, or when opening hospitals or libraries.

There had been only one photograph of her in *People* magazine during the entire time she'd been in college, taken while she attended a football game with one of her royal British cousins, a handful of photographs in *Harper's Bazaar* and *Vogue,* and a lovely one of her in *Town and Country,* in a ballgown, in an article about young royals. Christianna kept a low profile, which pleased her father. Freddy was entirely another story, but he was a boy, as Prince Hans Josef always pointed out. But he had warned him that when he returned from Asia, there were to be no more supermodel capers or starlet scandals, and if he continued to draw attention to himself, his father would cut off his allowance. Freddy had gotten the point, and had promised to behave when he came home. He was in no hurry to return.

"I'll see you tonight, my dear," Prince Hans Josef said as he gave her a warm hug, and then left the dining room as the footmen he walked past all bowed low.

Christianna went back to her own apartment on the third floor of the royal palace. She had a large beautiful bedroom, a dressing room, a handsome sitting room, and an office. Her secretary was waiting for her, and Charles was lying on the floor. He had been groomed and coiffed and bathed, and didn't look anything like the dog she had run in the woods with that morning. He looked gravely subdued and somewhat depressed over whatever they had done to clean him up. He hated being bathed. Christianna smiled as she glanced over at him, feeling more in common with the dog than with anyone else in the palace, or maybe the entire country. She disliked being coiffed and groomed and tended to as much as the dog did. She had been much happier running with him that morning, getting soaked and covered with mud. She patted him and sat down on the other side of the desk, as her secretary looked up at her and smiled, and handed Christianna her dreaded schedule. Sylvie de Maréchale was a Swiss woman from Geneva, in her late forties, whose children had grown up and gone. Two were living in the States, one in London, one in Paris, and for the past six years she had handled everything for Christianna. She was enjoying her job much more now that the princess was home. She had a warm, motherly style, and she was someone Christianna could at least talk to, and if necessary, complain to, about the boredom of her life.

"You're opening a children's hospital today at three, Your Highness, and you're stopping at a home for the elderly at four. That should be quite a short stop, and you don't need to make a speech at either place. Just a few words of admiration and thanks. The children at the hospital will give you a bouquet." She had a list of names of the people who would be escorting her, and the names of the three children who had been chosen to present the bouquet. She was impeccably organized, and always gave Christianna all the essential details. When necessary, she traveled with her. At home, she helped her organize small dinners of important people her father asked her to entertain, or larger ones for heads of state. She had run an impeccable home for

years, and was teaching Christianna to run hers, with all the details
and attention to minutiae that made each event go well. Her direc-
tions were seamless, her taste exquisite, and her kindness to her
young employer without limit. She was the perfect assistant to a
young princess, and she had a nice sense of humor that brightened
Christianna's spirits when her duties weighed heavily on her. "You're
opening a library tomorrow," she said gently, knowing how tired
Christianna was of doing things like that, after being home for only
three months. Christianna's return to Vaduz still felt like a prison sentence to her. "You'll have to make a speech tomorrow," she warned
her, "but you're off the hook today." Christianna was looking pensive,
thinking of her conversation with her father. She didn't know where
yet, but she knew she wanted to go away. Maybe after Freddy got
back, so her father wouldn't feel so alone. She knew he had hated it
when she was gone. He loved and enjoyed his children, and royal or
not, he enjoyed his family more than all else, just as he had loved his
marriage, and still missed his wife. "Do you want me to write your
speech for tomorrow?" Sylvie offered. She had done it before and was
good at it. But Christianna shook her head.

"I'll do it myself. I can write it tonight." It reminded her of her
homework in her college days. She found she even missed that now,
and it was something to do.

"I'll leave the details about the new library on a sheet on your
desk," Sylvie said, then looked at her watch, startled by the hour.
"You'd better dress. You have to leave in half an hour. Is there anything you'd like me to do for you? Or get out?" Christianna shook her
head. She knew Sylvie was offering to get jewelry out of the vault for
her, but all Christianna ever wore were her mother's pearls, and the
earrings that went with them, all of which had been a gift to her
mother from Prince Hans Josef. Wearing them meant a lot to her. And

it always pleased her father to see Christianna in her mother's jewels. With a nod at Sylvie, she went to change, and Charles got up and followed her out of the room.

Half an hour later Christianna was back in the office, looking every inch a princess in a pale blue Chanel suit with a white flower and black bow at the neck. She was carrying a small black alligator handbag that her father had bought for her in Paris, with matching black alligator shoes, her mother's pearls and earrings, and a pair of white kid gloves tucked into the pocket of her suit.

She appeared elegant and youthful, with her long blond hair pulled neatly back in a long smooth ponytail. She was impeccable as she got out of the Mercedes sedan in front of the hospital and was warm and gracious as she greeted the head of the hospital and its administrators. She spoke a few words of thanks, acknowledging the work they would do there. She stopped to chat and shake hands with all the people pouring down the front steps to see her. They oohed and aahed at how pretty she was, how young and fresh she looked, how elegant her suit was, how unassuming her manner, and how unpretentious she was in every way. As she always did when she made public appearances, representing her father and the palace, Christianna went to considerable effort to make a good impression on all who met her, and as she drove away, everyone standing outside waved, and so did she, wearing the impeccable white kid gloves. Her visit to the hospital had been a complete success for all of them.

She laid her head back against the seat for a minute as they drove to the home for the elderly, thinking about the faces of the children she had just kissed. She had kissed hundreds of others like them, since she had assumed her duties in June. It was hard to believe, and even harder to accept, that for the rest of her life this was all that she would do—cut ribbons, open hospitals and libraries and senior centers, kiss children and old ladies, shake hands with dozens of people, then drive away and wave. She didn't mean to be ungrateful for her blessings, or disrespectful to her father, but she hated every moment of it.

She knew full well how lucky she was in so many ways. But thinking about it, and how futile her life was becoming and would continue to become over the years, depressed her profoundly. Her eyes were still closed as they pulled up in front of the senior center, and as the bodyguard who went everywhere with her opened the door for her, he saw two tears roll slowly down her cheeks. With a smile at him and the people waiting for her with looks of excitement and anticipation, with a white-gloved hand, she brushed the tears away.

# Chapter 2

Prince Hans Josef stopped by Christianna's apartment that night, after his dinner for the ambassador to the UN. It had been an elegant party for forty people in the palace dining room and although he would have liked her there, Christianna wasn't missed. He had invited an old friend to help him host the event. They had gone to school together years before, she was a widow, and he thought of her as a sister. She was Freddy's godmother and had been a family friend for years. She was an Austrian baroness and had helped him to keep the conversation lively, not always an easy task at official events.

Once outside Christianna's apartment, her father found the door open. He could see her on the living room floor, with her arms around her dog, playing the music she had brought back from America full blast. The dog was sound asleep in spite of the noise. The prince smiled when he saw them, and walked quietly into the room. Christianna looked up and smiled when she noticed him observing her.

"How was dinner?" Christianna asked. He looked distinguished and tall in his dinner jacket. She had always been so proud of the fact that he was such a good-looking man. He was truly the epitome of the handsome prince, and beyond that, a profoundly wise and kind man, who loved her more than life itself.

"Not nearly as interesting as it would have been if you had been there, my darling. I'm afraid you would have found it very dull." They were in full agreement on that. She was happy not to have gone. Her two official functions that afternoon, at the hospital and the senior center, had been enough. "What are you doing tomorrow?"

"Opening a library, and then I'm reading books to blind children, at an orphanage."

"That's a nice thing for you to do." She stared up at him for a long moment, and didn't comment. They both knew that she was agonizingly bored and aching for something more important to do. She could see her life stretching ahead of her now, like an endless, bleak, and nearly intolerable road. Neither of them had anticipated how difficult her adjustment would be once she got home. It made him regret now that he had allowed her to go to California to college. Perhaps Freddy had been right. He had always said that he thought it was a bad idea. As outrageous as he was in his own life, Freddy had always been far more protective of her. And he was well aware of what a taste of a freer life could do to her. In the end, it had. She no longer felt suited to the life she was born to lead. She was like a beautiful racehorse trapped in a stall that was too small for her. Looking down at her, her father was acutely aware that she looked like any other young girl, playing her music too loud on her stereo. But they both knew all too well that she was no ordinary young girl. All Hans Josef could hope for her was that she would soon forget the inebriating taste of freedom she had become addicted to in the States. It was his only hope. If not, she would be miserable for a long time. Or even the rest of her life, which would be an awful fate for her.

"Would you like to go to the ballet with me in Vienna on Friday night?" her father asked solemnly, desperately trying to think of things she might enjoy doing, to enliven her solitary life. Liechtenstein had strong ties with both Switzerland and Austria, and the prince frequently went to Vienna for the opera or ballet. Until just before the Second World War, the reigning princes of Liechtenstein had lived in Vienna. When the Nazis had annexed Austria in 1938, Hans Josef's father had moved his family and the court back to Liechtenstein's capital to watch over the country's "Honor, Courage, and Welfare," according to the princely "house laws." They had been there ever since. Christianna's father was the embodiment of the family code of ethics, and the sacred oath he had taken when he became reigning prince.

"That might be fun," Christianna said, smiling up at him. She knew how hard he was trying to make her feel comfortable again. However much he loved her, his hands were tied. There was only so much he could do to ease her pain. To others, their lives may have looked like a fairy tale, but Christianna was in fact the proverbial bird in the gilded cage. And her father had begun to feel like her jailer. He had no easy solution at hand. It was going to be more fun for her when her brother got home from his extended stay in Japan, but having Freddy back always brought problems of a different kind. Life at the palace was a great deal quieter with the young prince away. They hadn't had a scandal to dissipate since he left, much to his father's relief.

Hans Josef then came up with another idea. "Why don't you go to visit your cousin Victoria in London next week?" It might do her good to get away. The young marchioness of Ambester was a first cousin of the queen, and exactly Christianna's age. She was full of mischief and fun, and she had just gotten engaged to a Danish prince. Christianna's face lit up as soon as he suggested the idea.

"That would be a lot of fun, Papa. You wouldn't mind?"

"Not at all." He beamed at her. It pleased him to think that she might have some fun. There was nothing very exciting for her to do in Liechtenstein. "I'll have my secretary arrange it in the morning." Christianna quickly got up and put her arms around his neck, as Charles groaned, rolled over, and wagged his tail. "Stay with her for as long as you like." He didn't worry about her getting out of control in London, as he did about his son. Christianna was a very well-behaved young woman, who was always cognizant of her responsibilities to her position and to him. She had had fun in Berkeley, for four years, but had never gotten even remotely out of hand, at least as far as her father knew. The two devoted bodyguards who had gone to Berkeley with her had managed to keep a lid on things once or twice. Nothing serious, but like any girl her age, even a royal one, there had been a few brief romances, and a night or two of too much fun with more than a little wine involved, but she had come to no harm, and never to the attention of the press.

Her father kissed her goodnight, and she lay on the floor for a while longer, listening to the music, and then she got up and checked her e-mail before she went to bed. She had e-mails from her two college friends, checking in and asking her how her "princess life was going." They loved to tease her about it. They had looked up Liechtenstein on the Internet, and had been stunned when they saw the palace in which she lived. It was beyond anything they could have imagined. She had promised to visit them both at some point, but for the moment had no plans to do so. Besides, she knew it would be different now. Their days of innocence and easy fun were over. Or at least hers were. One of her friends was already working in Los Angeles, and the other was traveling with friends for the summer. She had no other choice than to make peace with her own life, and make the best of it. She liked her father's suggestion of going to see her cousin in London.

On Friday morning she drove to Vienna with her father. They had to travel across the Alps, and it was a six-hour trip to the family's previous seat, Palace Liechtenstein in Vienna. It was spectacularly beautiful, and unlike the palace at Vaduz, which was their main residence, parts of the palace in Vienna were open to the public. The part that she and her father occupied was heavily guarded and somewhat secluded. Her apartment there was far more ornate than her rooms in Vaduz, which were beautiful but somewhat more human scale. At Palace Liechtenstein, she had an enormous bedroom with a huge canopied bed, mirrors and gilt everywhere, and on the floor a priceless Aubusson carpet. It looked like a museum, and a huge chandelier hung overhead, still lit by candles.

The familiar servants she had known all her life were waiting for her there. An ancient ladies' maid who had served her mother twenty years before helped her dress, while a younger woman drew her bath and brought her something to eat. She went to meet her father in his rooms at exactly eight o'clock wearing a black Chanel cocktail dress she had bought in Paris the year before. She was wearing small diamond earrings, her mother's pearls, and the ring she always wore, a *chevalière* with the family crest on it, on the little finger of her right hand. It was the only symbol she wore as a sign of her royal birth, and unless one was familiar with the crest, it was no more impressive than any other signet ring. The crest was carved into a simple oval of yellow gold. She had no need for symbols indicating who she was, everyone in Liechtenstein and Austria knew, and recognized her when they saw her, as they did throughout Europe. She was a remarkably pretty girl, and had appeared with her father just often enough to have caught the attention of the press for the past several years. Her brief disappearance to the States to study had been perceived only as a hiatus. Whenever she returned to Europe she was photographed, no matter how diligently she avoided it. And ever since she had come back for good, the press had been watching out for her. She was far more beautiful than most of the other princesses in Europe, and more appealing because she was so shy, reticent, and demure. It only excited journalists more because that was the case.

"You look beautiful tonight, Cricky," her father said affectionately as she walked into his room, and helped him with his cufflinks. His valet was standing by to assist, but Christianna liked taking care of him, and he preferred it. It reminded him of the days when his wife was alive, and he smiled as he looked at his daughter. He and her brother and cousins were the only people in Europe who called her Cricky, although she had used the name in Berkeley when she went to school. "You look very grown up," he said, smiling proudly at her, and she laughed.

"I am grown up, Papa." Because she was so small and delicate, she had always looked younger than her age. In blue jeans and sweaters or T-shirts, she looked like a teenager instead of the twenty-three-year-old she was. But in the elegant black cocktail dress, with a small white mink wrap on her arm, she looked more like a miniature of a model in Paris. She was graceful and lithe, her figure perfectly proportioned for her size, and she moved with grace around the room, as her father continued to smile.

"I suppose you are, my dear, although I hate to think of you that way. No matter how old you are, in my mind, you will always be a child."

"I think Freddy thinks of me that way, too. He always treats me like I'm five."

"To us you are," Prince Hans Josef said benevolently. He was just like any other father, particularly one who had been obliged to raise his children without a wife. He had been both father and mother to them. Both agreed he had done a remarkable job, and never failed them once. He managed to juggle his duties to the state and those as a father with affection, patience, wisdom, and an abundance of love. And as a result, all three members of their immediate family were extraordinarily close. And even though Freddy was badly behaved much of the time, he had a profound love for his father and sister.

Christianna had spoken to her brother in Japan that week. He was still in Tokyo and having a wonderful time. He had been visiting temples, museums, shrines, and incredibly good although very expensive nightclubs and restaurants. Freddy had been the guest of the crown prince for the first several weeks, which had been too restrictive for him, and now he was doing some traveling on his own, with assistants, a secretary, a valet, and bodyguards of course. It took at least that many people to keep Freddy in even moderate control. Christianna knew what he was like. He told her the Japanese girls were very pretty, and he was going to China next. He still had no plans to come home, even for a visit, until the following spring. It seemed an eternity to her. While he was gone, she had no one even close to her age to talk to at home. She shared all her deepest confidences with her dog. She could talk to her father, of course, about important things, but for the daily banter that occurred among the young, she had no one at all. She had had no friends her own age as a child, which had made Berkeley even more wonderful for her.

Christianna and her father arrived at the ballet in the chauffeur-driven Bentley limousine, with a bodyguard in front as well, in which they had traveled earlier that day from Vaduz. There were two photographers waiting outside, who had been discreetly informed that Prince Hans Josef and the princess would attend the performance that night. Christianna and her father didn't stop to speak to them, but smiled pleasantly as they walked in, and were greeted in the lobby by the ballet director himself, who led them to their seats in the royal box.

It was a beautiful performance of *Giselle,* which they both enjoyed. Her father nodded off to sleep for a few minutes during the second act, and Christianna gently tucked her hand into his arm. She knew how heavily his duties weighed on him at times. He and his father before him had turned the country from an agricultural center into a major industrial force with a powerful economy and important international allegiances, like the one with Switzerland, that benefited them all. He took his responsibilities very seriously, and during his reign the country had flourished economically. In addition, he spent a considerable amount of time on his humanitarian interests. At the time of her death, he had established a foundation in his late wife's memory, and the Princesse Agathe Foundation had done an enormous amount of good work in underdeveloped countries. Christianna had been planning to talk to him about it. She was becoming more and more interested in working for the foundation, although he had discouraged her from doing so at first. He had no desire to allow her to join their workers on site in dangerous places. She wanted to at least visit them, and perhaps work in the administrative office if he allowed it, if she didn't go to the Sorbonne. He had made it clear that he preferred her to pursue her studies. She was hoping that if she started working for the foundation at the administrative level, she might be able to convince her father to let her take an occasional trip with the directors now and then. It was just her cup of tea. Theirs was one of the most prosperous and generous foundations in Europe, in great part funded by her father from his personal fortune, in memory of his late wife.

They returned to Palace Liechtenstein shortly before midnight. The housekeeper had tea and small sandwiches waiting for them, and Christianna and her father chatted as they ate them, talking about the performance. They often came to see the opera in Vienna too, and symphonies. It was close enough and provided a break from their otherwise serious routines, and Prince Hans Josef loved his little trips with his daughter.

He encouraged her to do some shopping the next morning. She bought two pairs of shoes and a handbag, but she was saving her energy for London. The kind of things she bought in Vienna were what she wore at state appearances and formal ceremonies like the ribbon cutting. The clothes she bought in London she wore at home in Vaduz, or in her private life, when she had one, which she didn't at the moment. She had spent the last four years in jeans, and missed them now that she was at home. She knew her father didn't want her leaving the palace in them, unless she was driving out in the country. Christianna had to think of everything ten times before she did it— what she said, what she wore, where she went, with whom, even the casual comments she might make in public that could be overheard and misquoted later. She had learned already as a very young girl that there was no such thing as privacy or freedom for the daughter of a reigning prince. It would have been far too easy to embarrass him or cause a difficult diplomatic situation if she offended someone. It was something Christianna was acutely aware of, and made every effort to respect, out of love for her father. Freddy was far more casual about it, much to everyone's chagrin, when he found himself in the midst of some mortifying situation, which up to now he had done often. Freddy just didn't think. Unlike him, Christianna always did.

She was also very interested in women's rights, which was a sore subject in her country. Women had only had the vote for just slightly over twenty years, since 1984, which was unthinkable. She liked to say that her arrival had brought them freedom, since the year of their emancipation was the one in which she'd been born. In many ways, it was still an extremely conservative country, in spite of her father's very modern ideas about economics, and his politically open-minded views. But it was still a small country, bound by traditions that had existed for nine centuries, and Christianna felt the weight and burden of them all. She loved the idea of bringing fresh ideas back from the States with her, and developing more job opportunities for women, but with only thirty-three thousand subjects, and fewer than half of them women, there were painfully few women who would be affected by Christianna's youthful, energetic outlook. Nonetheless, she wanted to try. Even the fact that she could never inherit the throne was an archaic tradition. In other monarchies and principalities she would have been as eligible to rule as Freddy, although inheriting the throne was the last thing she wanted. She had no desire to reign, but she thought the traditional discrimination was inappropriate in a modern country, on principle. She mentioned it to her father's twenty-five members of Parliament, whenever she saw them, just as her mother before her had hounded them about giving women the right to vote. Little by little they were coming into the twenty-first century, but far too slowly for Christianna, and in some ways even for her father, although he was less a rebel than she was. Ideologically, he still had deep respect for their old traditions, but he was also three times her age, which inevitably made a difference.

They talked about her trip to London in the car on the way back to Vaduz. Her father had brought a briefcase bulging with papers to read on the trip, but the drive was long enough that he had time to chat with Christianna, too. She was going to visit Victoria on Tuesday. She cautiously suggested going alone, without guards, and her father was adamant about it. Ever worried about potential violence, he wanted her to take at least two bodyguards with her, maybe even three.

"That's silly, Papa," she complained. "I only had two in Berkeley, and you always said America was much more dangerous. Besides, Victoria has one of her own. I only need one."

"Three," he said firmly, frowning at her. He hated even the remotest chance of her being in danger. He preferred to be overly cautious than to be cavalier.

"One," Christianna bargained, and this time he laughed.

"Two, and that's my final offer. Otherwise you stay home."

"All right, all right," she conceded. She knew her brother had three with him in Japan, and a fourth for relief. Other royal families sometimes traveled with fewer bodyguards, but because it was public knowledge that their family and country were immensely rich, it put all of them at greater risk. It was about wealth, as much as about who they were, perhaps even more so. The prince's greatest fear had always been that one of his children would be kidnapped, and he was exceptionally cautious as a result. Christianna had long since made her peace with it, as had Freddy. He used his bodyguards to fetch and carry for him, albeit good-humoredly, and to get him out of messes he created, usually with women, or help him escape from a nightclub late at night when he was too drunk to walk. Christianna had far less use for hers, as she was much better behaved, and she had a comfortable, easy relationship with them, as they were very fond of her, and very protective. But she still preferred to go out alone, and almost never could. Her father simply wouldn't allow it, with good reason in some countries. He wouldn't even think of letting her travel to South America, although she had always wanted to go there. The stories about kidnappings of the wealthy and powerful were legion, and a Serene Highness with a vast fortune behind her would be a plum they couldn't resist. Prince Hans Josef preferred not to put temptation in their path in the form of his daughter. He forced her to confine her travels to the United States and Europe, and he had taken her to Hong Kong himself, which she loved. She said she wanted to travel to Africa and India next, which made him shudder. For the moment, he was relieved that she was satisfied with a week in London, staying with her cousin. That was as exotic as he wanted her to get, which was exotic enough. The young marchioness was extremely eccentric, given to outrageous behavior, and for several years had had both a python and a cheetah as pets. The prince had flatly forbidden her to bring them to Vaduz. But he knew that Christianna would have fun with her, and he knew also how much she needed it.

They returned to the palace in Vaduz after ten o'clock that night. The prince's assistant was waiting for him. Even at that hour, he had work to do. He was going to have a late supper at his desk, and Christianna decided to skip the meal entirely. She was tired after the trip and went to look for Charles in the kitchen, where he was sound asleep near the stove, and was instantly excited to see her when he heard her step. They went upstairs together, where her lady-in-waiting was sitting quietly, expecting her, and offered to run a bath.

"I'm fine, Alicia," Christianna said with a yawn. "I think I'll go straight to bed." The bed was already open, impeccable, and waiting for her. There was a large embroidery of their crest on her sheets. And there was nothing more for the woman to do, so with a curtsy she withdrew, much to her charge's relief. She had been lying when she said she was going to bed. She had every intention of taking a bath, but wanted to draw it herself. She preferred to be alone in her rooms.

After her lady-in-waiting left, Christianna stripped off her clothes and walked through her bedroom in her underwear, and went to check her e-mail in her small, elegant office. It was all done in beautiful pale blue silks. Her bedroom and dressing room were pink satin. The room had been her great-great-grandmother's, and Christianna had lived in it since birth with her nanny, until she retired.

She had no e-mails from America that night, and only a brief one from Victoria, which said how much fun they were going to have that week. She had all sorts of mischief planned, she hinted darkly, which made Christianna laugh. Knowing Victoria, she was sure she did. She had no doubt of that.

She wandered back to her bedroom then, still in her underwear, and finally went to run her bath. Wandering around with no one else in the room with her was a huge luxury and her only freedom. There were almost always servants, ladies-in-waiting, assistants, secretaries, and bodyguards around her. Privacy was a rare gift, and she enjoyed every minute of it. For a moment, it almost felt like being in Berkeley, although her surroundings were certainly very different. But it was that same sense of peace and freedom and being able to do whatever she wanted, even if all it meant was being able to take a bath, and listen to her favorite music. She put some CDs on from her student days, lay down on her bed for a minute while she waited for her enormous antique tub to fill, and closed her eyes. If she thought about it hard enough, she could almost feel herself back in Berkeley . . . almost . . . but not quite . . . thinking about it, she wanted to spread her wings and fly, or turn the clock back. It would have been so wonderful if she could. But those heavenly days of freedom were over. She was here now. Much to her chagrin, she had grown up. Berkeley was nothing more than a memory. And she was a Serene Highness forever.

# Chapter 3

On Tuesday morning, bright and early, Christianna left the palace at Vaduz for London, and stopped in to see her father on her way out. He was already hard at work in his office, going over a stack of folders with a look of concern. He and his chief finance minister appeared to be having a serious discussion, and neither looked pleased with the result. Had she been staying home, she would have asked her father about it that night. She loved hearing about his policies and decisions, the shifts in palace positions, and the economic issues that came up. It was the only reason why she would have agreed to study political science at the Sorbonne, but she still hadn't decided yet. She loved the idea of getting out of Vaduz, but she wasn't enthusiastic about going back to school, even in Paris. She wanted to do something more important for humanity. She was currently more drawn to the foundation than to the Sorbonne.

"Have a wonderful time," her father said warmly. He and the minister had stopped their discussion the moment she entered the room. The finance minister had no idea how much her father shared with her, or how much she knew. She was far more aware of the inner workings of the principality than her brother, and far more intelligent about them. All Freddy wanted to do was drive fast cars, and chase girls, or even faster women than the Ferrari he drove. "Give my best to our cousin. What do you and Victoria have planned, or do I even want to know?" he teased with a loving smile.

"Probably not." She smiled back. But he wasn't worried. Whatever mischief Victoria had in store, he knew that Christianna was a very sensible girl. He was never even remotely concerned about that. "I'll be back in a week, Papa. I'll call you tonight." He knew she would. She always did what she said, and had since she was a child.

"Don't worry about me. Just have fun. What a shame," he then said, pretending to lament. "You're going to miss a state dinner on Friday night." He knew just how boring she thought the dinners were.

"Do you want me back?" she asked seriously, her disappointment not showing on her face. If he wanted her to, she would have come back for him, although she would have been disappointed to cut her London visit short. But for both of them, responsibility and duty were the name of the game, and the code by which they lived.

"Of course not, silly girl. I wouldn't dream of it. Stay longer if you like."

"I might," she said, looking hopeful. "You wouldn't mind?"

"Stay as long as you like," he reassured her, as she hugged him again and shook hands with his minister politely, and then with a last wave at her father, Christianna left.

"She's a lovely girl," his finance minister said to him, as they went back to their work.

"Thank you," Hans Josef said proudly. "Yes, she is."

Her driver took Christianna to the airport in Zurich with her two bodyguards, and four security officials put her on the plane.

Once on board, it was obvious that someone important was traveling, all the flight attendants appeared to be buzzing around her. They offered her champagne, which she declined, and immediately after takeoff, they brought her a cup of tea. One bodyguard was sitting next to her, the other was across the aisle. All the way to London she read a book about the application of economic policies, which her father had recommended to her. And an hour and a half later they landed at Heathrow Airport, where a limousine was waiting for her. She was whisked through customs, with nothing to declare, and two airport security police joined forces with her bodyguards, and took her to the limousine. They took off immediately, and less than an hour later, the car pulled up in front of Victoria's small, elegant house on Sloane Square. She was one of the few titled women in London who had an enormous fortune, thanks to an American mother, an heiress who had married a title and left her daughter a vast inheritance when she died two years ago. Victoria was having a fabulous time with the money, and didn't mind it at all when people said she was spoiled. She knew she was, and was having so much fun she was never embarrassed by her extravagant way of life, and she was extremely generous with her friends.

She opened the door for Christianna herself, and stood there in blue jeans, a T-shirt, and high-heeled red alligator shoes, with huge diamond earrings and a stunning tiara sitting slightly askew on her bright red hair. She squealed the moment she saw her cousin, threw her arms around her, and escorted her inside, as Christianna's two bodyguards carried in her bags, and the butler ushered them upstairs.

"You look *fabulous!*" she said to Christianna, as the tiara slid slowly toward her ear, and Christianna started to laugh.

"What are you doing with that thing on? Should I have brought mine? Are we going somewhere tonight?" Christianna couldn't think of a single place she would have worn a tiara, except maybe to a ball given by the queen. And Victoria hadn't warned her of anything important going on.

"It just seems too stupid to leave it sitting in the vault. I thought I'd get some use out of it. I wear it all the time." It was so typical of her.

She was wild, eccentric, and beautiful. She was extremely tall, nearly six feet, and completely undaunted, she went everywhere in six-inch heels, platforms preferably. She wore either miniskirts or jeans, her skirts were so short they almost looked like belts, and she was always swathed in diaphanous tops that seemed to drip and fall and were always slipping to reveal one breast and her creamy white skin. She was a spectacular-looking young woman. She had done some acting and modeling, gotten bored with it, and tried painting for a while. She was actually quite good at it, but she never stuck with anything for long. She had just gotten engaged to a Danish prince, whom everyone said was totally besotted with her, but knowing her as well as she did, Christianna was not entirely convinced that the engagement would last long either. Victoria had been engaged twice before, once to an American, and the second time to a well-known French actor who had left her for someone else, which Victoria said was incredibly rude. She had had a new boyfriend herself by the following week. She was by far the most eccentric person Christianna knew, but she loved spending time with her. They always had so much fun together. They stayed up all night, went to parties, and danced at Annabel's. Christianna always met interesting people with her. Victoria also drank a lot and smoked cigars. She lit one now as they sat down in her living room, which was a jumble of both modern and ancient art. Her mother had left her several Picassos, and there were books and art objects everywhere. Christianna was ecstatic just being there with her. It was the exact opposite of her quiet life in Vaduz with her father. Being around Victoria was like watching a circus act on the high wire. You never knew what would happen next. Watching her was breathtaking.

They chatted for a few minutes about their plans for the next week. Victoria said her fiancé was in Thailand on an official tour, and she seemed to be taking full advantage of it, going out every night, although she claimed to Christianna that she was madly in love with him, and this one would stick. Christianna wasn't as sure. Victoria mentioned in passing that they were having dinner at Kensington Palace that night, with several of their cousins, and afterward they'd all go out.

The phone must have rung ten times during their conversation, and Victoria answered it herself. She gushed and laughed and teased as her two pugs, four Pekingese, and a chihuahua ran around the room barking. She no longer had the cheetah or the snake. It was a total madhouse, and Christianna loved it. She loved visiting her.

Victoria asked Christianna about her love life, as a maid quietly served them lunch. They had oysters and salad, which was a new diet the already-too-slim redhead said that she was on.

"I don't have a love life," Christianna said, looking undisturbed. "There's no one for me to go out with in Vaduz. I don't really care." There had been someone she liked in California, but it had ended when she went home, and it hadn't been serious, just good company while she was there. They had parted good friends. And as he had told her before she left, "the princess thing" would have been too much for him. Most of the time it was for her, too. It was a heavy burden to live with.

"We'll have to find you someone fabulous here." Victoria's idea of fabulous wasn't exactly Christianna's, although she did know some very interesting people, most of whom were a lot of fun, but no one Christianna would have taken seriously. They were usually a very exotic bunch. Victoria knew everyone who mattered in London, and everyone else was dying to meet her.

The two young women went upstairs after lunch. One of Victoria's maids had already unpacked Christianna's bags, and hung everything neatly in the closet. The rest was impeccably put away in drawers. Victoria's guest room was decorated in leopard and zebra patterns, with red roses everywhere. It was all done in beautiful French fabrics, with stacks of books on every table, and a huge four-poster bed. She had enormous style, and always managed to pull off things no one else could have, in her decorating and everywhere else. Her own bedroom was done in pale lavender satin, with a huge white fox blanket on the bed. It had the look of an extremely expensive brothel, but in spite of the flamboyant taste, she had exquisite antiques and everything she owned was of impeccable quality. There were a life-size silver skull and a pair of gold handcuffs sitting on a table next to her bed. The table itself was made entirely of crystal, and had belonged to the maharajah of Jaipur.

As promised, they went to Kensington Palace to dine that night. A number of Christianna's royal cousins were there, and everyone was happy to see her. She hadn't seen any of them since she got back from Berkeley in June. They went to a private party afterward, stopped at two nightclubs, Kemia and Monte's, and wound up at Annabel's at the end of the night. Christianna had loved every minute but was getting tired by then. Victoria was still going strong, with the help of a considerable amount to drink.

It was five o'clock in the morning when they got back to the house in Sloane Square, and both girls walked slowly up the stairs to go to bed. Christianna's bodyguards had been with them all night, and had just retired to their rooms on the top floor. It had been a typical night in Victoria's life, and one Christianna knew she wouldn't forget for a long time. Spending time with Victoria was always unforgettable, and a far cry from sleepy Vaduz.

The rest of the week was equally exciting, with parties, people, shopping, an opening of a gallery, a constant round of cocktail parties, dinners, and nightclubs, and inevitably the two young women wound up in the press. Victoria had been wearing her tiara and a leopard coat. Christianna was wearing yet another black cocktail dress, with a mink jacket she had bought the day before. She didn't feel too extravagant since she knew she would have plenty of opportunities to wear it at home. The rest of what she bought was mostly fun, and she had to buy another suitcase to take it all home. In the end, she stayed ten days, and would have loved to stay longer. But she felt guilty leaving her father alone. She looked happy and relaxed, and delighted with her visit the day she left, and she hated going back to Vaduz. Victoria made her promise to come back soon. The parties to celebrate her engagement hadn't even begun. They were waiting for her fiancé to come home from his extended tour.

Christianna couldn't help wondering if his family had sent him away to get him out of her clutches. Victoria was not exactly anyone's idea of the ideal wife for a crown prince, no matter how besotted he was. Everyone who knew her said it wouldn't last. But she was having fun making plans for a wedding to be attended by a cast of thousands. It was definitely one Christianna didn't want to miss. The two cousins hugged and kissed as she left, and as soon as she arrived back in Vaduz, Christianna had to dress for a state dinner her father was giving that night, for visiting dignitaries from Spain. It was a formal dinner in the state dining room, with dancing afterward in the palace ballroom.

She joined her father that night in a white chiffon evening gown and silver high-heeled sandals she had just bought in London. As always, she looked delicate, elegant, and exquisite. She smiled to herself, thinking of Victoria, as she walked downstairs to join her father. She wondered what he would have said if she had worn a tiara like their cousin. On Victoria, with her wild red hair, and smoking cigars, it looked just right. Christianna would have felt silly wearing one of theirs from the vault, or pretentious at the very least. Victoria had worn hers even at breakfast, and whenever they went out.

Christianna hadn't seen her father yet in the brief time she'd been home. She had gone straight upstairs to dress, so she wouldn't be late for dinner. And as always, she was at his side, at precisely the right time. He smiled down at her with unconcealed pleasure. He was thrilled to see her back, and hugged her the moment he saw her.

"Did you have fun in London?" he asked with interest just before the guests arrived.

"It was fantastic. Thank you for letting me go." She had called him several times, but didn't dare tell him all they were doing. She knew he'd worry, and all of it was harmless. But trying to explain it to him would have made it sound too racy. And everything had been fine. Better than that, it had been fabulous. Her cousin had been the perfect hostess, and had seen to it that Christianna had fun every minute she was there.

"How serious do you think her engagement is this time?" her father asked, looking skeptical, and Christianna laughed.

"Probably about as serious as the others. She says she's crazy about him, and she's planning the wedding. But I'm not buying a dress yet."

"That's what I thought. I can't imagine her as Queen of Denmark one day, and I'm sure her future parents-in-law can't either. They must be terrified." Christianna laughed out loud at what he said.

"She must be practicing to wear the crown. She wore one of her mother's tiaras the whole time I was there. I think she's setting a new fashion."

"I should have sent you with one of ours," he teased her. He knew Christianna would never have worn it.

The guests began to arrive then, and it was a serious, extremely circumspect evening. Christianna worked hard at dinner, speaking to the dignitaries on either side of her, one in German, and the other in Spanish. And she was relieved to dance with her father at the end of the evening.

"It's not as exciting as London, I'm afraid," he said apologetically, and she smiled. It had been a painfully dull evening for her, but she had expected it to be. It came as no surprise, but she attended many events like it to please her father. He knew that, and was touched by the effort she made. She was so diligent about her official duties and obligations, no matter how tiresome they were. She never complained. She knew there was no point, she had to do them anyway, and accepted it with grace.

"I had enough fun in London with Victoria to last me for a while," she said generously. She was actually exhausted after all the late nights she'd had. She had no idea how Victoria did that as a constant way of life. She was a seasoned partyer in London, and had been doing it for years. Unlike Christianna, she had never gone to college. She always said there was no point, she knew she'd never use anything she learned there. She attended art classes instead, and was actually a fairly decent artist. She especially loved to paint dogs dressed up as people. A shop in Knightsbridge was selling her paintings for a fortune.

The guests at the palace in Vaduz went home long before midnight, and she followed her father slowly up the stairs afterward. They had just reached the door to her apartment when one of the prince's aides came looking for him. He looked as though it was urgent, and Prince Hans Josef turned to him with a frown, waiting to hear what it was.

"Your Highness, we just got a report of a terrorist attack in Russia. It appears to be a very serious hostage situation, similar to the one in Beslan several years ago. It appears to be almost an exact duplicate, in fact. I thought you might like to watch it on CNN. Several of the hostages have already been killed, all children." The prince hurried into Christianna's living room, and turned on the television set. All three of them sat down to watch in silence. What they saw was horrendous—children who had been shot and were bleeding, others being carried out of the building, dead. Nearly a thousand children had been taken hostage, and over two hundred adults. The terrorists had taken over a school, and wanted political prisoners released in exchange for the children. The army had surrounded the place, and there seemed to be chaos everywhere, with crying parents outside, waiting for news of their children. The prince watched the broadcast unhappily, and Christianna stared in horror. It was a grisly scene. They sat watching for two hours, and then the prince got up to go to bed. His assistant had long since left.

"What a terrible thing," her father said sympathetically. "All those poor parents waiting for their children. I can't imagine a worse nightmare," he said, as he hugged her.

"Neither can I," Christianna said quietly, still wearing the white chiffon gown and silver sandals. She had cried several times as she watched, and her father had been moved to tears as well. "I feel so useless sitting here, all dressed up and unable to help them," she said, as though she felt guilty, and he hugged her again.

"There's nothing anyone can do, until they get the children out of there. It'll be a bloodbath if the army forces their way in." The thought of that was even more upsetting, and Christianna dabbed at her eyes again. The terrorists had killed dozens of children. There were already a total of a hundred fatalities by the time they turned off the TV. "This is the worst situation I've seen since Beslan." They kissed each other goodnight, and Christianna went to undress and put on her nightgown. A little while later, already in bed, she felt compelled to turn on the television again. By then the situation had gotten worse, and more children had been killed. Parents were frantic, the press was everywhere, and soldiers were milling in groups, waiting to be told what to do. It was mesmerizing watching it, and horrifying. It was easy to guess that many more lives would be lost as the night progressed.

In the end, she lay awake all night and watched it, and by morning she had dark circles under her eyes, from the many times she'd cried, and lack of sleep. She finally got up, took a bath and dressed, and found her father having breakfast in his office. She was wearing a heavy sweater and jeans when she walked in. She had made a number of phone calls, before she went to look for him. And when she found him, he looked every bit as distressed as she did. By then the death toll had doubled, almost all of them children. As half the world did, her father had the TV on, and had been watching when she came in. His food was virtually untouched. Who could eat?

"Where are you going at this hour, all dressed?" he asked, looking distracted. Liechtenstein had no official role to play here, but watching the tragedy unfold was leaving everyone feeling frantic and upset. This was no made-for-television movie. This was all too real.

"I want to go there, Papa," Christianna said quietly, with eyes that bored deep into his.

"We have no official involvement or position on this situation," he explained to her. "We're a neutral country, we have no reason to work with Russia on solving this, and we don't have an antiterrorist team."

"I don't mean in an official capacity. I want to go as me," she said clearly.

"You? How else would you go except in an official capacity, and we don't have any there."

"I just want to go as one human being helping others. They don't have to know who I am."

He thought about it for a long moment, pondering the situation. It was a noble thought, but he didn't think it was a good idea. It was too dangerous for her. Who knew what the terrorists would do next, particularly if they found that a young, beautiful princess was afoot? He didn't want her there.

"I understand how you feel, Christianna. I'd like to help them, too. It's an absolutely terrible situation. But officially, we don't belong there, and on a private level, it would be too dangerous for you." He looked grim as he said it.

"I'm going, Papa," Christianna said quietly. This time, she didn't ask him, she was telling him. He could not only hear it in her words, but sense it in her voice. "I want to be there to do whatever I can, even if only to hand out blankets, pour coffee, or help dig graves. The Red Cross is there, I can volunteer to work for them." She meant it. He knew it. He suddenly suspected it would be hard to stop her, but he knew he had to try, as gently as he could.

"I don't want you to go." It was all he could say. He could easily see how distraught she was. "The area is too dangerous, Cricky."

"I have to go, Papa. I can't sit here any longer, feeling useless, watching it all on TV. I'll take someone with me if you want." It was obvious from the look in her eyes and what she was saying to him that she felt she had no other choice.

"And if I say no?" He couldn't tie her up and have her carried to her room. She was a grown woman, but he was adamant that she not go.

"I'm going, Papa," she said again. "You can't stop me. It's the right thing to do." It was. But not for her. He would have liked to go too, but he was long past the impetuous compassion of youth, and too old to take the risk.

"It is the right thing, Cricky," he said gently. "But not for you. It's too dangerous. If they find out who you are, they could take you hostage, too. I don't think terrorists respect neutral countries any more than they do anyone else. Please don't argue with me about this." She shook her head then, obviously disappointed by his reaction. But he felt obliged to protect her from herself. "You have a responsibility to our people here," he said sternly. He tried everything he could. "You could be killed, or get hurt. Besides which, you have no technical or medical skills to offer. Sometimes untrained civilians, however well-intentioned, only make situations like that worse. Christianna, I know you mean well, but I don't want you to do this." His eyes burned into hers.

"How can you say that?" she said angrily, with tears swimming in her eyes. "Look at those people, Papa. Their children are dead and dying. Probably many more will die today as well. I have to go there. There must be something useful I can do. I'm not going to sit here, just watching it on TV. That's not who you taught me to be." She was pulling at his heart, harder than she knew. She always did.

"I didn't teach you to risk your life foolishly, for God's sake," he said, angry in his turn. He was not going to allow her to bully him into it, no matter how hard she tried. The answer was still no. The problem was that she was not asking him, she was telling him. In Christianna's mind, there was no other choice.

"You taught me about 'Honor, Courage, Welfare,' Papa. You taught me to care for and be responsible for others. You taught me to reach out to those in need, and do all I could to help them. What happened to honor, courage, and welfare, *your* family code? You told me that our lives are dedicated to duty and responsibility for all those who need us, no matter how much courage it takes, to stand for what I believe. Look at those people, Papa. They need us. I'm going to do what I can for them. That's what you taught me ever since I was a little girl. You can't change that now because you don't want me there."

"It's not the same when there are terrorists involved. They don't play by any rules." He looked at her miserably, his eyes begging her not to go. And then she reduced him to tears, by turning her face up to his and kissing his cheek. "I love you, Papa. I'll be all right. I promise. I'll call you when I can." He saw then that two of her bodyguards were standing in the doorway, wearing rough clothes. She had organized them to travel with her, even before she came to see him. She had meant every word she had said. And he knew then that unless he physically restrained her, she was going with or without his permission. For a moment he bowed his head, and then raised it again to look at her.

"Be very careful," he said gruffly, and then he looked at the guards with daggers in his eyes. He was every inch the reigning prince, and even if Christianna defied him, the two men knew there would be hell to pay if anything happened to her. "Don't let her out of your sight for a minute. Do you understand that? Both of you."

"Yes, we do, Your Highness," they said rapidly. It was rare to see him angry, but he looked it now. In fact, he was not angry but worried. More than that, he was terrified for her. He couldn't have tolerated losing this child he loved so much. Thinking that made him

realize how the people must have felt losing their children as the terrorists were murdering them one by one, in order to get their friends
released from prison. It was an exchange of terrorists for children, a
horrifying exchange, and an impossible situation for all involved. And
as he thought of it again, he knew she was right. He didn't like it for
her, but he admired her courage and her desire to go. She was doing
just exactly what he had taught her: to lay down her life if need be in
service to others. Indirectly, her wanting to go there was entirely his
fault.

After Christianna went back to her bedroom to get her backpack,
her father walked her and her two bodyguards to the car.

"Go with God," he said as he hugged her, with tears in his eyes.

"I love you, Papa," she said calmly. "Don't worry about me. I'll be
fine."

She got in the car then, with the two men. All three of them were
wearing boots and warm jackets. She had called for a reservation on
the flight several hours before. She was planning to find the Red
Cross, and volunteer once she got there. She had seen on CNN that
they were on the scene, doing whatever they could.

The prince stood watching until the car went through the gates.
She hung out the window and waved to him with a victorious smile.
She blew him a kiss and mouthed the words *I love you,* and then they
turned the corner and were gone. He walked back into the palace with
his head bowed. He was sick over her going, but he knew there had
been absolutely nothing he could do to stop her. She would have gone
in any case. All he could do now was pray for her safety and safe return. More than she knew, he admired her with all his heart. She was
a remarkable young woman, and as he walked into his office, he felt a
thousand years old.

# Chapter 4

Christianna and her two bodyguards drove to Zurich and flew from there to Vienna, where they boarded a flight to Tbilisi in Georgia, which was a five-and-a-half-hour flight.

They landed in Tbilisi at seven o'clock that night, and half an hour later, they took an ancient, worn-looking small plane to Vladikavkaz in the southern Russian territory of North Ossetia. The plane was crowded, the interior looked threadbare and poorly maintained, and the turbo-prop plane shuddered noticeably on takeoff. It had been a long day on the first plane, and all three of them looked tired when they got off the final flight just before nine o'clock that night.

The bodyguards she had brought with her were her two youngest ones. Both had been trained in the Swiss Army, and one of them had served before that as an Israeli commando. She had chosen the right men to accompany her.

She had no idea what she would find when she reached Digora, where they were going, some thirty miles from Vladikavkaz, where they had landed. Christianna had made no definite arrangements beyond the flight. She was going to look for the Red Cross as soon as they arrived at the scene of the hostage situation in Digora, and offer them whatever assistance they needed. She assumed they would be allowed at the scene, and hoped she was right. She was not afraid of what would happen, and had made no efforts to secure a place to stay or a hotel room. She wanted to work at the scene, around the clock, if necessary. She was prepared for long hours on her feet, and no sleep, while she helped either the frantic parents or the wounded children. She had taken first-aid training in school, but other than that she had no specific skills, other than youth, a good heart, and a willing pair of hands. And in spite of her father's frantic warnings, she wasn't worried about whatever potential dangers she might encounter. She had been willing to take the risk, and she was sure that for those outside the school the terrorists had taken over, the risk was slight. In either case, she wanted to be there. And she knew her bodyguards would protect her, so she felt safe.

Her first run-in with an unexpected stumbling block happened as she came through immigration at the airport. One of her bodyguards handed the customs officer all three of their passports. Her agreement with them had been that under no circumstances were they to reveal her royal identity once they got to Russia. She hadn't anticipated it being a problem before that, and was startled when the customs official stared at her passport at length, and then at her. The photograph was a good likeness, so it was obviously not that.

"It's you?" he asked, looking slightly belligerent. He was speaking to her in German, as he had heard her speak to one of her bodyguards in German and the other in French. She nodded assent, forgetting the difference between their passports and hers. "Name?" And then she knew what it was.

"Christianna," she said quietly. There was only a single name on her passport, her first name, as was the case with all royals. Queen

Elizabeth of England, Princess Michael of Kent, who was Marie Christine. All passports issued to royals in every country showed only their first name, but not their title or surname. The Russian customs official looked angry and confused.

"No name?" She hesitated and then handed him a brief letter issued by the government of Liechtenstein explaining the circumstances of her passport, and her full identity as a Serene Highness of the principality. She had needed the letter while she was studying in California and had had similar problems going through U.S. Immigration. The official letter was written in English, German, and French, and she kept it in her travel pouch with her passport. She only presented it if asked. He read it carefully, glanced up at her twice, then at the bodyguards, and back at her. "Where are you going, Miss Princess?" She tried not to smile. He was obviously not familiar with titles, having grown up in a Communist state, but looked moderately impressed. She told him their destination, and he nodded again, stamped their passports, and waved them through. Hers was a neutral country, like Switzerland, which often opened doors for her that another passport would not have been able to do. And her title usually helped. He questioned them no further, and they went to a car rental office and stood on line for half an hour with everyone else.

All three of them were starving by then, and Christianna handed the two men a small package of biscuits, and two bottles of water she had carried with her in her backpack, and opened a third for herself. It seemed like an eternity to get their turn. And when they finally did, all that was available was a ten-year-old Yugo, at an astronomic rate. Christianna agreed to take it, since there was nothing else, and handed her credit card across the counter, which once again had no last name. The woman asked if she had cash. Christianna had brought some with her, but didn't want to give it up so early in the trip, and the woman finally agreed to accept the credit card, after offering them a better deal if they paid cash, which Christianna declined.

She signed the agreements, took the car keys, and asked for a map. Ten minutes later she and the two bodyguards, Samuel and Max, went out to the parking lot to find the car. It was tiny and looked battered. The two men barely fit into the car, as Christianna slipped easily into the backseat with her backpack, grateful that she was small. Samuel started the car, as Max opened the map. From what the woman at the car rental had said, they had a thirty-mile drive ahead, and would probably arrive at eleven o'clock that night. Samuel was driving, and once in the parking lot, they had taken their weapons out of the bag they'd checked, and put them on. Max loaded them for both of them, as they drove out of the parking lot, and Christianna watched. She had no qualms about guns, and had been around them all her life. Her bodyguards were useless to her without them. She had even been taught to fire weapons herself, and was an unusually good shot, better than her brother, who found weapons offensive, although he liked the social aspects of duck and grouse hunting and went often.

They were starving by the time they left the airport, and stopped for dinner halfway through the trip in a small restaurant by the roadside. Samuel spoke a few words of Russian, but mostly they pointed at what others were eating, and sat down to a simple, rugged meal. The other diners were mostly truck drivers, traveling at night, and the pretty young blonde and two powerful healthy-looking men were instantly noticeable among them. They would have been even more so if any of them had even imagined that she was a princess. But all she looked like was a pretty young girl, in jeans, the heavy workboots she'd had in Berkeley, a thick sweater, and a parka. She had her blond hair pulled back. The men were similarly dressed and had a military look about

them. Others would have guessed easily that they were security of
some kind, but no one questioned them here. After eating, they paid
and drove on. They noticed a number of Daewoo minivans on the
road that were used as shared taxis and were called "Marshrutkas,"
Christianna learned later. They were a favorite form of transportation.

Unable to read the signs and confused by the map, they took several wrong turns and arrived at their destination at nearly midnight.
They were quickly stopped by a roadblock manned by Russian soldiers in riot gear. They were wearing helmets, face masks, and carrying machine guns, as they questioned why Christianna and her
guards were there. Christianna spoke up from the backseat and said
in German that they were looking for the Red Cross representatives in
order to work with them. The sentry hesitated, told them in halting
German to wait, and consulted his superiors, who were conferring at
a short distance. One of them talked to him, and then approached the
car himself.

"You're Red Cross workers?" he asked, frowning at them, and looking at them intently with suspicion. He wasn't sure what they were,
but they didn't look like terrorists to him. He had a sixth sense for
that, which told him that the threesome in the Yugo were there for the
reason they said.

"We're volunteers," Christianna said distinctly, and he hesitated,
continuing to look them over. Nothing he saw set off red flags for him.

"From where?" The last thing he wanted was tourists wandering
into the mess they already had on their hands. Like the first man they
had talked to, he looked tired. It was the second day of the siege, and
a dozen more children had been killed that afternoon, and dumped in
the schoolyard, which had demoralized everyone. Two others trying
to escape had been shot. The entire situation was a copycat event of
the similarly awful hostage crisis that had happened several years

before in Beslan, in the same region of North Ossetia. This was nearly an exact duplicate, on a slightly smaller scale. But the death toll was rising daily, and it wasn't over yet.

"We're from Liechtenstein," she said clearly. "I am. The two men are Swiss. We're all neutrals," she reminded him, and he nodded again. She had no idea if it would make any difference or not, but she thought it couldn't hurt to remind him.

"Passports?" The guard in the driver's seat handed them to him, and he had the same reaction as the customs official to Christianna's. "Yours has no surname," he told her, sounding annoyed, as though it were a mistake she had made in the passport office when she got it. But this time she didn't want to hand him the letter, she didn't want people in the area knowing that she was there, or making a fuss about it.

"I know. My country does that sometimes. For women," she added, but he remained unconvinced, and began to look suspicious. He had to be, given what was going on. Reluctantly, she handed him the letter. He perused it carefully, stared at her, then at the two men, back at her, and then looked at her in astonished admiration. "A royal princess?" He seemed utterly amazed. "Here? To work with the Red Cross?"

"I hope we will. That's what we came to do," she explained. The officer then shook hands with her driver, told them where to find the Red Cross enclave, handed them a pass, and waved them through. It was a most unusual occurrence, to give them access to a hostage scene, and Christianna had the feeling that if she hadn't been a princess, they wouldn't have let them in. The officer respected her, and the two men who had accompanied her to Russia. He even gave them the name of the person in charge. And before they drove on, Christianna asked him quietly not to explain to anyone who she was. She said it would mean a great deal to her if he didn't. He nodded, still looking impressed as they drove off. She hoped he'd be discreet. Having people know who she was would spoil everything for her, or certainly make it difficult. Anonymity in these circumstances was far easier for her. And if the press caught wind of her presence, they would pursue her everywhere, and she might even have to leave. That was the last thing she wanted. She wanted to be useful, not cause a journalistic feeding frenzy, fed by her.

As they approached the school, there were police cordons, military barricades, riot police, commando squads, and soldiers with machine guns everywhere. But having made it through the initial barricade, they were no longer checked as closely. Their passports, when asked for, were only glanced at and no longer thoroughly inspected. They looked at the makeshift passes, and nodded. Most of the civilians they saw were crying, either parents or relatives of children or teachers still inside. It was so exactly reminiscent of the earlier hostage situation in Beslan that it was hard to believe an almost identical event had occurred, in the same state. And finally, after searching thoroughly, and drifting past a fleet of ambulances, they found four large Red Cross trucks, with an army of workers around them, wearing the familiar red and white armbands to identify them in the crowd. Several of them were holding children. They were serving coffee, tending to frantic-looking parents, and standing quietly in the crowd.

As soon as she saw them, Christianna got out of the car, and Samuel, the bodyguard with the commando training, followed her closely, while Max went to park the car in a field that had been designated for families and press. The car had been tight for them to ride in, but at least it had gotten them there. Christianna asked for the name that the officer at the barricade had given them, and was directed to a cluster of chairs standing near one of the trucks. There was a woman with white hair sitting there, speaking to a group of women in Russian. She was reassuring them as best one could. There was very little one could see of what was happening inside, only the constant shifting and moving of soldiers, standing ready and alert. And all of the Russian women were crying. Christianna didn't want to interrupt and stood off to one side, waiting until the older woman finished talking to them. She knew it might be hours before the woman was free to check them out. Christianna stood patiently by until the woman in charge of the Red Cross team noticed her, glanced up, and met her eyes with a questioning look.

"Are you waiting for me?" the woman asked in Russian, sounding surprised.

"I am," Christianna answered in German, hoping they would find a common language. Usually, in cases like that, it was English or French, and she was fluent in both. "I can wait." She wasn't going anywhere and didn't want to interrupt. The senior Red Cross member excused herself, patted one woman's arm consolingly, and stepped aside to where Christianna stood.

"Yes?" It was obvious that Christianna was neither a local nor a parent. She looked too clean, not disheveled enough, her clothes were still neat, and she didn't have the worn-out look that everyone else had all around them. The strain of watching the scene unfold had taken a toll on them all. Even the soldiers had cried as they brought back the bodies of the children who had been shot.

"I would like to volunteer," Christianna said quietly, looking calm, quiet, self-possessed, and competent in the way she addressed the older woman, who had no idea who she was.

"Do you have Red Cross identification?" the woman asked. They had settled on French. The woman in charge looked like she had been through the wars, and she had. She had helped to wrap the bodies of dead children, held sobbing parents in her arms for two days, tended

wounds until the paramedics could get to them. She had done everything possible since arriving there within two hours of the attack,
even served coffee to exhausted, crying soldiers.

"I'm not a Red Cross worker," Christianna explained. "I flew here
today from Liechtenstein with my two . . . friends . . ." She glanced
at the two men beside her. If necessary, she would volunteer as a
humanitarian emissary of her country, but she greatly preferred to do
so as an anonymous individual, if they would allow her to help on
that basis. She wasn't sure they would. The older woman hesitated,
looking at Christianna carefully.

"May I see your passport?" she said quietly. There was something
in the woman's eyes that gave Christianna the feeling the woman
knew who she was. She opened the passport, glanced at the single
Christian name, closed the passport again, and handed it back to her
with a smile. She knew exactly who Christianna was. "I've worked
with some of your British cousins in the African states." She didn't
mention which ones, as Christianna nodded. "Is anyone aware that
you're here?" The young woman shook her head. "And I assume those
are your guards?" She nodded again. "We can use the help," she said
quietly. "We lost twenty more children today. They just made another
request for prisoner exchange, so we may be seeing some more casualties in a few hours." She signaled for Christianna and the two men
to come with her, stepped up into their truck, and came back with
three faded armbands. They were running out. She handed them to
Christianna and her men, and they each put one on. "I'm grateful for
your help, Your Highness. I assume you're here in an official capacity?" she inquired in a tired, gentle voice. There was something so
kind and compassionate about this woman that just talking to her
was like an embrace. Christianna was profoundly glad that she had
come.

"No, I'm not," Christianna answered. "And I'd rather no one know who I am. It gets too complicated. I would appreciate it if you would just call me Christianna." The woman nodded and introduced herself as Marque. She was French, but spoke fluent Russian. Christianna spoke six languages, including the dialect spoken in Liechtenstein, but Russian wasn't among them.

"I understand," Marque said quietly. "Someone may recognize you anyway. There's a lot of press here. You looked familiar to me the moment I saw you."

"I hope no one else is as astute," Christianna said with a rueful smile. "It ruins everything when that happens."

"I know it must be very difficult." She had seen press feeding frenzies like it before, and agreed with Christianna that if no one knew, it would be simpler for them all.

"Thank you for allowing us to work with you. What can we do to help? You must be exhausted," she said sympathetically as the woman nodded.

"If you go to the second truck, we need someone to help make coffee. I think we're almost out. And we have a stack of boxes we need to move, with medical supplies in them, and bottles of water. Maybe your men could help us with that."

"Of course." She told Max and Samuel what was expected of them, and they quickly disappeared toward where the boxes were, as Christianna headed to the second truck, as directed by Marque. Her bodyguards were reluctant to let her go alone, but she insisted she would be fine. There was so much armed protection in the area that she was certainly not at risk, whether they were with her or not.

Marque thanked her again for her help, and then walked away to check on some of the women she had been talking to before Christianna arrived.

It was hours before Christianna saw her again, while she was handing out coffee, and later bottles of water. There were blankets for
those who were cold. Some people were sleeping on the ground. Others sat rigid or sobbing, waiting for news of their loved ones inside.

As Marque had predicted, the terrorists' demand for prisoner exchange had a violent outcome within almost exactly three hours. Fifty
children were shot and thrown from windows of the school by hooded
men. The bodies of the dead children flew to the courtyard below like
rag dolls, as people screamed, and finally the soldiers were able to re-
trieve them under heavy fire to cover them. Only one child was still
alive when they brought her back, and she died in her mother's arms,
as soldiers, locals, and volunteers alike stood by and sobbed. It was an
atrocity beyond measure. And it wasn't over yet. By then nearly a
hundred children had died, almost as many adults, and the terrorists
were still in full control. A rabid Middle Eastern religious group had
taken responsibility for the attack by then, with ties to Chechen
rebels. It was a joint effort to have thirty terrorists released from
prison, and the Russian government was standing its ground, much to
the anger of the crowd. They preferred to have thirty terrorists released, and spare the lives of their children. There was a sense of despair and helplessness around them everywhere in the crowd, as
Christianna stood with the other Red Cross workers and sobbed.
What was happening was beyond imagining.

She had done very little since she arrived, other than hand out water
or coffee, and then suddenly she saw a young Russian woman standing
next to her crying inconsolably. She was pregnant, and holding a toddler by the hand. Her eyes met Christianna's then, and as though they
were long-lost relatives, they fell into each other's arms and cried.
Christianna never knew her name, and they shared no language in
common other than the bottomless sorrow caused by watching children

die. Christianna learned later that she had a six-year-old in the school, who had not as yet been seen or found. Her husband was a teacher there, and he had been one of the first fatalities of the previous night. She was praying that her son was still alive.

The two women stood side by side for several hours, alternately hugging and holding hands. Christianna brought some food for the two-year-old, and a chair for the pregnant woman to sit down, while she continued to cry. There were so many others like her that it was hard to distinguish them in the crowd.

It was after dawn when soldiers in commando uniforms told them to clear the area. The entire group of waiting people and workers had to move well back. No one knew what was happening, but the terrorists had just made what they said was their final demand. If that one was not met, they said they were going to blow up the entire school, which seemed entirely plausible by now. They were people without conscience or morality, with no value whatsoever for human life, apparently even their own.

"We need to get in the trucks," Marque told her quietly as she passed by, rounding up her troops, and Christianna was now counted among them. "They haven't told us, but I think they're going to go in, they want everyone as far away as we can get." She had been moving among the locals and telling them the same thing. People were walking and running across a field behind newly formed riot police lines. It made the parents' hearts ache to put even more distance between them and their children trapped inside. But the soldiers were pushing the crowd back now with force, as though they were running out of time.

Christianna picked the toddler up, put an arm around her young pregnant friend, and helped her into one of the trucks. She was no longer in any condition to walk, or tolerate what was happening. She looked as though she was going to give birth at any moment. Christianna was no longer aware of it, but her bodyguards were watching her from close by. They were well aware that the local troops were about to go in, and if something dire happened, they wanted her within their reach. Marque had noticed them as well, and understood why they were keeping Christianna in their sights. No one wanted a dead princess on their hands as well as more dead children. The death toll was already far too high. It would have been a further victory for the terrorists to kill a royal even from a neutral country. Her anonymity as well as her safety were vital. And Marque was impressed by how hard Christianna had worked all night. She had been tireless, with the zeal, passion, energy, and caring of youth. Marque suspected that, if she had time to get to know her, Christianna was a young woman she would have liked. She seemed very down to earth and real.

Everyone waiting moved far back across the field, and within half an hour there were explosives, machine-gun fire, tear gas, and bombs going off, as commando squads and riot police stormed the building. It was impossible to determine who was in control, as the crowd watching from the distance just stood there and cried. It was hard to believe that there would be anyone left alive after it was over, on either side.

Christianna left her young pregnant friend lying down on a cot in one of the trucks, as she continued to ask what had happened, but no one knew yet. It was too soon to tell, as the battle raged on. Christianna joined the other Red Cross workers handing out blankets coffee, water, and food in the crowd. They had put small children, shivering in the early morning chill, in two of the trucks. It was hours later before the gunfire stopped. It was almost more frightening when it did than when it started. No one knew exactly what that meant, or who was in charge. They could still see troops moving in the distance, and then from an upstairs window, a white flag. The crowd at the far edge of the field shivered in the cold, and continued to wait for news.

It was another two hours before a group of soldiers crossed the field to bring them back. Tragically, there were hundreds of children's bodies to identify, and the screams of anguish all around them seemed to ebb and flow for hours, as families identified and mourned their dead. All but two of the terrorists had committed suicide. The bombs in the school had not been detonated, and were being dis-armed by bomb squads. The remaining two terrorists had been taken away in armored cars, before the anguished crowd could tear them apart. Military intelligence wanted to interrogate them. And in all, there were five hundred children dead, and almost all of the adults. It was a hideous tragedy that no one would soon forget. And now that it was over, suddenly there was press everywhere. The police were trying in vain to hold them back.

Along with the other Red Cross workers, Christianna walked with parents, among the lifeless children, while they identified them, then helped the parents wrap them and place them in small wooden coffins that had appeared from somewhere. A sob caught in her throat for the thousandth time as she spotted her pregnant friend, clutching her son to her as she cried. The boy was nearly naked, but alive and covered with blood from a cut on his head. Christianna walked over to her and hugged both mother and child. There was no stopping the tears, and Christianna took off her own jacket and put it around him, as the young woman smiled at her through her tears, and thanked her in Russian. Christianna hugged her again and helped her get the boy to a paramedic to check him. In spite of the obvious trauma, and the cut on his head, surprisingly, he was all right. The scene had not gone unnoticed by Marque, working alongside the other workers herself,

helping people to identify bodies, and closing coffins. It was a devastating day and night, even for the soldiers, and those who had seen
scenes like this before. There had been few in the recent history of ter-
rorism that had been quite this bad. And for Christianna, it was an ini-
tiation by fire. As she stooped to help someone else, she noticed that
she was covered with blood. Everyone seemed to be covered with it
from the children they had held, both dead and alive.

Throughout the afternoon and night, many more ambulances arrived, hearses, trucks, vehicles, and people came from neighboring
towns and far away. It felt as though all of Russia had come to be with
these people, help them bury their dead, and mourn. By late that
night, they seemed to have a clear idea of who had been killed, and
who had been saved. Almost all the missing children were accounted
for, although a few had been rushed to hospitals while no one knew
their names. It was midnight when Christianna and her two bodyguards helped Marque and the others load their trucks. The volunteers' work was done, the rest would be handled by the professional
members of the Red Cross, who would help locate the children who
had gone to hospitals in other locations. Christianna stayed till the
bitter end. She stood outside the last truck, hugged Marque, and
burst into tears of grief and exhaustion. They had all seen too much in
the past few days. Christianna had only been there since the night before, and knew without question that her life had been forever
changed. Everything she had seen or done or experienced before this
seemed irrelevant to her now.

Marque knew better than anyone that that was how it worked. Her
own two children had been killed in an uprising in Africa while she
and her children were living there, and had stayed too long in a time
of political unrest. It had cost her children's lives, something for which
she had spent a lifetime trying to forgive herself, and eventually it had

also cost her marriage. She had stayed in Africa after that, and started a Red Cross chapter to help the locals. She still went back often, had worked in the Middle East, during various wars and conflicts, and in Central America. She went wherever she was needed. She no longer had a country. She was a citizen of the world, her nationality was the Red Cross, her mission helping all those who needed her, in whatever situation, no matter how uncomfortable, debilitating, or dangerous. Marque feared nothing and loved all. And she stood with her arms around Christianna now, while the young woman cried like a child. They had all been through too much.

"I know," Marque said gently, indifferent to her own exhaustion, as always. This was her life's blood, and she gladly shared it with others who needed it more than she did. She wasn't afraid of dying in the course of her work. This was her family now, and all that she loved. "I know how hard it is the first time. You did a wonderful job," she praised her, as Christianna stayed buried in her arms. She was hardly bigger than a child. Her bodyguards had also cried many times that night and were no longer ashamed of it. It would have been stranger if they hadn't. Christianna loved them for it. Just as Marque had come to love her for all she'd done. It was a long time before Christianna wiped her eyes and emerged from the older woman's arms. She hadn't had a mother's embrace for most of her lifetime, and this felt the way she imagined it would have. Someone holding you until you felt ready to face life again. Christianna wasn't sure she was yet. She would never forget the tragedies she'd seen that night, or the pure rejoicing of parents who found their children alive and were reunited. She had cried just as hard at that. It had all been heart-wrenching beyond anything she could have imagined. She had expected to work hard, but not to have her heart torn from her body and ripped apart.

"If you ever want to come to work for us," Marque said quietly, and meant it, "call me. I think you have a gift," she said honestly. She had discovered her own after her children had died, and she had made the children of Africa her family. In her years of service, she had loved and comforted children all over the world. She had turned her own devastating loss into a blessing for others.

"I wish I could," Christianna said, still looking shaken. She knew too well that working for them wasn't even a remote possibility. Her father would never allow it.

"Maybe you could for a short time. Think about it. I'm easy to find. Call the International Red Cross office in Geneva—they always know where to find me. I don't stay anywhere for long. If you want to, we'll talk."

"I'd love that," Christianna said sincerely, wishing she could convince her father, and knowing at the same time that there was absolutely no chance she ever would. He would have gone insane at the thought. But this was so much more meaningful than anything she could do at home, or even through the foundation. For the first time in her life, she had felt alive and useful that night, as though her existence were not an accident but had a purpose. And she knew that even if they never met again, for the rest of her life she would remember Marque. There were people all over the world who felt that way about her.

The two women embraced again, and as the Red Cross trucks began to leave at dawn, she, Max, and Samuel went back to where they had left the car. It had several bullet holes in it, and the windshield had vanished, smashed into tiny pieces on the floor of the car. The two men cleared it out as best they could. It was going to be a chilly ride back to the airport. They left not long after the Red Cross as the sun streaked across the sky. There were still soldiers and police in the area. All the bodies had been removed. The ambulances were gone. And the children who had died there would never be forgotten.

It was a long silent ride back to Vladikavkaz. Neither Christianna nor her bodyguards said more than a few words to each other. They were too exhausted, and too shaken by what they'd seen. Max drove this time, while Samuel slept in the front seat, and Christianna stared out the window. They had been there for one day and two nights, which seemed like an eternity. Christianna stayed awake for the whole trip, thinking about the young pregnant girl, a widow now, with three children. She thought of Marque and the gentleness of her face, her limitless kindness and compassion. She reflected also on what she had said at the end, and wished that there were some way to convince her father to allow her to do this kind of work. She had no desire whatsoever to get a "license," a master's degree, at the Sorbonne. It meant nothing to her. But most of all, she thought of the faces she had seen that night, the people who had died, the faces of those who had survived as they wandered shell-shocked among their families and parents . . . the gifts, the losses, the tragedies, the terrors, the terrible people who had done this to them, and their complete lack of conscience. She was still silent and wide awake when they reached the airport. They returned the car and assured the rental company that they would be responsible for the damage. Christianna said to put it on the credit card she had given them initially. She saw people staring at her as they walked through the airport and had no idea why, until one of her bodyguards put his own jacket around her shoulders.

"It's all right, I'm not cold," she assured him, and handed it back to him, as he looked at her sadly.

"You're covered with blood, Your Highness," he said quietly, and as she looked down at the sweater she had worn, she saw that she was. The blood of hundreds of children, and nearly as many adults, as many of them as she had touched. She glanced in a mirror and saw that it was in her hair as well. She hadn't combed her hair in two days, and she no longer cared, about anything except the people she had seen in Digora. Now they were all that mattered.

She went to the ladies' room and tried to make herself look respectable, which was relatively hopeless. Her shoes were covered with mud from the fields she had stood in. Her jeans and sweater were caked with blood. It was in her hair, under her nails, she could still smell it. It had seeped into her soul. She showed her passport as they left, and this time no one commented. On the way out, it didn't seem to matter as much. And late that night they were home.

The bodyguards had called ahead, and her car and driver met them at the airport. They had asked the driver to cover the seats with towels, which mystified him until he saw her. At first he didn't realize it was blood. He looked shocked when he did, and said nothing. They rode to the palace in Vaduz in silence. As the gates opened, they entered, and she looked at the place where she lived, had been born, and would probably die one day, hopefully when she was old. But all she knew now to her core and soul was that nothing there had changed in the past three days, but she had returned a different person. The girl who had left Vaduz three days before no longer existed. The one who had come home after the siege of Digora was forever changed.

# Chapter 5

Christianna did not see her father the night she got home. He was in Vienna for a diplomatic dinner at the French embassy, and had stayed at Palace Liechtenstein, just as he had when he went to the ballet with her. He knew before he left for Vienna that she was safe. Their cell phones hadn't worked while they were in Russia, but her bodyguards had called him from the airport to reassure him. Until then, he had been wild with worry. And he came to find her the moment he got home. It was twenty-four hours after she had returned from Russia. She looked immaculate in jeans, loafers, and a Berkeley sweatshirt. Her hair was freshly washed and brushed. There was no sign of what she'd been through, or how harrowing it had been, until he looked into her eyes. What he saw there terrified him. She didn't look dead, but more alive than he had ever seen her, wiser, older, sadder, deeper. Just as she had known herself when she came home, after all she'd seen during those three days, she was no longer the same person. Looking at her, he was frightened. He knew everything had changed since he had last seen her.

"Hello, Papa," she said quietly as he put his arms around her and kissed her. "I'm so happy to see you." She seemed more adult than she ever had been, more of a woman. He wanted to hold her in his arms and keep her, and suddenly he knew he couldn't. The child he had known and nurtured was suddenly gone, and in her place was a woman who had learned and seen things that no one should ever have to know.

"I missed you," he said sadly. "I was so worried about you. I watched the news constantly, but I never saw you. Was it as awful as it looked?" he asked, sitting down next to her and taking her hand in his. He wished she hadn't gone, but there had been no stopping her. He knew he couldn't. And he knew the same now.

"It was worse. There was a lot the press wasn't allowed to show, out of respect for the families." Tears rolled slowly down her cheeks as his heart ached for what she'd been through. He would have done anything to protect her from it. "They killed so many children, Papa. Hundreds of them, as though they were just sheep or cattle or goats."

"I know. I saw some of it on television. The families' faces were so terrible. I kept thinking of how I would feel if I lost you. I couldn't bear it. I don't know how those people will survive, and go on. It must be so hard." She thought of her young pregnant friend then, the one she had never been able to talk to, but they had just held each other and cried . . . and Marque . . . all of them who had crossed her path in those few days. "I was relieved that the press never got you. Did they ever find out that you were there?" He assumed they hadn't or he would have heard about it, and she shook her head.

"No, they didn't, and the woman in charge of the Red Cross was very discreet. She knew it the moment she saw my passport. She said some of our cousins have worked with her before."

"I'm glad she didn't say anything. I was afraid someone would." If so, it would have been the least of her problems, although she wouldn't have liked it either, and was glad that she had been able to do her work undiscovered and undisturbed. It would have been such an intrusion to have photographers in her face, and offended all the grieving people. She had been lucky to remain anonymous through-out the trip.

She looked at her father long and hard then, and he sensed that something was coming that he wouldn't like. She tightened her grip on his hand and looked into his eyes. Hers were two bottomless pools of bright blue sky, very much like his, except that his were old and hers were young. And in hers he saw twin pools of hope and pain. She had seen too much for a girl her age in those three days. He knew it would take her a long time to forget all that she'd seen.

"I want to go back, Papa," she said softly, and he looked startled, shocked, pained. "Not to Russia, but to work with the Red Cross again. I want to make a difference, and I can't do that here. I know I can't do it forever, but I want a year, six months . . . after that I'll do whatever you want. But for once in my life I want to do something that makes a difference, a big one, to someone else. Papa, please. . . ." Her eyes were filled with tears as he shook his head and shifted un-comfortably in his seat.

"You can do that with your mother's foundation, Cricky. You've had a shocking experience. I know what that's like." He had gone to disas-ter scenes before, and seen the agony of people's grief. But he could not do as she asked. "There are many things you can do here. Work with handicapped children, if you like, or the poor in Vienna. Volun-teer at a hospital for burn victims. You can soothe many sorrows, and console many aching hearts. But if what you're asking me is to go to dangerous countries, in high-risk situations, where you yourself are at risk, I just can't allow you to do that. I would worry about you too much. You're too important to me, I love you too much. And I owe your mother a responsibility here, too. She would have expected me to keep you out of harm's way."

"I don't want to do those things here," she said petulantly, sounding like a child again, but she felt like one with him. This was an argument she didn't want to lose, nor did he. "I want to go out in the world for once in my life, be like everyone else, work hard, and pay my dues, before I settle into this comfortable life forever, like Victoria, trying to decide which tiara to wear, and which dress, cutting ribbons at hospitals or visiting orphans and old people for the rest of my life." He knew how much that life chafed, and he didn't disagree. But particularly as a woman, she couldn't go running around the world, risking her life in war zones, or digging ditches for the poor, to atone for the sins of being royal and rich. He knew better than anyone that she had to make her peace now with who she was.

"You've just come back from four years in the States. You had a great deal of freedom there"—in fact, more than he knew—"but now you have to accept who you are and all that goes with it. It's time for you to come home, not time to run away. You can't run away from this, Christianna. I know. I tried myself when I was young. In the end, this is who we are, and all that comes with it is what we must do." It sounded like a death sentence to her as tears rolled down her cheeks, grieving the freedom she would never know or taste, the things she would never do. For this one year of her life, she wanted to be just like everyone else. Her father was saying that it was impossible for her. This was the one gift she wanted from him now, before it was too late. If she was ever going to do it, this was the time.

"Then why is Freddy still running around the world, doing whatever he wants?"

"For one thing"—her father smiled at her—"your brother is immature," as they both knew, and then her father's face grew serious again. He knew this was an important subject to her. "For another, he's not in dangerous areas, or at least not technically or geographically, or due to circumstances like the ones you just experienced in Russia. Your brother creates his dangers himself, and they are far more harmless than anything you would encounter working for the Red Cross. You would spend a year, or however long, doing things like what you just went through. Nothing untoward happened this time, thank God, and you came to no harm. But you could have. If they had in fact blown up the school, without announcing it first, you could have gotten hurt, or worse." He shuddered thinking of it. "Christianna, I am not sending you out into the world to be killed, or mauled, or exposed to tropical diseases or natural disasters, political unrest, or violence of any kind. I simply won't do it." He was adamant about it, as she had known he would be, but she wasn't ready to give up yet. It meant too much to her now. And she knew that even if she went to work at her late mother's foundation, he would not allow her to travel to rigorous areas with them, even for visits. All he wanted was to protect her, but that was exactly what she was so tired of and didn't want.

"Will you at least think about it?" she begged him.

"No, I won't," he said, and then stood up. "I'll do anything I can and everything you want to make your life better and more interesting here. But forget the Red Cross, Christianna, or anything like it." He looked at her sternly, bent to kiss her, and before she could say more, he strode out of the room. The discussion was over. And for hours afterward she sat alternately depressed and angry, fuming in her room. Why was he so unreasonable? And why did she have to be a princess? She hated being royal. She didn't even answer her e-mails from the States that night, which she usually loved to do. She had too much else on her mind, and had seen too much.

She avoided her father entirely for the next two days. She rode her horse, and went running with her dog. She cut ribbons at an orphanage and another home for the elderly. She read on tape for the blind, and spent time at the foundation, and hated all of it. She wanted to be anyone other than who she was, and anywhere other than at home in Vaduz. She didn't even want to go to Paris. Above all, she hated her life, her ancestors, the palace, her father when she dared. She didn't want to be a princess anymore. It felt like a curse to her, and surely not a blessing, as she had been told all her life. She called Victoria in London to complain to her, and she told her to come back. But what was the point of that? She'd just have to come back to Vaduz again, and everything waiting for her there. Her German cousins invited her to come and stay, but she didn't want to go there either. And she refused to join her father for a trip to Madrid, to visit the king of Spain. She hated them all.

She had been raging for two weeks, in a deep gloom, when her father came to her. She had been avoiding him assiduously for days. He was well aware of her misery, and looked bitterly unhappy himself, as he sat down in a chair in her bedroom. In deference to him, she turned the music down. She had been using it to drown out everything that was in her head, and her sorrows. Even Charles looked bored, as he looked up at her, wagged his tail, and didn't bother to get up.

"I want to talk to you," her father said quietly.

"About what?" she asked, still sounding petulant and surly.

"About your insane idea of signing up with the Red Cross. I want you to know I think it's an extremely bad idea, and if your mother were alive, she wouldn't even have considered talking to you about it. In fact, she'd have killed me for talking to you at all on this subject." Christianna frowned as she listened to him. She was tired of his trying to convince her of what a bad idea it was. She had already heard it, several times too often, which was why at the moment she wasn't speaking to him at all.

"I know how you feel about it, Papa," she said somberly. "You don't have to tell me again. I've heard it."

"Yes, you have, and so have I. So you can listen to me one more time." He almost smiled to himself, thinking that he might rule a country and thirty-three thousand subjects, but he was having a much harder time reigning over one daughter. He sighed, and then went on. "I spoke to the director of the Red Cross in Geneva this week. We had a long talk. In fact, at my request, he came here to see me."

"You're not going to buy me off by having me volunteer in an office," she said angrily, glaring at him, as he fought not to lose his temper, and succeeded. "And I'm not going to give a ball for them, here or in Vienna. I hate things like that. I find them disgustingly boring." She crossed her arms across her chest as a signal of her refusal.

"So do I, but they're part of my job. And one day they may be part of yours, depending on who you marry. I don't enjoy all that either, but it's expected of us, and you can't simply decide that you don't want to be who you are. Others have done that before you, and made a mess of their lives. Christianna, you have no choice but to accept your fate here. We're very fortunate in many ways." His voice mellowed a little as he looked at her. "Besides, we have each other, and I love you very much. And I don't want you to be unhappy."

"I am unhappy," she stressed again. "I lead a thoroughly useless, stupid, spoiled, indulgent life. And the only time I've ever done anything meaningful or worthwhile was two weeks ago in Russia."

"I know that. And I know you feel that way. I understand. A lot of what everyone does, in any job, is meaningless and superficial. It's very rare to have an experience like the one you just had, where you are truly helping people in their direst moments. You also can't make a life of that."

"The woman who ran the Red Cross operation in Russia does just that. Her name is Marque, and she's an amazing woman."

"I know all about her," her father said calmly. He had spent many hours with the head of the Red Cross who had come to see him from Geneva, and ultimately the prince had been satisfied with their conversation, although with grave reservations. "Cricky, I want you to listen to me. I don't want you to be miserable, or even unhappy. You absolutely must accept who you are, and understand to your very soul that you can't escape it. It is your fate, your destiny, and your obligation. And also a great blessing in many ways, although you don't see that yet. And part of that is that you must be a blessing to others, as you are, where you are, and not just try to deny it. You are a blessing to me as well, and one day, you will be to your brother. You know a lot more about this country than he does. And you will help him run it, even if from behind the scenes. In fact, I'm counting on you to do that. He will be reigning prince, but you will be his mentor and adviser. He can't run this country without you to guide him." It was the very first time he had ever suggested that to her, and she was shocked. "How you deal with your responsibilities, your life, what you do about it, how miserable you make yourself ultimately is up to you. I want you to spend some time thinking about it. You cannot now, or later, or ever, escape who you are. I expect a great deal of you, Christianna. I need you. You are a Serene Highness. It is part of you, both your heritage and your job. Do you understand me?" He had never before made himself as clear in her entire life, and it frightened her and made her want to run away.

She wanted to avoid what he was saying but didn't dare, he was her father after all, whether a reigning prince or not. And she hated hearing what he said, because it was so painfully true, and she loathed being reminded of it. It was a burden she could not lighten, remove, or take off. Ever. And now he wanted to add Freddy's duties to her own. "I understand you, Father," she said grimly. She only called him Father and not Papa when she was very angry. Just as he used her title, although rarely, when he was furious at her, which was rarer still.

"Good. Then if you understand me, we can go on," he said, undaunted. "Because ultimately, you have no choice here. I will only discuss this with you if you truly accept who you are, and resign yourself to what you eventually must do. If you can't do it now, then I will give you some time to adjust to the idea, but sooner or later, you must come home to your responsibilities in Vaduz. To your own duties and obligations, and to help and guide your brother with his." It was an awesome burden for her to hear what he expected of her, and would one day. It was worse than she had feared.

"I don't want to go to Paris," she said, looking stubborn.

"I wasn't going to suggest Paris. And I don't like what I am going to suggest. But the Red Cross director himself has agreed to take full responsibility for you. He assured me, in fact he swore to me, that if I entrust you to him, you will come to no harm, and I intend to hold him to it. If even the slightest incident occurs, or any political situation becomes unpleasant, then you are coming home on the next flight without further discussion. But until then, I am agreeing to allow you to join one of their projects for the next six months. At most a year, if it goes smoothly. But after that, no matter what, you come home. And for now, I am only committing to six months. We'll see what happens after that. They have a project in Africa that they think might appeal to you. It was started by your friend Marque. It's primarily a center for women and children with AIDS, and it's one of the few peaceful parts of Africa at the moment. If that changes at any time, it's over and you come home. Is that clear?" There were tears in his eyes when he finished speaking to her, and she stared at him in amazement. She had never in a million years expected him to change his mind about what she wanted to do.

"Are you serious? Do you mean it?" She got up and threw her arms around his neck, unable to believe it. There were tears in her eyes too as she hugged him and kissed him. She was ecstatic. "Oh, Papa!" she said, moved beyond words, as he hugged her tightly.

"I'm probably completely insane to let you do this. I must be getting senile," he said in a shaken voice. He had thought long and hard about it, and had remembered how anguished he had been himself at her age, wanting to do something more meaningful with his life. It had been an agonizing few years for him, and as crown prince he had been utterly unable to free himself from his duties, and had to live with his frustration. And then he had met her mother and married her and everything had changed. His father had died soon after, and he had become reigning prince. He had never had time to look back at those early unhappy days again, but he remembered them well when he jogged his memory, which was what had finally convinced him. And Christianna would never have the burden or responsibility of reigning. That lot would fall to her brother, and never to her, since women could not reign in Liechtenstein. All of that had finally led to his decision, although he had done so with enormous trepidation, and only because he loved her so much, which Christianna always knew, even when she was angry at him. She wasn't angry at him now. She had never in her life been as grateful or as happy.

"Oh, Papa," she said, her voice filled with emotion. "When can I go?"

"I want you here for the holidays. I'm not going to be here without you, selfish as it sounds. And it is. I told the director you can go in January, or later if you prefer, but not before. They need time to get ready for you anyway. They're setting up some new programs there, and they don't want any new volunteers until at least then." She nodded. She could live with that. It was less than four months away. She could hardly wait.

"I promise, I'll do everything you want me to, until I leave."

"You'd better," he said with a rueful grin at the daughter he loved so much, "or I might change my mind."

"Please don't!" she said, looking like a child again. "I promise I'll behave."

The only thing she regretted about it was that she would be leaving before her brother returned. But she would see him when she got back, or perhaps he'd come to visit, since he had very little to do in Vaduz, and loved to travel. He had been to Africa himself several times. She could hardly wait for her adventure to begin. She had never been so happy in her life. And afterward, when she had to come home, she would have to make her peace with it. As her father said, it was her destiny, and her lot in life. And maybe then, she'd go to work for the foundation, and one day run it, since her brother had no interest in it, and when he succeeded their father, he would no longer have time. The thought of guiding him still frightened her. It was something she'd have to face eventually, she knew. But first she had her time in Africa to think about. She could think of nothing else.

"You have to do several weeks of training in Geneva before you leave. I'll give you the director's number, and you can have your secretary set it up with him. Or perhaps they can send someone to train you here." She didn't want special favors from them, she wanted more than anything to be the same as everyone else. If only for this one precious year. It was her last chance.

"I'll go to Geneva," she said quietly, without telling him why.

"Well then," he said, standing up. "You have much to think about and much to celebrate." He paused in the doorway and looked back at her, and for just a moment he looked like an old man. "I'll miss you terribly while you're gone." And worry about her constantly, but he didn't tell her that. He looked tired and sad as he stood at the door.

"I love you, Papa . . . thank you . . . with all my heart," she said, and he knew it was heartfelt. He knew he had done the right thing for her, no matter how hard it was for him. And he would send people to protect and safeguard her, there would be no argument with that.

"I love you too, Cricky," he said softly, nodded, smiled at her, and left the room with tears in his eyes.

# Chapter 6

Once her father had agreed to let her work for the Red Cross, Christianna threw herself into her duties in Vaduz with renewed energy, cutting ribbons, visiting the sick and elderly, reading to orphans, and attending diplomatic and state events with her father, without a single word of complaint. He was touched by the efforts she made, and hopeful that she would be ready to adjust to the duties of her royal life with more equanimity when she got home. She could hardly wait to leave for Africa in January, and had had a note from Marque, who had heard via the grapevine that Christianna would be going to Africa. She thanked her again for her efforts when they had met, and wished her well on her new adventure. She was excited for her. She said it would be an experience she would never forget. Marque still went to Africa herself at every opportunity, and said she might come to visit while Christianna was there.

Neither Christianna nor her father was prepared for Freddy's reaction when Christianna sent her brother an e-mail, telling him her plans. He was incensed, and violently opposed to the idea. He called their father, and did everything he could to convince him to change his mind. But much to Christianna's relief, her father held firm. After arguing with his father about it unsuccessfully, Freddy decided to call her himself.

"Are you out of your mind?" he said angrily. "What are you thinking, Cricky? Africa is dangerous, you have no idea what you're doing. You'll get killed by natives in some local uprising, or you'll get sick. I've been there, it's not a place for you. Father must be insane." She was relieved that Freddy hadn't been able to make him renege, although he had certainly tried.

"Don't be silly," she said blithely, although his fury unnerved her a little. "You spent a month there last year, and you had a wonderful time."

"I'm a man," he said stubbornly, as she rolled her eyes. She hated it when he said things like that.

"Don't be stupid. What difference does that make?"

"I'm not afraid of lions and snakes," he said, sounding cocky. He felt sure she would be terrified of both.

"Neither am I," she said bravely, although she definitely wasn't enthused about snakes.

"Like hell you're not. You nearly had a heart attack when I put a snake in your bed," he reminded her, and she laughed.

"I was nine."

"You're hardly older than that now. You should be at home where you belong."

"Doing what? I have nothing to do here, and you know it."

"You can go to dinner parties with Father, or find a husband. Do whatever princesses are supposed to do." She was still trying to figure that out herself. "I hear Victoria just got engaged again, by the way. The crown prince of Denmark? That won't last." Christianna didn't argue with him, they both knew her too well. In fact, Christianna had just heard from one of her German cousins that Victoria was getting bored with him, although everyone said he was a very nice man. Christianna couldn't actually imagine her marrying anyone, at least not for a long time. "Stupid girl," Freddy muttered. "She's obsessed with getting married. I don't see how any man could stand being married to her, although I have to admit, she's a lot of fun."

"What about you?" Christianna asked plaintively. "When are you coming home? Aren't you bored yet?"

"No," he said, sounding mischievous, "I'm having way too much fun."

"Well, it's not fun around here without you. I'm bored to death."

"That's no excuse for you to go running off to Africa, and trying to get yourself killed." He actually sounded worried about her. Although he teased her constantly, and had tormented her as a child, he adored her, and had been sorry to hear she'd be gone by the time he got home. He was seriously thinking of going to visit her, if she actually persisted in what he considered her totally mad plan.

"I'm not going to get killed," she reassured him. "I'm not joining the army. I'll be working for the Red Cross in a facility for women and children."

"I still think you should stay home. How's Father?" he asked casually. He was feeling mildly guilty for having been gone so long, but not guilty enough yet to come home.

"He's fine. Working too hard as always. Why don't you try and come home for Christmas before I leave?"

"I have too much to see in China. Hong Kong, Beijing, Singapore, Shanghai, and I want to stop in Burma to see friends on the way back."

"We're going to be sad here without you, we already are."

"No, you won't," he said, laughing. "You'll be too busy having fun in Gstaad." They always went there for Christmas and New Year, but even that was going to be less fun this year without him. She loved skiing with him, although Christianna and her father saw friends and relatives there every year. It was a very pleasant part of their life. And she'd be leaving shortly after that.

"I really miss you, you know," she said, feeling nostalgic for a minute. It was nice talking to him, even if he did disapprove of her plans. He was very protective of her, and had been ever since he had grown up. It was still hard for her to imagine, though, that he would be reigning prince one day. She didn't like to think about it, since more than likely that would happen only when her father was no longer around, hopefully not for a very long time. And in the meantime, all Freddy did was play. He had no desire to spend time in tiny Vaduz either. He was even more bored than Christianna whenever he was there, and he did far fewer official duties than she did. He had never been interested in mundane things like that. He happily shirked his responsibilities and escaped, every chance he got.

"I miss you, too," Freddy said gently. "And what did I hear about your going to Russia? Father said something to me about it, but I didn't quite get it. What were you doing there?" She told him about the terrorist attack on the school in Digora, the hostages they'd taken, the horrifying death toll, the shocking things she had seen while she was there. He sounded shocked, and understood better what had led her to volunteer for the Red Cross. "What's happening to you, Cricky? You're not going to go and become a nun or something like that, are you?" He couldn't even begin to imagine her flying off to Russia and spending three days in a hostage crisis, working for the Red Cross. He had seen the attack on the news, but it would never have occurred to him in a million years to jump on a plane, and go to the scene to help out. It would have been the furthest thing from his mind. And although she loved him madly, Christianna also knew that he was an extremely spoiled, self-indulgent man.

"No, I'm not going to become a nun," she laughed.

"Any bad boys I need to chase off when I get home?"

"Not a one," she said, smiling. She hadn't had a date since she had left Berkeley in June. She had been away for four years and had lost touch with the few friends she had at home. Hers had always been an isolated life. "You're the only truly bad boy I know."

"Yes," he said proudly, "I suppose I am, aren't I?" Her calling him that always amused him. He had no desire to be anything other than that, and maybe wouldn't for a long time. At least for the moment, in Tokyo, he was staying out of the press. He hadn't been involved in a scandal, or a hot romance, for at least two months. "And don't think you've gotten away with your African caper," he suddenly remembered, and scolded her again. "You're not going to get me off that subject as quickly as that. I have every intention of calling Father again!"

"Don't you dare!"

"I'm serious. I think it's a perfectly awful plan."

"Well, I don't. I'm not going to just sit here cutting ribbons, while you have all the fun, running around the world. How many geisha girls are you bringing home?" she teased him back.

"None. And besides, I haven't been to China yet. I hear the girls are absolutely beautiful in Shanghai. And I just got invited to Vietnam."

"You're hopeless, Freddy," she said, sounding more like a big sister than a younger one. Sometimes she felt that way. He was so lovable and irresistible, while being completely irresponsible at the same time. She wondered if he'd ever get married. She truly couldn't imagine it, and in recent years, he had become one of the most notorious playboys in Europe, a fact that did not please their father. He expected

Freddy to marry someone worthy of him one of these days, and stop chasing models and starlets. The only princess he'd ever been involved with had been married. He was a total reprobate. The husband of the princess he'd been involved with had called him a scoundrel in the press, to which Freddy had responded that he was flattered that the man thought so highly of him. In some ways, Christianna knew, it was better that he was not at home. As long as he continued to behave that way, all it did was upset their father. At least in Tokyo, whatever mischief he was up to was not under everyone's nose. "Think about coming home for Christmas," she reminded him before they hung up.

"You think about coming to your senses and staying home. Forget Africa, Cricky. You'll hate it. Just remember all the snakes and bugs."

"Thank you for the encouragement. And you think about coming back before I leave. Otherwise I won't see you for at least eight months."

"Maybe you ought to think about becoming a nun" was his parting shot. She told him to behave himself, blew him a kiss, and hung up. She worried about him at times. He was so totally uninterested in the job that their father did so well, and that he would inherit one day. She just hoped he would manage to grow up sometime before he did. Their father cherished the same hope but grew more worried about it each year.

Christianna mentioned that evening that she had spoken to him, and her father sighed and shook his head.

"I worry about what will happen to the country when he takes over the reins." Although a tiny country, Liechtenstein had a booming economy, which had not happened by accident. Christianna knew far more about their policies and economy than her brother did. Her father thought at times that it was a shame that their ages, sexes, and personalities were not reversed. He would have hated to have a profligate daughter, which she wasn't, but he hated just as much the thought of having an irresponsible playboy as reigning prince. It was a problem he had yet to solve. But so far, time was on their side, and fortunately, although he had just turned sixty-seven, Prince Hans Josef was in good health. Presumably, Freddy would not be reigning soon.

The next two months flew by as Christianna attended to her duties with renewed zeal. She wanted to do everything as perfectly as possible, before she left for Africa, if nothing else than to show her father how grateful she was for letting her go. She spent two weeks in Geneva, for her Red Cross training. She already had a certificate in advanced first aid. Most of her briefings were about the country where she would be living, the local tribes, their habits, the potential dangers of the current political situation, the things she had to look out for, the faux pas she had to be careful not to make, so as not to offend the locals. She got an intense crash course about AIDS, since the facility where she would be working was specifically for that purpose. And then there were several warnings about insects to be aware of, diseases she had to be vaccinated against, and how to identify a wide variety of poisonous snakes. It was only during that part of her training that she wondered, though only for a fraction of an instant, if Freddy was right. She hated snakes. They told her what kind of equipment she needed, what her responsibilities would be, and what kind of clothes to bring. Her head was swimming with all the information by the time she got back to Vaduz. The palace doctor had already begun giving her the necessary vaccinations. In all, she would have to have nine, several of which she had been told might make her sick. She was having vaccinations for hepatitis A and B, typhoid, yellow fever, meningitis, rabies, and boosters for tetanus, measles, and polio. And she had to take antimalarial drugs while she was away, as well as before and after. It all seemed worth it to her. The only thing that still worried her a bit were the snakes. She had already ordered two pairs of stout boots, and had been told to shake them out when she got out of bed, before putting them on, in case something unpleasant had crawled into them during the night—not an appealing thought. But everything else they had told her sounded fine, particularly the work. She was going to be helping the professional medical and other workers, as a kind of general assistant during the time she was there. As a result, her job was a little hard to define, and she would learn more about it once she was there. She was ready, able, and willing to do any task she was assigned. In fact, she could hardly wait.

Two weeks before Christmas, right after her training in Geneva, she and her father went to Paris for a wedding. One of her Bourbon cousins, on her mother's side, was getting married. A princess was marrying a duke. The wedding itself was spectacular, at Notre Dame, and the reception was in a beautiful *hôtel particulier* on the rue de Varenne. The flowers were exquisite, every possible detail had been thought of. The bride wore a magnificent lace gown by Chanel Haute Couture with a cloud of veil that covered her face. There were four hundred people at the wedding, which was attended by royals from all over Europe, and the cream of *le tout Paris,* the most fashionable people in Parisian society. The wedding was at eight o'clock at night, and the groom and all the male guests wore white tie. The women wore spectacular evening gowns. Christianna wore a deep blue velvet dress trimmed in sable, with her mother's sapphires. She saw Victoria there, who had just broken her engagement to the Danish prince. She was wilder than ever, and single yet again, she claimed much to her relief.

"When's your naughty brother coming home?" she asked Christianna, with a wild look of mischief in her eye.

"Never, at this rate," Christianna answered. "He says not till spring."

"Damn. What a shame. I was going to invite him to come to Tahiti with me over New Year's." She said it in such a way that Christianna suddenly wondered if Victoria was zeroing in on him for a fling.

"Maybe he'll meet you there," Christianna said, glancing around. It was one of the prettiest weddings she'd ever seen.

The bride had been attended by a flock of little children, carrying satin baskets filled with flower petals, as was the custom in France. "I think he's already in China," she said vaguely. She had just spotted a friend across the room, whom she hadn't seen in years. Her father left at two in the morning, while the party was still in full swing. Along with most of the young people, Christianna stayed till nearly five A.M. The bride and groom were still there at that hour as well, dancing up a storm. The car was waiting for Christianna outside, with her bodyguards, and she got back to the Ritz, where she and her father were staying, at nearly six A.M. It had been a fabulous event, and she hadn't had as much fun in years.

Christianna couldn't help thinking, as she took off her sapphires and evening gown and laid them on a chair, that the life she led in Europe was about as far as one could get from the life she was about to lead in Africa while working for the Red Cross. But as much fun as this was from time to time, the life she would be embarking on was exactly the one she wanted. Still thinking about it, she slipped into her bed with a smile.

She and her father spent the rest of the weekend in Paris. He reminded her somewhat wistfully, while walking through the Place Vendôme on the way back to the hotel, that it wasn't too late to change her mind about working for the Red Cross. She could still change her plans and go to the Sorbonne. As soon as he said it, she looked up at him and smiled.

"Papa, I won't be away for that long." Although she was hoping to stretch the six months to a year, if he allowed it.

"I'm going to miss you so much," he said sadly.

"So will I. But it's going to be so exciting. And when could I ever do this again?" Now was the time, while she was still young. Later, when she took on more of her responsibilities, it would be even less likely that she could get away, and they both knew it. He had promised her, so he wouldn't go back on his word. But he hated to see her leave.

Her father encouraged her to stay in Paris for an extra day after that, or more if she wanted. But knowing she was leaving for Africa soon made her feel guilty leaving him alone for long. He was so attached to her, and missed her terribly when she was gone. Her Berkeley years had been hard for him. He was much closer to Christianna than to his son, and particularly enjoyed discussing the business matters of the principality with her, and valued her opinions.

She and Victoria went shopping on the Faubourg St. Honoré and the Avenue Montaigne on Monday. They had lunch at L'Avenue, where Freddy normally loved to pick up models. His favorite haunts were Costes, Bain Douche, Man Ray, and the Buddha Bar. Freddy had a particular fondness for Paris, but so did Christianna. She and Victoria fell into her room at the Ritz at the end of a long day, and ordered room service. They were both still tired after the wedding. And they parted company finally on Tuesday morning at the airport. Christianna flew to Zurich and Victoria to London, promising to meet up again soon. Victoria had already said she would come to Gstaad, to stay with her, if she didn't go to Tahiti. Now that she was no longer engaged, she was slightly at loose ends, and Christianna was hoping to see her again before she left.

She had a lot to do in Vaduz these days. There had been an official announcement from the palace that she was going to be traveling for the next several months, with no specifics about her plans or destination. It made security issues simpler that way, and she was determined that no one know that she was a princess while she worked for the Red Cross. Once word was out that she was leaving, suddenly everyone wanted her for ceremonies, openings, groundbreakings, parties, and blessings. She tried to do as many as she could, and she was exhausted when she and her father left for Gstaad the following week. They always had fun there. It was a very fashionable ski resort, filled with Americans and Europeans, playboys, beauties, movie stars, and assorted royals. It was one of the few vacation spots that catered to the extremely rich that Christianna actually enjoyed. She and her father were both avid skiers, and they had a wonderful time there every year.

She and her father celebrated Christmas quietly together, they went to midnight mass afterward, and she tried to call Freddy in Hong Kong but he was out. It seemed odd not to have him there with them, and he called them both the following morning. He asked about the Bourbon wedding in Paris, and she told him of Victoria's somewhat offhand invitation to him for Tahiti. He said he was sorry to miss it, but maybe he'd go with her for Easter, and after begging his sister to reconsider her plans again, he wished them both a Merry Christmas and hung up.

Christianna and her father stayed in Gstaad, as they always did, till just after New Year, and she was startled to realize once they got back that she only had four days left in Vaduz before she left. And for her father's taste, the last days flew by much too fast. He wanted to savor every moment he could with her. But his own responsibilities intruded too much of the time. He walked into her room on the last day with a mournful look. She was busy packing her bags, and looked up as he came in. Even the dog was lying near her suitcase, looking sad.

"Charles and I are going to miss you," he said, looking unhappy.

"Will you take care of him for me?" she asked, giving her father a hug. She was going to miss them, too. But she couldn't wait to leave on her big adventure.

"Yes, I will. But who will take care of me?" He was only half-teasing. He relied on her company for more than he would have, if his wife were still alive, or if Freddy were more of a presence in his life or a better companion. He was never around, and when he was, he provided more aggravation and concern than companionship or support. Christianna's father spoke to her, and opened up to her as he did to no one else in his life.

"I'll be back soon, Papa. And Freddy will be back in another month or two." Her father rolled his eyes, and they both laughed.

"I don't think your brother will ever take care of me, or anyone else. And I think I'd be frightened if he did. The rest of us will be taking care of him." They both knew he was right, and Christianna laughed again, although they both shared the same concern about what would happen to the country when Freddy would be the reigning prince. Christianna's father had begun to hope that she would become her brother's principal adviser, when that happened, and was trying to teach her all he could. She was a willing student, loving daughter, shirked no responsibilities, and never failed him, which would make her absence more acute, although admittedly even he knew that at times he put far too much burden on her.

"I'm sure he'll grow up one of these days, Papa," Christianna said, trying to sound confident and hopeful, however undeserved.

"I wish I shared your optimism. I miss the boy, but I don't miss the chaos he creates while he's here. It's awfully peaceful around here without him." He was always honest with her, as she was with him.

"I know. But there's no one like him, is there?" she said, sounding like an adoring sister, which she was. He had been her hero when she was a little girl, although he had always teased her, and still did now. "I'll call you whenever I can, Papa. Apparently they have phones at the post office there, although they're not very reliable, I'm told, and sometimes the lines are down for weeks. Then all we can do is radio out. But I'll get word to you somehow, I promise." She knew her bodyguards would work something out, so she could get messages to her father to reassure him. They wouldn't have dared to do otherwise, or he might force her to come back, if she caused him to worry too much. She was going to do everything she could to stay in touch, whatever that had to be. She was still hoping he would allow her to extend her trip. She wanted to stay the full year.

Their last night together was bittersweet. They had dinner in the private dining room, and talked about her plans. She asked him about some new economic policies he had just introduced, and what the parliament's reaction had been to them. He was pleased that she had asked, and enjoyed discussing it with her. But then it only reminded him again of how lonely his life would be without her. She hadn't even left yet, and he couldn't wait for her to get back. He wanted the coming months to speed past, and he knew they wouldn't. Without the bright sunshine she provided in his life, the days would drag. Selfishly, he was thinking of insisting that she come back after the initial six months, and when he mentioned it to her, she asked him to wait to decide. She might be ready to come back then herself, or need a few more months to finish whatever she started. She asked him to keep an open mind, and he agreed. Their exchanges were always reasonable,

affectionate, and adult. In many ways, she was one of the main reasons he hadn't remarried. With Christianna to keep him company, and
talk to him, he didn't need a wife, nor want one. And besides, he felt
it was too late in his life to start again. Before that, he had been too
busy. He was comfortable now as he was, although he would be far
less so when she was gone. He kissed her goodnight, already mourning her absence, and they had breakfast together the next morning.
She was wearing blue jeans for the long flight, and would probably
wear nothing else for the next year. She had packed only one dress,
just in case, two peasant skirts she had brought back from California,
several pairs of shorts she had worn at school, a stack of jeans and
T-shirts, hats, mosquito netting, insect repellents, her malaria medication, and sturdy boots and shoes to protect her from the dreaded
snakes.

"This is no worse than when I used to go back to school in California
after the holidays, Papa. Think of it that way," she tried to console him.
He looked so mournful and so sad before she left.

"I would prefer to think of you right here."

He could barely speak when he said goodbye to her. He held her in
a long hug, and she kissed his cheek lovingly, as she always did. "You
know how I rely on you, don't you, Cricky? Take care of yourself."

"I will. I'll call you, Papa. I promise. Take good care of yourself,
too." It was harder leaving him than she thought it would be, as a sob
caught in her throat. She knew how much he needed her, and she
hated leaving him alone. She knew how lonely it would be for him.
But just this once, this one last time, before she took on her royal duties forever, she needed her own life.

"I love you, Cricky," he said softly. And with that, he turned to the
two bodyguards standing next to her, with a stern look. "Stay close to
her at all times." There was no mistaking his orders. They were the

same two young men who had accompanied her to Russia, Samuel and Max. They were as excited as she was about their new adventure, and she was comfortable and resigned about having them with her. Her father had been intransigent about that. It was the one condition on which he would not relent, so Christianna did at last. She felt slightly foolish having two bodyguards with her, but the director of the Red Cross camp had said he perfectly understood the need for it. He was extremely sensitive to her situation, and had assured her by e-mail that he would not divulge who she was. He was the only one who would be aware that her passport bore no last name, which might have given her away to those who were aware of such things, though they were usually rare. Marque had been singularly aware of that, as she had worked with royals before. Others weren't. But Christianna was taking no chances. The one thing she didn't want anyone to know was that she was a princess. She wanted to be treated the same as everyone there. She didn't want anyone calling her Your Serene Highness or ma'am, and surely not her bodyguards, who were masquerading as fellow volunteers, friends who were coming with her. Christianna had thought of everything and covered all her bases. And thus far, the director of the facility had been totally cooperative with her to that end.

"I love you, Papa," she said as she got into the car, and her father closed the door. He had wanted to come to the airport with her, but had to meet with all his ministers that morning, about the economic policies he and Christianna had discussed the night before. So he was saying goodbye to her at the palace.

"I love you too, Cricky. Don't forget that. Take good care of yourself. Be careful," he warned again, and she smiled, and leaned out the window to kiss his hand. The bond they had formed in the years since her mother's death was unseverable, and unusually close.

"Goodbye!" she called out and waved as they drove away. He stood and waved until the car went through the gates, turned, and disappeared, and then with his head bowed, he walked slowly back into the palace. He had done this for her, allowed her to go to Africa, to make her happy. But for him, it was going to be a miserable six months or year without her. And as he walked into the palace, the dog walked sadly behind him. Without Christianna's lively presence, they both already looked like a sad, lonely pair.

# Chapter 7

Christianna's flight from Zurich took off promptly for Frankfurt that morning. Her bodyguards were in business class, and she was in first. And although she had warned them not to, the palace had discreetly let the airline know that she was on the flight. It was exactly what she didn't want, and it annoyed her. All she could do was console herself with the knowledge that she would not be "special" for the next year. She didn't want to be. This time away in Africa, working for the Red Cross, was her last opportunity to be an ordinary person, with none of the burdens that automatically came with her station in life. For the next months, she wanted none of the privileges of being royal. None at all. She wanted her experience there to be exactly the same as it was for everyone else, for better or worse.

When she changed flights in Frankfurt, she was grateful that no one appeared to know who she was. There was no one to meet or greet her, no one to help her transfer planes, no special attention. She picked up her backpack and handbag, while the two bodyguards managed their luggage and hers. They chatted amiably for a few minutes between flights, and tried to imagine what it was going to be

like. Sam thought it was going to be rugged. He had been to Africa before. The director in Geneva had assured her it would be comfortable,
and Christianna had insisted, and meant it, that she didn't care. She
was more than willing to rough it with everyone else, if that was the
case. He had promised her anonymity, and she was counting on that.
Otherwise, it would spoil everything for her. In her mind, this was her
last chance at real life, before she dedicated herself to the heavy
weight and restrictions of her royal duties forevermore.

Samuel had been collecting data from the U.S. State Department
for weeks about the political situation in Eritrea, in East Africa, where
they were going. It bordered on Ethiopia, which had caused Eritrea
serious problems over the years. The two countries had finally signed
a truce several years before, and all was peaceful now. The border
skirmishes that had occurred with Ethiopia previously had stopped.
Samuel had promised to alert the prince if anything changed, or anything worrisome happened anywhere around them, and if necessary,
he would get the princess out of the country in that case. But there
seemed to be no concern for now, just as the Red Cross director
had promised as well. Eritrea would be interesting and safe. All
Christianna needed to do was concentrate on the work at hand. She
was leaving the security issues up to them, to be handled as discreetly
as possible. They were claiming to be three friends from Liechtenstein, who had signed up for the year together. It was a plausible story
they intended to stick to, and there was no reason why anyone at the
camp should suspect otherwise. And Christianna knew how discreet
the two men were.

After the ten-hour plane trip from Frankfurt, to Asmara, via Cairo,
they barely glanced at her passport in Asmara. They didn't even notice the absence of a surname, much to Christianna's relief. She didn't
want the press notified anywhere on her route, as word of her pres-

ence in the country might follow her to her final destination, and she wanted to avoid that at all costs.

By now, they had been on the road for fourteen hours, and Christianna was tired. The two men had slept on the long flight. As they walked out of the airport, they looked around. Max had gotten an e-mail before they left, confirming that they'd be picked up. No one had been sure at the time who would come to meet them, or which of the camp's vehicles they'd bring. They'd been assured someone would be there, but no one seemed to be waiting for them.

They walked into a small grass thatched hut, and bought three orange sodas. The drinks were made by an African company, and tasted sickly sweet, but they drank them anyway, as it was hot and they were thirsty, although it was winter in East Africa, but the weather was warm. The scenery around them was beautiful, the air was dry and the terrain flat. There was a soft hazy light that seemed to wash over everything and reminded Christianna of the warm luminosity of her mother's pearls. There was a gentleness to their surroundings, as they waited for someone to come. Eventually, they sat on their bags outside the hut, and half an hour later an ancient battered yellow school bus rolled up. It had a Red Cross flag taped to each side, and other than that looked entirely disreputable, and as though it couldn't possibly have gone a mile. In spite of that, it had driven all the way from Senafe, and the trip had taken five hours.

The door opened and a tall, disheveled-looking, dark-haired man stepped out. He looked at the three of them sitting on their bags, smiled, and rushed over to help them, with apologies for his tardiness. Looking at the ancient yellow bus, one could easily see why he'd been late.

"I'm so sorry, I'm Geoffrey McDonald. I had a flat tire on the way, it took forever to change. Not too tired, Your Highness?" he asked optimistically. He had recognized her from a copy of *Majesty* maga-zine someone had lying around, although she looked younger than he'd expected, and still fresh and beautiful after the long trip.

"Please don't call me that," Christianna said instantly. "I hope the director in Geneva warned you. Just Christianna will be fine."

"Of course," he said apologetically, taking her backpack from her, as he and the bodyguards shook hands. In theory, he wasn't supposed to extend a hand to her, unless she did so first, and as he was British he was apparently aware of the etiquette involved, but she was quick to extend her hand. He shook it cautiously with a shy smile. He looked like an absentminded professor, and she liked him instantly, as did the two guards.

"I hope no one is aware of all that here," she said, looking worried.

"No, not at all," he assured her. "In fact, I'd been warned. I just for-got. It's rather exciting to have a princess coming to stay with us, even if no one knows. My mother would be very impressed," he confessed, "though I won't tell her till after you leave." There was an awkward boy-ishness about him that would have been hard not to love. Christianna felt instantly at ease with him. He was friendly and warm.

"I don't want the others to know," Christianna explained again as they walked toward the bus, with both bodyguards just behind her, carrying their bags.

"I understand. We're very excited to have you here. We need all the help we can get. Two of our people got typhoid and had to go home. We've been short-handed for eight months." He had a slightly dis-tracted, rumpled quality to him, and looked as though he was in his early forties. He said he had been born in England, but had lived in Africa all his life, and had grown up in South Africa, in Capetown, but he'd run the camp in Senafe for the past four years. He said the facil-ity had grown by leaps and bounds since he'd started. "They've gotten used to us by now. The locals were a little leery of us at first, although they're very friendly people here. In addition to the AIDS facility, we basically run a medical aid station for them. A doctor flies in twice a month to give me a hand." He added that the AIDS facility they ran had been a considerable success. Their goal was to prevent the spread of the disease, as much as to treat those who already had it now. "The center has been overflowing. You'll see when we arrive. And of course we treat all the local diseases and ailments as well." He got off the bus again before they left, and bought a soda himself. He looked dusty, and tired, and slightly haggard, as though he worked too hard, and Christianna was touched that the director had come himself.

It was exciting just being there, trying to absorb the unfamiliar sights and sounds, although they were all feeling somewhat dazed by the long trip. Samuel and Max were quiet, studying their surroundings, ever on the alert, and constantly aware that their mission was to protect her. So far so good.

When Geoff got back, he started the bus, as it made a series of horrible coughs and groans, backfired, and then shook alarmingly as it came to life. He turned to Samuel and Max with a broad grin. "I hope one of you is a mechanic. We need one desperately at the camp. We have medical personnel, but no one knows how to fix our cars. They're overeducated, the lot of them. We need plumbers, electricians, and mechanics." The bus took off rattling down the road, stopped and then started again, as though to illustrate his point.

"We'll do our best." Max smiled. He was much more capable with weapons, but he didn't say that. He was willing to give it a try. The bus nearly stopped again while going up a hill at a snail's pace, as Geoff chatted with all three of them. He looked as though Christianna made him slightly nervous, as he cast shy glances at her and smiled. It was impossible for him to forget who she was.

She asked him questions about the AIDS facility, the crisis of AIDS in Africa, and the rest of the medical care they provided. He explained that he was a doctor himself. His specialty was tropical medicine, which was what had led him here. As they talked, she watched the scenery drift by. There were people walking on either side of the road in brightly colored clothes, with swaths of white cloth. A herd of goats walked right across their path. The bus stopped for it, and then wouldn't start again, as a man in a turban leading a camel tried to help a young boy herd the goats. Geoff flooded the engine trying to bring it back to life, and then had to let it sit for a while as the goats finally left the road. It gave them a further chance to talk.

He was extremely informative in his data and assessments. He said they were not only treating young women, but children as well in the AIDS facility, many of whom had been raped, and then shunned by their tribes once they were no longer virgins, worse yet if they got pregnant. Their families could no longer marry them off, so they were useless in trade for livestock, land, or currency. And once they got sick, they were almost always abandoned. The number of AIDS-affected men and women was shocking, and the fact that it continued to rise was even more alarming. He said their patients were also suffering from tuberculosis, malaria, kala azar (a form of black fever), and sleeping sickness.

"We're emptying the ocean with a thimble," he said, outlining the situation for them in words that left no doubt as to how desperate the situation of their patients was, many of them refugees from border disputes with Ethiopia in the years before the truce. He also said the truce was somewhat uneasy as Ethiopia continued to lust after Massawa, Eritrea's port on the Red Sea. "All we can do is care for them, make them comfortable, and help some of them until they die.

And try to educate others about the prevention of disease." It was a daunting prospect, as Christianna listened to him, and Samuel and Max also asked him a number of questions. Theirs wasn't a dangerous mission, but it was a depressing one. Their mortality rate was high, a hundred percent among those with AIDS. Most of the women and children who came to them were too far advanced in the disease for it to be arrested, controlled, or forced into some form of remission. One of their main goals, he said, was to prevent new mothers from passing on AIDS to their newborns, by giving both mother and infant medication and convincing them not to breast-feed. Culturally and practically difficult since many of them were so poor, they sold the formula given to them and continued to breast-feed because it was cheaper, and then the babies got AIDS too. It was a constant uphill battle, according to him, to educate and treat them, when they could. "We do what we can for them, but we can't always do a lot, depending on the situation. Sometimes we have to accept that too." He also mentioned that Doctors Without Borders came through the area frequently and gave them a hand. They were grateful for help from other organizations as well, not just the Red Cross, although a hundred percent of their funding came from them. The local government was too poor to be of any help. He said they were planning to ask some foundations to contribute, but they hadn't had time to write the grant requests yet. Christianna thought she'd like to help eventually, thinking of their own foundation, which contributed generously to situations similar to this. She would learn more about their needs in the coming weeks and months, and talk to the foundation about it when she went back.

It took them five hours to reach the camp. They talked almost all the way. Geoff was a pleasant, obviously kind and compassionate, interesting man, with a vast knowledge about the continent where he lived, and the agonies that plagued it, most of which could not be fixed, for now, and probably wouldn't be for a long time. But he and those he worked with were doing all they could to change that.

Christianna finally fell asleep for the last few minutes of the bus trip, despite the constant rattling, shaking, noise, and appalling fumes that the bus emitted. She was so tired she could have slept through a bomb at that point. She woke up with a start when Max touched her arm. They were in the camp, and the bus was surrounded by Red Cross workers, watching with curiosity to see the three new workers who were about to arrive. They had all been talking about them for weeks. All they knew was that they were two men and a woman, and that they came from somewhere in Europe. There was some vague rumor that they were all Swiss, someone else said they were German, then they thought the men were German, the woman Swiss. No one had mentioned Liechtenstein to them. They were perhaps confused since their stay and arrival had been set up by the Geneva office. But whoever they were, they were more than welcome, and desperately needed at the camp. Even if not doctors or nurses, at least they were willing hearts and hands.

As Christianna looked around, she saw a dozen people staring at her, all of them in assorted informal garb. Shorts, jeans, T-shirts, hiking boots, the women with short hair, or tied up under scarves, several of them had white doctors' coats on, the women as well. She saw one middle-aged woman with a weathered face, a warm smile, and a stethoscope around her neck. There was a very pretty one, tall, with dark hair, who was looking into the bus intently with a native child in her arms. There seemed to be roughly an equal division between women and men. And the age range seemed to span from Christianna's age, or somewhere in that vicinity, to a few faces that looked nearly twice her age. Standing among them were a handful of local workers wearing colorful native garb, some of whom were holding children by the hand. The center itself, at the hub of the compound, looked like a cluster of freshly painted white huts. And on either side were a series of large, almost military-looking tents.

Geoff held a hand out to her, in spite of her lofty position, to steady her as she got out of the bus onto uneven ground. Christianna smiled at him, and then glanced at the others shyly, as Samuel and Max came out of the bus carrying their bags. Christianna looked just rumpled and sloppy enough after the long trip not to stand out, as one by one the waiting band of workers approached.

Geoff introduced the older woman first. Her name was Mary Walker, and as the stethoscope suggested she was a physician. She was British, and the head of their program that dealt with AIDS. She had white hair hanging in a long braid down her back, a heavily lined smiling face, and piercing blue eyes. She reminded Christianna instantly of Marque. She shook Christianna's hand with a strong, sure handshake of her own and welcomed her warmly to the camp. There were two other women standing beside her, one a pretty young Irish girl with curly black hair and green eyes. She was a midwife, and drove all over Debub, in the outlying areas, delivering babies, and bringing them, or their mothers, back to the camp when they were sick. Next to her was a young American woman, who, like Geoff, had grown up in Capetown. She had gone to college in the States, but missed Africa too much, as they all did when they left.

And once they met, and he had told her about the place where he was working, she had agreed to join Geoff here. Her name was Maggie, and Christianna rapidly realized, as Geoff put an arm around her once she approached, that Maggie and Geoff were romantically involved. Maggie was a nurse. She gave Christianna a warm hug of welcome. The Irish girl introduced herself as Fiona with a broad, mischievous grin. She was quick to shake Christianna's hand and welcome her.

The four men who were standing around introduced themselves in rapid succession. Two were German, one was French, and the fourth was Swiss, and all appeared to be somewhere in their thirties: Klaus, Ernst, Didier, and Karl. And finally, the tall dark-haired young woman with the child in her arms came forward and shook hands with Christianna and the two men. She had beautiful eyes and a serious face. Her name was Laure, and she was French. She seemed much more reserved than the others, and Christianna wondered if she was shy. She spoke to her in French, but even then the tall beautiful young woman didn't warm up much. Her attitude bordered on hostile. Geoff explained that she had been with UNICEF for several years, and had been in Senafe with them for several months. Geoff and Mary were the only doctors in the group, Fiona the only midwife, Maggie the only nurse. The others were all benevolent, caring, hardworking, conscientious people who had come to Senafe to make a difference, in whatever way they could, like Christianna herself.

The camp was actually on the outskirts of Senafe, in the subzone of Debub, in the north, near the Ethiopian border, which would have been worrisome in the years before the truce, but no longer was. It was peaceful here now, and fairly remote. As Christianna continued to look around, she was struck by the beauty of the African women who were standing just beyond the group, smiling shyly, in colorful costumes, with lots of jewelry in their hair, on their ears, and around their necks. There were six more residents working at the center, four women and two men, all of whom were talking to women or children in the huts, and hadn't been able to come out and greet the new arrivals. But there was an ever-growing group of exotically dressed

African women who stood staring and smiling at the threesome that had just gotten off the bus.

The African women who stood watching them were wearing the most exotic costumes Christianna had ever seen. They had tightly braided hair in tiny rows strung with beads and jewels that hung on their faces. They were heavily adorned, and draped in interesting fabrics, some of them woven with gold or metallic threads. Some of the women were fully covered, and others stood watching her with bare breasts. Their elaborate costumes and efforts to adorn themselves were in sharp contrast to the plain, unattractive clothes worn by the Western workers, who looked anything but sexy or even attractive in their T-shirts, shorts, jeans, and hiking boots. Geoff explained to her that there were nine ethnic groups or tribes, in Eritrea, the Tigrinya, Rashaida, Afar, Tigre, Kunama, Saho, Nara, Bilen, and Hedareb, and she was struck almost immediately by the warmth of the African women's smiles. One of them came up and embraced her, explained that she was from Ghana, and said her name was Akuba, and proudly told Christianna that she was a Red Cross volunteer. Christianna also met one of the African men who helped them at the center, whose name was Yaw. It was a lot of information to absorb all at once, a lot of people, a brand-new place, an entirely different culture, a whole new life, an unfamiliar job. Christianna felt overwhelmed as she looked around, and tried to take it all in. It would have been almost impossible to explain to anyone what a feast it was to the senses, how exciting it was, or how gentle and sweet the Africans seemed. Their faces were faintly similar to Ethiopians, they definitely looked related in spite of the hatred and long history of warfare between them. A fifth of Eritrea's population had fled the country, during those battles, before the truce five years before. But none of the faces Christianna saw around her appeared embittered. On the contrary, the people were beautiful, and seemed very warm.

"You must be exhausted," Geoff interrupted the many introductions. He could see that she was tired, and they had been driving for nearly five hours. She had come to the farthest reaches of the world. But Christianna had never been happier, and like a child at a birthday party, she wanted to drink it all in.

"I'm fine," she said gamely, chatting for a moment first with Akuba, and then speaking to the Eritrean women, and finally with the people she would be working with for the next months. She could hardly wait to get to know them, and to start work herself.

"Come on," Fiona said with a broad smile. "Allow me to escort you to the Ritz." She pointed to one of the large tents on one side of the cluster of huts, where they worked. They lived in the tents, the women on one side, the men on the other, and for those who wished to combine forces like Maggie and Geoff, they had separate, smaller tents. The men's tent was referred to as the George V, after the illustrious hotel in Paris, and the women's tent was the Ritz.

Christianna took her valise from Samuel, and he looked instantly unhappy about it. He didn't like her going off alone, before he and Max had assessed the place, and they hadn't had time to yet. She gave him a nod and a smile, firmly took the bag from his hand, and set off after Fiona. Real life had begun.

The tent Fiona took her to was larger than Christianna had expected, and airier than it looked from the outside. It was a heavy canvas tent they had bought from the military, they had put a wooden floor in it, and there were eight cots, one of which had been unoccupied since Maggie moved out to live in a separate tent with Geoff. And with the new arrivals, there would be eight men in the men's tent. The Africans who worked for them at the center lived in huts they built themselves. And Maggie and Geoff had their own tent, which Geoff had bought himself.

Fiona walked Christianna over to the far corner. There was a small night table with a drawer in it next to her cot, with a battery-operated lamp, and there was a battered military-surplus footlocker at the foot of the bed.

"That's your closet," Fiona said with a burst of laughter. "Don't ask me why, but I came here with a full wardrobe six months ago. I finally sent it all back. I haven't worn anything but jeans and shorts since I got here. Even if we go into Senafe for dinner, which we don't do often, no one gets dressed up." Christianna had worn jeans, a long-sleeved white T-shirt, an old denim jacket she had bought in a thrift shop in Berkeley, and running shoes, which had been comfortable for the trip. But in spite of that, there was something stylish about her. She had worn no jewelry other than her family signet ring and a tiny pair of silver earrings. The African women she had just met were wearing far more jewelry than she. Christianna had done everything she could to look plain. She learned a few minutes later that Fiona was thirty, although she looked fifteen. Christianna had incorrectly guessed that they were the same age. She said that Laure, the tall dark-haired girl, was twenty-three. Almost everyone else was in their thirties, except Klaus and Didier. And she said they were a great team.

Christianna sat on her cot as she listened to her, and a moment later Fiona flopped down onto the cot, too, like the seasoned girl at boarding school, welcoming the new girl as she came in. It was all a little daunting at first, and although Christianna had been desperate to come here, she had to admit that she was still feeling more than a little overwhelmed, with culture shock, if nothing else.

"What are your two friends like?" Fiona asked her with a giggle. She admitted that she and Ernst had gone out to dinner a few times, but in the end they had decided not to pursue a romance, and had wound up friends. It was a lot easier to do that here. Geoff and Maggie were rare. Most of the time the entire group preferred the camaraderie of being coworkers, without complicating it with romance, but now and then it happened. They also knew that sooner or later most people would move on. They rarely stayed for more than a year, and things changed when you went back. "So tell me about Sam and Max," Fiona persisted, and Christianna laughed. Technically, for the next six months or year in East Africa with her, they were on duty, and not supposed to indulge in that sort of thing. But she certainly wouldn't have objected or told anyone if either or both of them had a fling, or even a serious romance. It was a long time for them to be abstinent otherwise. They were both young men, after all. And they could keep an eye on her, as they were assigned to do, and still manage to have some fun, too. Christianna was more than willing to turn a blind eye. "They're both really nice men. Reliable, conscientious, responsible, honest, trustworthy, hardworking, kind." She listed their many virtues as Fiona laughed. She looked like a dark-haired elf sitting on Christianna's cot, with dancing green eyes. They seemed and felt like two kids, and Christianna hoped they'd be friends, despite the difference in their ages. Laure, who was her own age, didn't appear nearly as friendly, and had barely said a word to her when they met. In fact, she had glared at her as soon as Christianna got off the bus. She had no idea why. Everyone else in the camp had been lovely to her.

"That sounds like a job reference," Fiona teased her, more accurate than she knew or than Christianna would admit. "I mean what are they like? They're gorgeous—are they nice guys?"

"Very. Samuel used to be an Israeli commando. He's amazing with weapons." She realized she had slipped again, and reminded herself to be more careful in future. She was tired after the trip.

"That sounds scary, unless we have another Ethiopian war, in that case he might come in handy. I assume they're not married, or they wouldn't be here." Although she knew Mary Walker had been at first. She had come for a ninety-day tour of duty, had never gone back, and got divorced. She loved East Africa and its people too much to leave it. She was the only doctor on the team other than Geoff, and she specialized in AIDS. She had a passion for the people she took care of, more so than her marriage, which she realized once she got there had been dead for years, so she stayed. "Do they have girlfriends at home?" Fiona inquired, and Christianna shook her head and then hesitated.

"I don't think so. I never asked." Even she had to admit, it sounded odd, if they were claiming to be friends. The problem was that it was a charade, and Christianna didn't want to get caught.

"How do you know them?" Fiona asked, hopping onto her own bed like an elf. It was the one next to Christianna's. They could whisper secrets at night like young girls.

"Actually I've known them for a long time. They work for my father." She had finally been honest, which was something at least. "When I told them I was coming here, they both volunteered to come, too." And had subsequently been assigned the job, which of course she couldn't say. "We went to Russia together, during the hostage crisis in Digora. The woman who was running the Red Cross station there was remarkable. I fell in love with her and what she was doing. I decided after that to come here, and so did they." Christianna's face grew serious and sad. "I think that night changed a lot of things for all three of us. So here we are." She smiled at her new friend. She liked

Fiona a lot. Everyone in the camp did. She was a warm, easy, open person, and worked tirelessly at her job, which she said she loved. Like many of the others, she was in love with Africa, too. It was a magical place, and addictive once it got into your blood.

"What was the woman's name?" she asked with interest.

"Her name is Marque."

"Of course. I know her too. Everyone does. She comes here sometimes. She is Laure's aunt, that's why she's here. Laure had some sort of broken engagement, or failed marriage or something. She never talks about it. But the rumor is she came here to recover. I'm not entirely sure she loves it, or maybe she's just unhappy. That sort of thing is hard. I was engaged once, too"—she giggled again—"for about ten minutes. To a terrible man. I ran off to Spain for a year to get rid of him, and he married someone else. Terrible bloke. He drank." Christianna smiled and tried to look sympathetic. It was a lot of information to digest at once, and she was so jet-lagged and tired, she was afraid that she would inadvertently say something she shouldn't that would give her away, that she was a princess and lived in a palace. The thought of doing that made her shudder. She didn't want any of that infringing on her life here, and hoped it wouldn't. It shouldn't happen if she was careful. She just had to be aware of what she said at first until she got used to her new life.

"Do you have a boyfriend at home?" Fiona asked her then with interest.

"No, I don't. I just finished college in the States in June. I've been hanging around home since then, and then I came here."

"What sort of work do you want to do when you go back? Medicine? I love midwifery myself—maybe you should come out with me and have a look. It blows me away every time to see a new life come into the world. It's truly a miracle, and always exciting, even though once in a while it's sad, when something goes really wrong. It happens. But most of the time it's happy."

Christianna hesitated at her question. "I was thinking about public relations. My father does that, and actually he's in politics and economics a bit, too. I like business a lot. I majored in economics in school." It was all true, to a degree, depending on how you viewed it.

"I can't do math at all. I can barely count," Fiona said, not entirely accurately. Christianna knew it had taken her seven years to become a midwife, including nursing school, so she must have been a decent student, or at least a persevering one. And she obviously loved her work. "I think business would be too boring," Fiona said honestly. "All those numbers. I love working with people. You can never predict it, especially here." She lay back on her bed with a sigh. She was going out that evening to visit patients, and usually tried to rest for a while before that, so she would be fresh and alert. She had a number of patients who were about to deliver at any moment. They were planning to send runners if she was needed, and she would go out to them in the ancient Volkswagen bug that had been at the camp for years. For Fiona, it was a thrill each time a new life came into the world. And here in Africa, she saved babies' and mothers' lives more often than not. The conditions she worked in were primitive beyond belief. She was good at what she did.

Christianna lay on her cot quietly for a few minutes. She wanted to get up and unpack and look around. She was too excited to sleep, but for a moment, her body felt heavy, and her eyelids began to flutter. Fiona looked over at her and smiled. She seemed like a sweet girl, and Fiona had to admire her for coming to East Africa at her age. It was a pretty brave thing to do, and just as she looked over at her, Christianna's eyes opened wider again, as she glanced at Fiona on the next cot.

"What about the snakes?" She sounded worried, and Fiona laughed out loud at the question.

"Everyone asks that the first day here. They're scary, but we don't see a lot of them." She didn't tell her that a puff adder had slithered into the tent two weeks before, but usually they didn't. "We'll show you pictures of which ones to look out for. You get used to it after a while." Fiona saw more snakes than most of the workers in the camp, since she was out in the bush a lot, visiting her patients.

Both women lay quietly for a few minutes, and without wanting to, Christianna drifted off to sleep. She was absolutely exhausted, and when she woke, Fiona was gone. Christianna went outside to look for the others. There were several people walking around the compound.

Christianna saw Akuba and smiled at her. She was leading a child by the hand into one of the huts. And the man called Yaw was hammering something intently. She looked around her, and there was a beauty to the night that she had never seen in her life before, that African light that people talked about, and the air was like a caress on her cheek. She noticed then that there was another tent, behind the huts. She followed the sounds she heard from there, and discovered the entire Red Cross crew, sitting at long refectory tables with rough-hewn benches, eating. Christianna looked instantly embarrassed, though far more rested than when she left them earlier. She had needed the sleep, but was afraid it made her look lazy, which was no way to start.

"I'm so sorry," she said apologetically when she saw Geoff and Maggie. The full crew was there, minus Fiona, who was out in the bush delivering a baby, and had been gone for hours. Including Christianna, Max, and Samuel, they were seventeen now, of actual Red Cross workers. There were at least a dozen local Eritreans who worked with them, and Akuba and Yaw, who were from Ghana. "I fell asleep." She looked mortified, but Samuel and Max looked pleased to see her, as did the others. They had just started eating. They were eating chicken and vegetables, and a huge bowl of rice with fruit mixed into it. They worked hard, and the quantities were generous enough to keep them going.

"You needed the sleep," Geoff said sensibly. "We'll show you everything you need to see tomorrow. I've already given Sam and Max the tour." They had discreetly asked him to see everything, which was part of their duties as security covering her. But they had been fascinated by what they'd seen, and both men had been enchanted by the children, who seemed to be everywhere in the camp, dozens of them, all smiling, laughing, giggling, playing, as were some of their elders. The locals seemed like an exceptionally happy people, smiling or laughing all the time. Even the sick ones staying at the center were friendly and good-humored.

Mary indicated an empty place for her to sit, next to Laure, and Christianna climbed over the bench and sat down. Didier was on Laure's other side, chatting to her in French, and Ernst was on Christianna's other side. He had been making idle chitchat with Max and Sam, in Swiss German since they were all Swiss by nationality, although Samuel was half Israeli and had served in both armies. Christianna understood them and laughed a couple of times. Then she turned to Laure and said something in French. There was no response. She blatantly ignored Christianna, and continued talking to Didier. She obviously had a chip on her shoulder, and Christianna had no idea why. She had done nothing to offend her.

Christianna chatted easily with Mary Walker across the table instead. She was explaining the AIDS epidemic they were dealing with, and then went on to explain to Christianna what kala azar was, which was actually black fever, and sounded more like the plague, which involved blackening of the feet, face, hands, and abdomen. It sounded awful to Christianna, especially over dinner. Geoff added a few more gory details. But Christianna found it all fascinating, particularly their AIDS work. Mary mentioned that the Médecins Sans Frontières team, Doctors Without Borders, would be coming back in a few weeks. They flew in once a month, bringing a larger medical team than the one they had on hand at the camp in Senafe. When necessary, they brought surgeons, and did surgery as needed. They flew in for emergencies as well, although most of the time Mary and Geoff handled everything that came up, including emergency appendectomies, and cesarean sections. They were a full-service operation, Geoff said, teasing. He spoke highly of the Doctors Without Borders teams, which flew all over Africa in small planes, and delivered medical services wherever required, even in war zones, or the most remote places.

"They're an amazing bunch," he commented, as he helped himself to a huge portion of dessert. He was rail thin, and obviously burned off whatever he ate. He had eaten a healthy dinner, as had all the men at the table. The women seemed to eat less, although they ate well, too. They all worked hard, and enjoyed their evenings talking and laughing together over dinner. Most of them ate lunch on the fly, and Mary told Christianna that breakfast was served in the same tent at six-thirty. They started work early. Local women did the cooking, and had learned the kind of European dishes they all liked. Maggie was the only American on the team, and said the only thing she really missed from home was ice cream. She said she dreamed of it sometimes. She was a long, long way from home, but seemed immensely happy. They all were, except Laure, whom Christianna had noticed all through dinner. She always looked sad, and spoke very little. The only one she spoke to, in undertones in French, was Didier. She said very little to the others, and nothing at all to them throughout dinner. The others were all making an obvious effort to get to know Christianna and the two men who had come with her. Geoff had poured her two glasses of wine they had served in celebration of their arrival. And Max and Sam already seemed to be integrated into the group, among the men. There was a lot of bantering during dinner, and bad jokes in French, English, and German, all of which she spoke. It was a wonderfully international group.

It was late when they all finally got up, and walked out into the warm African night, still talking and laughing. The men invited Max and Sam to play cards with them, and they accepted and said they would be back in the tent in a few minutes. They couldn't say it, of course, but they had to be sure that Christianna had settled into her tent for the night, which was after all why they were there. Geoff and Maggie went back to their tent arm in arm, and the cluster of women wandered slowly toward theirs, still chatting. Fiona hadn't come in yet, and the others assumed she was delivering a baby somewhere. The mortality rate among newborns in East Africa was terrifying, mostly in the twenty-four hours immediately before or after delivery. Fiona was single-handedly trying to improve those statistics, and she had convinced many of the local women to get prenatal care, and at-tended every delivery she could.

Christianna asked if they worried about her traveling around alone at night. Mary Walker commented that she was fearless and the sur-rounding areas were pretty safe. They were close to the Ethiopian bor-der, which was always somewhat concerning, but there hadn't been any problems or overt violations of the truce in several years, not that it couldn't happen. She said that the truce between the two countries was always tense, and the Ethiopians continued to feel that they had gotten a bad deal. They still wanted Eritrea's ports, but there had been no problems in Senafe, and the young Irish midwife was much loved by all those she tended. One of the other women Christianna had met that night, Ushi, was a German woman who was a teacher, and worked with the local children. She said that Fiona always had a gun on her, when she traveled at night, and she wasn't afraid to use it, although she'd never had to. Carrying weapons wasn't encouraged, but Fiona did it anyway, and given the circumstances, it was probably smart. Ushi, short for Ursula, had been warm and welcoming to Christianna and the two men. They all were, except for Laure, who walked back to the tent ahead of them in silence. She seemed like a very unhappy girl, and she had continued to glance at Christianna with inexplicable but visible dislike.

The women chatted once they were in the tent, and put on their pajamas. Christianna would have loved a bath, or a shower, but had already been told it wasn't possible. There was an outdoor shower they all used in the morning, or early evening, as young local girls poured water over them, and boys did the same for the men. It was primitive, but Christianna had been told about it beforehand, so she wasn't surprised. She wasn't afraid of the discomforts she might encounter, and the other women teased her about snakes and lions, and told her they might get into the tent at night. They teased everyone about it when they arrived. They were all like girls at camp, and Christianna loved it. It was everything she had hoped for, and she already loved the gentle Senafe women she'd seen. They were so beautiful and exotic and always smiled.

Christianna was asleep the moment her head hit the pillow. Some of the women read in the light of their battery-operated lamps. Others slept. They had taken her to the bathroom outside, and one of them had stayed with her, because she was still afraid of snakes, but nothing terrible had happened. It was a rudimentary outdoor affair that in essence was nothing more than a hole in the ground with a seat over it, a shovel, and a big bag of lime. That was going to take some getting used to, Christianna thought to herself with a small shudder, but one did what one had to. She suspected she'd get used to it in time. She was sound asleep before any of the others, some of whom talked in quiet whispers, and said they liked her. She seemed like a very sweet girl, and would be a good addition to the team. They had the feeling she came from a good family, probably from money. She was well spoken, discreet, polite, and spoke several languages fluently, but she was also without artifice or pretension and seemed extremely straightforward and natural, and they liked that about her.

Laure shrugged as she listened and said nothing. Mary wondered if she was jealous, since they were about the same age, but she wasn't close to the others in the camp either. Laure was the only squeaky wheel in the group, and seemed unhappy most of the time. She was going home in two months, according to plan. She was one of those rare people who hadn't fallen in love with Africa, neither the continent nor the people, and hadn't enjoyed much or anything about it. She had brought her problems and sorrows with her. Mary knew from Laure's aunt, Marque, that she had been jilted nearly at the altar, two days before her wedding, and her fiancé had run off with her best friend and married her. Laure had been miserable ever since, and still was, and even the distraction of working there hadn't helped her much. She was going back to working at UNICEF in Geneva, and seemed to have benefited little from the extraordinary experience she'd had here. She was surprisingly cynical, and even bitter, for someone so young.

Fiona came in at four in the morning, and the others were all asleep by then. She had delivered two babies that night, and everything had gone well. She got into her bed, and was asleep within minutes. At six o'clock, their alarm clocks started going off, and the women began to stir. They were all good humored when they got up, and headed to the shower together, in their bathrobes, with their towels over their arms. Fiona was up and on her feet with the rest of them, and in good humor, after two hours of sleep. She was used to it, and did it often. She almost never slept in, unless she'd had an exceptionally rough night. But even then, she was usually in good spirits. She loved to sing old Gaelic songs in the shower at the top of her lungs, just to annoy them, and they always groaned and told her how awful her voice was. She loved it. She was the camp clown.

Christianna was dressed and in the dining tent promptly at six-thirty. She ate a hearty breakfast of porridge and eggs, with a bowl of berries that had been grown in the camp. She drank an enormous glass of orange juice and smiled at Max and Sam when they walked in. Breakfast was quick since everyone was busy, and by seven o'clock everyone was doing their jobs and hard at work. Christianna saw Max leave in an old car shortly after that, and Samuel told her quietly that he was going into Senafe, to the post office, to call her father and report in. She nodded, and as directed, followed Mary into the main hut, where the women and children with AIDS were treated and housed.

Mary explained to Christianna, as Geoff had during the bus trip, that they gave pregnant women with AIDS a single dose of the drug nevirapine four hours before delivery, and the baby a small dose during the first few days after its birth. In most cases, that reduced the risk of AIDS by fifty percent, according to studies. The real problem came when they had to convince the mothers to feed their babies formula, not by breast. If they breast-fed their babies, they almost inevitably gave them AIDS, but formula was a foreign concept to them, and they were suspicious of it. Even if the volunteers gave them formula at the center to take home with them, often they didn't use it, sold it, or traded it for other things they needed more. It was an uphill battle, Mary said. And AIDS education for prevention of the disease was an important part of what they did. She had been thinking that Christianna might be good at that. She had a pleasant, gentle way that the women she stopped and spoke to seemed to like, as Mary watched her and translated for her, as needed, until she learned the local dialects. She had an almost professional way of going quietly from bed to bed, saying a few words, offering comfort, and dealing with the African women with warmth, kindness, compassion, and respect.

"Have you ever worked in a hospital?" Mary asked with interest. She had no way of knowing how many hospitals Christianna had visited in her life as a princess. This was standard fare for her. She knew just how long to stay and chat, without wearing the patients out, but still giving them the impression that she was interested in what they said, and making each one feel as though they had her undivided attention.

"Not really," Christianna said vaguely. "I've done some volunteer work."

"You have a lovely bedside manner," Mary complimented her. "Maybe you should think about being a doctor or a nurse."

"I'd like that," Christianna said, smiling, knowing only too well that there was no chance of it. Mary had been impressed as well that she didn't seem to flinch at the sight of the worst sores, or the ugliest of wounds. Whatever she saw before her, she remained gracious, warm, and seemingly unaffected. "My father expects me to go into the family business when I get home" was all she said.

"Shame. Something tells me you've got a gift for this." The two women smiled at each other, as Mary continued to introduce her to patients, and then walked her into another hut, where Geoff was doing check-ups, and giving vaccinations. The tiny waiting room was full of patients, and playing children. Once again Christianna stopped to talk to each of them briefly, as though she had done this before.

Fiona took her off to meet some of her pregnant patients after that. Mary stopped to talk to Geoff for a few minutes after Christianna left with Fiona.

"She's awfully good at this," Mary commented briefly. "She has a lovely way with people. It's almost as though she's not new at it. She's wonderful with the patients. I think I'd like her to do AIDS education for me. And she can work with Ushi with the kids."

"Whatever you like," Geoff said over the howls of a screaming child who had just gotten a shot. He wasn't surprised that Christianna was good with patients. Knowing what he did of her, and the others didn't, he assumed correctly that she had visited hospitals all her life. She didn't need to use her title of princess, he could see by watching her that she was royal to her core, and had lovely, gentle ways. She made everyone feel comfortable around her, and yet she wasn't afraid to have fun, to tease and laugh and joke, just like everyone else. He was very glad she'd come, although he'd had some trepidations about it. He could see now what a good addition she was to the team, how well she fit in, and they needed the extra pair of hands, not only hers, but those of her two men. And much to Geoff's surprise, she wasn't difficult, demanding, or spoiled. She was in fact, open, interested, and humble.

Christianna spent the rest of the morning with Fiona, talking to pregnant women. She helped herself to some food in the dining tent at lunchtime, and didn't bother to sit down to eat it, but ate it on the run. And then she spent the rest of the day with Ushi, teaching the children. Christianna loved doing it, and had taught them two new songs in French before they left. Ushi looked at her with a broad smile as they went outside for some air, and complimented her generously, as the others had.

"You know, you have a gift," Ushi said, as she lit a cigarette.

"No," Christianna said quietly, "being here in Africa is the gift." She said it with such obvious gratitude to be there that Ushi leaned over and gave her a hug.

"Welcome to Africa," Ushi said, as she hugged her. "I think you're going to love it here, and you're right where you belong."

"So do I," Christianna said almost sadly. She had only just arrived and was falling in love with it. She was already sad, knowing that one day she would have to leave. She had found the life she wanted, and knew just as certainly that one day she would have to give back the gift. Thinking about it, she was quiet all the way back to the women's tent.

"What are you looking so depressed about?" Fiona asked her when she saw her. She had just come in herself, and was going out to patients again that night.

"I don't ever want to leave," Christianna said, looking mournful, as Fiona grinned.

"Uh-oh, everybody, she's got it," Fiona said to the room at large, as the other women glanced over. Most of them had just finished work, and were enjoying a break before dinner. "She's got African fever! Quickest case I've ever seen." Christianna laughed at the description, as she sat down on her bed. She had worked for ten hours straight and loved every minute. "Just wait till you see a snake."

The others laughed, and so did Christianna. She played Scrabble after that with Ushi in German, while Fiona did her nails. She wore bright red nail polish even here. She said it was the one indulgence she couldn't give up. And as she looked around the room at the other women, Christianna knew she had never been happier in her life.

# Chapter 8

As Christianna headed for the dining tent the next morning at
six-thirty, Max was waiting for her discreetly outside her tent.
She was surprised to see him, and he spoke to her in a whisper.

"Your Highness," he whispered, and she stopped him almost as
soon as the words came out of his mouth by habit and reflex. She
looked instantly upset.

"Don't call me that," she whispered back. "Just call me Cricky, like
everyone else does." She had told them all her nickname the day
before.

"I can't do that, Your . . . oh . . . sorry . . ." He blushed.

"You have to," she said to him, and whispered even lower, "that's a
royal order." He grinned. "Why were you waiting for me?" It looked
like a serious conspiracy between them as Maggie and Fiona walked
by on the way to breakfast.

"I spoke to your father yesterday. I didn't get a chance to tell you
last night." They had never been alone.

"Is he all right?" She looked momentarily worried until Max
nodded.

"He's fine. He said to send you his love. If you want to talk to him, I can drive you to the post office sometime. It's not too far."

"Maybe in a few days. I don't have time right now. There's too much to do here."

"I'm sure he understands. I told him you were fine."

"Good. Was that all?" He nodded. "Thank you, Max." She smiled.

"You're welcome, Your—" He stopped himself before he said it, and she laughed.

"Practice saying it, Max. *Cricky*. Or you're fired." They both laughed, and he followed her to breakfast. The others were already in the tent eating when they arrived.

"Slowpokes," Fiona teased them. "We ate everything." She was flirting with Max, which Christianna thought was funny. He seemed to be enjoying it. Samuel smiled about it, too. They were both already comfortable in the group.

Christianna enjoyed sharing breakfast with the others, and half an hour later she reported to work. Mary had given her a stack of books to read about AIDS, and some guidelines about what to teach. She wanted Christianna to design her own course, and improve on what they had. She was flattered to be asked. She was going to teach the class in Tigrinya, with a local interpreter beside her to translate. She read as much as she could of the material that morning, visited some of the patients with Mary, went back to her reading, and skipped lunch entirely. She reported to Ushi in the schoolroom after that. She was falling in love with the children. They were beautiful and loving, and they loved talking to her. She read the youngest ones a story after school, and then went outside to the compound for some exercise. She had been inside all day.

She saw Laure sitting quietly by herself when she went out, as Akuba walked by, holding one of her children by the hand. Christianna waved and smiled. Christianna had only been there for two days, but she already felt at home. It was all new and exciting, but she felt so at ease there, and so enamored of the people and the country that it was almost as though she'd been there before. She was about to go for a walk outside the compound, and then decided to turn back and talk to Laure. She had already begun making friends with the others, and she wanted to at least try to reach out to the sullen French girl. She had looked miserable ever since Christianna had arrived. It was hard not to wonder why. The only time Christianna had ever seen her smile was when she was talking to a child. Laure's job was doing administrative work in the office, and filling out and filing medical records. It was tedious work, but apparently she was good at it. Geoff had said she was thorough and precise.

"Hello," Christianna said cautiously. "Would you like to take a walk? I need some air." The air there was delicious, no matter how hot it was. There was always a smell of flowers around them. The tall dark-haired French girl seemed to hesitate for a moment. Christianna thought she would decline, and was startled when she nodded. She stood up to her full height and looked down at Christianna. And then they set off on their walk in silence.

They walked past women in their beautiful costumes, and down a path that Laure seemed to know that led past a small river, which suddenly made Christianna anxious.

"Should I be worried about snakes? I'm terrified of them," Christianna confided.

"I don't think so," Laure said with a shy smile. "I've been here before and I've never seen one." Laure looked more relaxed with her than she had before.

They continued walking, and Christianna was startled to see a wart hog in the distance. It reminded her that they were in Africa, not just some pleasant countryside that could have been in Europe. Here everything was exciting and different. It was hard to believe she had only been there for two days. After a while the two women sat down on a log, and watched the stream drift by. It felt very peaceful and somewhat surreal. Christianna just hoped that a snake didn't appear at their feet.

"I met your aunt Marque in Russia," she said finally, not knowing what else to say to her. She looked as though she had a lot on her mind, or a thorn in her side somewhere. It was obvious that something was bothering her, and maybe had been for a long time.

"It's amazing how many people know her," Laure said quietly.

"She's a lovely woman," Christianna said with feeling, remembering when they had met in Russia.

"She's more than that. She's a saint of some kind. Did you know she lost her husband and both her children? She stayed too long when war broke out in the Sudan. And in spite of that, she still loves it here. She has Africa in her blood. And now she devotes her life to other people. I wish I could be more like her, giving to others the way she does. I hate it here." Christianna was startled by the words. For Laure, it was a long speech and a surprising admission.

"There aren't many people who can do what she does," Christianna said gently. She was flattered that this woman who seemed to be sealed so tight had opened up to her. "I think it's a gift."

"I think you have that same gift," Laure said quietly, as Christianna stared at her in disbelief.

"How can you say that? You don't even know me." She was flattered by the words. It was a huge compliment, particularly from her.

"I watched you coming out of the classroom yesterday with Ushi. You spoke to everyone, you had children hanging all over you. And when I picked up the records at Mary's office, all her AIDS patients were talking about you. That's a gift."

"You're good with children, too. I see you smile every time you talk to them."

"Children are always honest," Laure said sadly. "It's the adults who never are. They lie, they cheat, they wound. I think most people are profoundly bad." It saddened Christianna to hear her say it, and was a sad statement about the young woman's life and the experiences she must have had.

Listening to her, and seeing the look in her eyes, Christianna decided to take a risk. "Betrayal is a terrible thing, particularly by people we love."

There was a long pause as Laure watched her, as though deciding whether or not to trust her, and then finally she did. "They told you why I came here. I suppose it's not a secret. Everyone in Geneva knew it . . . and Paris . . . and everywhere else . . . even here. I was engaged to a man who made a total fool out of me, with my supposedly best friend." She sounded bitter as she said it, but even more than that, wounded and sad.

"Don't give him the satisfaction of letting it destroy you. He doesn't deserve that, and neither does your so-called best friend who ran off with him. Sooner or later they'll pay a price for that. Things like that come back to haunt you in the end. You don't find happiness at someone else's expense." There was something quietly reassuring about what Christianna said. She had been praying to find the right words to say to this injured girl.

"They're having a baby. She was already pregnant when they ran off. He got her pregnant while he was engaged to me. I didn't find that out till later. To add insult to injury."

As Christianna listened to her, she suddenly thought of words she had heard almost daily in Berkeley, and there was no way to translate them into French. She asked Laure cautiously if she spoke English. She nodded seriously and said she did. Christianna looked at her and smiled.

"In that case, all I can say about them is, 'that sucks.' It was a disgusting thing for them to do to you." Laure smiled too as she heard the words, and then suddenly she grinned, and finally started to laugh.

"That's the silliest thing I ever heard," Laure said, laughing. She was even more beautiful when she laughed. She was a striking-looking girl, and it was hard to believe she'd been jilted. He had to have been a fool to leave her, particularly as he did.

"It is silly, isn't it?" Christianna said, giggling. "But it kind of says it all, doesn't it? That *sucks*," she repeated with vigor, and suddenly they were just two young girls sitting by a stream, and life seemed suddenly simpler. They were like two kids who had just finished school. "He must have been a fool. When we drove up in the bus two days ago, I thought you were the most beautiful woman I'd ever seen." It was true. Laure was a spectacular-looking girl.

"Don't be silly." Laure looked embarrassed. "I look like a tree. I've hated being tall all my life. I always wanted to be small like you. In fact, the woman he ran off with, my so-called best friend, looks a lot like you. It upset me the moment I saw you. And then when you just asked me to go for a walk with you, I told myself that she's not you. I'm sorry if I've been rude. At first, every time I looked at you, I saw her, and I was angry at you."

"You weren't rude," Christianna lied to her, "you just looked sad."

"No," Laure insisted. "I was rude. But you reminded me so much of her."

"Sucks for me," Christianna said again in English. It had been her favorite expression in school. The two young women leaned against each other, laughing.

"No, it sucked for *me*," Laure added in her heavy French accent, and they had tears running down their cheeks, as Yaw rode by them on the path. He was riding his bicycle somewhere, heard them laughing, slowed down, rode past, looked up at the tree, and then shouted at them, as they waved at him. They thought he was just saying hello.

"Go!" he shouted at them. "Go away!" He was waving frantically, and they looked at each other, still laughing, and got up. He was waving them away. They weren't sure what he wanted or what he was saying, but he kept yelling at them. They were still giggling, as they walked back onto the path and he pointed to the tree. An enormous green mamba snake had been lying right above them, sunning himself on the thick branch of the tree, and almost as though on cue, it dropped on top of the log where they'd been sitting, and slithered toward the stream. As they saw it, both girls screamed and ran away, waving at Yaw as he laughed and rode away.

"*Merde!*" Christianna said, and was still screaming, as both girls ran nearly all the way back to the compound, and then they stopped and started laughing again. "Oh my God, did you see that thing?" They had run so fast that Christianna's side ached. "You told me you'd never seen any snakes there," Christianna said, still shaken.

"Maybe I never looked up at the tree," Laure said with a grin. "That was the biggest snake I've ever seen."

"Sucks for us," both girls said in unison, and then laughed again.

"Thank God I'm going home soon," Laure said as they walked back more slowly, in deference to the stitch in Christianna's side from running so hard. She had never run so fast in her life as after they'd seen the snake. It was her worst nightmare come true. Or would have been if not for Yaw. And then as they walked along, Laure suddenly real-ized she'd be sad to leave. Christianna was the first friend she had made here. The others had been nice to her, and pleasant to work with, but Christianna was the first person who had genuinely reached out to her. And surely the first person who had ever made her laugh as hard. Even if she looked shockingly like the woman who had betrayed her, she was a nice girl. It was written all over her. "Do you have a boyfriend?" Laure asked her with interest, as they walked into the camp.

"No, I have a brother, a father, and a dog. For now, that's it. I had one in Berkeley, but it wasn't a serious thing. He e-mails me some-times, or he did before I came here."

"Your two friends seem nice, the ones you came with." Christianna nodded, not sure what to say. Sometimes they were hard to explain, other than that they were just two friends who had wanted to come to Africa, too.

"They were in Russia with me, and they met Marque, too." Laure nodded, and as they headed toward the women's tent, she stopped and looked at Christianna for a long moment.

"Thank you for asking me to take a walk with you. I had a good time, Cricky." She had heard the others call her that, and felt comfort-able doing so herself now.

"I had a good time, too." Christianna smiled at her warmly. Making friends with Laure had been a victory of sorts for her, and was an unexpected gift. It had been hard earned. "Except for the snake," Christianna added, and they both laughed as they walked into the tent everyone called the Ritz. The others were all back from work, in varying degrees of undress, relaxing after a long day.

"Where have you two been?" Mary asked them, surprised to see them together. Everyone had noticed the chill between the two, and how unpleasant Laure had been to Christianna till then.

"We went out looking for snakes, and we found a big one, lying in a tree." Christianna grinned, and Laure smiled, too.

"You don't sit under trees in Africa," Mary scolded her with a stern look, and then she glanced at Laure with the same disapproving look. "You know better than that. We can't let you girls go anywhere, can we? I'm going to have to send you to your room." Both young women laughed, and Laure announced that she was going to take a shower before dinner, which they all knew was not as simple as it looked. But she was sure she could still find someone to pour the water for her. She put on her bathrobe and left the tent, as Christianna lay down on her bed, trying not to think of the enormous snake they'd seen. She'd never screamed as loud in her life or run as fast. Thank God for Yaw.

"What on earth did you do to her?" Fiona asked with a look of amazement. She looked tired. She had delivered three babies in a row that afternoon, and one had died. It always depressed her when tragic things like that happened. She had done everything she could to save the infant, and Geoff had helped, but there was nothing they could do. It happened that way sometimes, but it always weighed heavily on her.

"We just went for a walk," Christianna said calmly. "I think she needed someone to talk to."

"Well, she never talked to any of us until you got here. You must have special powers."

"No, she was just ready to talk." Christianna had sensed it, although she hadn't expected it to go as well as it did. She just didn't want an enemy living with her in the same tent.

"You have a way with people, Cricky," Fiona said with a look of admiration. Everyone in the camp had noticed it, and talked about it. It had been obvious to all of them, even in the short time since she arrived. Christianna had a special kind of grace—as Laure had said that afternoon, a "gift."

Laure came back from the shower shortly after. She looked happy and relaxed, and when they all left for dinner that night, she and Cricky were laughing about the snake. And for the first time since she'd been there, Laure joined in the general conversation at dinner that night. Everyone was surprised to discover that she had a sense of humor. She teased Cricky liberally about how loud she'd screamed and how fast she ran away.

"I didn't see you sticking around to take pictures of him," Christianna answered, and then they laughed about it again, still shuddering over what it would have been like if he'd fallen out of the tree while they were still sitting there. It didn't bear thinking.

They walked back to the tent together that night, and Christianna asked her quietly why she hated Africa. It had struck her when Laure said it that afternoon.

"Maybe I don't hate Africa as much as I think I do," Laure said pensively. "I've been so unhappy here. I suppose I brought it all with me, all the misery that happened before I came. I don't know . . . maybe I just hated me."

"Why would you do that?" Christianna asked her gently.

"I don't know . . . maybe because he didn't love me enough to stay with me and be faithful to me. Maybe I thought that if he didn't love me, why should I . . . I kept looking for what was wrong with me to make them do a thing like that. It's complicated, I guess."

"They were bad people to do that to you," Christianna said simply. "Good people don't do things like that. You don't believe it now, but you'll be glad one day, when you find someone else. Next time you'll find a good man. I truly believe you will. Lightning like that doesn't strike twice. Once in a lifetime is enough."

"I can't even imagine trusting someone again," Laure said as they walked into the tent. The others weren't back yet, so they were alone.

"You will. You'll see."

"When?" Laure asked, looking sad again. The pain of the betrayal she'd lived through was still in her eyes, but now she had a friend.

"When you're ready. It was probably good for you to come here, and get away from all of it."

"That's what I thought. But I brought it all here with me. I haven't been able to think of anything else."

"When that happens again," Christianna said quietly, "do you know what you have to do from now on?"

"What?" Laure was expecting pearls of wisdom from her new friend's mouth. She had been wise and accurate so far, and Laure was impressed.

"Just think of the snake that nearly fell on us today, and be glad we're alive. That's two snakes you've narrowly missed. Him, and the one today." Laure laughed out loud. She was still laughing when the others came in, and looked at them in amazement again. None of them could even remotely imagine what Christianna had done to the girl who never talked. But whatever it had been, it worked. They all agreed. There was no question about it. Christianna had a gift. They felt lucky to have her in their midst. And she even more so to be there with them.

# Chapter 9

The day before Doctors Without Borders came, everyone was always busy. Geoff lined up cases he wanted them to see. There were a few small surgeries he suspected they would perform there. They had two serious cases of tuberculosis he was worried about, and there had been a small outbreak of kala azar that he wasn't panicked about yet, but he was always grateful for their presence and consultation, particularly in malaria season in September, which fortunately was still a long way off. There would be four physicians and two nurses joining them for the week, which always took some of the burden off Geoff's and Mary's shoulders. And there were always their AIDS patients to consult about. The Doctors Without Borders brought new medications for them. And it was always nice to see familiar faces and new ones. They had already radioed the camp several weeks before to say that they had a new doctor with them, who was interested in spending a month or so with them. He was a young American, doing AIDS research at Harvard. Geoff had responded that he'd be grateful to have him around for a month, if he'd enjoy it. It would raise their number of camp residents to eighteen, and Geoff had promised to set up an additional cot for him in the George V, since they were already full up.

Christianna had spoken to her father twice by then, and he said he missed her terribly. It was only February, and he couldn't imagine another five months without her, let alone longer. He said he wanted her to come home at the end of six months, and not stay the full year, and she didn't comment. She didn't want to argue about it with him yet. She was planning to do that later in the year. She had no desire whatsoever to leave East Africa a moment earlier than she had to. He was relieved at least that she was well and happy, although even he knew it didn't bode well for her coming home early. Christianna felt guilty leaving him alone in Liechtenstein, but this time was sacred to her. She knew only too well that she would never get a chance like this again.

She had completed her plan for the AIDS education program by then, and had started small classes for the local women, with her translator at her side, a sweet girl who spoke adequate English, taught to her by missionaries. And often her translations made Christianna and her students laugh. They tittered and giggled at the funny things Christianna said, and seemed to take her seriously about the rest. Mary thought she was doing a fine job and said that to Geoff often, and also to Christianna, although she thought Mary was only being kind.

She was still teaching with Ushi every afternoon, and the children adored her. She had brought Laure in several times to help, and she loved it. With a friend to confide in, and take walks with in the afternoon, the previously dour French girl had begun to flourish. When the others commented on the miraculous transformation that had occurred, Christianna insisted that it had only been a matter of timing. Laure had been ready to open up, and Christianna had just been there at the right time, like an accident of friendship. The others didn't buy it. They could see what had happened, better than she could perhaps, and how gently Christianna had drawn her out of her shell. The angry, taciturn girl she had been for months had vanished. Now she talked, laughed, and made jokes like the others. She even played cards with the men at night, and was delighted when she came back to the women's tent with a handful of *nakfa,* the local money.

And even more than Laure, the girl they all called Cricky was thriving. Even Geoff forgot now that she was a Serene Highness, which made it easier to keep the secret. She had become one of them in barely more than a month. They could no longer imagine life without her, nor could she. She felt as though she had truly found herself in East Africa, and wished she could stay forever. She couldn't bear thinking of leaving, and wanted to hang on to every moment and savor its delights to the fullest.

The morning the Doctors Without Borders came, Christianna was doing rounds with Mary, before teaching her AIDS prevention class, and when the head of the visiting team walked in with Geoff, he introduced him to Christianna. As always now, he just called her Cricky. The head of the visiting team was Dutch, and spoke to her in German. He was an interesting-looking man who had worked for Doctors Without Borders for years. In the Sudan at one time, then Sierra Leone, Zaire, Tanzania, and finally Eritrea. During the border war with Ethiopia, he had treated a great many casualties on both sides, and was relieved that it was over, as were the locals. Many of those who had fled at the time and migrated elsewhere, had come home to Eritrea now.

He and Geoff were old friends and always happy to see each other, and he was substantially older than Geoff. He always claimed to be too old for this work now, but no one believed him. He was a youthful-looking, vital man, and enjoyed flying the plane himself. He had flown for the British at the very end of World War II, after fleeing Holland. He was a very interesting man, and Christianna was delighted to meet him. She had been hearing about him since she arrived.

They had a lively dinner in the dining tent that night, combining both groups, as the doctor in charge regaled them with funny stories, and the various younger members of the group mingled, and enjoyed getting to know each other or renewing old friendships. It was always nice to have new faces in camp, just as it had been when Cricky and her two men arrived. The young American had sat next to Mary at dinner, and they were talking intently about the new protocols for AIDS being tested at Harvard. He was young but extremely knowledgeable in his field, and Mary thoroughly enjoyed hearing all the latest developments and picking his brain about her current caseload. He had examined all of her patients with her that afternoon, and had made some excellent suggestions. For Christianna, listening to them all around her was like being at a medical convention, but she found it fascinating. And there were lots of times at dinner when they all talked about other things. There seemed to be endless laughter peppered among the more serious topics.

Christianna was also pleased to see that Laure was enjoying talking to one of the young French doctors. They seemed to be having a serious conversation through most of dinner, and after dessert Laure started a lively game of poker. She had turned into the camp's hottest and most successful gambler, and tonight was no exception. She glanced over at Christianna several times, and when no one was looking, Christianna gave her a thumbs-up over the young French doctor, and Laure laughed. She looked happier than she had in a long time, and Christianna was glad.

It was the end of the evening, with the poker game still in full swing, when Christianna was introduced to the American doctor who would be staying with them. His name was Parker Williams, and she had heard him say to someone that he was from San Francisco. While they were chatting over coffee, she told him that she had gone to Berkeley. He very politely said it was a great school, although she knew he had gone to Harvard.

"How did you wind up out here?" he asked with interest. She told him about the siege at the Russian school, meeting Marque, and realizing that she wanted to spend a year of her life doing something like this before settling into her family business. And in response to her questions, he said that he wasn't really part of Doctors Without Borders, he was just following them as part of his research project on AIDS for Harvard, but he said that he was thoroughly enjoying it, and looked forward to the time he would spend in Senafe.

"I love it here," she said quietly, and from the look in her eyes he could see that she did. Laure had already commented earlier on how attractive he was and how much he looked like Christianna. He was equally blond, had the same deep blue eyes, although he was tall, and she was tiny. But there was nothing small about her spirit, as her coworkers there had already discovered.

She and Parker chatted for a little while, about the camp, the people in Senafe, the work they were doing there. She told him about the AIDS prevention program she had developed with Mary's help. And after listening to her describe the ground she was covering, he said he liked it and was impressed with the progress she had obviously made in a short time.

He joined Laure's poker game after that, and most of the men stayed in the dining tent, while Christianna and the other women went back to their tent.

"He's a cutie," Fiona cackled to Christianna as they walked back to the Ritz.

"Who?" Christianna said innocently, momentarily distracted. She was thinking that she hadn't called her father for several days, and should probably go into Senafe to do so the next day. He got upset when she didn't call him.

"Don't give me that," Fiona snorted at her. "I saw you talking to him. You know who I mean. The young doctor from Harvard. Hell, if you don't want him, I'll have a go at him myself." Fiona always had an eye out for new men, although she was more talk than action. None of them had many opportunities for such liaisons. And other than Maggie and Geoff, most of them steered clear of romances in the camp. It got too complicated later, and they lived together like sisters and brothers. But the arrival of Doctors Without Borders always caught everyone's attention.

"You can have him," Christianna said, laughing at her, although Fiona was still flirting with Max, but so far it had gone nowhere. It was just talk, and something they both played at.

"Don't you like him?" Fiona asked, referring to Parker Williams again.

"He seems fine. I just haven't been thinking about things like that here. There's too much work to do, to worry about all that." Christianna was engaged in other pursuits here, and finding a man was the last thing on her mind. She was well aware that it would only complicate her life. It had been different in Berkeley when she was a student. But not here, at the far end of the world, particularly given the burdens of her real life. If she got involved with someone here, it would just have to end when she went back. And this time it might hurt. Last time it hadn't.

All of the women got undressed and went to bed, and an hour later Laure joined them. She'd had a good time, and everyone teased her in the morning about how much money she'd made. She'd cleaned them all out.

"You'll be the only person I know to leave Senafe a rich woman," Geoff said, as Laure grinned. She'd had fun, and the French doctor was nice.

As always, they were all hard at work at their various jobs by seven. Parker Williams was doing rounds with Mary, the head of the team was seeing patients with Geoff, and the other doctors who'd flown in were helping them see patients and restock their supplies. Christianna was in the tiny office she used for her AIDS prevention class, when Mary came by to ask her if she'd like to join them, and she looked surprised. She wasn't part of the medical team after all, and it was a compliment to be included in medical discussions, even when they were over her head. She always learned something from them, and in the short time she'd been there, she'd learned a lot.

By now she knew all of their AIDS patients fairly well, especially the children. She visited everyone on the ward every day, and brought them little treats, fruit for the women, games for the children. She put fresh flowers in the ward for them, always nicely arranged. She had a way of making everyone's life better, as Mary constantly observed. But she was quiet when she joined them. She didn't want to interfere with Parker's dialogue with Mary. And she only asked him a question once, about a certain medication she had heard about from the others but didn't understand. He explained it to her carefully, and then spoke to the patients. On two occasions, Christianna translated for him, when the patients only spoke French. They had two women from Mozambique on the ward.

"Thanks for the help," he said casually when she left to teach her class.

"Anytime." She smiled and went to do her own work. She skipped lunch entirely that day, and went straight to the schoolroom to help Ushi, and when she finished, she dropped by to see Laure in her office. The young French doctor happened to be there, chatting with her. Cricky smiled at her, and rapidly disappeared. And then she went outside to take a walk on her own. Fiona had been gone all day, so she had no one to talk to or walk with. The others had already gone back to the tent to relax.

"Thanks again for your help this morning," she heard a voice call out to her, and she turned to see who it was. It was Parker. He had worked hard all day, and they had finished at the same time.

"That wasn't a big thing." She smiled pleasantly, and then to be polite, because she didn't want to just stand around, she asked him if he'd like to take a walk, and he said he would. He thought the area was beautiful, and it was totally unfamiliar to him. He said he had only been in Africa for a month.

"Me too, or just a little longer," she said pleasantly, as they headed in the same direction she usually went with Laure.

"Where are you from?" he asked with interest. He had thought she was French, but Mary said she wasn't.

"A tiny country in Europe," she smiled at him. "Liechtenstein."

"Where exactly is that? I've always heard about it, but to be honest, I wouldn't know where to place it on a map." He had a nice easy way about him and a warm smile.

"Most people wouldn't. It's landlocked between Austria and Switzerland. It's only a hundred and sixty square kilometers. Very tiny, which is why you didn't know where it is." She smiled back. They weren't flirting, far from it, they were just making idle conversation as they walked. She thought he looked a little bit like her brother Freddy, but it seemed safe to assume that he was much better behaved. Most people were.

"What do they speak there?" He seemed to soak up information like a sponge. "German?"

"Mostly, and a dialect that derives from it but is very hard to understand."

"And French?" Hers had seemed perfect to him that morning, and now he was impressed, if it wasn't her native tongue. It had sounded like it to him.

"Some people do. Though most speak German. I just always spoke French at home. My mother was French."

"Was?" he asked, looking sympathetic.

"She died when I was five."

"Mine died when I was fifteen." It was something they had in common, although she didn't pursue the subject. She didn't want to be rude or intrusive and ask painful questions. "My brother and I grew up alone with my dad."

"My brother and I did, too." She smiled.

"What does your brother do now, assuming he's old enough to be doing something?" He laughed, she looked very young to him, mostly because she was so small. She was barely taller than a child, although if she was working for the Red Cross in Africa, he knew she had to be a reasonable age, at the very least over twenty-one.

"He's old enough," Cricky said ruefully. "He's thirty-three. Actually, most of the time, he travels, chases women, and drives fast cars."

"Nice work if you can find it," he teased. "Mine is a doctor, and so is my dad. My father is a surgeon in San Francisco, and my brother is a pediatrician in New York. And I live in Boston." He supplied all the relevant information, as some Americans did, far more so than

Europeans, who gave much less personal information away. But Christianna didn't mind it. She liked the open, friendly American ways. She had missed that since she left Berkeley in June.

"I know you live in Boston." She smiled pleasantly at him, he seemed nice. "You do research at Harvard." He seemed pleased that she knew.

"What do you do in Liechtenstein . . . what's your hometown called, by the way?"

"I live in the capital, Vaduz. And I'm going to work for my father when I go home. But I'm hoping to stay here all year first. If he lets me. He gets a bit nervous when I'm away. But my brother will be home from China soon . . . that will distract him, I hope. Or drive him insane, depending on what my brother does." They both laughed.

"Is he a race car driver? You mentioned fast cars."

"No." She laughed harder this time, as they walked down a path bordered by bushes, flowers, and trees. The smell of the flowers was heavy and sweet, and one that she would always associate with Africa now. "He's just a very bad boy."

"Doesn't he work at all?" He looked surprised. That concept was new to him, though not to her. Most princes didn't, especially crown princes like her brother, although most were far more respectable than he was, and found tamer ways to fill their time.

"Actually, he works for my father sometimes, too, but he doesn't like it much. He prefers to travel. He's been traveling in Asia now for several months. He was in Japan before, and now China. He's planning to stop in Burma on his way home." They sounded like an interesting family to him.

"And your father?"

"He's in politics and PR." She had it down pat now, and had said it often enough. She had almost convinced herself. "I'll work for him in PR when I go home."

"That sounds like fun," he said generously, and she groaned.

"I can't think of anything worse. I'd much rather be here."

"And what does he think of that?" he asked, looking at her cautiously. She was beginning to intrigue him. She was a very bright girl.

"He's not too pleased. But he let me come. He agreed to six months, but I'm going to push for a year." He realized that she was still young enough to be ruled by her father, and somewhat dependent on him. He had no idea to what extent she was bound by her father's rules, and the duties imposed on her as a princess. He would have been stunned had he known.

"I have to be back at Harvard in June, but I love it here, too. It's the most interesting place I've ever been. Africa, I mean. I did some research in Central America a few years ago. My specialty is AIDS in developing countries. This has been a terrific opportunity for me."

"Doctors Without Borders is a wonderful group. Everyone respects them a great deal."

"It will be interesting for me in Senafe, too, and nice to stay for a while. What I've been doing for the past month was a little more hit and run, although I've been very grateful that they let me tag along." She nodded as they slowly turned back. It had been a very pleasant walk with him. He asked her about Berkeley then and if she liked it, and she said she did, very much.

"I was very sorry to go home in June."

"It doesn't sound like you or your brother like being home a lot," he said with a mischievous grin.

"You're right. Liechtenstein is a very small place. There's not much to do. There's far more for me to do here." She was enjoying her AIDS work, and the children she was teaching in the afternoon. She felt useful here, which meant a lot to her.

"I'll have to visit there sometime," he said politely. "I've been to Vienna, and Lausanne and Zurich, but I've never been to Liechtenstein."

"It's very pretty," she said loyally, not sounding convinced herself.

"And very dull," he added for her.

"Yes, *very* dull," she admitted with a smile.

"So why go back?" He looked puzzled. In the States, if people didn't like where they lived, they moved, just as he and his brother had. He liked San Francisco, but it was too quiet for him, too.

"I don't have any choice," she said sadly, but there was no way she could explain. He assumed from what she'd said that her father was pressing her into the family business, particularly if she had an irresponsible brother. It didn't sound fair to him. And the truth of her situation was the farthest thing from his mind. He couldn't have imagined it in a million years. "That's just the way it is. Now I have this year off, and then I have to go back for good."

"Maybe you can rethink that while you're here." She laughed out loud at that, and shook her head.

"I'm afraid there's no way I can do that. Sometimes you just have to accept your responsibilities and do what's expected of you, no matter how tedious it is."

"You can do anything you want in life," he insisted, "or not do what you don't want. I've never believed you have to play by other people's rules. My father taught me that when I was very young."

"I wish I could say my father thought that way, but he doesn't. Very much the opposite. He believes in duty before anything. And tradition." He sounded tough, maybe even unreasonably so, Parker thought, but he didn't say it to her. She looked so happy to be here.

They were back in the camp by then, and Parker said he was going to shower before dinner, as though he were going back to a hotel room.

"You'd better hurry before the water boys go home," she told him, and explained the system they used to bathe. He had experienced it that morning, but hadn't realized that after a certain hour you could no longer shower, once the water boys left. He thanked her for the information and the pleasant walk, and then hurried back to the tent. And as Christianna wandered back to her own tent, she thought about how easygoing and likable he had been. She didn't know for sure, but she suspected he was about Freddy's age. She was still thinking about him when she went back to her tent, and lay down for a few minutes before dinner.

She was lying on her bed, staring into space with Parker in her mind's eye, and before she knew it, she felt so peaceful she fell asleep.

# Chapter 10

The team from Doctors Without Borders stayed with them for a week. The Senafe Red Cross team worked hard with them, and their combined efforts benefited the patients they were treating, particularly in the AIDS unit, with Parker's help. And every night the combination of the two groups in the dining tent made for a festive atmosphere. They had a wonderful time together. Particularly Laure and the young French doctor. By the time the visiting medical team left, there was obviously a spark between Laure and her new friend, and when she talked to Christianna about it, she was beaming.

"So?" Cricky asked her expectantly, as they followed their usual path toward the stream. They no longer sat under the trees, however. Neither of them had forgotten the snake that Yaw had spared them from.

"I like him," Laure admitted with a shy smile, and then just as quickly looked nervous and afraid. "But what do I know? He's probably a liar and a cheat like all other men." Christianna was sad to hear her say it, and particularly to see the wounded look in her eyes that went with it. Her fiancé had left her with an ugly gift—the gift of distrust for any man who came near her.

"Not all men are liars and cheats," Christianna said cautiously. The two young women had become fast friends in the short time they'd known each other, and confided much to each other, mostly about their hopes and dreams and fears for the future. Christianna would have liked to share more with her, about her own particular situation, but didn't dare. Her secret was a big one, and she couldn't share it with anyone here, not even Laure, no matter how much she liked her. She was afraid that it would change everything between them, so she continued to keep what she considered her dark secret to herself, the fact that she was a princess. "Some men are actually honorable and decent, Laure. Look at the life he leads, and what he's doing for humanity. That has to say something about him, don't you think?"

"I don't know," Laure said sadly, and then with tears in her eyes, "I'm afraid to trust him. I don't ever want to be that hurt again."

"And then what?" Christianna said practically, in her gentle, measured tone. "You enter a convent? You never date again? You give up on life? You stay celibate forever, afraid to go out with anyone or trust any man? That's a lonely life for you, Laure. Not everyone is as rotten as the man who let you down." Or the best friend who had gone with him. "This one may not be the right man, or it may just be too soon for you to trust again, but I'd hate to see you close that door forever. You just can't. You're too wonderful a person, and much too beautiful to let that happen."

"That's what he says," Laure said, drying her eyes. "I told him about what happened. He thought it was awful."

"It was awful. It was a totally rotten thing to do to you. He was a real cad, in every sense of the word," Christianna said vehemently, and Laure smiled at her. She loved her new friend.

"He had a right to change his mind about marrying me," Laure said, trying to be fair. "And even to fall in love with someone else."

"Yes, but not in the order he did it, and not with your best friend. He must have known sooner than two days before the wedding that he had grave doubts, and he had obviously been involved with her for a while. Any way you look at it, it was a rotten thing to do. But that doesn't mean that someone else will do the same thing again." She was trying to divide the two issues so Laure could see it more clearly.

"The same thing happened to Antoine," she said quietly. He was the young doctor in question. "They weren't engaged, but he went out with her for five years, all through medical school and after. She also went off with his best friend, and then married his brother, so he has to see her all the time. That's why he came here to Africa and joined Doctors Without Borders, so he wouldn't have to see them. He hasn't spoken to his brother since they got married, which must be sad for him."

"She sounds like a piece of work. It sounds like you both got lucky, getting rid of people like that, even though it may not seem like it right now. I really think you should give this guy a chance. When can you see him again after he leaves?" She didn't know exactly when the team was coming back this way again, although they came to the camp roughly once a month, and Laure was leaving in a relatively short time, in about a month, so she might miss him, if the Doctors Without Borders didn't come back before she left. It seemed a shame to Christianna for them to miss an opportunity to get to know each other. There was obviously something there or she wouldn't be so troubled. She clearly felt a pull toward this man, and at the same time felt vulnerable and afraid.

"He wants to see me in Geneva. He's leaving Africa in a few months. He's accepted a job in a hospital in Brussels, specialized in tropical medicine. He said he'd come to visit me when he gets back. I'm going back two months before him."

"That gives you time to adjust to the idea. Why don't you see how you feel about it when you go back? Maybe the two of you could correspond or something in the meantime." Laure laughed in answer, and Christianna had to admit that it wouldn't be easy for them to contact each other in Africa, given their locations and the nature of their jobs. But three months wasn't long to wait, and Laure needed the time to heal. "I think you should give it a shot, or at least leave the door open, and see what happens. You don't have much to lose at this point, you haven't invested anything in it. Let him prove to you that he's a good guy. Be cautious, but at least give the poor man a chance, he's been through a lot, too."

"I don't want to get my heart broken again," Laure said, still looking worried. But there was no question, she was tempted, and everything Christianna had said to her made sense.

"Nothing is whole that has not previously been rent," Christianna offered. "That's a misquote, and I think it's Yeats. All hearts get broken at some point, in the end it makes us stronger."

"And yours?" Laure smiled at her.

"My heart is a virgin," Christianna answered. "I've liked some people, a lot even, but I don't think I've ever been in love. In fact, I know I haven't." She had so little opportunity, except for her years in Berkeley, but other than that the scope of her world was so small, the options for her so narrow as to be almost nonexistent. In order to satisfy her father, it would have to be a prince, or at least someone titled, from her own world. If not, it would cause a huge explosion. Despite other young royals marrying commoners in recent years, her father had always insisted that she had to marry another royal. It was a promise he had made her mother before she died, a tradition that meant much to him, and he always pointed out that few royal marriages to commoners had been successful. It was not only about bloodlines for him, he had a profound belief that it was essential not to marry someone too different. And he had always made it clear to her that he would never give her his approval unless she married another royal. She believed him. And she could not conceive of getting married without her father's blessing. She couldn't say as much to Laure.

"I don't recommend it, falling in love, I mean. I've never been so miserable in my life as after he canceled the wedding and ran off. I thought I was going to die."

"You didn't though. That's a good thing to remember. And if this man, or another one, is a better man, then you were blessed."

"I suppose you're right," Laure said, looking more philosophical, and a little braver. Christianna had made some excellent points, and they hadn't fallen on deaf ears. Laure was ready to hear them, although frightened. She truly liked the man she had just met, a lot. There had been an instant attraction and understanding when they met, almost like soulmates, although she wasn't entirely sure she believed in that anymore. She had been convinced her ex-fiancé had been her soulmate too, although he turned out to be anything but and in fact someone else's. But this man was different, and he seemed vulnerable and cautious, too, also with good reason. They were perfectly matched in many ways, and respectful of each other. "Maybe I will see him when I go back," she said with a shy smile.

"Good girl," Christianna said, and hugged her as they walked back to the camp. They passed several of the local women, walking with their children. They both commented on how friendly the people of Eritrea were, even among themselves. They spoke nine different languages in the country, but no matter what they spoke, they always wore a smile, and were constantly helpful. They wanted everyone to feel warmly welcomed and comfortable. It made every encounter with them a joy.

The one thing that always pained Christianna when she saw it were the children with malnutrition, usually from outlying rural areas, but sometimes even here in Senafe. They had had years of starvation and drought, and the distended bellies of starving children brought to them for medical treatment never failed to make her cry. There was so little one could do for them to solve all the ills and sorrows and poverty they had endured and faced so courageously. The Red Cross was doing all they could for them, as were other groups, but the country needed more than a handful of compassionate people caring for them. They needed political and economic solutions that were beyond anyone's control. There was a sense of helplessness being there, while at the same time a sense of gratitude and joy just to be among them. Christianna intended to speak to her family foundation about an enormous grant for their benefit when she got home. And in the meantime, she was giving them her time, her heart, her soul. Just being there was an enormous gift to her, and she would be forever grateful to them for welcoming her so generously, to the Red Cross for allowing her this experience, and to her father for letting her come. Sometimes just thinking about it, her heart overflowed.

They reached the camp in time to shower before dinner. The water girls were gone, but the women poured the water for each other, and

Fiona joined them when she heard them laughing outside the tent in the makeshift shower.

"Okay, what's happening, girls?" Fiona asked with her standard look of mischief. She was currently having a hard time trying to decide whether to chase Max or one of the visiting doctors she thought was gorgeous. But he was leaving the next day, which didn't give her much time. Max was a better long-term investment as he was going to be around for quite a while. Christianna and the two men weren't planning to go home for months, hopefully not till the end of the year, so he was a much better bet than a one-night stand, however cute. She discussed it with both women, who laughed at her dilemma.

Fiona was single-handedly changing the face of obstetrics in the area of Debub, particularly Senafe. Before her arrival, women had had to travel three days by donkey to give birth in a hospital far from home, and often delivered their babies by the side of the road. With Fiona's help, far fewer infants were dying in the days immediately before and after birth. And when she sensed a problem that would require a physician on hand at the delivery, she insisted that they give birth at the center. The locals were vastly impressed by her kindness and competence, her energy, and how much healthier their infants were when they were born. Both mothers and babies did well in Fiona's care. She was becoming legendary and much loved.

"What have you two been up to?" Fiona asked with interest as she dried off, after showering at the same time as Cricky and Laure.

"Just talking," Laure said quietly, but she was friendlier with all of them now. Ever since her friendship with Christianna had blossomed, she had been more open with everyone. To Fiona, it seemed a miraculous change, which no longer surprised her. Christianna seemed to have that gift with everyone. "About Antoine," she confessed with a blush. "He's very nice."

Fiona laughed. "He's a lot better than that. He's a very handsome man, and I think he's totally smitten with you." And Laure with him.

"I might see him when I go back," Laure said quietly, with a glance at her other friend. Christianna had convinced her that afternoon. She was going to at least leave the door open for him, and see what happened after that. It was a major step for her.

Dinner in the dining tent that night was a festive affair. The residents at the camp on the outskirts of Senafe were sorry to see the others leave. It was so much livelier when they were there. There was a great deal of talk and laughter, the food seemed exceptionally good, and Geoff contributed several bottles of decent South African wine. They all had a good time, and afterward Laure and Antoine stood outside the tent and talked. After Laure's conversation with Christianna, she seemed to have opened up considerably. When Christianna and Fiona wandered out of the dining tent, they glimpsed Antoine and Laure kissing at a little distance. They said nothing, hoping not to disturb the young lovers, and walked back to the Ritz in silence, touched by what they'd seen. It was nice to know that after months of grief over her broken engagement, Laure was finally healing. They both hoped that she and Antoine would see each other again once back in Europe. They seemed to be crazy about each other.

"I'm glad somebody is getting kissed around here," Fiona said with a grin, and Christianna laughed, as they walked into their tent. "I'm sure not getting any," she complained good-naturedly. They lived in such close quarters and knew each other so well that they were more like sisters and brothers, and romances didn't flourish or even happen. It seemed simpler like that. She was even losing interest in pursuing Max, and was becoming friends with him. He and Samuel had gotten comfortable with everyone and fit right in. They worked every bit as hard as the others, mostly handling and unpacking supplies, making repairs, filling out requisition slips to replace whatever they were running out of, and going to the market for emergency supplies. Everyone appreciated their help and their tireless efforts. They checked in with Christianna several times a day, and were never far from wherever she was, but they didn't hover over her, or intrude on what she was doing. They had managed to achieve the perfect balance. There had been no slips about her identity, either by them or by Geoff.

"So what about you and our new American doctor?" Fiona asked Christianna, as they got into their beds. "I think he likes you," Fiona assessed. She loved imagining sex and romance all around her, although there was little or none of it in the camp. They all had other things on their minds, and had set romance aside for the duration of their stays, much to Fiona's chagrin.

"He likes everyone." Christianna smiled at her with a yawn. She was sorry to see the visiting medical team leave, too. They had been good company while they were there, and had done a huge amount of impressive work. "That's how Americans are. I loved going to school in America. I had a wonderful time while I was there."

"I've never been," Fiona commented. "I'd love to go one day, if I can ever afford it." She made a pittance as a midwife in Ireland, and was making even less here, but it was for a good cause. She had a real calling to do what she was accomplishing with the local women, and had already saved many lives. "I'll probably be poor forever." She didn't know why, but she always had the sense that that was not the case with Christianna. She wore simple clothes and no jewelry, but she was obviously educated and she had lovely manners, and was kind to everyone around her. Everything about her suggested a genteel background. Fiona had long since observed that she had the generosity of someone very comfortable in her world and in her own skin. There was nothing in her that was jealous or resentful. She seemed to care about everyone, and never spoke of money or the advantages she did or didn't have at home. In fact, she almost never spoke of her home, except now and then her father with great admiration. Fiona suspected but had no way of knowing that she came from a very easy life. It was that word that Mary used when she spoke of her that everyone agreed described her best. Christianna had grace, it was just an air about her, like the smile on her face.

"Maybe we can go to America together one day, if I ever leave Africa, which I'm beginning to doubt. Sometimes I think I'll stay here forever, and maybe even die here," Fiona said with a dreamy look, as Christianna smiled at her, her head on her pillow, her arms behind her head.

"I wish I could stay, too. I love it here. Everything makes sense here. I always feel like this is where I'm meant to be. For now anyway."

"It's a good feeling," Fiona said as she turned off her light. The others still weren't back. Mary had stayed out to enjoy a last night of talking to the doctors. Laure was still somewhere with Antoine, maybe still kissing him, or getting to know him better before he left. The two women could hear laughter outside. And both were sound asleep when the others came in.

Everyone was on hand to say goodbye to the Doctors Without Borders team the next morning. It was one of those gorgeous golden days typical of Africa that kept them all in love with the place. They all hated to see the visiting doctors leave. It had been so much more fun at the camp with them around. And Christianna noticed as she said goodbye to them that Antoine was holding Laure's hand, and she was smiling up at him. Whatever had happened between them the night before seemed to have been a good thing. Laure looked as though she was about to cry when he left.

"You'll see him again soon," Christianna said confidently as they both walked to work, after saying goodbye to the team. Laure headed toward the office, and Christianna toward the hut, where she visited the AIDS ward every morning.

"So he says," Laure muttered under her breath, and Christianna grinned.

She found Mary doing rounds with Parker when she went in. He had just finished examining a young mother whose baby had contracted AIDS. Further conversation with her revealed that she hadn't used the formula they'd given her and had given the infant the breast instead. She said her husband had been suspicious of the formula, thought it might make the baby sick, and had thrown it away. It was a tragedy Mary saw every day. AIDS and malnutrition were the curses she was constantly fighting there.

Christianna moved quietly past them to visit the women and children she knew. She didn't want to disturb Parker or Mary, and went about her business in silence, whispering gently in the bits of Tigrinya and Tigre that she had already learned. Both languages accounted for ninety percent of what was spoken in Eritrea. There was some Arabic spoken as well, although Christianna hadn't learned any yet. She was working hard learning the other two, and Fiona was helping her as she was fluent in both, given her extensive work in the field delivering the babies of the local women. The women Christianna spoke to in the AIDS ward had names like Mwanaiuma, which meant "Friday," Wekesa, which she had been told meant "harvest time," Nsonowa (seventh born), Abeni, Monifa, Chiumbo, Dada, and Ife, which meant "love." Christianna loved the sound of their names. The women laughed at her efforts in Tigre, which she didn't speak as well yet, and nodded their approval as she tried to master at least the rudiments of Tigrinya. They certainly weren't languages she'd ever speak again once she left. But they were useful here, for her work with the local women and children, and whenever she moved around Senafe. And the women loved her for the effort she made, even when she made embarrassing mistakes. When she did, everyone giggled in the ward. After she had finished delivering baskets of fruit to each of them, and set out two vases of flowers she'd picked herself, she went to her office to meet with half a dozen young women, to teach them the AIDS prevention course she'd designed.

She was just finishing with the women when Parker walked in, just in time to see her hand each of the women a ballpoint pen and several pencils as they left.

"What was that about? The pens I mean." He was looking at her with admiration. He had been touched earlier by how kind and attentive she was to everyone in the ward. And he thought the AIDS prevention class she had designed was very impressive.

Christianna smiled before she answered. He was wearing baggy shorts to his knees, and his white coat over a T-shirt. Everything was informal here. "I don't know why, but everyone here loves pens and pencils. I buy them by the case in town." Actually, Samuel and Max did, and gave them to her when they came back, so she could give them out, on nearly every visit to the ward, and to everyone after each class. "They'd rather have a pen than almost anything except food." The entire country was fighting a battle with malnutrition. Food was the greatest gift, and the center handed out a lot of it. It was their most important supply.

"I'll have to remember that," Parker said, watching her. She seemed to have learned a lot in the short time she was there. He had been particularly impressed by her efforts to speak to them in their native tongue. Their languages sounded nearly impossible to pick up to him. He couldn't even imagine managing as well as she did after being there little more than a month. Christianna had been working hard with her translator to learn essential words and phrases in the most common local dialects. "Are you heading over to the tent for lunch?" he asked with a friendly smile. She wondered if he was lonely now that the visiting medical team was gone.

"I teach a class in a few minutes," she explained, "with Ushi in the classroom. The kids are really cute."

"Do you speak the local dialects to them, too?" he asked with interest.

"I try to, but they usually laugh at me, a lot more than the women." She smiled thinking about it. The kids always erupted in gales of giggles whenever she said the wrong thing, which she did often. But she was determined to learn their language so she could speak to them directly.

"Do you give them pens, too?" He was beginning to find her intriguing. She had a kind of quiet, gracious poise that appealed to him, more than he wanted it to. The last thing he wanted to do was get involved with someone here. It would be a lot simpler to just be friends, and he had the impression she'd be good at that, too. She was a good listener, and seemed interested in people.

"Yes, I do," she said in answer to his question. "Max and Sam buy them for me in cases. Colored pens are always a big hit."

"I'll have to buy some, too, to give to patients. You'd think they'd want something more useful."

"Pens are a big status symbol here. They suggest education, and that you have important things to write down. Maggie told me about it when I came."

"What about lunch?" It was six hours since they'd last eaten, and he was starving. He was holding a nutrition clinic with Geoff that afternoon, where they were going to be giving out food.

"I don't have time," she said honestly. "I'll grab something on my way to class. I usually just eat fruit at lunch. But they put sandwiches out every day, not just when the visiting team is here." He was still new to the camp and its habits.

"I was hoping they would. I get so hungry here, it must be the air." Or how hard they worked, they all did, and he had, too. She had also liked his manner with people. He seemed gentle and competent, and deeply interested in every case. He seemed to respond easily to the warmth of the people he treated. It was easy to see that he was good at what he did. He exuded quiet confidence, and had a manner that assured people he knew what he was doing.

They walked over to the dining tent side by side, and once there, Christianna grabbed a handful of fruit from an enormous basket. There were yogurts there, too, which the camp cook bought in Senafe, but she never touched them. She stayed away from dairy products in Africa. A lot of people got very sick, not just from the major diseases that plagued the area, but also from simple dysentery. She hadn't suffered from it yet, and was hoping to keep it that way. Parker helped himself to two sandwiches, wrapped them in a napkin, and took a banana.

"Since you won't have lunch with me, Cricky"—he smiled—"I guess I'll take mine back to work, too." The others had come and gone. None of the workers ever lingered at lunchtime. He walked her to the classroom where she and Ushi taught, and then went back to the other hut, to discuss a number of their cases with Mary. "See you later," he said pleasantly, and then wandered off, looking casual and happy. It was obvious to Christianna that he was trying to make friends, but Ushi didn't think so. She thought he had something a little more personal in mind.

"A lunch date?" Ushi teased her.

"No. I didn't have time. I think he's just lonely without his friends."

"I think it might be more than that." Ushi had been watching him for days, and actually found him very attractive herself, but like Christianna and most of the others, she didn't want the complications of a camp romance. And he seemed far more interested in Cricky than in her, she realized. He had made that pretty clear through his friendly overtures to her, and had barely said a word to Ushi.

"I don't have time for more than that, nor the interest," Christianna said firmly. "Besides, Americans are that way. They're friendly. I'll bet you that in spite of the scheming in the camp, he's not even remotely interested in romance. Just like the rest of us, he's here to work."

"That doesn't mean you can't have a little fun, too," Ushi said with a smile. She liked going out with men, but had met no eligible ones for her here. Parker was the first truly attractive candidate who had come along, other than the visiting team every month, although she thought he was too young for her. He was the same age as Max and Samuel, whom she had overlooked romantically for the same reason. She knew from seeing Parker's records in the office that he was thirty-two years old. Ushi was forty-two. Age didn't matter here, and most of the time they hung out as a group. But she had a gut feeling he was interested in Christianna, although there was no serious evidence of it yet, despite his seemingly casual efforts to make friends. She had noticed Parker watching Christianna quietly at dinner, although she seemed oblivious to it. She didn't have romance on her mind, only work, and she had a polite, somewhat reserved, conservative style about her, particularly with men, almost as though she were constantly aware of not exposing herself in any way. She was far more relaxed and outspoken with the women. "I think he has a crush on you," Ushi finally said openly, and Christianna firmly shook her head.

"Don't be silly," she brushed off the suggestion, and a moment later they went back to work, but Ushi was convinced her assessment was correct.

She and Fiona chatted about it idly a few days later, as Parker continued to chat with Christianna at every opportunity and had started borrowing books from her, and consulting her about several of the AIDS patients, whom she seemed to have come to know well. He always seemed to have something he needed to ask her about, tell her, lend her, borrow from her. And at her suggestion, he had started handing out pens to everyone he saw. The patients loved him for it, and he became much loved by all within weeks of his arrival, for his gentle ways. He stayed up late at night in the men's tent, poring over the notes he made for his research project. Fiona often saw his portion of the tent lit up when she came home late from deliveries nearby. Often when he heard her, he came out and said hello to her, and they chatted for a few minutes, even at three and four in the morning. And remarkably, he always seemed fresh and good humored the next day.

He often invited Christianna to go on walks with him at the end of their workdays. She saw no harm in doing so, enjoyed his company, and together they discovered new paths and fresh terrain previously undiscovered. They agreed that they both loved Africa, its people, the atmosphere, the excitement of being able to improve conditions for people who were invariably so kind and open to them, and so desperately needed their help.

"I feel as though my life finally has some meaning to it," she said one day, as they sat on a log before turning back. There was no tree overhead, and she had told him about her experience with Laure when the snake fell out of the tree, some months back. It was nearly April by then, and Laure was getting ready to leave any day. Her correspondence with Antoine had flourished, and she was looking forward to seeing him in Geneva in June. They had already made plans to meet again. "I never felt that way before," Christianna continued. "I always felt as though I was wasting my time, and never did anything useful for anyone . . . until that night in Russia . . . and when I came here."

"Don't be so hard on yourself," Parker said generously. "You just finished school, Cricky. No one your age has set fire to the world yet, or cured all its ills. I'm nearly ten years older than you are, and I'm just getting started myself. Helping people is a life's work, and it looks to me like you're off to a hell of a good start here. Is there something like this you can do in Liechtenstein when you go back?" Although they both knew that there were few opportunities in a lifetime like the one they were experiencing here.

She laughed wryly at his question, forgetting for a moment that he didn't know who she was. Talking to Parker was like talking to a brother, though not necessarily her own. "Are you kidding? All I do at home is cut ribbons and go to dinner parties with my father. I was leading a totally stupid life before I came here. It was driving me insane," she said, sounding frustrated again, just thinking about it.

"What kind of ribbons?" he asked, looking puzzled. "Cutting ribbons" meant nothing to him. The concept of a princess cutting a ribbon to open a hospital or a children's home was inconceivable to him and the farthest thing from his mind. "Is your father in the ribbon business? I thought he was in politics and PR," and even that explanation had been vague.

Christianna laughed out loud in spite of herself. "I'm sorry . . . that made no sense. It doesn't matter. I just go on the jobs he sends me on . . . you know, like an opening ceremony for a shopping mall. Sometimes he sends me in his place when he's too busy. That's the PR part. The political side is more complicated to explain." She was momentarily horrified that she had almost slipped and spilled the beans.

"It doesn't sound like fun to me," he said sympathetically. He had felt the same way about joining his father's practice in San Francisco. He much preferred the research project he was working on at Harvard, and now the time he was spending here. Christianna had explained many things to him, and had been very kind about introducing him to life in Senafe, and the others had been equally helpful and hospitable.

"It isn't fun," she said honestly, looking pensive for a moment, as she thought about her father and the dutiful life she led in Vaduz. She had talked to him the day before. Freddy had finally come back from China a few weeks earlier, in March, as planned, and according to her father, he was already getting restless. He'd been staying at Palace Liechtenstein in Vienna and giving parties there. He said he'd go mad if he had to stay in Vaduz. She suspected, as her father did, that once Freddy inherited the throne, he would probably move the court back to Vienna, where it used to be, for generations before them. It was far more accessible and sophisticated, and he had a lot more fun there. Though once he was the reigning prince, he would have to be far more serious than he had ever been. She was thinking about all of it with a quiet frown, while Parker watched her.

"What were you thinking about just then?" he asked quietly. She had been silent for several minutes.

"I was just thinking about my brother. He's so impossible at times, and he always upsets my father. I love him, but he's just not a responsible person. He got back from China a few weeks ago, and he's already in Vienna, playing and giving parties. We all worry about him in the family. He just refuses to grow up, and for now he doesn't have to. But one day he will, and if he doesn't, it will be just terrible." She was going to add "for our country," but she caught herself and didn't.

"I assume that's why so much is expected of you, and why you feel you have to go home and help your father with the business. What if you didn't go home, and stopped enabling your brother? Maybe then he would have to grow up and take some responsibility off you." It was a sensible solution, and an unfamiliar subject to him. His own brother had been a remarkable student, and was a highly respected physician with a wife and three children. It was hard for him to relate to the tales she told him about her brother.

"You don't know my brother," she said, smiling sadly. "I'm not sure he'll ever grow up. I was only five when my mother died, he was fifteen, and I think it upset him very badly. I think he runs away from everything he feels. He refuses to be serious or responsible about anything."

"I was fifteen when my mother died. It was terrible for all three of us, and you could be right. My brother went a little crazy for a while, but he settled down in college. Some people just take a long time to grow up, your brother may be one of those. But I don't see why you have to sacrifice your life for him."

"I owe it to my father," she said simply, and he could see that it was a bond and duty she felt strongly about. He admired her for it, and was also surprised she had been able to come here. He asked her about it, and she explained that her father had finally relented, after endless badgering from her, and given her six months to a year with the Red Cross, before coming home to her responsibilities in Vaduz.

"You're too young to have all those expectations put on you," Parker said, looking concerned as her eyes met his. There was something deep within them that spoke of things he didn't know, and the look of sadness in her eyes touched him profoundly. Without thinking, he reached out and took her hand in his own. He suddenly wanted to protect her from all the intolerable burdens put on her, and shield her from all those who might hurt her. His eyes never wavered and hers never left his, and almost as though it had been meant to be that way since time began, he leaned over and kissed her. She almost felt as though someone else had made the decision for her. There had been no decision, no choice, there was no fear. She just melted into his arms and they kissed until they were breathless. It was comfort, desire, and passion blended into something very heady that dizzied both of them. They sat looking at each other afterward in the hot African sun, as though seeing each other for the first time.

"I didn't expect that," Christianna said quietly, still holding his hand, as he looked at her ever more gently. There was something about her that reached deep into his heart, and had almost since the day they met.

"Neither did I," he said honestly. "I've admired you a lot ever since I met you. I love the way you speak to people, and play with the children. I love the way you seem to take care of everyone, and always respect who they are." She was both grace and gentleness itself.

It was a lovely thing to say about her and she was touched, but even as they began something that might turn out to be beautiful, she was fully aware that if it had a beginning, it would have an end, too. Whatever they decided to share could only exist here in Africa. Their lives were too different, and would be surely once they got home. There was no way she would ever be allowed to pursue a relationship with him. She was just old enough now to be under constant scrutiny, at home and in the press. And a young American doctor, however intelligent or respectable, would never fit the rigid criteria set by the reigning prince for her. He wanted her to marry nothing less than a prince. When the time came for all that, if she was to follow her parents' wishes and family tradition that had existed till now, she would be obliged to ally herself with someone of noble birth. Given his antiquated and rigid ideas, her father would never tolerate a commoner as an acceptable husband for her. So whatever they started now could live only as long as they were both in Senafe. Carrying it beyond that would start a war with her father, which was the last thing she wanted. His approval meant the world to her, and she didn't want to upset him. Freddy did enough of that, and their father didn't deserve that after all he'd sacrificed for them. Christianna had been convinced for years that he had never remarried because of her and Freddy, which had been a sacrifice for him, maybe even a big one. Given how her father felt, once home again, her relationship with Parker would become forbidden fruit for her. It was not just about following rigid guidelines her father set for her. For Christianna it was also about respecting hundreds of years of tradition, however old-fashioned, and the country she loved so much, and even about respecting her father's promise to her dying mother.

She looked at Parker, not knowing how to say that to him, or if she should. But like a married woman, she felt she owed it to him to explain her circumstances, as best she could. One way or the other, Christianna was married to the throne of Liechtenstein, and even if she was not eligible for the throne herself, she was bound to it nonetheless, and everything her father and countrymen expected of her. She felt she had to set an example of how royals behaved. In spite of her own conflicts about it, she was a princess to her core.

"You look so sad. Did I upset you?" Parker asked her, looking worried. He didn't want to do anything that didn't appeal to her, too. He had been smitten by her for weeks, but if she wasn't open to it, even if disappointed, he would have understood. He liked her too much to do anything that might make her unhappy or uncomfortable.

"No, of course not," she said, smiling at him, her hand still resting in his. "You made me very happy," she said simply, and it was true. The rest was not as simple. "It's hard to explain. All I can say is that whatever happens between us will end here." It was the only way she could think of to say it. "I want to be fair, saying that to you now. The person I am here will have to disappear when I leave. There is no room for her once I go home. Once back in Liechtenstein, this will never be possible for us." He looked worried as she said it. It was too early for them to worry about the future after one kiss, but he could sense that what she was saying had far deeper meaning to her.

"It sounds like you're going back to prison or the convent," he said with a troubled look, and she nodded, drawing closer to him on the log, as though to hide in his arms. He put them around her and looked deep into her eyes to see what he could find there. They were two deep pools as blue as his.

"I am going back to prison," she said somberly, it was exactly how she felt about it. "And when I do, I have to go back alone. No one can come with me."

"That's ridiculous," he said, chafing at what she told him. "No one can imprison you, Cricky. Unless you let them. Don't let that happen to you."

"It already did." The day she was born. And the day five years later when her dying mother extorted the promise from her husband that he would never allow Christianna to marry anyone but a royal.

"Let's not worry about that right now, shall we? We have lots of time to talk about that later on." Parker was already determined that if he fell in love with her, as he was already starting to, he was not going to let her slip away from him. She was far too lovely and unusual a person for him to be pursuing just a fling. He wasn't asking her for her hand in marriage, but he was absolutely certain that he wasn't going to let her run away from him, no matter what she thought her obligations were to her father and the family business. It made no sense to him. And rather than arguing with her about it, he pulled her tightly into his arms again and kissed her, as Christianna felt she was slipping into a dream. She told herself that she had warned him, she had tried to be fair to him, or even warn him off. But having done that, she abandoned herself to his kiss, and had no desire whatsoever to resist.

# Chapter 11

The romance that began between Parker and Christianna was at first invisible, and then it grew, as they got closer and more intimate, passionate, and discreet. It wasn't just a sexual adventure for either of them. They were falling in love. In fact, by May, they had fallen. Hard. They spent all their off-duty hours together, checked in with each other several times a day, sat together at every meal. Living as closely together as they did in the camp outside Senafe, it was inevitable that the shift in their relationship came to everyone's attention within weeks, if not days.

As usual, Fiona was the first one to observe it. She knew Christianna well by now, or so she thought, and she had a keen eye for human interchanges. She had thought Christianna was quieter these days, and less communicative. At first, she was afraid that she was getting sick. Sometimes it started that way. She had been watching her closely for several days, out of concern, several weeks into the romance, when she saw the two lovebirds walking back to camp after one of their afternoon strolls, and both were wearing happy faces and guilty grins. Fiona chuckled to herself and couldn't resist teasing Christianna about it that night.

"Here I thought you were coming down with malaria or kala azar, the black fever, and I was worried about you . . . and all it is is a bit of romance. Well, well, my little Cricky, spot on! Good on you!" Christianna blushed at first and was about to deny it, but after one look at the knowing expression in Fiona's eyes, all she could do was smile.

"All right, all right . . . it's not a big deal. It's just something nice for now."

"The way you two look? Not likely, my dear. I've seen people leave on their honeymoon looking a lot less goo-goo-eyed than that. If a lion had come after the two of you today, I don't think either of you would have noticed . . . or even a snake!" she teased, and she wasn't far off the mark. Christianna had never been happier in her life, but she reminded herself every day that eventually it would have to end. And besides, he was going back to Harvard in June. They had two months to enjoy idyllic bliss in the magical setting where it had started, and then it would be over. It was something Christianna allowed herself to forget when she was with him.

"He's so wonderful," Christianna confessed, looking like a little kid. Fiona was pleased. It was nice to see people happy, and she was thrilled for her friend.

"If looks are anything to go by, and I trust my instincts on this one, he's just as crazy about you. When did that all start?"

"A few weeks ago." They had had a particularly nice time the night before Laure left. The camp gave her a party, and she had left looking like a different woman than the one who had arrived. She had cried when she embraced them all as she left, promising to stay in touch with all of them, particularly Cricky, whom she fully credited with giving her the courage to open her heart to Antoine. "I don't know. It just happened," Christianna tried to explain. She wasn't even sure she could explain it to herself. She was truly in love for the first time.

And Parker said he was as well. He said he had had one serious romance in medical school, and lived with her for a while. She was a resident when he was an intern, but within a few months they had both figured out it was a mistake and parted friends. According to him, and Christianna believed him, there had never been anyone serious in his life, before or since. With the work he had undertaken at Harvard, he didn't have time. And now, in Senafe, he was discovering love for the first time, and so was she. It was written all over her face.

"Oh my God," Fiona said, looking suddenly thunderstruck, "is this serious?" The look in Christianna's eyes, and Parker's when she'd seen them together that afternoon, said that it could be.

"No," Christianna said firmly, looking sad. "It isn't. It can't be. I told him that when we started, before we started, I have to go home to my responsibilities. I could never live in Boston, and he can't come home with me. My father would never approve." There wasn't even the remotest doubt of that on Christianna's face.

"Of a doctor?" Fiona looked shocked. Her parents would have been thrilled. "It sounds like he has unreasonably high standards to me."

"Maybe he does," Christianna answered quietly, just as she had said to Parker in similarly veiled terms. "But that's the way he is. He has many reasons for how he feels. It's complicated," Christianna said sadly.

"You can't live your life for your father," Fiona scolded her, upset by what she'd said, and her willingness to accept it unconditionally. "This isn't the dark ages, for heaven's sake. He's a wonderful man, he has a terrific job. He's trying to save the human race from the scourge of AIDS, at one of the most respected medical and academic institutions in the world. How much better does it get?"

"It gets better than that." Christianna grinned, the dark clouds suddenly gone from her face. "He is also an incredibly decent, wonderful person, and I love him . . . and he loves me." She looked totally mad about him.

"Then what nonsense are you talking about it having to end here?"

"That's a different story," Christianna said with a sigh, as she sat down on her cot, and took off her boots. Once in a while, she really missed wearing pretty shoes. She would have liked to wear high heels for him, but there was no chance of it here. "It's too complicated to explain," Christianna said again, and went on rhapsodizing about him, as Fiona looked amused.

"It sounds to me like you'd better run away from home when you get back. I hear Boston is a very nice place. I have relatives there," which was no surprise to Christianna since everyone the world over knew that most of Boston was Irish. "If I were you, I would go."

"He hasn't invited me," Christianna said primly, but they talked about a vast range of topics, including their respective plans when they got back. Parker hated hearing about hers. It continued to sound like a prison sentence to him.

"He will," Fiona said confidently. "He looked totally besotted when I saw you with him today. And come to think of it, he's looked like that for a while. I thought he was just overwhelmed by the unfamiliar surroundings and the work. Now I realize it was you." They both laughed at the idea. "So what are you going to do about it, Cricky?" She gave her a searching look.

"It's way too soon to worry about that now." But they both knew that, for whatever reason, Christianna was putting up some kind of wall, not between her and the young American doctor, but between them and any future they might have. Fiona had no idea why she was doing it, but it was clear that Christianna was convinced that their love affair could go no farther than the time they shared in Senafe. And thinking about it made Fiona sad. She liked both of them a lot.

The romance between Parker and Christianna flourished. They spent hours together at night after they had dinner with the others. They walked, they talked, they told each other stories about their childhoods and their pasts. Christianna always had to modify hers somewhat, for obvious reasons, but above all she shared the essence of what she felt, and her every thought. They met early in the mornings for breakfast, grabbed lunch together on the fly. The romance was in full bloom in May, as the African spring ended and moved toward summer, and no matter how in love they were, neither allowed it to interfere with their work. If anything, they worked harder, happier than each of them had ever been in their life. Together they were a force greater than even the sum of their parts that could not be ignored or denied. Being with either or both of them made everyone else happy, and everyone agreed that both were exceptional individuals who brought something special to the camp. Where Christianna had kindness, grace, compassion, and a remarkable way with people, Parker had gentleness, intelligence, and an extraordinary expertise in his field. Both of them bright, each of them funny, they added both spice and balm to every group they joined. As Fiona said, they were the perfect couple, but whenever she said it to Cricky, there was a sad look in her eyes. Something was stopping her from thinking about or talking about the future. All she was able or willing to do with Parker was live in the here and now. He had learned to stay off the subject of any future time with her, or what they would do about seeing each other when they went back. They simply lived day by day, more in love with each other by the hour, and happy sharing their work and their lives in this remarkable place, with people they loved so much.

Their relationship remained chaste for the first month, and then finally both Parker and Christianna asked if they could take a weekend off together. People rarely left the camp during their time off, although there were some wonderful places to visit in the area. But most of the time people who worked in the camp ended up spending time assisting the locals in their free time in whatever way they could. Geoff said he had no problem giving them a few days off, since neither of them was essential to the camp medically. Christianna was a willing, devoted and loving, hardworking spare pair of hands. And although Parker saw patients with Mary and Geoff and offered diagnoses frequently, most of his work was directed toward research. Fiona would have been much harder to spare as the only midwife. Or Mary or Geoff, as the two camp doctors, or Maggie, the only nurse.

After talking to people and doing a little local research, they decided to visit both Metera and Qohaito, which were both within twenty miles of the camp. Metera was known for its remarkable ruins, which were two thousand years old, and Qohaito had equally beautiful ruins, from the Aksumite kingdom. In addition, in Qohaito, they wanted to see the Saphira Dam, which was also over a thousand years old. Eritrea was sitting on the remains of a number of ancient civilizations, many of which had been partially excavated, and some of which had still been only minimally revealed. It sounded like an exciting trip to both of them. And a wonderful first adventure, almost like a honeymoon. They were told about a couple of tiny hotels where they could stay, which sounded very romantic. Klaus and Ernst had made several similar trips when they first came, and highly recom-

mended it to Parker and Christianna. The other two trips they wanted
to make later were to Keren, north of the capital, and to the port town
of Massawa, where they could go water-skiing in the Red Sea.

The only obstacle Christianna had to deal with before the trip was
a brief secret pow-wow with Samuel and Max. She knew she was going to have a serious problem leaving with Parker, without them.
They argued about it for two hours, and neither of her bodyguards
would relent.

"Why can't you just tell him that we'd like to go on the trip?"
Samuel said with a determined look. They had been like bulldogs so
far, but she knew they had to answer to the prince. And it wasn't fair
to ask them to keep her secret, but she was doing it anyway. They
were well aware that if anything untoward happened to her, even ac-
cidentally, they would be fully blamed, and perhaps even imprisoned.
She was asking a lot of them, although they hadn't told her father
about the romance yet. They had agreed between themselves to say
nothing about Parker to the prince. It was their gift to her.

"No!" Christianna continued to argue with them. "I don't want anyone with us, and neither does he. It would spoil everything." And
Metera and Qohaito were only a few miles away from the camp. She
was nearly in tears, and already had been twice, but they were relent-
less anyway. Their necks were on the line.

"Look, Your Highness." Max turned to her finally, realizing it was
time to be blunt with her. Nothing else had worked so far. "We don't
care who you go with, what you do, what your reasons are for the
trip. That's your business, and Parker's, not ours." Fortunately, they
were extremely fond of him, but she was asking them to risk their
jobs, and worse, perhaps her life. "We're not going to give your father
any details about the trip. Just a touristic weekend. He doesn't need
to know more than that. But if we don't come along, and something

happens to you . . ." He didn't finish his sentence, but she got the point. What he was saying was entirely reasonable. Living with it as a twenty-three-year-old woman in love with a man, was not.

"Why do you have to tell my father that I'm going, or even leaving the camp? And don't call me Your Highness again," she reminded him, and he nodded. "There have been no political problems in Eritrea in years. The truce with the Ethiopians may be uneasy, but no one has done anything objectionable or even frightening since we've been here and long before. Nothing is going to happen, I promise you. Parker and I will be fine. I'll call you if I can, and if I feel uneasy, you can join us then. But please, I am begging you, let me have these few days, for once in my life. Max . . . Sam . . . this is truly my last chance. Once I go home, I will never have anything like this again . . . I'm begging you . . . please . . ." As she looked at them imploringly, tears ran down her cheeks, and both men looked agonized. They wanted to help her out, but were afraid.

"Let us think about it," Samuel said finally, unable to think clearly in the face of her distress. They both liked her enormously, and respected her, but she was asking them to violate the conditions of their jobs, and their entire reason for being in Senafe with her.

Christianna walked away in silence, deeply disturbed. Fiona saw her as she walked back to the tent, obviously in tears.

"What's wrong?" She was instantly sympathetic as she put an arm around Cricky's shoulders. "Did you and Parker have a fight? Did you cancel the trip?" She couldn't tell her what had happened, she just shook her head in answer to Fiona's well-meaning questions. She didn't say anything to Parker either, but she was obviously subdued at dinner, and he was worried.

"Are you all right?" he asked her gently, and she had to fight back tears again. But she couldn't tell him what was happening, and didn't want to share with him the likelihood that Max and Sam would probably come on their trip, and in essence, ruin it for them. She didn't have the heart to tell him until she was sure. But she was almost certain now that neither guard would relent. There was just too much at stake for them, and potentially for her.

"I'm fine . . . I'm sorry . . . I just had a headache during dinner." It was a flimsy excuse and he didn't buy it. He knew her better. He wondered if she was coming down with some tropical disease, but she looked fine to him. She was usually so good humored that he found it instantly suspicious that she was so glum.

"Are you worried about our trip?" he asked gently, wondering if suddenly the idea of going away with him didn't appeal to her. He hadn't asked but suddenly wondered if maybe she was even a virgin and was nervous about sleeping with him. He kissed her, and then put his arms around her before she answered. "Whatever is bothering you, Cricky, I'm sure it's something we can work out together. Why don't we give it a try?" He looked down at her with the love and tenderness of a father for his child, which made her heart ache even more. All she wanted was to take this trip alone with him.

She was about to tell him that he didn't understand when Max signaled to her from behind Parker's back, and there was a definite urgency to his gesture. She stood there with Parker's arms around her and nodded to Max, trying to suggest that she would be with him in a minute. She slowly unwound herself from Parker's arms, and much to his consternation, said she would be back in a minute, she had to say something to Max that she had previously forgotten, and it was urgent. Something about a medication they were trying to get for him in town. Parker didn't question it, but went to sit down on a chair while he waited. Ushi came by soon after that with Ernst, and they had a pleasant chat, while Cricky disappeared into the deserted dining tent with Max and Sam.

"What?" She looked anxious, and both men looked nervous. Max spoke for both of them.

"We should probably be committed for this, but we're going to let you do it." What had decided it for both of them was that she was going to peaceful areas, and they were both well aware that this was a once-in-a-lifetime chance for her. Once back in Liechtenstein, she would never be alone again. Forever. Letting her go away with Parker was their gift to her. And given the circumstances and the location of their intended trip, they both felt that she would be safe with Parker, and he would take care of her. He was a totally responsible man, and they knew she would be in good hands. "There's only one condition, two actually." He smiled at her, and Samuel was smiling, too. "One is that you absolutely must take a radio, and a gun." The radio might be unreliable in the area, and unable to reach them. But they knew the gun was failsafe, and that she was well able to use it if she had to. She was an excellent shot and knew a fair amount about guns.

"The second condition is that we want you to be aware that if anything happens to you on this trip, we're going to shoot ourselves rather than go back and face your father. So you have two lives on your hands as well as your own." They both knew that it was a completely insane thing for them to do, and defeated their whole purpose in coming here, but they had decided to take a risk for her, and give her and Parker this opportunity to be alone. She was well aware of what they were doing, and threw her arms around first Max's neck and then Sam's, with tears running down her cheeks again. This time, tears of joy.

"Thank you, thank you . . . thank you . . ." They left her breathless with excitement and delight, and she ran out of the dining tent and back to where Parker was sitting with the others. He could instantly see the happiness in her eyes.

"Well, you look happy, Cricky," he said, looking pleased. All her anxiety seemed to have dissipated, although he had no idea why. "What did Max tell you that made you look like that?"

"Nothing. I got his medication for him, so he paid me back my poker earnings that he owed me. I'm a rich woman now!"

"I'm not sure the rate of exchange on *nakfa* is that great these days to justify looking like that, but far be it from me to burst your bubble, if it makes you that happy." Whatever it was, he was delighted that she seemed so comfortable again. She was floating on a cloud until they left. And they set out for Qohaito two days later. Just as Fiona had predicted it would, it felt like a honeymoon to her, and even to him.

They had borrowed one of the old dilapidated cars at the camp and made their way slowly through the countryside, feeling like children on an adventure. It was the most romantic trip Christianna had ever taken, and with each day she came to know Parker better and love him more. They made love the first night in a tiny hotel, with total abandon, and all the love that had grown between them since their whirlwind romance began.

It was almost like a honeymoon, as they drifted from one fascinating location to another, and collected memories like flowers. It was the perfect time. They planned to spend three days together before going back to Senafe. And it was on the second night of the trip that Parker found her gun, in a small case in her suitcase. She had asked him to hand her her nightgown, forgetting what she'd concealed in it, and he looked a little stunned as he held it in his hand.

"Do you always carry a gun?" he asked, gingerly setting it back in her suitcase. He had no idea if it was loaded or not, nor how to tell.

Guns were definitely not his thing. He repaired people, not destroyed them. Although she hadn't seemed the type for guns either. He was truly surprised.

"No," she laughed at him, taking the nightgown from him as she got out of the bath in their hotel. She didn't know why she was bothering with the nightgown, it would be somewhere on the floor for the rest of the night, five minutes after they got into bed. "Of course not. Max gave it to me in case we have a problem."

"I'm not sure I would feel comfortable shooting someone," he said, sounding a little nervous. "Would you?" She didn't tell him she was an excellent shot, although she wasn't fond of guns herself. But her father had forced her to learn.

"Not really. But he meant well. I just threw it in the suitcase and forgot about it," she said blithely, putting her arms around his neck, and kissed him.

"Is it loaded?" He was still uneasy about it, and her explanation seemed a little casual to him, and offhand.

"Probably." She knew it was, but didn't want to scare him. He pulled her close to him then, held her, and looked into her eyes. He knew there was something deeper there than what she was telling him. He already knew her well.

"Cricky, there's something you're not telling me, isn't there?" he asked calmly. Her eyes never left his, she hesitated for a long time, and then nodded. "Do you want to tell me what it is?" He never loosened his grip, on her body, or her heart, or this time her eyes.

"Not now," she said in a whisper, clinging to him. She didn't want to spoil everything, and it would. It had to. One day she had to tell him that she was going back to her life as a princess, to serve her country and her father as reigning prince, and there would be no room for him. She couldn't bring herself to say the words. "Not yet."

"When are you going to tell me?"

"Before we leave Senafe, whichever of us leaves first." Presumably, it would be him. He nodded. He had decided not to press her about it. He sensed that it was something deep and sad for her that troubled her a great deal. It was the sadness he saw in her eyes sometimes. A look of loss, sorrow, and resignation. He didn't want to pry her secret from her, he wanted her to give it to him willingly, when she was ready. And she was deeply grateful for his understanding. He was truly an amazing man, and she loved him more than ever, in gratitude for the gentle way he loved her.

The rest of their trip was even more beautiful than they had hoped for or expected. They headed back reluctantly, had taken a million photographs on the way, and rolled slowly back into camp late Monday afternoon, feeling as though they had been gone for months. It really felt as though they were returning from their honeymoon. Christianna felt married to him in her very soul. He kissed her as they got out of the car, and he carried her bag to the women's tent. She hated the idea that she wouldn't be able to sleep with him that night, and wake up beside him in the morning. That felt like punishment to her now.

Fiona was the first to see them when they got back, and she smiled at them both. She had just gotten back from a difficult delivery that had taken all day but went well in the end. She looked tired but happy to see them, as she always was.

"How was the trip?" she asked with a tired smile. She was almost envious, but liked them both too much to be truly jealous. And it was so nice to see them happy, which they obviously were. They were both beaming as they walked in.

"It was perfect," Christianna said, glancing over her shoulder at Parker for confirmation.

"Yes, it was," he said, smiling proudly at her.

"You lucky dogs!" Fiona complained good-naturedly, and they told her about the travel details of the trip, but obviously not the rest.

Everyone teased the young couple that night at dinner, and Max and Sam looked particularly relieved. She had thanked them profusely moments after they returned, and had returned the gun to Max. They had both hugged her fervently, immensely happy to see her in one piece. They had spent a tortured weekend, worrying about her, and she told them again what an incredible gift it had been, to let her go away with Parker alone.

"Let's not do it every weekend," Max said wanly, putting the gun back in his own pocket.

"I promise," she said, although she and Parker had said on the way back that they wanted to go away again. Next time to Massawa, to enjoy the water sports there. It was the port that the Ethiopians had coveted for years.

Dinner was festive that night, and everyone was in good spirits. Parker and Christianna seemed particularly close. The three days alone, staying in hotels together, had cemented the bond of their love. Christianna had to almost tear herself away from him that night, to go back to her own tent, and she slept poorly without him. They met at the dining tent at six the next morning, and were the first ones there. They fell into each other's arms like lost lovers, and Parker told her he couldn't even imagine a life without her anymore. Worse yet, neither could she, and it was dangerous for her to feel that way. In the long run, becoming that attached to him would break her heart. But it was already too late for those concerns.

In late May, Parker went to the post office with Max and Sam one day when they were calling her father. He called his supervisor at Harvard, and got an extension to stay until late July. He told him that he felt the work he was doing, and data he was gathering, was important, and it would be a mistake to leave prematurely in June as planned. The supervising doctor of his project took his word for it, and granted him an extension till late July, even August, if he felt he had to. He gave out a war whoop of glee when he hung up the phone. All he wanted was to stay in Senafe with Christianna. Sam walked him outside to celebrate, so Max could talk when he made his call. Sam didn't want Parker hearing Max call the palace, or asking for His Serene Highness. Parker gladly followed Sam outside, and Max made the call to give Christianna's father their usual report, that all was well and she was fine. She made the trip into town to speak to him herself roughly once a week, and he always told her how much he missed her and couldn't wait for her to come back. It made her feel guilty to hear his voice, but never guilty enough to want to leave. Far from it. And she was far too happy with Parker to go anywhere without him. She was doing all she could to hang on to their little world for as long as possible. One day the end would come, inevitably, but she wasn't ready for it yet, and couldn't even remotely imagine getting there. But at some point, they would have to face it, and she knew she would have to tell him the truth. She just prayed that that moment wouldn't come soon.

Parker was in a celebratory mood as they drove back to the camp outside Senafe. He immediately ran to find Christianna to tell her the good news. She was as excited as he was. She threw her arms around his neck, and he lifted her easily off the ground and spun her around. Their mail had come that day, and everyone was in a good mood. Christianna took a walk with Parker once she finished work, and they talked about their plans to go to Massawa, which they hadn't managed yet, but still intended to do.

When they got back from their walk, Parker went back to his own tent, and Christianna to hers, an arrangement they still found irksome. She was dying to spend the night with him again, and leave on another trip. They were also talking about getting a tent of their own. But she was thrilled with his good news, and the extension granted by Harvard. She was about to tell Fiona, who was lying on her bed reading a magazine, when she noticed that the little Irish woman she was so fond of was very pale. She worried for a moment that she was sick, as Fiona raised her eyes to her friend's. And for a long moment, she said not a word. Her milky-white skin became almost translucent easily, whenever she didn't feel well, or was upset, or enraged. She had a fairly hot temper, and the whole camp teased her about it. Once in a total fury, she had even stamped her feet, and then finally laughed at herself. She was looking every bit as pale as that day now.

"Are you okay?" Christianna asked her, looking worried. Something was very obviously wrong, as Fiona laid the magazine down and stared at her. "What's up?"

"You tell me," she said cryptically, and handed the magazine to her, for Christianna to see for herself. Christianna couldn't imagine what might have upset Fiona so much, and glanced across the page. And there she saw it. A photograph of herself, five months before, with her father, at the wedding they had attended in Paris before she left for Africa in January. She was wearing the blue velvet evening gown, with her mother's sapphires. And the caption under the photograph said simply, "Her Serene Highness Princess Christianna of Liechtenstein, with her father Reigning Prince Hans Josef." There wasn't much to say. It was all there. Christianna's face went instantly as white as Fiona's. There was no one else in the tent at the time, which seemed like a good thing to Cricky. This was not a piece of news she wanted to share with anyone, not even Fiona. She had been reading *Majesty* magazine, which listed all the doings of royals all over Europe.

Christianna had often been in it, and was obviously badly shaken that the magazine had fallen into Fiona's hands. Her mother always sent it to her from home. Christianna just hadn't expected to be in a current issue, or she'd have worried about it. But the photograph was five months old. She hadn't counted on that. "Would you like to explain this?" Fiona said, looking furious. "I thought we were friends. It turns out I didn't even know who you were. Your father is in PR, my blooming ass." In Fiona's mind, friends didn't keep secrets from each other. She was livid, and obviously felt betrayed. And if Fiona felt that way, Christianna was even more terrified of how Parker would react when he found out.

"Well, it is kind of like PR," Christianna said weakly, still just as pale. "And we are friends, Fiona . . . it changes everything once people know. I didn't want that to happen here. For once in my life, I wanted to be like everyone else."

"You lied to me," Fiona said, throwing the magazine on the floor.

"I didn't lie to you. I didn't tell you. That's different."

"My ass it is!" She felt utterly foolish and betrayed as she looked at Christianna with fire in her eyes and rage in her heart. "Does Parker know?" she asked, even more furious. Maybe they'd even been laughing at her because she didn't know, which was not the case.

"No, he doesn't," Christianna said with tears in her eyes. "Look, I love you, Fiona. You *are* my friend, but it wouldn't have been the same with you or anyone here, if they knew. Look at you now. You're proving the point."

"The hell I am!" she raged. "I'm pissed off because you lied."

"I had no other choice, or I might as well not have come. Do you think I want everyone here kissing my ass, waiting on me hand and foot, calling me Your Serene Highness, preventing me from doing any worthwhile work, or putting a doily under my sandwich at lunch?

This is my only chance in my *whole life* to be normal and real. I had to beg my father to come here. And when I leave here, it's all over for me. I am going to have to be that person for the rest of my life, whether I like it or not. And I don't. But it's my duty. This is the only moment of 'real life' I'll ever have. Can't you at least try to understand that? You don't know what it's like. It's like being in prison. Forever. A life sentence, until I die." It was how she truly viewed it, which was sad. There were tears pouring down her cheeks as she said it, and there was a long silence as Fiona stared at her, and the color slowly came back into her face. She had heard what Christianna had said, but said nothing as Christianna choked on a sob. She didn't reach out to the Irish woman again, she just sat there in tears, feeling the whole weight of the crown she wore, whether visible or not, crashing down on her head again, even here.

"And just exactly who are Max and Sam?" Fiona asked with a suspicious look, still angry, but less so. It was hard to understand the misery of her friend. It sounded like fun to her, but looking at the anguish in Christianna's eyes, she was beginning to understand that maybe it wasn't as much fun as it looked in a magazine. Until then, she had always envied the people she'd seen there.

"They're my bodyguards," Christianna said softly, as though confessing a terrible crime.

"Shit. And I was trying to get Max into bed for months. With no success, I might add," she said, her sense of humor returning slightly, but not fully yet. "He probably would have shot me if I'd had the balls to really make a pass at him."

"No, he wouldn't." And then Cricky had to smile herself at the memory of Parker finding the gun wrapped in her nightgown on the trip. She told Fiona about it, and this time they both laughed.

"You little shit," she said irreverently, not the least impressed by her title or allegedly lofty status. "How could you not tell me?"

"I couldn't. Think about it. And then what? If I did, sooner or later everyone would know."

"I would have kept it secret if you told me to. I can keep secrets, you know," Fiona said, looking insulted, and then she thought of something. "What are you going to do about Parker? Are you going to tell him?"

Christianna nodded miserably. "I have to. Before he goes, or I do. He has a right to know. I just don't want to tell him yet. It will ruin everything once he knows."

"Why?" Fiona stared at her blankly. It still sounded exciting to her, although Christianna was acting as though it was a fatal illness she had contracted at birth, genetically. And to her it was. "Maybe he'll like the idea of being in love with a Serene Highness. It sounds pretty cool to me, maybe it will to him, too. The fairy princess and the handsome young doctor from Boston."

"That's my point," Christianna said sadly. "It's all over when we leave here. It has to be. My father would never let me marry him. Never. I have to marry a prince, someone of royal birth. A duke, or a count at the very least, and he won't be pleased at anything less than a prince. He would never give me permission to continue seeing Parker. Never." And she didn't want to risk a permanent estrangement with her father.

"And you need his permission?" Fiona looked startled.

"For everything. And his members of Parliament as well, for anything even slightly unusual. There are twenty-five of them. And a hundred members of the Family Court, all of them related to me to some degree. I have to do as I'm told. I have no right whatsoever to

just do what I want, about anything. My father's word is law, literally." She looked devastated as she said the words. "And if I disobey
him, and cause an enormous scandal, it would break his heart. He's
had enough of that with my brother. He counts on me."

"So instead, he'll end up breaking your heart." It was slowly occur-
ring to Fiona what Christianna was dealing with, and would be forever. A hundred and twenty-six people decided her fate, if she played
by the rules. "Maybe it's not as much fun as it looks," she conceded as
Christianna nodded.

"I promise you, it's not." And then she reached out a hand and
touched Fiona's arm. "I'm sorry I lied. I didn't think I had any choice.
Only Geoff knows, and he's been very good about it. And of course
the director in Geneva."

"Wow! It's all very secret service." And then she reached out and
hugged her. "I'm sorry I got so angry. I just felt hurt that you hadn't
told me. You've got a hell of a problem on your hands with Parker. Are
you sure there's no way they'll ever let you see him when you go
back?"

"Never. Maybe once, for tea, if I say we were coworkers here, but
nothing more than that. My father would lock me up in a minute."

"For real? Like in a dungeon?" Fiona looked horrified for her
friend, and Christianna laughed.

"Not quite. But they might as well. He would tell me to stop immediately, and I would have no other choice than to follow his orders. If
I don't, it will create a scandal in the press, break my father's heart,
and break his promise to my mother. My father doesn't believe in all
these modern monarchies, where their children are marrying commoners. He believes in maintaining the sanctity and purity of royal
bloodlines. It's ridiculous, but ours is a backward country. Women
have only voted there for twenty-three years. It would take my father

an entire lifetime to see things differently." She looked devastated at the thought. She was desperately in love with Parker, and he with her. Their love affair had been doomed from the beginning, and he didn't know it. It sounded tragic to Fiona, like a very bad opera.

"What about all those badly behaved princes and princesses you read about in the press, who go around sleeping with people and doing silly things?"

"That would be my brother. It drives my father mad, and he would never tolerate it from me. Besides, he doesn't marry them, he just sleeps with them. I think if he actually married one of them, my father would disown him."

"I can't believe I never suspected," Fiona said again with a look of disbelief as Christianna asked her if she would mind ripping out the page so they could destroy it, before someone else saw it, especially Parker. Fiona agreed, and they tore it to bits. "He's going to be heart-broken when you tell him," Fiona said, suddenly feeling sorry for them both.

"I know," Christianna said, sounding tragic. "I already am. I proba-bly should never have started with him. It wasn't fair to him. But I couldn't help myself. We fell in love."

"It seems as though you ought to have that right, like anyone else." It all sounded so unfair to Fiona, now that she thought about it, and could see the pain in Christianna's eyes. She felt sorry for Parker, too, when he found out that their love affair could go nowhere, and would end in Senafe.

"I don't have that right," Christianna said, as Fiona reached out and hugged her.

"I'm sorry I got so mad. Maybe you can talk to your father when you go back."

"It won't make a difference. He will never allow me to be involved with a commoner, and especially an American. He's extremely old-fashioned about those things, and he's very proud of the fact that our bloodline is extremely pure, and has been for about a thousand years. An American doctor is not what he has in mind for me." It sounded stupid even to her and like something out of the dark ages, when she explained it, but it was reality for her.

"Well, pardon me," Fiona said, regaining her sense of humor. It had been a hell of a shock. For them both. Christianna was still feeling shaken by having been exposed, even if only by Fiona, whom she trusted. What if someone else got their hands on a copy of the magazine—there was always that risk—and then showed it to Parker? The thought of it made Christianna shudder, although she knew he had to find out sooner or later. Preferably from her at the right time, if there was one. And what if he reacted as Fiona had at first? He might walk away and never even speak to her again. Maybe in the end that would be better, and an easier way for them to leave each other, than distraught with grief.

"That reminds me," Fiona asked, looking at her with a puzzled frown. "What am I supposed to call you, now that I know?" She was teasing her, and Christianna laughed at the question.

"I thought 'you little shit' was rather good. What about that?"

"You serene little shit perhaps? Your serene shittiness? You big royal shit!" Despite the seriousness of what they were discussing, they collapsed on their beds in gales of laughter like two naughty kids. They laughed until tears of laughter, and not grief this time, rolled down their faces. They were still laughing when Mary Walker and Ushi walked in, and inquired about what was so funny. The two younger women were incoherent with giggles.

"Oh, I was just telling Cricky what a pain in the ass she is. She was reading my magazine and tore a page right out. She's such a princess sometimes," Fiona said, rolling her eyes, as Christianna stared at her in horror.

"You little shit!" Christianna said to her this time, and they collapsed in laughter again, as the older women looked at them, rolled their eyes, and went outside to take a shower.

"It must be the heat getting to them," Ushi said to Mary with a grin, as they left the tent, and Christianna and Fiona exchanged a long look. In the end, Fiona's discovery had tightened the bond between them. The one Fiona was worried about now was Parker. And so was Cricky. This was going to be devastating for him.

# Chapter 12

Christianna and Parker went to Massawa for a weekend, as they had hoped to, in June. Samuel and Max let her go alone again. They had an even better time the second time they went away. Every moment they spent together was idyllic, and this time when they got back from their magical weekend, Parker started hinting vaguely about marriage. It was everything Christianna would have wanted in other circumstances. But there was no question of it between them. She tried to avoid the subject, and then finally said that there was no way she could leave her father. He expected her to come home, and stay there, working in the family business with him. She had said all that to Parker before, but this time he was obviously upset and annoyed. It made no sense to him, or even to her now. But she felt bound by her father's wishes as much as by history and tradition. She had been taught since birth to sacrifice herself for her country, her subjects, and to obey her father's wishes on all decisions like this one. She knew that defying him would seem to him and even to her, the ultimate betrayal. She hadn't been brought up to be one of the young royals who married their trainer, a cocktail waitress, or even a respectable young doctor like Parker. If she was to proceed with this, she needed, and wanted, her father's approval, and she knew there was no way she would ever get it. It was simply not going to happen.

"For heaven's sake, Cricky, that's ridiculous. What does he expect you to do, stay home and become an old maid, working for him?" She smiled sadly at the question. In fact, her father expected her to marry, but it had to be someone he approved of, or even chose. Someone from a family comparable to theirs. Parker was from a very nice family, he was well educated. His brother and father were doctors. His mother had been a debutante, he told her once, laughing, because he thought all of that was so silly. Christianna was a Serene Highness, which was even sillier. But the result of it was not going to seem silly to him once he knew. It was going to seem tragic to him, too.

"That is what he expects of me," she said firmly. "And I'm not going to be able to marry for a long time. Besides, I'm too young," she said, trying to find plausible excuses to discourage him. She was turning twenty-four in a few weeks, which was not too young to marry. And her father was starting to make noises about her coming home. She had been gone for almost six months, and he thought it was long enough. Parker was still planning to leave in July. And if at all possible, Christianna wanted to finish out the year in Senafe. She had fought hard for it the last time she and her father talked, and things were at a standoff for now. With him at least. But Parker was starting to press her hard.

"Cricky, do you love me?" he finally asked her bluntly with a look of anguish in his eyes. He had never loved anyone as much in his life, nor had she.

"Yes, I do," she said solemnly. "I love you very much."

"I'm not suggesting we get married here, or next week. But I'm leaving soon, and before I go, I want you to know how serious I am.

You said you might go back to school. Why don't you come to Boston to do it? There are lots of schools for you to choose from. Harvard, Boston University, Tufts, Boston College. Your father let you go to college in the States. Why not graduate school, too?"

"I think I used up the last of my tickets here. He wants me to go to school in Paris now, because it's a lot closer to home, or settle down in Vaduz."

"Boston is six hours from Europe." And he had already understood that money was not an object to them. She had never bragged about it, but he could tell. His own father's circumstances were comfortable, too. Parker was no stranger to the good life, or a moneyed world. His father was very successful, as was his brother, and his mother had left him a small trust fund when she died. He was in good shape. Paying for his education had never been a problem. He even owned a small house in Cambridge, and if they married, he could offer her a good solid life. But not if she insisted on playing handmaiden to her father and letting him run her life. Hearing about it really upset him. "You have a right to your own life," he insisted.

"No, I don't," she said firmly. "You don't understand."

"No, I don't, dammit. Maybe if I meet him, he would understand that I'm a respectable person. Cricky, I love you . . . I want to know when I leave Africa that one day you'll be my wife." Her eyes filled with tears as he said it. This was awful. She realized more than ever that she should never have allowed this to start. The inevitable sad ending had been written from the first. She nearly choked on her response.

"I can't."

"Why? What is it that you've never told me? There is some dark, awful secret that you've been hiding from me all along. I don't care what it is. It can't be that awful. I love you, Cricky. Whatever it is, we'll work it out." All she could do was look at him and shake her head. "I want you to tell me now."

"It doesn't matter what it is. Believe me, Parker, all I want is what you're offering. But my father will never let me." She sounded absolutely sure, as Parker looked more and more upset by the minute.

"Does he hate Americans? Or doctors? Why are you so sure we can't work this out?" There was an interminable silence as she looked at him hopelessly. It was time. She knew she had no other choice but to tell him now. It took forever for her to open her mouth and form the words, and then finally she did.

"He doesn't hate anybody. And he wouldn't hate you. I'm sure he would like you very much. But not for me." The words sounded cruel, and the reality of her situation was cruel. For both of them. "My father is the reigning prince of Liechtenstein." There was an interminable silence as Parker stared at her, trying to absorb what she had just said. The concept was so foreign to him that he sat very still for a long time, looking at her with no expression on his face.

"Say that again," he said quietly, and she shook her head.

"You heard me the first time. I don't think you know what that means. I am entirely ruled by him, our constitution, and tradition. And when the time comes, he won't let me marry anyone who is not of royal birth. In some countries, they feel differently about those things. My father doesn't, he is very old-fashioned, and neither he nor the Family Court that makes those decisions will ever allow me to marry you, no matter how much I love you, and I do." Her voice was barely more than a whisper when she finished, as Parker stared at her in disbelief.

"The Family Court makes those decisions? You don't?" She shook her head.

"I make no decisions for myself. He does. And they do," she said, looking tragic. The full force of it began to hit him as he stared at her. "According to our constitution, all members of the princely house must approve a marriage, and it must not be detrimental to the reputation, welfare, or esteem of the Principality of Liechtenstein. The Family Court and my father would, I'm sure, consider our marriage detrimental to the country." Even to her, it sounded absurd, and that much more so quoting their constitution to him.

"Cricky, you're a princess?" His voice cracked as he said it, looking absolutely stunned. He was nearly speechless. And she was overwhelmed with a sense of loss and grief. "As in Your Royal Highness?" He stared at her in amazement, hoping she'd say no, but she didn't.

She smiled sadly at the man she loved so much, and shook her head. "Your Serene Highness. We're a small country. My mother was a Royal Highness, she was French, and a Bourbon. I suppose I could have the choice. I've always preferred Serene. And my father and brother are Serene, too." She was feeling anything but serene at the moment, and wished with all her heart that she weren't royal, but it did her no good.

"For God's sake, why didn't you tell me?" It was the same thing Fiona had said when she found out. And in Parker's case, he was right. She had owed him that. In his case, she had cheated him out of the absolutely certain knowledge that their romance could go nowhere, and would ultimately break their hearts. She realized, looking at him, how selfish she had been, as tears rolled slowly down her face.

"I'm sorry . . . I didn't want you to know . . . I just wanted to be me, with you. And now I realize what I've done. I had no right to do this to you." He stood up and began to pace, looking at her from time to time, as she watched him miserably, and then he came back and sat down next to her, and took her hands in his.

"I don't know how this stuff works. But people do walk away from all that. The Duke of Windsor did it when he abdicated to marry Wallis Simpson." And then suddenly Parker looked even more worried. "You're not going to be queen one day, are you, or take the throne? Is that why your father is so tough on you?" She smiled and shook her head.

"No, women can't reign in my country. They're incredibly old-fashioned, women have only had the vote for twenty-three years. My brother will rule the country one day, whether or not he chooses to grow up. But because he's so irresponsible, my father counts on me a lot. I can't let him down, Parker. I can't just run away. This isn't like a job that you quit. It's about family and tradition, and bloodlines, and honor, and thousands of years of history. This isn't something you take off, like a hat, or even a crown. It is who you are, and what you're born to, a country and people you serve as example to. It is about duty, not love. Love always takes a backseat to all the rest. It is about duty, honor, and courage. Not about love."

"My God, that's sick," he said, looking outraged. "And your father expects you to live like that, and give up who you are and who you love?"

"I have no other choice," she said, as though declaring her own death sentence. And for them, it was. "To make matters worse, he promised my mother that I would marry someone of royal birth. They were both incredibly old-fashioned and he still is. He believes in duty before love. Even for himself. And he counts on me even more now to uphold tradition and do the right thing because it's unlikely my brother will. I can't let him down, Parker. He will expect me, and demand of me, that I make this sacrifice for my country, my mother, and him."

"Will you ever see me again, after we leave here?" he asked, sounding desperate. He felt panicked by what she was telling him. She made it sound absolutely hopeless, because in her mind it was. He suddenly realized what they were facing, what it meant for them, and all because of who she was. She was fully prepared to sacrifice herself, and him, for her country and the wishes of its reigning prince. Parker didn't give a damn about her being a princess. All he cared about was being with the woman he loved. He had given her his heart, and now she was quietly giving it back to him, because of who she'd been born, and what was required of her as a result. For her, it was about honor, duty, sacrifice, and courage.

"I don't know," she answered his question, totally honest with him now. "I'm not sure I can see you again, or how often." She suspected Max and Sam would help her see him, at least once, but more than that would be very hard. If they did, it would create a scandal for sure. And one black sheep in the family was enough. Freddy already had that role. If she became one now, too, it would break her father's heart. She could not do that to him. "Maybe we could meet once somewhere. I don't think my father would let me come to the States. I just came back last year, and now I've been in Africa for months. After this, he'll want me home, or no farther than Paris or London."

"Could I meet you in Paris?" He looked so sad, every bit as sad as she felt. She felt as though she'd put a knife in his heart, and her own.

"I can't promise, but I'll try." She sounded worried and unsure. She had a feeling her father would want her to stay close to home when she got back. A weekend in Paris might not be too hard. Or perhaps she could go to London and stay with Victoria, and see him there. But the press always hung around her cousin like vultures, which would be disastrous for them. Paris would be infinitely better. "I'll do everything I can."

"And after that?" There were tears in his eyes now. None of this had been good news to him, just as it wasn't to her. But it was old news to her. It was all very new to him.

"After that, my love, you go back to your life, and I to mine. And we remember forever what we shared here, a memory we cherish . . . you will always own a piece of my heart, a very, very big one." She couldn't even imagine marrying someone else. Only him.

"This is the worst thing I've ever heard." He wasn't even angry at her. What was the point of that? He was just devastated right to his core. "Cricky, I love you. Will you at least ask him?" She thought about it for a long moment, and nodded yes. She could try. But once she did, her father would demand that she stop seeing Parker. As long as he didn't know, there was at least a chance that they could see each other. And she didn't want to give that up yet. Secrecy was the only possible path for now, and she told him that. This time he didn't disagree with her. He could only assume that she knew best. He was totally out of his league. This final twist of fate seemed like a very bad movie to him.

After that, he just sat with his arms around her, thinking about everything she'd said, trying to understand and absorb it, and realize what it meant for them. This was a terrible fate for them both. She was destined to be the lonely princess forever. And he the young doctor with the broken heart. He didn't like anything about the way this story was going to end. There was clearly not going to be a "happily ever after" for them.

They walked back to the camp afterward, both of them looking sad. They said very little. He just held her close to him, with an arm around her, and Fiona happened to see them wander into the camp. They both looked like someone had died, and she wondered. Parker didn't even say hello to her, which was rare for him. He kissed Cricky without a word and went back to his tent.

"What happened?" Fiona asked her, looking worried.

"I told him," Christianna said, looking bereft.

"About you?" Fiona whispered, and Cricky nodded. "Oh, shit. How did he take it?"

"He was wonderful, because he is wonderful. But the situation sucks." Fiona smiled at her choice of words.

"Yes, it does. Was he angry?" He didn't look it. He looked destroyed, which was worse.

"No. Just sad. So am I."

"Maybe the two of you can figure something out."

"We're going to try to meet in Paris after I go back. But that won't change anything, it will just drag it out. In the end, he has to go back to Boston and lead his life, and I'll be in Vaduz, with my father, doing what I'm supposed to do for the rest of my life."

"There has to be a way," Fiona insisted.

"There isn't. You don't know my father."

"He let you come here."

"That's different. He knew I was coming back. And I wasn't going to be marrying anyone here. This was supposed to be a sabbatical. My deal with him is that I take up my duties when I go back. He's not going to let me marry an American doctor, a commoner, and live in Boston. That's just not going to happen," she said miserably, and Fiona had to admit it didn't sound hopeful, even to her.

"Talk to your father. Maybe he'll understand. True love, and all that." She had never seen two people love each other more, or happier together than Cricky and Parker. It was hard to ignore, and tragic for it to end so senselessly.

"I'll talk to him eventually. But I don't think it will get me any-where." Fiona nodded, and walked quietly back to the tent with her. There wasn't much she could say, and she was sad for both of them. It was a sad story, not a happy one.

That night Parker and Cricky sat close together, and for the next weeks they were together more than ever. If anything, what she had shared with him, and its tragic implications, only made them love each other more. They were virtually inseparable until the end of July. And then the first of their agonizing hurdles had to be faced. He had to go back. There was no delaying any further. The director of his re-search program had asked him to come back on the first of August. Their last days were bittersweet beyond belief, and their last night had an unreal quality to it. Christianna thought it was the saddest night of her life. They sat outside her tent all night, as he held her in his arms. They had had a farewell dinner for him that night, and Parker and Cricky looked as though they were going to burst into tears at any moment. The others in the camp had no idea why it was so tragic, but they sensed easily that something difficult had hap-pened, and that it was an exceptionally hard time for them.

Many of the people he had treated had come to bring him gifts be-fore he left, carvings and statues, bowls and beads, and beautiful ob-jects they had lovingly made for him. He thanked them all, and had tears in his eyes every time. The AIDS patients he had met and treated there had touched his heart.

He and Cricky sat together all through the night, and watched the sun come up together. They took a walk in the gentle early morning light, under the splendor of the African sky. She knew as she walked with him that she would never forget this moment, or this time in her life. She wanted to stop time, and stay there forever with him.

"Do you have any idea how much I love you?" he asked before they walked back.

"Maybe half as much as I love you," she teased him, but there was nothing funny about it, or easy. When they went back, the others had gotten up and were moving around the camp. Akuba and Yaw were busy. The others were eating breakfast. Cricky and Parker joined them, but ate nothing. They drank coffee, and sat there silently holding hands. Even Max and Sam looked sad. They knew better than anyone there what lay ahead for her, a life without this sweet man that she loved. And he was truly a good man, though even that would do them no good. He wasn't the husband her father wanted for her, and had no hope whatsoever of becoming it. When he left Senafe, the death sentence for their love would have begun. And no one knew that better than the two of them.

Geoff was driving Parker to Asmara in one of the camp cars, and he had invited Cricky to come along. Their romance was no secret, and everyone heartily approved of it. They weren't sure why, but they all seemed to know that Cricky was not going to be able to pursue it when she went back. They assumed from what she'd said that she had a tyrannical father, who wouldn't approve, and expected her to dance attendance on him. They didn't consider it insurmountable, but difficult certainly. Only Fiona, Geoff, Max, and Sam knew the truth, and the two lovers themselves. The others assumed there was still hope for them. Those who knew who she was knew better, and that in fact there was no hope at all, unless she was prepared to defy her father and walk away from all she was, which seemed unlikely to those who knew her well.

Everyone embraced Parker warmly when he left. Mary particularly thanked him for his invaluable help, and he for hers with his research.

He had taken a last walk through the ward, and said goodbye to all the patients there. His heart was aching as he left. He and Cricky got in the car with Geoff, and began the long ride to Asmara. Cricky knew the drive would seem even longer on the way back, without him. Now at least she could touch him, talk to him, see him, feel him near her. She had never been as sad in her life. And finally, after a while, they said nothing and just held hands as Geoff drove. He had a feeling from bits and snips of the conversation between them that Parker now knew who she was, but he didn't ask. He had promised to keep her secret for the duration of her stay, and he had. If she had chosen to tell someone, that was up to her. Even now, he remained discreet.

They arrived in Asmara an hour before Parker's flight. The timing was perfect, and as she and Max and Sam had done when they arrived, they stood waiting, this time for the plane to land. Her heart ached even more when it did. She had been hoping it would be late. Every minute was precious, every ounce of her longed to go with him, and to disappear forever into his life. She had never been as close to running away, even if it meant breaking her father's heart. She was torn between two men she loved, what each needed from her, and what she wanted herself.

They had another half-hour after the plane landed, as people lined up, carrying boxes and bags. She and Parker stood quietly to one side, holding hands, as Geoff stood at a discreet distance, sorry for them. Knowing the truth about her, he knew full well what this moment meant.

And then it came. The final moment, final touch, final kiss, final feel of his arms around her and hers around him.

"I love you so much," she whispered, as they both fought back tears.

"It'll be all right," he said, wishing it were true. She knew better and said nothing. "I'll see you in Paris as soon as you get back. Take care of yourself." He smiled down at her. For this one last moment she was his, and perhaps never again. It was almost beyond bearing, for both of them. "And watch out for snakes!" he teased.

One last kiss, and he walked down the tarmac to the waiting plane. She stood staring at him, without moving, her eyes glued to him, as he walked up the stairs to the plane, stopped, and looked at her for an endless moment in time. Her eyes were riveted to him. She blew him a kiss and waved. He touched his heart and pointed to her with a sad smile, and then he was gone. She stood there, with tears running down her face. Geoff continued to stand at a discreet distance, wanting to leave her alone with her private grief, the reality of what they both had to face.

They watched the plane take off and circle high in the sky, on its way to Cairo, Rome, and then Boston. She followed Geoff quietly back to the car. Neither of them spoke for a long time.

"Are you all right?" he asked quietly, and she nodded. She felt as though someone had torn her heart out with their bare hands. She spoke little and never slept all the way back. She just sat, looking out the window at the African landscape sliding by. It looked so different to her now, without him. Everything would for a lifetime. He was gone out of her sky. They would never again have what they had shared for the past six months. It had been an incredible gift, and one she knew she would cherish forever. Their days together in Senafe had been more precious to her than diamonds.

Fiona was waiting for her when she got back. She saw the dazed look on Christianna's face and said nothing to her. She put an arm around her, took her into their tent, and put her to bed. Christianna looked up at her with the broken-hearted eyes of a child. The two women's eyes met, and Fiona smoothed her hair on the pillow and told her to close her eyes and go to sleep. Christianna did as she was told, as Fiona sat and watched her for a while, to make sure she was all right. Later, Mary came in and spoke to Fiona in a whisper.

"Is she okay?"

"No," Fiona said honestly, "and she won't be for a while." Mary nodded and went to bed. No one fully understood it, but they all knew something sad had happened, more than Parker just going home. As surely as if she had gone back to Liechtenstein, her life sentence without him had begun.

# Chapter 13

Christianna moved through the next two weeks in a daze. She had a letter from Parker after ten days. All he could talk about was meeting her in Paris. He said he had never hated Boston so much in his life. He was pining for her, just as she was for him. She wrote him two letters, but she didn't want to make this harder for him than it already was. It was unfair enough, and she had caused him enough misery with her impossible situation. She told him how much she loved him, but held out no hope.

On the third week after he left, there was a sense of unease one morning when she went to work. She wasn't sure what it was. It was almost palpable in the air. Everyone looked serious at breakfast, and she noticed that Akuba and Yaw weren't outside as she walked to the dining tent. Christianna glanced at Fiona, who looked as mystified as she did. Geoff explained the situation to them before they left for work. There had been an attack on the Ethiopian border the night before. An ambush. It was the first flagrant violation of the truce in many years. Geoff said he hoped it was a single occurrence, but they all had to be aware. If the war began again between Eritrea and

Ethiopia, it could become dangerous even for them. But that was still a long way off. This wasn't a war, it was a skirmish, and hopefully nothing more than an unfortunate incident. Geoff said that UN troops were on hand at the border, as well as those of the African Union, to keep the peace. But everyone looked concerned as they went to work, not so much for themselves as for these people they loved so much. They had suffered so terribly during the last war, all the workers at the camp hoped that the breaking of the truce would not light the fires of war again. It was everyone's dearest hope.

The patients were all upset that morning, there was much talking, and a sense of near panic. They had all lived through it before. In addition, the workers at the camp were worried about malaria season, which would be upon them in the next month. They had enough to worry about with that.

The consensus of opinion was that they just had to keep an eye on the situation, and be aware. For the moment, it posed no threat to anyone in the camp. But they were close enough to the border to have some justifiable concern. And after breakfast, Max and Sam came to talk to Christianna.

"Your father won't like this, Your Highness. We have to report to him." That had been one of the principal conditions of their being with her, and it had even been her agreement with him herself, that if the political situation ever got dicey, she would agree to leave at once.

"It was just a skirmish," she pointed out to both of them. "We're not at war." She had no intention of leaving now, particularly with malaria season coming, they needed her more than ever. And there were reports of a fresh outbreak of kala azar.

"It could worsen at any moment," they said, looking deeply concerned, "and once it does, it could get out of hand very quickly." Neither of them wanted to be in a situation where they couldn't get her out.

"Let's not panic yet," she said tersely, and went to work.

Nothing further happened for the next two weeks. It was the first of September by then, and the first cases of malaria began to come in. It was a grueling time for all of them, compounded by heavy rains. It was miserable in the camp, even in their tents, as they waded through heavy mud. She had been in Africa for eight months by then, and it had already seeped into her soul. With the heavier workload, and the miserable weather, they all fell into bed exhausted every night. And her father had been railing at Max and Sam for weeks to get her home, ever since the border skirmish, which he didn't like at all. But Christianna was refusing to go anywhere. They needed her, and she was staying. She sent the message to him via Sam and Max. She no longer had time to go to the post office to talk to him herself, which was just as well. She didn't want to argue with him. She was still too upset about Parker, and had too much on her mind.

"God, don't you hate this bloody weather?" Fiona said one night as they got back to the tent. She had been out delivering babies all day. Christianna had been helping with AIDS and malaria patients, and two more cases of kala azar had come in, and Geoff was deeply concerned. They didn't need a major outbreak of that on their hands as well.

Fiona had been back for less than an hour, when they called her out again. A woman not far from the camp was delivering twins. Still soaked to the skin, she went back out, praying her little car wouldn't get stuck in the mud, which it had already done several times. One night she had had to walk home in the pouring rain, well over two miles. She'd had a cough ever since.

Christianna saw her go out and waved with a tired smile. "Have fun!"

"Sod off!" Fiona said gamely. "At least you'll be dry in here." At certain times, it was a hard life, and this was one of them. And Fiona worked as hard as all the rest, often harder. She never complained, she loved what she did, and knew how badly they needed her.

Christianna heard the little car drive off, and finally went to sleep. They were all exhausted, from the weather and increased workload. And it didn't surprise her when she didn't see Fiona in her bed in the morning. She often stayed out all night, especially if the delivery was rough, or the baby frail. And with twins, it was bound to be hard.

Christianna went to breakfast with the others, and as he glanced around, Geoff looked suddenly concerned.

"Where's Fiona? Asleep or still out?"

"Out," Christianna answered as she poured herself a cup of coffee.

"I hope her car didn't get stuck in the mud." He said something to Maggie, and then decided to drive out himself and check. The rains hadn't let up all night, and still hadn't. Max volunteered to go with him. If the car was stuck, he could help push it out of the mud. A few minutes later, the two men set off. Christianna and Maggie went to the AIDS clinic, Ushi to her classroom, and everyone to their respective jobs. It was a morning like any other in the rainy season, except wetter and darker.

Christianna was in her office doing some paperwork later that morning when Max and Geoff got back. They had found the car, and Fiona wasn't in it. They had gone to the house where the twins were born, and were told that Fiona had left hours before.

It was the first time that anything like that had happened. Max came to tell her, and Christianna wondered if she had tried to walk home, and either got waylaid, or took shelter in someone's house. She knew just about everyone in the area, since she'd been delivering their babies for several years.

Looking grim, Geoff organized a search party, and assigned drivers to all their cars. Max drove one, Sam another, Ernst, Klaus, and Geoff jumped in the school bus. And Didier managed to start their worst and most unreliable car. Two of the women went with them, and at the last minute, Christianna jumped into the passenger seat beside Max. They had agreed to fan out, and comb the area, stopping at every house to see if she was there. Knowing Fiona, Christianna felt almost sure that she had done something like that. She was a practical, independent woman, and she wouldn't have spent the night in a car stuck in the mud. She would have gotten to a house and knocked on the door. She felt sure they would find her soon enough. Everyone in the area was so friendly. She was probably sitting cozily by the fire in one of their homes, until the rain stopped or she could get a ride back to the camp.

Max said nothing as they drove up one road and down another. They saw the school bus after a while, and conferred with the others. No one had seen anything, and the people in the houses where they stopped hadn't seen her either, although they all knew who she was.

They were out for well over two hours, and Max was still driving diligently, as Christianna looked intently at the side of the road. And then suddenly Max stopped. Something had caught his eye. He said nothing to Christianna, so as not to worry her unduly. He got out, ran through the rain, and then stopped. There she was, lying by the side of the road, like a rag doll, naked, her hair matted, her face half in the mud, her eyes wide. Christianna ran up behind him and saw her, and was horrified by what she saw. Fiona had obviously been raped and murdered, stabbed dozens of times. It was the most horrifying thing Christianna had ever seen. Max pushed her gently away, and told her to go back to the car.

"No!" she screamed at him. "No!" She crouched in the mud beside her friend, took her own coat off and covered her, and gently lifted her face out of the mud and cradled her head, as she herself was soaked by the rain. Christianna was nearly lying in the mud, holding her, sobbing and screaming, while Max tried to pull her away and couldn't. A few minutes later the school bus drove by and he flagged them down. Everyone ran out and saw what had happened. Klaus and Ernst gently helped Max pull Christianna away. They radioed to the others, and someone brought a tarp. Christianna was led away, sobbing, and they gently wrapped Fiona, put her in the bus, and drove back to camp.

The rest of the day was a blur for everyone. The authorities were at the camp all day. They combed the area, but no one had seen anything or anyone. No one knew anything, and the local authorities insisted it had been done by marauding Ethiopians, which seemed unlikely to everyone in the camp. It was obviously some local madman who had gone undiscovered. It was the first violence they had ever experienced in the camp. Geoff went to the post office in Senafe to notify the family by phone himself. They were devastated, predictably. And even though Christianna begged them not to, Max and Sam went to the post office with Geoff to call her father.

His response was exactly what they had expected. "Bring her back. Now. Tomorrow. Today. Get her out." They came back and told Christianna, but she was in no condition to leave, she was devastated by the death of her friend, and the agonizing way she had died. Conditions being what they were in Africa, Fiona's family had reluctantly agreed to have her buried there. They were still in shock, but it would have been complicated and expensive to bring her home. And she had loved Africa so much. It seemed right and fitting to bury her there.

Christianna wanted to talk to Parker, but she was too distraught to go to the post office with Sam and Max, and she didn't want to talk to her father. She didn't care what he said. She wasn't going home, at least until they buried Fiona. The scene around her was suddenly a jumble and a blur. Everything had gone so wrong, and now suddenly they were all afraid.

They buried Fiona the next day, with the entire camp still in shock. Word spread in the surrounding areas. There was a sense of outrage and horror among the locals, as well as among the workers in the camp. After her brief funeral service and burial, the residents of the camp huddled in the dining tent, crying and looking grim. There was no sense of an Irish wake, which she would have liked. Instead, there were crying, angry, frightened people, unable to believe that they had lost their beloved friend. Christianna and Mary hugged, sobbing. Ushi was inconsolable. Geoff and Maggie were shaken beyond words. It was a terrible time at the camp. And then suddenly the roof caved in.

Two days after they buried Fiona, there was another border skirmish, and within three days Ethiopia and Eritrea were once more at war. This time there was no conversation. Sam and Max did not go to the post office to call her father or discuss it with Christianna. Sam packed her bag, and Max waited outside while she dressed. There was no choice. They were going to carry her out if they had to. She insisted she didn't want to leave her friends. She had come to love this place and the people in it. Everyone gathered around her, and they all cried when she left. Geoff was in full agreement with Sam and Max. The others were all going to have to make their own decisions as to whether they stayed or left. But Geoff told Christianna himself that she had to leave. She had served them well, given richly of herself, and they all loved her for it. But as much as Sam and Max and her father did, he wanted her out. This was not her job, it was a piece of her heart and soul she had given, and he did not now want it to cost her her life. The other workers accepted the risk as part of their mission.

Christianna's mission was very different. The time she had spent with them in Africa was a gift to them and for herself.

They all said tearful goodbyes, she made a last tour of the patients in the AIDS clinic to say goodbye to them, and Geoff drove them to Asmara. Once there, they stood in the pouring rain, and she clung to Geoff like a crying child. So much had happened, and she was so frightened for all of them. She felt like a traitor leaving them now. UN and African Union troops had been arriving in the area for days.

"You have to leave, Your Highness," he said as though to remind her of who she was. "Your father would never forgive us if something happened." She had been there for nine months, and she still wasn't ready to go home, and knew she never would be. Her heart was here, and a piece of her life she would never forget.

"What about the rest of you?" she asked as the plane landed.

"We'll see what happens in the next few days. It's too soon to say. We'll see what they decide in Geneva, and what the others want to do. But it's definitely time for you to go home." In the end, this was their home and not hers. She hugged him tightly before she left, and thanked him for the happiest months of her life. He thanked her for all she'd done and all she'd given. He told her she was an extraordinary young woman and wished her well. He knew none of them would forget her, or her loving, selfless grace.

And then she, Max, and Sam got on the plane. She saw Geoff watching them as she looked out the window. He waved, and then ran back to the bus. Moments later, the plane took off for the endless flight back to Frankfurt, and then the short hop to Zurich, and finally home.

She sat staring into space for a long time on the flight, thinking of Fiona, and Parker, Laure before that, Ushi and all the children they had taught, Mary and all the women and children in the AIDS ward. She had left behind so many people that she had come to love. And poor Fiona left with her, forever in her heart. For once, she said absolutely nothing to Sam and Max. She sat on one side of the aisle, and they sat on the other. This time they had done their job. They would have carried her out, if they had to. With a war starting, there was no question in their minds, or her father's, where she belonged. Even Christianna didn't fight them this time, She knew she had no choice.

She slept most of the way to Frankfurt, and then looked out the window in silence. She was thinking of Fiona . . . then Parker . . . she called him in Boston the moment she got off the flight in Frankfurt, and told him everything that had happened, to Fiona, the border skirmishes, and the beginning of another war. He was stunned, as she sobbed.

"My God, Cricky, are you all right?" He couldn't believe what she'd told him about Fiona. She had described how they found her, and as she told him she cried all over again. She sounded completely overwrought.

"I love you," she said over and over again, unable to stop crying. "I love you so much." She hadn't seen him in nearly two months. It felt like centuries after everything that had happened.

"Cricky, I love you, too. I want you to go home and calm down. Rest. And as soon as you can get away, I'll meet you in Paris."

"All right," she said weakly, feeling as though she couldn't live another day without him. It had already been too long, and far too many terrible things had happened. He sounded as badly shaken as she was.

"Just go home, sweetheart," he said gently. "Everything will be all right," he reassured her, wishing he could put his arms around her. She sounded as though she were in shock.

"No, it won't," she sobbed. "Fiona's dead, Parker. It won't ever be all right for her."

"I know," he said, trying to soothe her, unable to believe what had happened. It seemed impossible to believe that lively, fiery, wonderful, loving Fiona was gone. "I know. But everything will be all right for us. I'll see you in Paris very soon." But she just cried harder knowing that it would probably be for the last time. She couldn't stand any more goodbyes or losses. She had to leave him then to catch her next flight, to Zurich. And he was worried about her. She sounded awful, and badly shaken, but who wouldn't have been, after everything she'd been through. "Can I call you at home?" he asked cautiously. She had given him the numbers before he left, but told him not to use them unless he had to. She didn't want to arouse suspicions. But this time Parker wanted to check on her. He was seriously worried about her, with good reason. She had never been so upset in her life.

"No, don't. I'll call you," she said, sounding nervous. Everything in her mind was a jumble. Fiona was dead. Parker was in Boston forever. Her friends in Senafe were going to be in a war zone. And now she had to face her father, when she didn't even feel ready to go home. In the space of seventeen hours, she had gone from one side of the world to another, she felt like a plant that had been ripped out of the rich African soil and had been suddenly uprooted. Liechtenstein no longer felt like home to her. She felt as though she belonged in Senafe. And her heart was in Boston with Parker. She was utterly confused, and as she and Parker hung up, she couldn't stop crying. She looked at Sam and Max, and they looked nearly as unhappy as she did. They had loved it there, too, but there had been no question in their minds that morning, and they had a single-minded goal. They had to get her out.

"I'm sorry we left like that, Your Highness. We had to do our jobs this time. It was time to leave."

"I know," she said sadly. "It went so wrong in the end, with Fiona and the breaking of the truce, and the border skirmishes. What will happen to all those people if they have to live through another war?" It made her heart ache to think about it, they were such kind, loving people. And she missed all her friends in the camp as though they were her brothers and sisters.

"It will be very hard for them if this war really takes hold," Max said honestly. He and Sam had talked about it at length on the flight. The UN was trying to step in, but they hadn't been able to stop it last time.

"I worry about the people in the camp, too," Christianna added.

"They'll know when to get out. They've been through this before." But there had been no question that she needed to get out sooner than they did. Max and Sam were both well aware that if something happened to her, it would have been disastrous. The prince would never have forgiven them, nor would they ever have forgiven themselves.

She was quiet on the last leg of the flight, from Frankfurt to Zurich. She had nothing left to say. She was so grief-stricken she was numb. The loss of her friend, the absence of the man she loved, how hopeless their situation was, no matter how much they loved each other, and being torn from the place she had come to love for the past nine months—all of it together was almost more than she could bear. And now, in spite of the joy of seeing her father again, she felt as though she were going home to prison, to be trapped in Vaduz for eternity, doing her duty to her father and their country, sacrificing herself more than ever before. She felt as though she were being punished for having been born royal. It had become, and had always been for her, an intolerable burden. She felt torn between what she had been taught she owed her ancestors, her country, and her family, and what her heart longed for, Parker, the only man she had ever loved.

The plane landed in Zurich, and her father was waiting for her at the airport. He put his arms around her, and there were tears in his eyes. He had been so desperately worried about her in those final hours. He couldn't have borne it if he had lost her. He looked gratefully at Max and Sam for getting her out before something terrible had happened. The news reports he had been following closely had gotten worse since she left Asmara.

She looked up at him, and smiled, and he could see instantly that a different person had come home. She was a woman, and not a girl anymore. She had loved and lived and worked and grown. And as it had done to others before her, the beauty of Africa and all she had learned and discovered there had crept into her very soul.

They waved her through customs in Zurich as they always did. They never even glanced at her passport. They didn't need to. They knew who she was and smiled at her. This time she looked at them and didn't smile back. She couldn't.

She got into the Rolls beside her father, with his familiar driver, and the bodyguard in the passenger seat. Sam and Max were following in another car, with two other bodyguards who were happy to see them. They weren't as devastated as Christianna was. It had been a job to them, although they had come to love it, too. And they were also sad to be back. Their old familiar world suddenly looked so different to them, just as it did to Cricky.

Cricky said little on the drive to Liechtenstein. She held her father's hand in silence and looked out the window. It was autumn and the weather was beautiful. But she missed Senafe. He knew everything that had happened, or thought he did. He knew about Fiona, and of Christianna finding her. He thought what he was seeing was her deep shock over that. He had no idea that what he was seeing was her sense of desolation over losing Parker too. Even if she hadn't completely lost him yet, she knew she would. And even if they met in Paris, there was no way they could continue doing so, without creating a scandal, like one of Freddy's, and she wouldn't do that to her father. She couldn't. She owed him more than that.

"I missed you, Papa," she said, as she turned to look at him. He was looking at her so tenderly that she knew yet again that she couldn't break his heart by betraying everything she'd been born to. So she was offering her own heart as a sacrifice instead, and Parker's. Two hearts for one. It seemed a terrible price to pay for duty.

"I missed you, too," her father said quietly. She held his hand, and once they reached Vaduz, she saw the familiar palace where she had grown up. But it no longer felt like coming home to her. Parker was home. Senafe was home. The people she had loved there had been home. The people in the life she had been born to had all become strangers to her in the last nine months. She had come home a different woman. And even her father knew it.

She got out of the car quietly. The servants she had grown up with were waiting for her. Charles came bounding up to her, and as he put his paws on her and licked her face, she smiled. And then she saw Freddy, waving to her from the distance. He had come from Vienna specially to see her. And in her heart of hearts, she felt nothing. The dog followed her inside, and she heard someone shut the door behind her. Freddy put his arms around her and kissed her. Charles barked. Her father smiled at her, and she smiled sadly at all of them. She wanted to be happy to see them, but she wasn't. She had been deposited in a family of strangers. Everyone who spoke to her called her Your Serene Highness. It was exactly who she didn't want to be, who she hadn't been for nine extraordinary months. She didn't want to be Christianna of Liechtenstein again. All she wanted to be was Cricky of Senafe.

# Chapter 14

Once home, Christianna continued to follow news of the situation in Eritrea with intense interest. She was worried about her friends. And the situation did not sound good. There were continuing border violations, and many people had already been killed. Eritreans were starting to flee the country again, as they had before. The war was slowly getting under way, and although she hated to admit it, her father had been right to force her to come home.

Her heart still ached over Fiona. She thought constantly about the laughter they had shared, how angry Fiona had been when she found out that Christianna was a princess, and she felt that she'd been holding out on her by keeping it a secret. She thought of all the good times they'd had together, and that terrible morning when they'd found her, and how horribly she had died. Christianna could only hope that the end had come fast. But even if in seconds, she must have faced such agony and terror. It was hard to get that hideous image out of her head, of Fiona, naked, like a rag doll, lying facedown in the mud and rain, having been stabbed again and again.

In both good and bad ways, Christianna had changed forever in

Eritrea. She had loved every moment of it, the people she'd met, worked and lived with, the places she had seen. It was all woven into the fiber of her being, and now she felt more like a stranger here than there. In Senafe she had been herself, the best self she had ever been. In Vaduz she had to be the one she had resisted all her life. In fact, she had to give herself up almost completely to be there. She had to surrender to duty and history. And worst of all, in order to be who she was destined to be, she had to give up the man she loved. She couldn't think of a worse fate. It felt like a living death to her every day. She loved her father and her brother, but being back in Vaduz continued to feel like a life sentence in prison to her. She had to force herself to get out of bed every day and do what was expected of her. She did it, by sheer force and self-discipline, but she felt as though a piece of her died every day. No one saw it, but she knew it. She was withering inside.

She and Parker wrote to each other by e-mail every day. She called him in Boston a few times once she was back, but he was afraid to call her. Christianna didn't want anyone aware of him, nor for anyone, particularly her father, brother, or security, to see his name on a message lying somewhere. E-mail was the only communication that was safe. And even there she held out no hope for the future to him. There wasn't any. And misleading him now, or harboring hopes herself, would have been too cruel. They had no hope, all they had now were memories of a golden time, and the love they shared.

She loved her exchanges with him, their laughter, even if only on screen. He told her how his work was going, and she told him about her days. Most of the time she just told him what she felt. She was more than ever in love with him, and he with her.

She attended numerous state events with her father, and two dinners in Vienna. And they went to an enormously fancy party in Monte Carlo, given by Prince Albert. It was the Red Cross Ball, which had particular meaning for her, although she had had no real desire to attend the ball. She was back in her traces again, the yoke of duty on her neck, her father's hostess in Vaduz and Vienna, and ever on his arm when they went out.

Freddy was living in Liechtenstein Palace in Vienna, and playing all over Europe. He traveled on yachts with friends, and spent a week in St. Tropez in September. As always, the paparazzi followed him, hoping to get some tidbit or scandal. Lately, he had been better than usual, but the press knew, as Christianna and her father did, that with Freddy it was only a matter of time before he was in the soup again, and being served up on a silver platter by the press. He had visited Victoria in London several times, and she was engaged again, to a rock star this time, in honor of whom she had gotten a huge heart tattooed on her chest, and dyed her hair green. Freddy loved hanging out with her. She moved in a racy crowd that suited him. And once in a while, when he had nothing else to do, he came home for a visit to Vaduz.

It unnerved him to see how mature Christianna had become, how determined her efforts to please their father. She visited the sick in hospitals and orphanages constantly, went to see old people in convalescent centers, spoke at libraries, and posed constantly for photographs. She was doing exactly what she was supposed to do, without a single word of complaint, but when he looked into her eyes on one of his visits home, what he saw there made his heart ache. Even Freddy could see the price she was paying for the life she led.

"You need to have more fun," he told her one morning over breakfast, on a gloriously sunny day in Vaduz toward the end of September.

"You're getting old before your time, my love." She had turned twenty-four that summer, and he was about to turn thirty-four, with no sign whatsoever of his settling down or growing up.

"What do you suggest?" Christianna asked him practically.

"Why don't you go to the South of France for a couple of weeks? The sailboat races are next week. Victoria rented a house in Ramatuelle, and you know how much fun her house parties are." It was all he could think of to suggest. And there was no question, it would have been fun. But then after that, what? Back to Vaduz again, and the weight of painful duties forevermore. Christianna was depressed about it from the moment she came home, and Freddy's well-meant but superficial suggestions didn't help. In fact, there was no real solution to the problem, except resignation and surrender. And to add fuel to the fire of her despair and loneliness, she had been obliged to give up love, of her own accord.

"I feel as though I ought to be here to help Papa. I've been away for so long." And he enjoyed her company so much. He said it every day.

"Father can manage fine without you," Freddy said, stretching his long, elegant legs out before him. He was an incredibly handsome young man, and women fell into his hands like grapes dropping off the vine. "He manages fine without me," Freddy laughed, and his sister sighed. She had given up so much to be home and pick up the thread of her duties again. She wondered when he would do the same, if ever. And most of the burdens that rested on her, and were keeping her from Parker, were because her brother shouldered none at all. It was hard not to resent him for it.

"When are you going to grow up?" she asked him pointedly. Even she was getting tired of his constant partying and irresponsibility. It was tedious at their age, although previously she had forgiven him all. But his lifestyle no longer seemed as charming to her as it once had. She was shouldering his responsibilities as well as her own.

"Maybe never. Or not until I have to," he said honestly. "What do I have to grow up for? Father is going to live for a long time. I'm not going to be reigning prince for years. I'll grow up when I am." She didn't say it to him, but wanted to, by then it might be too late. He had developed bad habits over the years and was incredibly self-indulgent. He was the exact opposite of his extremely responsible sister. Her willingness to be there for their father enabled Freddy to be who he was, and wasn't.

"You could help Father more than you do," she said tersely. "He has an immense burden on him constantly, worrying about the country's economy, dealing with economic and humanitarian issues, keeping our trade pacts in order with other countries. It would make life much easier for him if you took an interest in some of it." She tried to encourage him, but as he had all his life, Freddy did nothing. He just played.

"You've gotten awfully serious while you were away," he said, looking slightly annoyed at her. He didn't like being reminded of his duties, or called to order. His father had all but given up on it, and rarely did now. He just relied more and more on Christianna and it didn't please Freddy to be reprimanded by his younger sister, particularly if she was right. "I find that very boring," Freddy said, with an edge to his voice.

"Maybe real life is boring," she said, sounding older than her years. "I don't think that grown-ups have fun every day, at least not those in our particular situation. We have a responsibility to Father *and* the country, to set an example for people, and do what's expected of us, whether we like it or want to, or not. Remember? 'Honor, Courage, Welfare.' "

It was the family code by which they lived, or were supposed to. Her father and Christianna did. It had never meant a lot to Freddy, in fact nothing at all. His honor was questionable. He was not courageous about anything. And the only welfare that had interested him so far was his own.

"When did you get so holy?" he asked her irritably. "What did they do to you in Africa?" He had recognized in recent weeks that she had changed. She was no longer the young girl she had been when she left. She was a woman now, in all senses of the word. And when he looked into her eyes, she seemed pained.

"I learned a lot of things," she said quietly, "from some wonderful people," those that she had worked with as well as those she had gone to help. She had fallen in love with both, and with a man she loved deeply, and had given up for her father and country. She had seen a beloved friend die, and the country erupt in war. She had seen a lot in the nine months she was gone, and had come home a different person. Freddy could see it, and wasn't sure he liked it. He was finding her ever-increasing sense of responsibility painfully annoying.

"I think you're getting a bit tedious, my darling sister," he said with an edge to his voice. "Perhaps you need to have more fun, and spend less time trying to curb mine." There was a tartness to his answer, as he stood up and stretched lazily. "I'm going back to Vienna today, and then I'm flying to London to see friends." It was an endless merry-go-round with him, from one entertainment to another. She wondered how he could stand it. It was such an empty life. How many parties could one go to? How many starlets and models could one chase? While everyone else did all the work.

He left that morning after saying goodbye to her, and there was an uneasiness between them. He didn't like her criticizing him or reminding him of his duties. And she didn't enjoy watching him waste his life in constant dissipation. She was still annoyed about it, when she got an e-mail from Parker that morning. He was suggesting they meet in Paris.

Her first inclination was to say no to him, although she had promised him she would one day. The downside of it was that they would only get more attached to each other, fall more in love, and suffer even more than they already had, when they had to leave each other. And how many times could she do that? At some point, someone would recognize her, the paparazzi would come, and she would become as big a disgrace as Freddy, perhaps even worse since she was a woman, and her country's attitudes about women were so archaic, possibly the most in Europe. She hesitated for a few minutes after she read his e-mail, and then picked up the phone to call him. She was going to tell him no. But the moment she heard his voice, she melted.

"Hi, Cricky," he said gently. "How's it going there?" She sighed, trying to know how to answer him, and decided to be honest.

"It's so hard. I just had breakfast with my brother. Some things don't change, or not much. All he does is play and party and fool around, and have fun, while my father works like a dog, and I do everything I can to help him. It's just not fair. He has no sense of responsibility at all. He's thirty-four, and acts like he's eighteen. I love him, but sometimes I get so tired of all his nonsense." And she knew her father did, too. It put that much more responsibility on her shoulders and his as well. She felt obliged to make up for him in every way she could, and was beginning to resent him for it. She had never felt that way about it before Senafe. But she hadn't been in love with Parker then. Before she left, her brother had seemed like a charming, naughty boy who, most of the time, amused her. Now, since she was giving up so much, it was far less amusing. Parker thought she sounded tired, and sad.

"What do you think about Paris?" he asked, sounding hopeful.

"I don't know," she said honestly. "I'd love to, but I worry that we're just delaying the agony." She didn't add the words "of pulling the plug," which was how she saw it. There was just no other solution. At some point, she could try to talk to her father about it, but she had virtually no hope. Given how her father viewed things, a commoner in Boston, even if a respectable young doctor, was not something he would allow. He was not a prince, or even a royal. Christianna being with him violated all her father's beliefs, and hopes for her. He didn't care how many other princes and princesses in other countries were marrying commoners these days. He had no intention of mitigating his opinions or compromising. And for the moment, he had no idea Christianna was in love. And once he did, she knew her father. In the end, he would ask her to give him up, and she would have to. In her position, she could not go against the tides of a thousand years of tradition, or the deathbed wishes of her mother. The currents were just too strong, and eventually the love she shared with Parker would have to die. Realizing that again made her heart ache every time. And trying to explain it to him was worse.

"I'm just trying to keep the patient alive until we find a cure for the illness," he said, still cherishing his hopes and dreams and love for her. He was not willing to give up, not yet at least, and hopefully never.

"There is no cure, my love," she said softly, longing to see him. She was twenty-four years old, deeply in love with a wonderful man. It was hard to explain even to herself why she should stamp it out, for a country and a series of ancient traditions, or even for her father, or because her brother was inadequate for the throne. She felt pulled a thousand ways.

"Let's just meet in Paris," he said gently. "We don't have to solve all the problems now. I miss you, Cricky. I want to see you."

"I want to see you, too," she said sadly. "I wish we could just go to Massawa for the weekend." She smiled, remembering their weekend there. They had had so much fun. Their days in Africa together had been so much easier than these.

"I'm not sure that's the place to be right now. I've been reading about it on the Internet. The border wars are getting worse." The Ethiopians wanted the Eritreans' ports. They always had, and had never fully accepted the terms of the truce. "I think you got out at just the right time." Even though she hated being home, she couldn't disagree. It had been wise.

"Have you heard from anyone at the camp?" She hadn't in weeks, not since a letter from Mary Walker, and a postcard from Ushi. Neither had said much, other than that they missed her. They were guardedly waiting to see what happened, and expecting orders from Geneva. Meanwhile they were sitting tight.

"I had a card from Geoff. He didn't say much. I don't think they know anything yet. But if there's a full-scale war there again, it's going to be a mess. They'll probably have to get out, or risk some real dangers if they stay. They might join up with the UN forces at the border, but that will put them right in the line of fire. If they do that, they'll probably close the base in Senafe." Just thinking of that made Christianna sad. She had been so happy there. And she was sadder still for the Eritreans she had come to love so much. Another war with Ethiopia would be a terrible thing for them. They had only just recovered from the last one. "Let's get back to us," Parker called her to order. He had to go back to work. "Paris. You, me. Us . . . dinner, walking along the Seine, holding hands, kisses . . . making love . . .

does any of that sound familiar or even enticing?" She laughed. It sounded irresistible, not just enticing. And all of it with the man she loved.

"Who can resist?" she asked with a smile in her voice.

"I hope you can't. When can you get away? What does your schedule look like?"

"I have to go to a wedding with my father in Amsterdam this weekend. The queen of Holland's niece is getting married, and my father is her godfather. But I think I'm free the following one," she said practically, and he was laughing at her.

"You're the only woman I know, or ever will I guess, whose social calendar is taken up by kings and queens and princes. Other people have tickets to baseball games, or church socials. You, my love, are truly my fairy princess."

"That is precisely the problem." And he was her Prince Charming.

"Fine. I'm perfectly willing to play second fiddle to the queen of Holland. How about the weekend after?" She quickly flipped through her social calendar and nodded.

"I could do it." She was free, and then she paused, worried. "I don't know what I'll tell my father."

"Tell him you need to go shopping. That's always a good excuse." It was, but she was worried her father would want to go with her. He loved taking her to Paris. And then suddenly she remembered, and her face lit up with excitement. She could do it.

"I just remembered. He's going to a sailing race in England that weekend, in Cowes. He'll be busy." It always impressed Parker how devoted she was, and dismayed him at the same time.

"So are we on?" he asked, sounding hopeful.

She laughed and sounded young and free again, for the first time since she got home. "We're on, my love." She felt like she had just gotten a reprieve. Three days in Paris with him. And after that, she'd live with all the burdens she had. Just three more days with him. It was like lifeblood to her. Seeing him was the air she needed to breathe.

They made their plans. And she told her secretary to make reservations at the Ritz in Paris. He was going to do the same. They couldn't risk sharing a room, in case someone squealed at the hotel. They could leave his room empty, or hers, but they had to register separately. She was grateful he had the money to do it, and was willing to.

She asked the head of security to assign Max and Samuel to her. She knew they would be discreet and leave her alone. It would be like a reunion for them after Senafe. She could hardly wait.

She left for her official duties that afternoon with a spring in her step. She was nicer than ever to the children, more patient than she'd ever been with the old people, kinder than she was usually with people who shook her hand, or gave her flowers or hugged her. And when she went out with her father to an official dinner that night, even he noticed how happy she was. He was relieved to see it. He had been worried about her. She had seemed so unhappy since she got home, even more so than before she left. He was almost beginning to regret he had ever let her go, if it had only worsened the problem, rather than curing it. She was tireless in her kindness to the people she spoke to that night, gracious, poised, patient, intelligent. She was the daughter to him he always knew she was. What he didn't know was all that she could think about now was Parker, and seeing him again. She was living for three days in Paris with him, and would have walked across burning coals to get there. Parker was the only thing keeping her going now, the strength he gave her fueled her, and the deep, heady essence of their love.

# Chapter 15

Max and Samuel accompanied Christianna in the car to the airport in Zurich, and teased her about what a hardship assign-
ment this was. They both loved traveling with her, enjoyed Paris, and
it was a nice break from routine for them as well. It was almost as
though the Three Musketeers were on the road again, even if not for
long. They had no idea she was meeting Parker in Paris. She hadn't
said anything to them. She didn't want anyone to know, not even
them. She wanted no slip-ups, no mistakes. This wasn't a weekend in
Qohaito, far from her father's eyes. This was very close to home for
her, and she knew that one slip would bring the press on her in a
minute. She and Parker were going to have to be infinitely careful and
relentlessly discreet.

They arrived at Charles de Gaulle Airport in Paris and were escorted through customs by the head of airport security, as they always
were. A chauffeured car was waiting for her, and Max and Sam got in
it with her. They no longer called her "Cricky" here, but had referred
to her respectfully as "Your Highness" ever since they got home. It
seemed strange to hear it from them now, but she accepted that.

One of the managers of the Ritz had already checked her in when she arrived, and she was taken to a beautiful suite looking out on the Place Vendôme. She stood impatiently, looking out at the beauty of the square, hung up a few things, ordered tea, paced nervously around the room, and then, almost like in a movie, there was a knock on her door. She opened it, and there he was, more beautiful than ever. Parker, in a blazer and slacks, open-necked blue shirt, and before she could even take a good look at him, she was in his arms. They kissed so passionately that the air nearly went out of both of them. She had never been so happy to see anyone in her life. They hadn't seen each other in two months. It was the end of September, and he had left at the beginning of August. She felt like a drowning person gasping for air. She was speechless with joy, when he finally pulled away a little to look at her.

"My God, you look so beautiful," he said, overwhelmed himself. He was used to seeing her the way she looked in Senafe, with her hair in a braid, in shorts and hiking boots, without makeup or elegance. Now she was wearing a pale blue wool dress the same color as her eyes, and pearls at her neck and ears. And even high heels, she pointed out. And they didn't have to worry about snakes, he teased.

Everything about seeing each other was perfect. She had planned to go for a walk with him, or stop at a small café on the Left Bank. He had had the same idea, and instead they were in bed, tightly in each other's arms within minutes. They were like starving people who needed to be fed before they could do anything else. And their passion for each other had only increased in the two months they hadn't seen each other.

Afterward they lay sated and comfortable on the impeccably pressed sheets of her bed at the Ritz, looking up at the splendid details of the ceiling, and then back into each other's eyes. She couldn't stop kissing him, and he couldn't keep himself from holding her close. It was late afternoon before they finally got up, and shared a bath in the suite's huge bathtub. Being together was almost like a drug to which they had both become addicted, and now could not live without.

They finally made it out of the room, and walked first around the Place Vendôme and then around the Left Bank. Sam and Max had been stunned and delighted when they saw him, and then realized what the weekend was about. They kept a discreet distance and followed the young lovers as they walked and talked for hours. It was as though they had never been apart. They talked about the same topics they used to, he told her about his research project, she told him what she'd been doing in Vaduz. They talked about their time in Senafe, the people they had come to love there, their concerns for the laughing, generous Eritrean people. Neither of them mentioned Fiona, because it was just too sad. This was meant to be a happy time for them, and it was.

They had coffee at the Deux Magots, talked some more, and then went across the street to the church of St. Germain des Prés, lit candles, and prayed. Christianna lit her candles for the people of Eritrea and Senafe, for Fiona, and one for them as well, hoping that somehow they would find a solution to their problem, that maybe by some miracle her father would be reasonable and allow them to pursue their love. She knew it would take a miracle for that to happen. She was relieved to know that Parker was also Catholic, because that would have been a stumbling block to her father, and a big one, probably insurmountable. At least that was one obstacle they didn't have to deal with. They had so many others to worry about, fortunately religion wasn't one of them. The throne of Liechtenstein had been Catholic since the sixteenth century, and her father was profoundly devout about their faith.

They went back to the hotel afterward, and had to delay dinner when they made love again. It was nine-thirty by the time Christianna was dressed in a white pantsuit and sweater she had bought the year before at Dior. She looked like a little angel, as she left the hotel again on his arm. Sam and Max were waiting outside with the car.

They drove until they found a bistro, and then sat there for hours, talking some more. They were tireless in their interest in each other, their passion for each other's projects, their concern for each other's well-being. It was a constant exchange of information between them, of laughter, jokes, and topics that fascinated them both. She particularly liked hearing about his AIDS project, since she had become knowledgeable about it in Senafe, and now it was dear to her heart, just as he was, and everything he touched.

"And what about you, sweetheart? How's the ribbon business going?" They had come to call it that once she explained to him what it was.

"I'm doing a lot of it these days. It makes my father happy, and the people I do it for. It makes them feel important if I open their buildings for them, or whatever they want." It was strange even to her to realize that it made a difference to them, that her presence cutting a ribbon, or saying a few words, shaking a hand, or gently touching a head, could make them feel as though they had shared in her grace and magic for a minute, and were somehow different as a result. It was something she had talked to him about at length by e-mail, the strangeness of being a person who was admired and sought out, without their truly knowing her, or if she was in fact worthy of the respect and admiration they gave her, simply because of who she had been born. It seemed magical to him as well, the fairy princess who blesses the people with her magic wand, casting a happy spell on them. She laughed when he said that to her, wishing she could do as much for herself and Parker. But in many ways, life had. Seeing him again was an enormous blessing in which they both shared. And sharing that blessing gave them more to share with others. In the warmth of Parker's love, Christianna felt she could do anything, and he said he felt the same way about her. The only problem they had, and it was an enormous one, was that they were living on stolen moments.

They fell asleep in each other's arms that night, like sleeping children, after they made love again. They couldn't get enough of each other, their thirst for each other's bodies and souls was bottomless and never quenched, or at least not for long. They had two months to catch up on, and the next morning Christianna teased him that they couldn't make up for all of it in one weekend.

"Then give me a lifetime," Parker said, looking serious, as she lay in bed beside him.

"I wish I could," she said, looking sad again. She hated thinking about how hopeless their situation was. Unless she was willing to walk away from her responsibilities and break her father's heart, she simply had no choice. "If it were in my power to say so, I would be yours. I am yours, in all the ways that matter." Save one. She could not agree to marry him, and probably never could because she knew without a doubt that her father wouldn't give his consent, and she didn't want to marry Parker without that. Breaking every belief and tradition she'd been brought up to respect seemed the wrong way to start. And Parker wanted to marry her more than anything in life. He had been in love with her for seven months, and it already seemed like a lifetime to him. He wanted more now, and so did she. They promised each other to try not to think about it that day, and enjoy the time they had. He was going back to Boston, and she was flying back to Zurich on Monday night.

They spent Saturday walking along the Seine, looking at the

bookstalls, playing with the puppies in the pet shops, taking a Bâteau Mouche for the fun of it, and having lunch at the Café Flore. She felt as though they had walked all over the Left Bank, into antique shops and galleries, before they let Sam and Max drive them back to the Right Bank across the Pont Alexandre III. They drove past the Louvre in all its splendor and talked about what it must have been like when it was a palace. She smiled and said that her mother had been both a Bourbon and descended from the house of Orléans. She was a Royal Highness, not a Serene one, on both sides. She explained to Parker that in order to be a "Royal" Highness, one must be directly descended from kings, which her mother was. Her father's lineage descended from princes, so he was Serene. For Parker, unfamiliar with all the royal traditions she had grown up with, it was heady stuff, in fact, a little dizzying, and so was she for him. It was the first time he had ever seen her passport, with only her Christian name.

"And that's it? No last name?" It seemed funny to him, and she smiled.

"That's it. Just Christianna of Liechtenstein. All royals have passports like that, with no surname at all. Even the queen of England, her passport just says 'Elizabeth,' and in her case it is followed by an R, for Regina, because she is the queen."

"I guess Princess Christianna Williams would sound a little strange," he said apologetically with a rueful grin.

"Not to me," she said softly, as he kissed her again.

On their way into the hotel, they stopped at the Bar du Ritz for a drink. They were both thirsty and tired, but had had a wonderful day. Parker ordered a glass of wine, and Christianna a cup of tea. He had learned in Senafe that she almost never drank. She didn't like it, and only did so at state occasions, when she felt obliged to toast someone with champagne. Otherwise she had no great fondness for alcohol.

And Parker always told her she ate like a bird. She was tiny, and had a slim but womanly figure, which he found irresistibly sexy, as he had proven often.

There was a man playing the piano at the bar of the Ritz, and as they sat there enjoying it, Christianna laughed.

"What are you laughing at?" Parker asked her with a happy smile. All he wanted was for their weekend in Paris to last forever, and so did she. They were totally in agreement on that concept.

"I was just thinking how civilized this is compared to Senafe. Imagine if we'd had a piano in the dining tent." It was after all where their romance began.

"It might have been a very nice touch," he laughed along with her.

"God, I miss it. Don't you?" she said longingly, with her love for Africa in her eyes.

"I do, but also because I could wake up every morning and see you, and end the day seeing you. But I have to admit that other than that, my work has been really interesting at Harvard," more so than it had been in Senafe, although he had loved the patients he saw there. In Boston he saw no patients, but was only coordinating research. He mentioned that he had had a letter from the Dutchman who was the head of the team he'd traveled with from Doctors Without Borders. Christianna said that she admired their work tremendously, and so did Parker.

"If I were a doctor, I would do that," she said, and he smiled at her.

"I know you would."

"I wish I could dedicate my life to helping people, as you do. The things I do for my father seem so stupid. The ribbon business. It means nothing, to anyone," least of all to her.

"I'm sure it means something to them," he said gently.

"It shouldn't. I'm nothing more than a hospitality committee. My father does the real work, he makes economic decisions that affect the country positively, or negatively if he makes the wrong decision, although usually he makes the right ones." She smiled loyally. "He makes humanitarian efforts, he makes things better for people. He takes his responsibilities so seriously."

"So do you." Parker was extremely impressed by that about her.

"It makes no difference. Cutting a ribbon will never change anyone's life." She wanted to start working at the foundation that winter, but hadn't had time yet. Her father was keeping her too busy making state appearances for him, many of which were things Freddy should have been doing, but never did. In some instances, Christianna was carrying the ball for all three of them. At least if she started work at the foundation, she would feel she was doing something useful. But going to state dinners, and all her other minor duties seemed meaningless to her. And for that, she was having to give Parker up. It seemed inordinately cruel to her, just so she could be a princess, obey her father, and serve the people of Liechtenstein.

"Does your brother do anything?" Parker asked cautiously. He knew it was a sore subject with her.

"Not if he can help it. He says he will wait to grow up until he is the reigning prince, and that could be a long time from now. I hope it will be." Parker nodded. Her brother sounded like a scoundrel and a black sheep, but he didn't say it to her.

Eventually, they went upstairs to change for dinner, but never made it out the door of their room. They wound up making love again, sitting in the bathtub together afterward, and ordering room service. And they fell asleep in each other's arms again. It was the perfect weekend.

The next day they went to mass at Sacre Coeur, and listened to a choir of nuns sing. It was a beautiful day, and they walked in the Bois de Boulogne, and smiled at people kissing and walking their babies and dogs. It was a perfect day. They went for ice cream, stopped for coffee, and finally, relaxed and happy, they drove back to the Place Vendôme, and walked into the Ritz. She had asked the concierge to make dinner reservations at Le Voltaire, which was her favorite small, chic restaurant in Paris. They had few tables, a cozy atmosphere, great service, and fabulous food.

At nine o'clock they left the hotel, dressed for dinner and in high spirits. Christianna was wearing a very pretty pale blue Chanel suit, with high heels and diamond earrings. She loved dressing up for him, although it was certainly different than when they had been in Senafe. And he loved how elegant she was now.

As they walked out of the lobby, he put his arm around her as soon as they came out of the revolving door. The air was balmy, and she was smiling at him lovingly—when suddenly like a rocket explosion there was a flash of lights in her face. She didn't even have time to register what it was and they ran to the waiting car, followed by a trail of paparazzi. Parker looked stunned, and Christianna instantly unhappy when Max whisked them away.

"Go! Go! Go!" Max told the driver, as Sam hopped in next to them in back, and within seconds they sped off but not before two more photographers got them.

"Damn!" Christianna said, looking at Max in the front seat. "How did that happen? Do you suppose someone called them?"

"I think it was an accident," he said apologetically. "I almost warned you, but you came out too fast. Madonna walked out of the hotel just before you did. She's staying at the hotel, too, and they were waiting for her. I think you were just a bonus." But they had obviously recognized her the moment she came out of the hotel, and they had caught her smiling adoringly up at Parker, with his arm around her. There was no mistaking what this was, or that it was a romance. "We'll go in the back way later."

"It's a little late for that," she said tersely, and looked at Parker, who was still stunned. He hadn't even had time to react yet, and his eyes still had spots in front of them from the strobes. There was no doubt in Christianna's mind that the photographs would turn up somewhere. They always did. At an inopportune time when it was embarrassing, or at the very least awkward. And if her father saw them, which he would if they came out, he was not going to like it. Particularly her lying that this was a shopping trip. And he didn't like her making a spectacle of herself in the press. They had enough of that with Freddy.

Christianna was quiet on the way to the restaurant, and Parker was sorry to see her upset. He tried to console her, and she was a good sport about it, but it was obvious that she was worried. "I'm sorry, baby."

"Me, too. We didn't need that headache. It was so nice while no one knew." And essential.

"Maybe they won't use them," he said, trying to sound hopeful.

"They will. They always do," she said sadly. "My brother makes such an ass of himself all the time that they always try to tar me with the same brush. The shocking Liechtenstein prince and princess. They love saying things about royals. And I'm so careful to stay out of the press that they always get excited when they see me."

"It was rotten luck that they were waiting for Madonna." She agreed with Max that he should have warned her, but he explained that she must have already left the room when he saw them, because she was out the door within seconds, and Madonna had just sped off in a limousine with her children.

She tried not to let it spoil dinner for them, but Parker could see that she was distracted and worried. They enjoyed it anyway, but it put a damper on the evening. She was worried sick about what her father would say when he saw the press, and once he saw Parker. It opened a whole can of worms she didn't want to have to deal with yet, and had taken the timing right out of her hands. But she was helpless to change it.

They went in through the service entrance of the Ritz, on the rue Cambon. It was the same entrance Princess Diana had used when she stayed at the hotel. Many celebrities and royals came in the back entrance, and rode up in the tiny elevator, to avoid the paparazzi waiting for them out front. And then finally they were back in the safety of her room, and she relaxed again in his arms. They made love again that night, and there was a bittersweet feeling to it. She was so afraid that the photographs that had been taken would be used to force her hand with Parker. Once her father knew, she would be entirely at his mercy, which was the last thing she wanted.

Still worrying about it, she slept fitfully that night, and woke up several times with nightmares. Parker comforted her as best he could, and they were both quiet over breakfast the next morning, as the room service waiter poured their coffee. They waited until he left the room to discuss it further. Christianna trusted no one now. She had been shaken by the paparazzi attack the night before. She dreaded discussing it with her father, if it actually hit the press.

"Sweetheart, there's nothing you can do about it," Parker said sensibly. "It happened. It's over. We'll deal with it if it comes out," he said calmly, sipping the hot coffee.

"No, *we* won't deal with it, if it comes out," she said, sounding strained and unhappy. She was tired after sleeping badly the night before, and obviously worried. "If it happens, *I'll* deal with it. And so will my father. I'll be dealing with him alone. I didn't want that to happen to us, until we were ready. Because I'll get one shot at this, to convince my father about us. He won't let me discuss it with him twice. And the way to start that conversation wasn't with a lie. I lied to him about coming to Paris." But as always, she'd had no other choice. Her range of options was always narrow, and limited at best. "I just don't like it. Being exposed in the press is so tacky and unpleasant." She had an aversion to that, unlike her brother, or perhaps because of him, and his frequent scandals, she was even more sensitive about it.

"Yes, it is." He didn't disagree with her, nor did he react to anything she'd said. "But all we can do is make the best of it. What other choice do we have?"

"None." She sighed, and drank her coffee, and made an effort not to beat him up about it. It wasn't his fault, but it was causing her grave concern, and he could see it.

After breakfast, they dressed and went out. They wandered down the Faubourg St. Honoré to look at the shops, and then went to L'Avenue for lunch. She relaxed finally and was relieved to see that no one had followed them. Max and Sam stayed close, and they continued to have Christianna and Parker use the back entrance of the hotel on the rue Cambon to go in and out. It was safer and more prudent.

After lunch, they went back to the hotel. They both packed, and then curled up on the bed. They had both booked the latest flights they could, so that they would have as much time together as possible. They didn't want to lose a minute with each other, or even less a lifetime, thanks to the paparazzi. Although she knew that her chances of convincing her father were slim to none, she didn't want anything to tip that balance further, and scandalous press in the tabloids would almost certainly do that.

They lay on the bed together for a long time, and eventually they made love for the last time, gently, slowly, tenderly, savoring their final moments together. And afterward she lay in his arms and cried. She was so afraid now that she would never be able to see him again. She wanted everything they'd had before, in Senafe, and all they had now were these tiny borrowed moments whenever they could find them. He made her promise that they would come to Paris again, whenever she could get away. He said he would arrange his schedule around her at a moment's notice. As a research doctor, and not one who saw patients regularly, he had more freedom to do that. She didn't know yet what effect the paparazzi's photographs would have, if any. She said they needed to lie low for a while and wait to see what happened. Hopefully, nothing. But that seemed too much to ask. If so, they had been lucky.

They got out of bed finally, showered together, and dressed. He had never used his room once during the entire weekend, but it had given them respectability, and he was perfectly happy to pay for it, even if for nothing. Especially if it made things better for her. Parker wanted to do everything possible to make this work. She was more familiar with the situation than he was, and the restrictions on her, so he was more than willing to play by her rules, or her father's. He was truly in love with her, and more than life itself, he wanted to see her again, and, if they were incredibly lucky and blessed, marry her one day. She said it was impossible, but he was willing to hang around and wait. She was the only woman he had loved that way. And she was just as in love with him.

They kissed long and hard before they left the room, and then left the hotel together through the back door. Max and Sam took care of all the necessary arrangements. They were driving to the airport in the same car, as their flights were almost at the same time, hers to Zurich, and his to Boston. And then finally, their last moments came. She kissed him before they left the car, and then only stood looking at him sadly in the airport. She could not kiss him there, and he understood that. It was the burden of who she was, which he now fully accepted.

"I love you," she said, standing two feet away from him and facing him. "Thank you for a wonderful weekend," she said politely, and he smiled. She was always gracious and polite, even when she was worried, like after the paparazzi.

"I love you too, Cricky. Everything's going to be all right. Try not to worry too much about the paparazzi." She nodded and said nothing. And then, unable to stop herself, she reached out and touched his hand, and he held it. "It's going to be all right," he told her in a whisper. "I'll see you soon, all right?"

She nodded, with tears in her eyes. She mouthed the words *I love you* again, and almost as though she had to tear herself away from him, she walked slowly to her plane, with Max and Sam carrying her bags, and Parker picked up his and went to check in for his flight. He turned to look at her as she walked away. She turned and smiled bravely at him, with one hand raised for him, and then touched her heart, as from across the airport and the worlds that separated them, he touched his.

# Chapter 16

Christianna had a busy week after she went back to Vaduz. She had a series of official engagements and appearances, and her father gave two dinner parties in Vaduz back to back on Tuesday and Wednesday nights. It was Thursday morning, as she dressed for an official lunch her father had asked her to attend, that her secretary walked in, and without a word handed her the British *Daily Mirror*. Until then, she and Parker had e-mailed each other constantly, and been reassured that nothing had turned up in the press. And now here it was. The British got it first. And they had a field day with it. They always did.

The headlines were glaring, and the photograph showed her beaming up at Parker, looking ecstatic and blissful, as he smiled down at her with an arm around her. It was instantly obvious that they were either madly in love, lovers, or both. She always felt stupid when she looked at photographs of herself on the front page. And normally, they were not in a romantic context. That had only happened to her once, and never again, and she had been very young. She had been extremely cautious since then. Except this one time with Parker, when it mattered so much, and she had walked right into them on the heels of Madonna. It was such rotten luck. She stared at it with a look of devastation.

The headline was succinct, and fortunately not seamy, although it might have been. But even what it said was not what she wanted said about them. "Hot new Romance in Liechtenstein: Princess Christianna . . . and who is her Prince Charming?" The text said that they had been seen leaving the Ritz Hotel in Paris, presumably during a romantic weekend. It commented that they made a handsome pair. And then it referred to the fact that her brother's romances were legion, and usually his sister's doings were more discreet, so this must be the The Big One. She could just imagine her father's face when he read it.

She quickly e-mailed Parker to give him a heads-up. She told him what newspaper and that it had made the front page. He could look it up on the Internet. That was all she said. She was in too big a hurry to say more, and rushed off to the official luncheon given by her father. As she would have expected, he said nothing about it during lunch. It wasn't her father's style to drop hints or do things by half measures. He preferred to confront things head-on, just as he did with her brother.

It was only after their guests had left the palace that he asked her if she could spare a few minutes of her time, and she knew what was coming. It had to be. She couldn't appear on the front page of a London newspaper, with a man he'd never heard of, caught during a romantic tryst, and have him choose to ignore it. That would be too much to ask.

She followed him to his private sitting room and waited till he sat down, and then she did the same. He glanced at her for a long moment with a look of displeasure mixed with grief. For an interminable amount of time, he said absolutely nothing and neither did Christianna. She wasn't going to bring the subject up, in case by some miracle she got a reprieve and this was about something else, but of course it wasn't. He finally began.

"Christianna, I suppose you know what I want to talk to you about." She tried to look expectant, innocent, and blank, but failed abysmally. She could feel guilt creep all over her face, and finally she nodded.

"I think I do," she said in barely more than a whisper. Her father was always kind to her, but he was nonetheless the reigning prince and could have a daunting way about him, when he chose to. And after all, he was her father, and she hated to incur his wrath, or even his displeasure.

"I assume you saw the photograph in the *Daily Mirror* this morning. I'll admit the photograph is lovely of you, but I was somewhat curious about the identity of the gentleman beside you. I didn't recognize him." So clearly he was not a royal, since her father knew them all. He somehow implied, without ever saying it, that it must have been a tennis teacher or something of the kind. "And you know, I'm not terribly fond of reading about my children in the press. We get an opportunity to do quite a lot of that with your brother. I don't usually recognize any of his friends either." It was a slam at Parker, suggesting that he was the male equivalent of the kind of lowlife Freddy went out with, which was not the case. Parker was educated and decent, a doctor, and from a nice family. All the women Freddy went out with were actresses, models, or worse.

"It's not at all like that, Papa," Christianna said, trying to sound calm, but feeling panicked. They were not off to a great start. She knew her father, and he was not at all pleased. "He's a lovely man."

"I hope so, if their report is accurate and you spent the weekend at the Ritz with him. May I remind you that you told me you were going there just to go shopping?" His eyes were filled with reproach and displeasure.

"I'm sorry, Papa. I'm sorry I lied to you." She figured that abject apology was the only way to go, and she was ready to grovel if he would allow her to see Parker. "It was wrong of me, I know."

He smiled gently at that. "You must really love this man, Cricky, if you're willing to eat that much crow." And it hadn't escaped him either that they looked ecstatic together, which was why he was so worried. "All right, let's get this over with. Who is he?"

She paused for breath for a long time. She was terrified she wouldn't do it right. And their whole future rested on whether or not she did. It was an awesome burden.

"We worked together in Senafe, Papa. He's a doctor, doing AIDS research at Harvard. He was with Doctors Without Borders, and then continued his research with us at the camp. Now he's back at Harvard. He's Catholic, from a solid family, and he's never been married." It was all she could think of to say at one gulp, but the data she offered her father was respectable at least, and painted a decent portrait of Parker.

The nature of the information she gave him was all he needed to know, particularly the fact that he was Catholic and had never been married. His heart sank. "And you're in love with him?" This time she didn't hesitate. She nodded. "Is he American?" She nodded again. It answered his most important question. He was an American commoner, and not suited to a princess, the daughter of a reigning prince, for anything other than as an acquaintance.

"Papa, he's a really lovely man. He comes from a good family. Both his father and brother are doctors. They come from San Francisco." He didn't care if they came from the moon by rocket ship. He had no title. It was an entirely unsuitable match for her, in his opinion. And he knew the Family Court and members of Parliament would agree with him, although he could have overruled them, if he wished. And Christianna knew that, too. She also knew that he would never use his powers to allow her to marry a commoner. It went against everything he believed.

"You know you can't do that," he told her gently. "You'll only make yourself, and him, miserable if you continue to see him. You'll wind up with a broken heart, and so will he. He's a commoner, Christianna. He has no title. He's not even European. It's out of the question, if you're asking me what I think you are." His face was rigid, and she was already in tears.

"Then let me just see him. I won't marry him. We could meet from time to time. I promise I'll be discreet."

"I assume you were discreet this weekend, in Paris, unless you're even more foolish than you've been, and I don't think you are. And the press still discovered you, and look at what it looks like. A Serene Highness having assignations with men in hotel rooms. That's not very pretty."

"Papa, I love him," she said with tears running down her cheeks.

"I'm sure you do, Cricky," he said gently. "I know you well enough, I think, to believe you wouldn't do this lightly. Which makes this even more dangerous for you. You cannot marry him, ever, so why would you carry on a romance that will only break your heart and his? It isn't even fair to him. He deserves to be in love with someone he can marry. And you're not that person. One day, when you marry, it will have to be a person of royal birth. It's in our constitution. And the Family Court would never in a hundred years approve him."

"They would if you told them to. You can overrule them." They both knew he could. "Other princes and princesses all over Europe marry commoners these days. Even crown princes. It happens everywhere, Papa. We're a dying breed, and if we find the right person, even if not of royal birth, wouldn't you rather have me marry a good man, who loves me and will be kind to me, than a bad one who happens to be a prince? Look at Freddy," she threw at him, and he winced. "Would you want me to marry a man like him?" Her father shook his head. That was a whole other subject, but she was using everything she could, knowing full well how much Freddy upset him.

"Your brother is a special case. And of course I want you to marry a good man. But not all princes are derelicts like Friedrich. He may grow up one day, but I'll confess, if you came home with a man with his habits, I would lock you up in a convent. And Christianna, I'm not going to do that here. I'm sure this young man is honorable and everything you say. But he is not eligible for your hand, and he will never be. I don't want you seen in public with him again. And if you do love him, I strongly advise you to end it with him before it gets worse. Both of you will only get hurt. As long as I'm alive, it will go nowhere. If you're lonely and unhappy here, we'll start looking around for a husband for you, a suitable one. But Christianna, this one isn't. You may not see him again." For the first time in her entire life, she actually hated her father. She was sobbing when she answered him, and she had never seen him so cruel. As kind as he had been to her all her life, he was now denying her the only thing she really wanted, a life with the man she loved, and his approval. And he had refused.

"Papa, please . . . this isn't the fourteenth century. Can't you be more modern about this? Everyone talks about what a creative, modern ruler you are. Why can't you let me be with a commoner, even marry him someday? I don't care if my children have titles, or are commoners. I'll even give up mine if you wish. I'm not in line for the succession. I could never reign here, even if Freddy didn't. So why does it matter who I marry? I don't care if I'm a princess, Papa, or marry a prince," she said, engulfed in sobs, as he looked at her miserably.

"But I do. We cannot ignore our own traditions, or our constitution, whenever it's convenient. That's what duty and honor are about. You must do your duty, even when it hurts, even when it means you must make sacrifices. That's why we're here, to lead the people and protect them and show them by our example what we expect of them, and what's the right thing to do." He was a purist and an idealist, for her and himself, bound by history and tradition. He made no exceptions to the rules, even for himself.

"That's your job, Papa, not mine. They don't care who I marry, and neither should you, as long as he's a good man."

"I want you to have a good prince."

"I don't. I swear, I will never marry if you do this." He looked anguished as he responded. She loved this young American even more than he had feared.

"That would be a grave mistake. For you, even more than for me. If he loves you, he shouldn't want you to violate your heritage, out of respect for you. You need to marry someone from your own world, who understands your duties, traditions, and obligations, who has led the same life as you, someone of royal birth, Christianna. A commoner would never respect your life. It would never work. Trust me on this."

"He's American, it makes no sense to him. Nor does it to me. This is completely stupid, and cruel." She disagreed with everything he had said, and knew Parker would have too. She was fighting a thousand years of tradition, to no avail.

"You're not American. You know better than to do something like this. You're my daughter and you know what's expected of you. If this is what happened when you went to Africa, I am very sorry I allowed you to go. You have violated my trust." It was everything she had told Parker, and all she had feared her father would say. In fact, it was worse.

He was completely intransigent and inflexible, living in another century, determined to follow tradition and the constitution and make no exception out of compassion for her. He was not even giving her a ray of hope. And worse, he was totally convinced that he was right. She knew he would never relent. She felt as though his words had broken her heart. She was almost in physical pain as she looked at her father in despair, and he looked at her in sorrow. He hated to cause her pain, but he felt he had no choice.

"I want you to stop seeing this man," he said finally. "How you end it is up to you. I will not interfere, out of respect for you. And he has done nothing wrong, so far. You were both foolish to go to Paris, and expose yourselves. You saw what happened, they caught you immediately. You must end it, Cricky, as soon as possible, for both your sakes. I leave the rest up to you." With that, he stood up and turned away. He did not come to put his arms around her because he knew how devastated and angry she was, and it seemed wiser to wait. She needed time to accept everything he had said, to make her peace with it, and tell this man. All he wanted and all he hoped now was that she would forgive him one day. But he was doing what he was convinced was right for her.

She stood up and looked at him in disbelief. She couldn't believe he was willing to do this to her. But he was. He felt it his duty, and had pointed out hers to her. And then, still crying, she turned and left the room without another word. There was nothing left to say.

When she returned to her apartment in the palace, she told her secretary to cancel her appointments and appearances for the rest of the
day, the rest of the week in fact. She closed her bedroom door then,
and called Parker in the States. He answered instantly, and had been
waiting to hear from her. He had suspected that since the photograph
had hit the newspapers, she would be talking to her father about it,
and he would have something to say. Christianna was sobbing when
he answered the phone. It didn't bode well for what her father had
said to her.

"It's all right," he said soothingly, "it's all right. Calm down." She
tried and failed miserably and finally caught her breath long enough
to tell him in halting words what her father had said.

"He said we have to stop seeing each other immediately." She
sounded beaten, frightened, and like a child again, and all he wanted
was to put his arms around her and console her and give her strength.

"And what do you say?" he asked, sounding anxious. He had been
afraid of this. She had warned him of it since Senafe. And she was
right. It was hard to believe that people in this century could take
such an archaic position, but apparently her father had. The entire
concept of Serene and Royal Highnesses was archaic. But she was in
fact a princess, and like it or not, she had to deal with it. And so did
he, and her father's insistence that she only marry a man of royal
blood.

"I don't know what to say. I love you. But what can I do? He totally
forbade me to pursue this with you. He said he'll never let us marry,
and I know he means it. He would have to override the parliament
and the Family Court to allow us to marry, and he won't." And she felt
wrong just running away. She couldn't do that. She wanted his permission. Parker believed it now, too, and he was as devastated as she
was. To him, this was insane. It made no sense. For a moment, he

thought of suggesting that they meet in secret until her father died, and once her brother ruled the country, she could sneak away. But realistically, Hans Josef could live another twenty or thirty years, and it would be no life for them. Her father had completely boxed her in, and him with her.

"Will you meet me again for a weekend?" There was a long pause while she thought about it. "I want to discuss this with you in person. Maybe we can figure out something." Although he had to admit now that it was unlikely he could come up with a solution that she could live with, and that would be acceptable to her father. She was not willing to just walk and defy him, although perhaps in time she would be. He also knew that the promise made to her mother mattered to her, as well as the approval of the parliament and Family Court. In order to marry Parker, she had to be willing to defy them all. He knew it was a lot to ask. And he was thinking of talking to her father himself, if Christianna was willing, and if the prince would see him. Other than that, he had no suggestions for right now. He just wished he could put his arms around her, and so did she. This was so much harder than he had hoped it would be. All her fears had been right.

"I'll try," she answered finally about the weekend. "I don't know when I can. I'll have to lie again. And we can't do this often." In truth, she suspected that if she met him again, it would be the last time she ever saw him. She could not hide from her father forever, and the paparazzi would never let her, no matter how careful they were. But she wanted to see him one more time. Even if only that, and she was not going to ask her father permission to do so. She was sure he wouldn't even grant her that. So she did not intend to ask. "I'll see when I can get away. It may not be for a while. I have a feeling he's going to watch me closely. We'll just have to e-mail and use the phone for a while."

"I'm not going anywhere," he said calmly. He was trying to sound calmer for her than he felt. He was completely panicked. Thanks to the archaic traditions of her father and country, he was going to lose her. Her father was breaking both their hearts. "I love you, Cricky. We'll see what we can come up with."

"I told him I would never marry," she said, sobbing again, and his heart went out to her. Her pain was as great as his, perhaps greater, because she felt betrayed by someone she loved.

"Let's both calm down before you become the virgin princess in the tower. Maybe if we're stubborn enough over time, we'll wear him down. What if I go to talk to him?" Parker suggested cautiously.

"You don't know him," she said somberly. "He won't see you, and we won't wear him down. He believes in what he's doing." She sounded lighthearted for a moment then, and giggled. "And by the way, I'm not a virgin."

"I won't tell if you don't," he laughed. He wasn't willing to give up on her yet, in spite of her father. It seemed a lot to ask her to run away with him and abandon everything, and he didn't think she would. She had far too great a sense of duty to defy her father and the traditions and constitution of her country. To her it seemed almost like treason. She wanted to win her father over, and convince him. And even Parker was coming to believe it was hopeless. And she had a strong distaste for scandal because of her brother. But Parker was determined to find a way. There had to be one. He refused to be defeated. He asked her to call him back in a few hours, just to talk, and told her to try and calm down. She felt better after talking to him, he was so solidly there for her, and such a good person. But she still couldn't see a way to improve their situation. She knew her father would never re-lent. She wanted to see Parker one more time, and then she suspected she had to do as she was told, and say goodbye to him. It truly broke her heart.

Christianna remained locked up in her apartment for five days. She opened the door to no one save her secretary once a day, when she accepted a small amount of food on a tray. She called Parker and e-mailed him. She took no calls, she went nowhere. And she had no contact whatsoever with her father. He inquired about her many times a day, and was always told the same thing, that she hadn't come out of her apartment. He was grief-stricken, but just as she had no choice in the face of his rigid disapproval, he felt he had no choice either, given the traditions he was bound to uphold, and even the promise he had made her mother. They were trapped in a piece of history, both of them, however painful. And Parker along with them, with disastrous results for all. But no matter how agonizing, there was still no way out, for now.

In despair one night, Christianna called her cousin Victoria in London. She was in high spirits, her new fiancé was there, and she sounded as though she'd been drinking, which was typical. So she was very little help to Christianna in her plight.

"Darling, I saw you in the paper . . . my Gawd, that man you were with is so handsome, why didn't you tell me? Where did you find him?"

"In Senafe," Christianna said dully. She was feeling awful, which was why she'd called. Facing the reality of her situation, she had cried for hours, and had called Victoria for comfort, which she was not very good at. She was too busy having fun to focus on anything else.

"Where?" Victoria sounded blank.

"In Africa. He was one of the doctors there."

"How sexy! Is your father having a fit?"

"Yes, he is," Christianna said miserably, foolishly hoping for some advice.

"Obviously, darling. He's so hopelessly uptight and old-fashioned. Just think how lucky he is not to have a daughter like me. But then again," she said whimsically, "he has Freddy. I suppose that's punishment enough, although I love the boy. He was here last night." Christianna had thought he was in Vienna, but hadn't talked to him in days, not since before her weekend in Paris.

"Papa says I have to end it, and I can never marry him because he doesn't have a title."

"How stupid. Why doesn't he just give him one? He could, you know. They do it all the time here, for the silliest of reasons. Well, not really, I suppose . . . but they could. I heard about an American who bought the title because he bought someone's house."

"My father doesn't do things like that. He ordered me to end it."

"What a nasty thing to do. I'll tell you what, why don't you meet him in secret here? I won't tell a soul." Except her drug dealer, her maid, her hairdresser, her ten best friends, her new fiancé the rock star, and probably even Freddy, some night when they got drunk together, which they apparently did often. Christianna liked the idea but knew it would never work. And if she became one of Victoria's permanent coterie, her father would have Christianna locked up. Victoria seemed to be getting worse, and constantly more outrageous. Christianna was never entirely sure if it was her personality or drugs. Even her father had commented since Christianna got home that from all he heard, Victoria seemed to be completely over the top and he thought Cricky should steer clear of her. Freddy, of course, loved her entire scene.

In the end, talking to Victoria gave her nothing, not even comfort.

She would have loved to talk to Fiona, with her bright mind, sense of justice, and practical ideas, but she was gone, and Christianna knew she would never have understood the delicacy of the situation. She knew nothing about royal life. She had no one to talk to, and no one to offer suggestions or comfort, except Parker, who was as distraught as she was. He was at his wit's end, and all he wanted from Christianna was for her to meet him somewhere, but she couldn't yet. She was waiting for things to calm down, so she wouldn't draw attention to what they were up to, whatever they decided at the time.

The topper, of course, was a call from Freddy. He had gone to Amsterdam, and blithely said he was having a fabulous time doing drugs, and Victoria and her fiancé were with him. Christianna was instantly sorry she had taken the call. He sounded high, and was.

"Well, don't give me shit anymore, my perfect little virgin sister. All those speeches you and Father make me about facing my responsibilities. What a crock that is, while you're sneaking off to Paris with your boyfriend. You're just as bad as I am, Cricky, you just cover your tracks better, with all that holier-than-thou garbage, while you kiss Papa's ass. And you didn't cover your tracks so well this time, darling, did you?" He was nasty all through the call, and a moment after she took it, Christianna hung up. She hated him sometimes. And now she hated them all, even her father. There was so much hypocrisy and tradition, and unlivable rules that bound them. The only one she didn't hate was Parker. He suggested that the sooner she came out of her locked room, the sooner everyone would stop paying attention to her, and the sooner they could meet.

The day after he made the suggestion to her, she unlocked her doors. She went back to doing the appearances she was committed to make. She did everything she was supposed to do, and was expected to. The only thing she wouldn't do was go to dinners with her father, or events with him. Nor would she sit in the dining room with him alone. She just couldn't do it. She was eating very little these days, her heart was aching, and she ate in her room on a tray, with the dog as company. Her father didn't press the point. They nodded to each other when they passed each other in the halls, but neither of them spoke.

# Chapter 17

For the rest of October and into the early days of November, Christianna performed her duties like the princess she was. She eventually began speaking to her father again, although with little warmth and great reserve. He had never hurt her so badly in her entire life, and what was worse, he knew it, and felt terrible about it himself. He was trying to give her as much space and time as she needed to heal. He was impressed that she was still fulfilling her duties, but deeply saddened by her continuing anger at him, although he fully understood why, and even sympathized with her. He just felt there was nothing he could do differently, due to the circumstances. It was an impossible situation even for him. He was locked in by his beliefs, and convinced he was doing the right thing for his daughter.

Freddy had caused one of his scandals by then. He had a fight with someone at Mark's Club. He had been frighteningly drunk, as usual, was asked to leave, punched the doorman, got in a fight with police on the street, and was taken to jail. In the end, they didn't arrest him, sobered him up, and her father's lawyers picked him up and brought him home the next day. He remained in Vaduz under house arrest for the next week, and then went back to Vienna to wreak more havoc. He was becoming a serious problem to his father, and after what he had said to her about Parker, for the moment she wanted nothing to do with him either. She was not on glowing terms with either her father or her brother. And her life in Vaduz got lonelier every day. She was pining for Parker, but he had not come up with any brilliant suggestions, as promised. There were none, and she knew it, but she still wanted to see him one more time, to say goodbye.

The opportunity came finally when her father went to Paris for a week, for UN meetings over the tensions in the Middle East. As a neutral country, Liechtenstein's contributions were valuable, despite its tiny size. And her father was a deeply respected man on the international political scene. He was well known for his integrity and sound judgment.

She called Parker as soon as he left. He was going to San Francisco for Thanksgiving in a few weeks, but he said he could fly to Europe to meet her first. Paris was out, because her father was there. London was always a hotbed of press. And Parker came up with a wonderful suggestion, which she loved.

"What about Venice?"

"It's cold in winter, but it's so beautiful. I'd love that." And there was a good chance it would be deserted and no one would discover them. It was a spring and summer destination for lovers, not a winter one. It seemed perfect to them, and particularly to Christianna. Venice in winter seemed like the perfect place to say a tragic last goodbye.

She made her own arrangements by phone, which was more complicated than she thought it would be. And finally she had to take her secretary Sylvie into her confidence, because she needed a palace credit card to pay for her tickets. She had agreed to meet Parker there.

Sam and Max had already said they would come with her, although they had some trepidation about it, once they suspected who she'd be meeting there. She told them she would take full responsibility for it, and two days later they were on the plane. Sylvie had been instructed to tell her father that she was going to a spa in Switzerland. But he was far too busy with the UN in Paris to call.

She left in darkest secrecy, and was more than a little nervous about it. But no matter what they did to her after this, or said to her, she had to see Parker one last time.

Sylvie had made reservations for them at the Gritti Palace. They had two rooms, as they'd done in Paris, but only planned to use one. And he was waiting for her at the hotel when she arrived. She called him, and he was in her room instantly, and she was in his arms. He had never looked more beautiful to her, nor she to him. She cried when she saw him, and moments later he had her laughing. They were days of laughter and tears, and endless love.

The weather was beautiful and sunny, they walked miles everywhere. They went to churches and museums, ate in tiny restaurants and *trattorie,* avoiding all the fashionable places where they might get caught, although Venice seemed almost deserted at that time of year. They walked through the Piazza San Marco, looking at the pigeons, went to mass in St. Mark's Cathedral, and took a gondola under the Bridge of Sighs, the Ponte dei Sospiri, as he looked at her happily. It was like a dream for both of them, and neither of them wanted to ever wake up.

"You know what that means, don't you?" he whispered, after they glided slowly under the Bridge of Sighs. The gondolier had sung to them, and Christianna was lying against him, totally content, covered in a blanket in the cool November air.

"What?" She looked peaceful and sounded dreamy as she looked up at him with a smile. They had been from Africa to Paris and now to Venice, but the journey they had shared would have to end here. She wasn't thinking about that then, just about how happy she was.

"Once we go under the Bridge of Sighs together, we belong to each other forever. That's what the legend says, and I believe it. Do you?" Parker asked as he pulled her close to him.

"Yes," she said quietly. She had no doubt that she would love him for the rest of her life, but doubted she would ever see him again after this. And then she turned to look at him and told him again how much she loved him, so he would never forget this moment either. The difference between them was that in her head and heart she was freeing him, to go on and lead a life without her, almost as though she were going to die. In fact, her heart was doomed, at her father's hands. She would live her dutiful life forever, and then one day she would retire quietly. She had no intention of marrying some prince her father might introduce her to at some later time. She knew without hesitating for an instant that Parker was the love of her life. And in his innocence, as they drifted through Venice, holding hands and kissing, Parker had no idea what was in her mind. She was planning to tell him on the last night.

On their second day in Venice, they wandered in and out of shops under the arcade. They were mostly jewelers and a few antique shops. They finally walked into one tiny little shop in the corner under the arcade. They had some crosses Christianna wanted to look at, and they walked in, hand in hand. The shopkeeper was ancient, and Christianna spoke to him in Italian about the crosses while Parker poked around, and then noticed something in a display case that caught his eye. It was a narrow gold band with tiny emerald hearts embedded in it. It was obviously antique and well worn, but the color of the stones was pretty, and he pointed it out to Christianna and told her to ask the man how much. He quoted an absurdly low price, and when they both looked startled by how cheap it was for something so pretty, he apologized and reduced the price further. Parker gestured for him to take it out of the case so Christianna could try it on, and she was touched. He slipped it onto her finger and it fit perfectly, as though it had been made for her or belonged to her in another lifetime. The tiny bright green emeralds came alive on her delicate hand. Parker beamed at her, and paid the man as she looked at him in amazement, and then at the lovely band she was wearing.

"I don't know what you call it when you ask a princess to marry you, particularly when you're about to be beheaded by her father."

"A guillotine ring, I think," she said, smiling, and he laughed out loud.

"Exactly. That's our guillotine ring, Your Highness," he said with a very creditable bow, as though he had done it a thousand times. "One day I'll replace it with a better one, if they'll ever let me. But in the meantime, that's so you know I love you, and I mean it. And if we go to the guillotine together, or I go by myself, at least you'll have something to remember me by."

"I'll always remember you, Parker," she said, with tears filling her eyes. And for the first time, as she looked at him, she realized that he knew as well as she did what this trip was. It was their goodbye, either forever or perhaps for a very long time. It would have been hard if not impossible for her to continue to sneak away to see him. It had been nothing short of a miracle for her to be able to do so this time. He knew perfectly what was happening, and so did she. They were storing away memories now, until they met again, if they ever could. Like squirrels in winter, gathering nuts to save for when they were starving. Their life of starvation would begin the day they left Venice. Until then, they were celebrating the abundance of their love. The little emerald ring served to confirm it, and when he slipped it onto her finger and told her he loved her, she vowed to herself and to him that she would never take it off. They referred to it after that as her guillotine ring, which always made her smile.

They visited the Doge's Palace and the Pisani Palace, and then the Pesaro Palace, and the Church of Santa Maria della Salute, and Christianna particularly wanted to visit Santa Maria dei Miracoli, because she wanted to pray for a miracle for them. It was the only thing that would help them now.

They shared their last dinner in a tiny restaurant on one of the smaller canals. A man sang love songs to them, with a mandolin, and whenever they weren't eating, they held hands. They took a gondola back to the hotel, and stood outside for a long moment, in the moonlight, looking at each other. Each moment they had shared in the past few days was etched forever in their minds.

"We're going to have to be strong, you know, Cricky," Parker said to her. Without her ever having said it to him in so many words, he knew exactly that this was the last time they would ever be together, ever or for a long time. "I'm always going to be with you, sometime, somehow. If ever you doubt it, look at your guillotine ring, remember this, and we'll find our way back to each other someday." As she listened to him, she knew that one day he would marry someone else, have children with them, and hopefully have a happy life. She couldn't even imagine doing that herself. She wanted no one in her life but him. And all he wanted was her.

"I'll love you till the day I die," she said, and meant every word of it, while he hoped that wouldn't be for a long, long time.

And then, walking slowly, they went inside for their last night. He made love to her, and afterward, wrapped in their robes, they stood on the balcony, and looked at Venice by moonlight. It was heartbreakingly beautiful.

"Thank you for coming to meet me here," she said, looking at him, and he pulled her slowly into his arms.

"Don't say that to me. I would cross the world for you. Whenever you want to see me, call me, and I'll come running." They had agreed to continue e-mailing each other. She couldn't even imagine a life without contact with him, even if she couldn't see him again. And she had promised to call him, she needed to hear his voice, too. Her father could prevent them from seeing each other, but he couldn't stop them from loving each other. Only time could do that. And for now, they were still deeply in love.

They slept in each other's arms that night, stirring occasionally, touching each other, feeling each other's breath on their cheek as they lay tangled and enmeshed. They couldn't get enough of the feel of each other's skin, or the look in each other's eyes.

They stood in the shower together in the morning, letting the water run over them, and then made love one last time. They were each taking all they could with them. It was going to be a long hard winter for a very long time without each other's touch. All they had now was each other's love.

There were no paparazzi when they left. No one had said anything to them, or asked questions. Max and Sam had left them alone for all three days. The two guards had had a good time visiting Venice together, and when they went under the Bridge of Sighs, Samuel had teased Max that it meant they'd be together forever. And Max had asked him if he wanted to be shot now or later. They were both saddened, though, when they saw the look on Christianna and Parker's faces as they left for the airport. There was total silence first in the gondola, then the car, as they left Venice, and both men walked away as the two lovers said goodbye.

"I love you," Parker said, holding her tightly in his arms. "Remember your guillotine ring and what it means. I would die for you, Cricky. And who knows what happens in life? Maybe one of those candles you lit will work."

"I'm counting on it," she said softly, clinging to him for the last few minutes, and then she had to leave. Her flight was first, and she kissed him again and again until Max and Sam thought they'd have to drag her away. "I love you . . . I'll call you when you get home."

"I'll be right there, whenever you want me, and right here." He touched his heart as he had when he left her in Africa. In his heart, he had never left her since, or even before.

They kissed one last time, and feeling as though she had wrenched her soul from his, she walked away toward the plane. She turned once, waved at him, her head held high, her eyes locked in his. She touched her heart and pointed to him. He nodded at her, never letting go of her eyes, and then she turned, and boarded the plane.

# Chapter 18

Christianna never said a word on the plane, on the way from Venice to Zurich. Several times she looked down and touched the little band on her hand with the emerald hearts. Both men noticed it, and wondered if they had gotten married in Venice, but they didn't think they had. It was obviously something that had some deep meaning to her. She smiled at them as they got off in Zurich, and thanked them both for coming to Venice with her. There was something very quiet about her, sad, distant, and strangely removed, as though her heart and soul had left with Parker, and only a shell was returning to Vaduz, which was in fact the case.

She was silent again when they reached the palace in Vaduz two hours later. They had driven slowly, and she was in no hurry to get home anyway. It had been a magical three days in Venice with Parker, and all she had now was the rest of her life here, in prison. She would have preferred the guillotine to this. A life of eternal duty, to a father who had denied her her dreams, all in honor of her royal lineage. It seemed a high price to pay for who she was, and didn't want to be.

The dog was outside in the courtyard when they arrived. He

bounded up to her, and she patted him. He followed her inside, and she went upstairs to her rooms. She'd been told her father was still away, and was due back that afternoon. They had timed it perfectly.

Sylvie was in her office and looked up at her. She didn't ask any questions. She didn't want to pry. She handed Christianna her list of appearances for the next day and the rest of the week. There was nothing unusual on the list, and all of it promised to be tedious in the extreme.

"I assume you haven't been watching the news," Sylvie said cautiously, as Christianna looked at her and shook her head. Sylvie noticed the narrow emerald ring too and said nothing. "Your father stunned everyone by making a fairly historic speech at the UN meetings." Christianna waited to hear the rest without comment. Sylvie had the same impression as Sam and Max, that Christianna's body had come back, but she wasn't really there. She looked like a robot as she went through the motions, and felt like one. Her heart and soul were on a plane to Boston with Parker.

"What kind of speech?" Christianna asked finally, without any particular interest. But she knew she was supposed to remain aware of her country's political positions, and the stands they took on international policies, particularly at the UN. The meetings in Paris had been important about dealings with the Arab world.

"He took a very powerful position, for a neutral country, on how some of the disputes should be resolved. There's been a lot of talk and comment about it. Every politician and head of state in the world has been asked for comment. He came out for some very strong measures. There's been a lot of criticism from some quarters, and a lot of praise from others. The press will be swarming once he's here. One of his secretaries told me that he has four interviews lined up today. The general consensus is that he was very courageous, and it needed to be said. I think the surprise was that no one expected it from him." In other circumstances, Christianna would have been proud of him. But she was so numb now, she didn't care.

There was also a state dinner scheduled for that night, at the palace, and for the first time in over a month, Christianna had agreed to be there. This was the life she had signed up for, and given up Parker for. Like her father, she was doing her duty. It was all she had left.

She stayed in her rooms after that, unpacked her bags herself, and looked at the photograph of Fiona she kept on her dresser. It was a picture of her laughing, with her eyes wide in surprised delight, her mouth open in gales of laughter. It was how Christianna wanted to re-member her. There were others of the whole team in Senafe, but that particular photograph of Fiona was especially dear to her. It made her think of her as happy forever. And there was another one of Parker, looking straight at her, in the shorts and hiking boots and cowboy hat he had worn at the camp. She looked at all the photographs, and then at her ring.

She didn't see her father until the state dinner that night. He was full of life and seemed very pleased with himself. His speech had caused a major stir at the talks in Paris and around the world. They were surrounded by press for days, which Christianna assiduously avoided. She went about her business quietly and did what she had to. Their eyes met once across the table at the dinner, and then she avoided him. She had asked not to be seated next to him, and in spite of her reluctance to be there, she had interesting dinner partners, and a pleasant evening. It was going to be a long lifetime of these evenings without Parker. It was hard to believe now that the night before she had been in Venice with him.

By sheer coincidence, she and her father were walking up the stairs to the private apartments at the same time. She heard his footsteps behind her, and turned to look, their eyes met and held, as she stopped on the stairs, and he walked up quietly and stood next to her.

"I'm sorry, Cricky," he said softly, and she knew what he was referring to.

"Me too." She nodded, turned, walked up the stairs to her own rooms, and softly closed the door, as he walked past to his own rooms.

She didn't see him again till two days later. She had to get a paper from his office, and saw him being interviewed. He was all over the papers these days, backing up the position he had taken, although it was becoming more and more controversial every day, and she had already noticed that they had discreetly increased palace security. He had three bodyguards with him everywhere he went, and Christianna suddenly had two. Although there were no direct threats, it seemed the prudent thing to do, and he always was, particularly about her. He had angered a lot of people, despite the fact that a vast number admired him for the position he had taken. Christianna was still angry at him, and would be for a long time, but she admired him for his courage at the UN. He was a man of integrity and strong beliefs.

She had spoken to Parker several times once he got back. He sounded tired, but always loving when she called him. His e-mails were funny and cheerful. Sometimes he sent her jokes that made her laugh out loud. Most of the time he told her what he was up to, how the research was going, and how much he missed her. She said the same things to him.

For the next two weeks she was busy at the palace. She had taken on some new projects, continued doing her usual obligations, and was starting to talk to the foundation about working for them. She had decided not to study in Paris in the spring. She wanted to go to work for the foundation that had been established in memory of her mother. It was the only thing that she was interested in, and made sense for her to do. The week she met with them, Parker was in San Francisco for Thanksgiving. It was a holiday she had enjoyed a great deal while she was in Berkeley. She had gone home with friends each year, and wished that she could be with him now with his father and brother. But that was never going to happen.

She had just spoken to him, when she went outside with the dog, and noticed that her brother had just arrived. He had driven up in a brand-new Ferrari, red typically, and when he saw her, he seemed in a good mood, although she was still angry at him too, over his comments about her getting caught by the paparazzi in Paris. They had seemed rude and unusually unkind to her, even for Freddy.

"How are you, Your Highness?" he teased her, and she gave him a haughty look and then laughed.

"Am I supposed to use your title now?" She laughed at him. He was truly impossible, but he was her brother.

"Definitely. I expect you to curtsy, too. I'm going to run this place one day, you know."

"I try not to think about that." He would never have had the guts to do what their father had just done on the world scene, or the knowledge of how to do it. Their father had skated a thin line between warring forces and opinions, and had come out looking like a hero. Even Parker had been impressed, although he wasn't happy with him these days either.

"What do you think of my new car?" Freddy asked her, changing the subject.

"Nice. It looks expensive," she commented with a smile.

"Rumor has it I can afford it, or our father can. I just bought it in Zurich." She had to admit it was a beautiful car, although he had two others almost just like it, in the identical color. He seemed to have an unlimited appetite for expensive, fast cars, and equally expensive, fast women. He had a new one in his arms at the moment, and probably others no one had yet heard of. It was a constantly revolving harem. "Want a ride?" he offered enthusiastically, as she laughed and shook her head. The way he drove always made her carsick. Even the dog ran away when he opened the car door.

"I'd love to. Later. I've got an appointment," she lied, and hurried back into the palace.

As it turned out, the three of them had dinner together that night. The atmosphere was a little strained, as their father was currently annoyed at Freddy about something, which he didn't want to discuss in front of Christianna. She sat quietly with both of them, enjoying their company for the first time in two months, since the incident with Parker. It was almost December, and they were talking about their plans for Gstaad over the holidays. They sounded like a normal family for once. No one was talking about politics, economic policies, or even what Freddy had most recently done wrong. They were very relaxed, Christianna laughed at her brother's jokes, and their father even guffawed a little, although some of the jokes were somewhat offensive, but as always, they were funny. Freddy was definitely the family clown.

As they got up from dinner, he tried to talk Christianna into taking a ride with him, yet again, in the new car. But it was cold outside, and the road was probably icy. They had had their first snowfall a few days before. Freddy looked profoundly insulted that she wouldn't accept his invitation, and turned to his father.

"What about you, Father? Want a quick ride before bedtime?" His Father was about to say no, but he spent so little time with him as a rule, and was so angry at him so often, that Hans Josef hesitated and looked like he thought he should make the effort. And he was always too busy to do things like that in the daytime.

"If you promise it's only for a few minutes. I don't want to wind up in Vienna, while you demonstrate the efficiency of the engine."

"I promise," Freddy said, looking delighted, with a smile at his sister. It was almost like old times that night, when they were both younger. Freddy had had a passion for great cars even then. Nothing much had changed, except that she had grown up and he hadn't. She had made a comment about it at dinner, and to get even, he had called her his older sister, although he was ten years older, the same age as Parker.

Their father went out into the hall, and asked one of the men in footman's livery to get him his topcoat, and he returned with it a moment later. Freddy had had enough to drink at dinner that he didn't need one. And Christianna followed them both outside. Charles, her dog, was sound asleep upstairs in her bedroom.

There were security guards outside, chatting easily. They had just changed shifts, and didn't notice them come out at first. Christianna thought that was unduly casual of them, given the current increase in their security concerns at the palace, due to the spotlight of world politics being focused on her father at the moment. Within a few minutes, the guards on duty came over to chat with them, but she thought it had taken them too long to get there. She didn't want to say anything then and embarrass them, but she was going to mention it to Sylvie in the morning and have her report it.

"May I assume I'm going to enjoy a civilized ride with you, Friedrich?" their father said with a jocular air. He was in a good mood after their pleasant dinner. "Or will I need a doctor to administer tranquilizers after I get back?" It was his way of warning him not to go 150 miles per hour.

"I promise, I'll be nice."

"Don't scare Papa too much," Christianna warned him, and with that the two men slid into the long, low, incredibly sleek-looking car. It looked almost like a bullet.

They closed the doors, her father waved with the window closed, and his eyes met hers for a moment. There was something sorrowful in them, as though he were telling her again how sorry he was about Parker. She knew he wouldn't change his mind, but he was sorry for the grief that he had caused her. As she looked at him and nodded, as though telling him she understood, she felt Parker's ring on her finger, and the highly sensitive machine took off, with Freddy's foot hard on the gas. She had never before seen a car start so quickly. She was about to go back inside because she was cold, but decided to stand and watch for a minute. She wondered if Freddy had managed to terrify her father yet. He too had liked fast cars in his youth— perhaps it was genetic—but in her father's case, never fast women, only her mother, even until now.

She was watching them, with a smile on her face, wondering when they would turn around, and as she stood there, Freddy slowed the car down, just enough to negotiate a turn in the road, and as he did, and the brakelight came on, there was the sound of an explosion so powerful that it sounded like the sky was coming down. At the same moment Christianna heard the sound, there was suddenly an enormous fireball where the car had been, and the car, her father, and Freddy literally vanished. Her mouth fell open as she looked at it, no one moved, and then suddenly everyone came running. The guards on duty flew down the road on foot as fast as they could, as others jumped into cars and sped toward the blaze, and Christianna began running. Her heart was pounding, and suddenly in her mind's eye, she saw Fiona lying in the mud . . . she kept running and running . . .

there were suddenly sirens in the air, whistles blowing, men speeding past her, and the roar of the fire. She reached the place where the car had been almost at the same time as the men did. They were dashing everywhere, the palace fire engines came, and men with hoses, water was shooting everywhere, and someone pulled Christianna backward. She was dragged away as she stared at all of them. And all she could see was the fire raging, seemingly in midair, there was no car, and beneath where it had been, a huge burning hole in the ground. Her father and Freddy had disappeared into the atmosphere. Someone had put a bomb under Freddy's car. Her entire family was gone.

# Chapter 19

Afterward Christianna could no longer remember what had happened, not unlike the day that Fiona had died. She remembered walking back into the palace, people running everywhere, two security guards taking her to her room and staying there with her. Sylvie appeared, other faces that she knew, and some she could no longer remember. Police came and went, bomb squads, soldiers. Trucks of men in riot gear arrived, Swiss police, ambulances, news trucks. The ambulances were unnecessary. Not even shreds of her father and brother could be found. In the early hours, no one claimed responsibility for the bomb, nor did they expose themselves later. Her father's act of courage at the UN meetings had come at a high price. They must have planted the bomb sometime between the time Freddy arrived and after dinner. But if they had put it under his car, clearly they hadn't intended to kill the reigning prince, perhaps only the crown prince as a warning to his father. With Freddy's excitement about his new car, and the friendly family dinner, they had managed to kill the reigning prince as well, by sheer blind luck.

The palace and the grounds were swarming with men in uniforms all night, and as though in a daze, Christianna insisted on leaving her room with her security guards and walked among them. And as soon as she left the palace, she saw Sam and Max running toward her. Without thinking or saying a word, Max took her in his arms and began crying, as Sam stood by with tears rolling down his cheeks. Both had been with the family for years, and all Christianna could do was stare once again at the still-burning blackened pit where the car had been when it exploded.

At first, only a few people had realized that Prince Hans Josef was in the car—they had thought it was only Freddy, which was bad enough. But news spread rapidly, passed by the guards who had seen him get in the Ferrari with his son. It had been a double tragedy and a double loss for the country, and the world, that night. Christianna was ringed with guards carrying machine guns, and Max and Sam on either side, as she wandered around. She refused to go back into the palace. It was as though by staying close to where they had been when they vanished into thin air, she could somehow bring them back or find them. It was impossible to understand the implications of all that had happened, and all it meant for Liechtenstein. She looked at Sam and Max, and seeing them cry, it began to dawn on her that she had lost her brother and her father. She was an orphan, and her country had no leader.

"What's going to happen?" she asked Max, looking terrified.

"I don't know," he said honestly. No one did. Aside from the personal tragedy it was for her, it was a huge political dilemma for the country. Freddy was the reigning prince's only male heir, and women were not allowed to be considered for the succession. There was literally no one to take his place.

Christianna never went to bed at all that night. It was still impossi-

ble to understand what had happened. Newscasters were everywhere, wire services were sending reporters. After his breathtaking
speech at the UN, Hans Josef was a major piece of news, and the car
bomb was considered important world news. Inevitably, the two
events were intimately linked. Mercifully, a fleet of guards shielded
Christianna from the news teams.

At some point in the middle of the night, Christianna went upstairs
and Sylvie helped her dress in somber black. She came back downstairs, and all of her father's assistants and secretaries were there,
frantically making notes and calls. She had no idea who they were
calling or what to do. His principal assistant came to her, as she wandered around like a ghost, and told her they had to make arrangements.

"Arrangements for what?" She looked blank. She was in shock. She
appeared competent and sane, even calm, but she couldn't get her
mind to understand what had happened. All she kept thinking was
that Papa was gone. She felt five years old again, and could suddenly
remember everything that had happened the morning her mother
had died . . . and now Freddy . . . poor Freddy . . . for all his foolish
ways, now he was gone, too. They all were. She was totally alone in
the world.

She was sitting in her father's office with his secretaries and armed
guards in the room when her father's members of Parliament arrived.
All twenty-five of them, wearing black suits and black ties, with
ravaged eyes. They had been up together, in little groups, in each
other's homes all night, alternately watching the news and crying,
and discussing what to do. They had an enormous problem, one the
country had never had before. They no longer had a reigning prince,
they had no one in line for succession, as he had died with the crown

prince, and women could not even be considered, according to their constitution. Aside from the overwhelming personal tragedy that had occurred that night, it was a disaster for the country as well.

"Your Highness," the prime minister spoke to her gently. He could see that she was in no condition to talk. But they had no choice. They had been together since four o'clock that morning, hours after they'd been called with the news, and had waited till eight o'clock to come to the palace. Everyone, including Christianna, had been up all night. The palace was ablaze with light in the November darkness. "Your Highness, we must speak with you," the prime minister said again. He was the senior member of all twenty-five, and had been her father's chief confidant. "Will you sit down with us?" She nodded, still looking dazed, and they cleared the room of everyone except the guards carrying machine guns. No one knew what to expect next, or if the car bomb had been a single act, a precursor to a broader offense, or even an ambush on the palace. There were Swiss soldiers carrying machine guns outside and in the palace. The Swiss government had offered them immediately and sent them from Zurich.

Christianna sat down, staring at the members of Parliament, and they all took chairs around the room. They were sitting in what had been her father's office, and it felt strange to her that he was not there. For a moment, she wondered where he was, and then like a second explosion in her mind, she remembered. More than anything, she remembered the look they had exchanged just before her brother drove him away. That look of apology and regret that would now haunt her for a lifetime, along with the bitter argument that had driven a wedge between them for two months. They had not even yet recovered, until the wounds began to heal that night, and now he was gone. She kept telling herself she would never see either of them again, and found it impossible to absorb it.

"We must speak to you. We are all beside ourselves with grief over your enormous loss. It is something so horrible that it is truly beyond thinking. Please accept our deepest condolences, from all of us." She nodded, unable to speak herself as tears came to her eyes. She was in fact a twenty-four-year-old girl who had just lost all the family she had. And there was no one to console her, only these men who wanted to talk to her. She recognized each and every one of them as she looked around the room. All she felt able to do was nod. It had been an immeasurable shock, as they were well aware. Her face was so pale, she almost looked transparent.

"But we must also speak to you about the succession. Our country has no leader. It's a situation that, according to our constitution, must be resolved at once. It is dangerous for us to have no one in charge, particularly now." For the moment, the prime minister was designated to handle any national disaster, which this certainly was. But all of them felt uneasy having no one to fill the seat her father had so unexpectedly and suddenly left empty. "Are you able to understand what I am saying to you, Your Highness, or are you too upset?" He spoke to her as though she had suddenly become deaf. In fact, she was overwhelmed at having been left so bereft. But she was still able to understand, if not respond.

She finally forced words from her mouth, for almost the first time since it had happened. "I understand," she was able to confirm.

"Thank you, Your Highness. What we want to discuss with you is who is to take the succession." He was well aware of her family history, and knew each member of the hundred-member Family Court. "You have several cousins in Vienna who are directly in the line of succession. They are related to you, of course, on your father's side. But in fact, when I went down the list last night, at least the first seven of them, or even eight or nine, are not appropriate to even consider. All of them are far too old and some quite ill. Several have no children, so the succession could not pass down through them. And a great many after that are women. And you know the rules about no female succession. We would have to go to well over the twentieth in line, even twenty-fifth, to find a man of appropriate age, in good health, and I am not even sure he would accept. They are all Austrian, and none has had close ties with Liechtenstein, which leads us to a very interesting place.

"Your father was a very modern man, or an interesting combination. He respected all of our venerable traditions, he believed in everything this country has stood for, for a thousand years. At the same time, he instigated a number of new and more modern positions, without ever sacrificing the old ones. He believed women should have the vote, in fact long before they actually got it. And Your Highness, he had great respect for you. He frequently told me how interested you were in our economic policies, and the very astute suggestions you made, particularly for a young person your age." He never mentioned her brother Freddy, it would have been inappropriate now, but the reigning prince had frequently said to several of his ministers that if it were not for their current laws, Christianna would have been far more able to reign than her brother. "We have an enormous problem here," he went on, pausing for breath. "We have no one in direct line to your father, who is truly the right choice for the succession. As we all know, these things are passed on by blood, and often not by skill. But if we are to follow bloodlines, to find someone the right age and sex, we would have to go far down the succession. I don't think it ever occurred to your father, nor should it have, that the crown prince would not reign. But with this tragedy that has befallen us tonight and you, Your Highness, with the greatest respect, I believe that I know what your father would do if faced with this situation. We discussed it at length, all through the night, and we all agree that the only right choice for the succession here is you." Christianna stared at him as though he were insane, and briefly wondered if she was. Perhaps she was dreaming all this, her father and brother hadn't died and she would wake up in a minute, after escaping this hideous nightmare.

"We are proposing to pass a new law, an emergency measure, to be confirmed and approved by the Family Court immediately, to change our constitution and amend it, to allow the succession to extend to women from now on, and in this case, specifically to you. Further to that, we discussed also tonight that we are equally aware that in your bloodline, on both sides of your mother's immediate family, you are related to the kings of France. If you accept the succession in your father's name, and become reigning princess of Liechtenstein, as we hope you will, and your people, I believe, will also hope you will, given your relationship as direct descendant of the kings of France, in this case, we would wish you to become reigning princess as a Royal Highness, and not a Serene one. I truly believe your father would have approved that too, and of course that also would have to be ruled on and confirmed by the Family Court, also immediately. We must fill the succession as soon as possible. We cannot leave Liechtenstein without a leader. Your Highness, I am asking you on behalf of all of us, as prime minister and one of your subjects and countrymen, in your father's name, will you do it?" There were tears literally pouring down Christianna's cheeks as she listened. She was a twenty-four-year-old girl they had just asked to become leader of her country, reigning princess in her father's shoes. She had never been so frightened in her life, and was shaking from head to foot, from terror, grief, and shock. Everyone in the room could see how hard she was shaking. She could barely speak. She was touched beyond words, but felt completely unequal to the job. How could she ever measure up to her father? And a Royal Highness? They might as well have asked her to be queen. And in a way, they just had. She liked the idea of women being accepted into the line of succession, and always thought they should be, but she felt so much less capable than one needed to be to take on such an overwhelming task.

"But how could I do that?" She was crying so hard she could barely speak.

"We believe you can. And I feel absolutely certain your father thought so, too. Your Highness, I am asking you, begging you, come to your country's aid tonight. We will do all we can to support you, and help you. No reigning prince has ever felt ready for the job. It is something that you learn and grow into. I truly believe you are capable of it, and that your father would want you to. Will you accept what we are suggesting to you? If so, Your Highness, it will be a blessing for us all, also for you, and surely for our country."

She sat rooted to the spot in her seat, looking from one face to another, and the answer was there in each pair of eyes. Had one of them looked doubtful or hesitant or angry, she knew without a moment's pause she would say no. But instead each of them looked at her expectantly, begging her to do as they asked. They were imploring her, and worse than that, she could almost hear her father's voice from the grave, asking her to do it. She sat staring at them miserably, still shaking, she had never been so frightened or sad in her life. And almost as though a power stronger than she were forcing her to, she slowly nodded her head, unable to believe what she was doing. This was for the rest of her life, until she died. Now she would have to carry the same burdens he had. She would have to live for her country and no longer for herself. Duty would no longer be just a word to her, it would be a way of life she could never escape. But even as she thought of it, backing away from it like a horse from its stall in terror, she looked the prime minister in the eye and spoke in the merest whisper.

She said a single word as she looked at them. "Yes."

As soon as she said the word, everyone in the room was smiling and looked relieved. In spite of the terrible tragedy that occurred that night, the members of Parliament were pleased. The prime minister reminded her that Elizabeth had become Queen of England at twenty-five, and it was a far bigger country and greater responsibility. There was no doubt in his mind or those of everyone else in the room that she could rule Liechtenstein, and well, at twenty-four. Christianna looked totally amazed.

He then told her what would happen next. "Each of us will call four members of the Family Court, to put both of these proposals before them. That you will be the reigning princess of Liechtenstein, as the first woman to do so, and hereafter women will be allowed the succession, and that your title will be Royal Highness now, due to your mother. There are twenty-five of us, and we will contact the entire Family Court today. If they vote in your favor, and ours, we will hold a private investiture tonight, in this office. It is my most ardent hope that that will happen. Liechtenstein cannot be without a leader, and we sincerely believe that you are the best person, the right person, and the only person for the job." He stood then, looked at her and around the room, and added, "May God be with us all, and with you, Your Highness. I will call you with the results this afternoon." And then, before she could catch her breath or change her mind, they filed out of the room. She stood there for a long moment after they left, and looked at the portraits or her great-grandfather, grandfather, and father that hung there. She looked into her father's eyes in the portrait that was so very like him, and sobbing, she left the room.

# Chapter 20

Three men with machine guns walked Christianna upstairs to her bedroom, where Sylvie was waiting for her. She looked as shaken as everyone else in the palace that night. She looked frightened and exhausted and grief-stricken. Prince Hans Josef had been a wonderful man. And before Christianna had even fully entered the room, she reminded her that they had a funeral to plan. A state funeral, for both of them, the reigning prince and the crown prince. Christianna couldn't even get her mind around it, let alone do it.

"Would you like to lie down for a few minutes, Your Highness, before we start?" Christianna nodded, thinking that this woman didn't even know what was coming. If the Family Court voted as the ministers wished them to, by that night she would be reigning princess. It was too terrifying to even think about.

A moment later Sylvie left the room, and said she would be back in half an hour. The three men with machine guns followed her, and stood right outside the door, while Christianna lay down. There was only one person she wanted to talk to now, the only person she knew would help her and support her. She didn't even check to see if she had an e-mail from him. She was sure he had heard by now. However tiny her country was, she was sure that the bomb that had killed her father and Freddy was an explosion that had been heard around the world.

She picked up the phone that sat next to her bed, and dialed Parker's cell phone. Even in her confusion and misery, she vaguely remembered that it was Thanksgiving and he was in San Francisco.

He answered on the first ring, and had been desperate for her call. He knew there would have been no hope whatsoever of reaching her if he tried. Everything he had seen on the news had suggested chaos at the palace in Vaduz.

"My God . . . Cricky? . . . Are you all right? . . . I'm so sorry . . . I'm so sorry . . . I heard it on the news." She listened to his voice and just sat there and sobbed. "Sweetheart, I'm so sorry this happened. I couldn't believe it when I saw it." The news had shown a blazing fire on the palace grounds, and soldiers and riot police running everywhere. The palace looked completely overrun. To Parker's dismay, there had been almost no mention of her whatsoever. All he knew was that she was alive.

"Neither could I," she said miserably, trying not to remember it again . . . that awful moment when the car had turned into a ball of flame, taking her father and Freddy with it. "I was standing right there when it happened."

"Thank God you weren't in the car with them." At first he had been afraid she was. And as he said it, she suddenly remembered that Freddy had offered her the ride first, and she had declined. It was the hand of fate. "Are you all right? I wish I were there to help you. What can I do? I feel so helpless."

"There's nothing you can do. I have to begin planning the funerals in a minute. They're waiting for me, but I wanted to talk to you first.

I love you . . . something else terrible has happened," she said, sound-ing mournful, and Parker braced himself for yet more bad news. It was hard to believe it could get any worse than this, or even come close. "There is no one else in direct line for the succession. All my fa-ther's cousins are terribly old . . . they're Austrian . . . Parker, they want to change the law about female succession. They're putting it to the Family Court today." She choked on another sob. "They want to make me reigning princess . . . oh my God, how could I ever do that? I don't know anything about it, I could never do the job . . . and my life will be ruined forever. I would have to rule the country till I die, or pass on the succession to one of my children one day . . ." She was crying so hard she could barely speak, but he had heard every word she said. Thousands of miles away, he looked as shocked as she had. He couldn't even begin to imagine what that meant.

"And they want to make me a Royal Highness, because of my mother, not Serene."

"You've always been royal to me, Cricky," he said gently, trying to soften the blow for her. It seemed like an awesome responsibility, even to him. But like her ministers, he didn't doubt for a moment that she could do the job. He knew she could, and would do it well. He didn't even have the remotest idea of what it meant for them. And all he could think about was how worried he was about her. Not only did she have to face the grief of losing her family, but now she had to take over running a country as well. It was truly beyond belief.

"Parker . . . ," she said, choking on sobs, "I'll die an old maid." She sounded like a child as she wailed, and all he wanted was to put his arms around her.

"I don't see why that has to be the case. Your father was married and had children. Queen Elizabeth of England was married and had four kids, and I don't think she was much older than you are when she became queen. I don't see why one has to exclude the other," he said sensibly, trying to calm her down. The one thing he didn't see was how he fit into the picture now. If anything, it seemed worse for them. With her new status as a Royal Highness and no longer a Serene one, he was even less likely to be considered suitable for her. The only difference now was that she would be making the rules, and he couldn't help wondering if that changed anything. Her father had had the power to allow her to marry a commoner, and refused to use it. But Parker had absolutely no idea if the prince could have married one himself, and in Cricky's current grief-stricken state, he wasn't about to ask. He knew that other monarchs had married commoners, particularly in Scandinavian countries, and he vaguely remembered they had given them titles and everything was all right. For the moment, Doctor was good enough for him, he wasn't going to worry about the rest. She had enough on her mind right now. He didn't want to add his concerns.

"Queen Elizabeth was twenty-five!" Christianna corrected him in a choked tone, and this time he laughed.

"I think you're up to it by a year. Do you want them to wait a year?" he teased.

"You don't understand," she said, sounding miserable and very young. "If the Family Court says yes, there will be a private investiture tonight . . . I will be reigning princess by tonight . . . how am I ever going to do that?" She was crying harder again. The poor thing had lost her father and her brother only hours before, and now they were putting a whole country on her back. It would have been a lot for anyone to swallow at one gulp.

"Cricky, you can do it. I know you can. And just think, now you can make all the rules."

"I don't want to make the rules. I hated my life before, now it will be worse . . . and I'll never see you again." She couldn't stop crying, and he wished more than ever that he could hold her and calm her down. She had so much to go through in the coming days.

"Cricky, now you can do anything you want. We'll see each other again . . . don't worry about it. Whenever you can see me, I'll be there. And if you can't, I love you anyway."

"I don't know what I can do. I've never been reigning princess before, and I don't want to be." But she knew she couldn't refuse. She felt as though she owed it to her father to take this on, so she had agreed.

Sylvie stuck her head in the door at that point, and tapped her watch. They had to get to work. They had state funerals to organize, two of them. Christianna was beside herself. She didn't even have time to properly mourn her father and brother, no chance to absorb what had happened, and within hours she would have a country to run, and thirty-three thousand people she would be responsible for. The very prospect of it was terrifying, and he could hear it in her voice.

"Cricky, you have to try to calm down. I can't even imagine how awful this must be. But you have to do everything you can to hang on now. You can't afford to do anything else. Call me anytime you want. I'm right here, sweetheart. I love you. I'm right there with you. Now try to be strong."

"I will . . . I promise . . . do you think I can do it?"

"I know you can." He sounded loving and calm.

"What if I can't?" Her voice shook as she asked.

"Then you fake it for a while and figure it out as you go. No one will ever know the difference. You're the boss. All you have to do is act like it . . . maybe start with a few beheadings. Something like that," he teased, but she didn't smile. She was completely overwhelmed.

"I love you, Parker . . . thank you for being there for me."

"I always am, baby . . . I always am."

"I know." She promised to call him back later, and went to find Sylvie in her office. She already had mountains of papers on her desk. Christianna had to make the decisions, and Sylvie and her father's staff would do the rest. All she had to do was plan their funerals right now. She would worry about the rest later. And everywhere she went, men with machine guns went with her. They were still on high alert.

The first thing Christianna did was plan two state funerals. One in Vienna, the other in Vaduz. There were no bodies to lie in state, she realized with horror. So she and Sylvie planned a mass at St. Stephen's Cathedral in Vienna, and the following day, they would have one at St. Florin's in Vaduz. It was Thursday, and they planned the first one for the following Monday, and in Vaduz the day after. She had to select the music and decide what kind of flowers. They decided to have two empty caskets at the service, and a reception afterward at Palace Liechtenstein. The security considerations were enormous, given what had happened. And the same would be true in Vaduz.

She worked on it all day with Sylvie and her father's staff, and was still hard at work on it, with no sleep the night before, when the prime minister called her, and Sylvie handed her the phone. She said that he wouldn't say what it was about. Christianna knew, but they had told no one yet.

"They approved it," he said in a serious voice, and as she heard it, Christianna gasped. In some tiny part of her, she had hoped they wouldn't. But they had. Now she had to live with the consequences of accepting their offer that morning. "They also named you a Royal

Highness. We are very proud, Your Highness. Can you do it at eight o'clock tonight?" It was already after six. "I thought perhaps we could do it in the chapel. Is there anyone you want there other than your ministers, Your Highness?" She wanted Parker there, but it wasn't possible. The only other people she wanted were Sylvie, Sam, and Max. They were her best friends now, and the only form of family she had left. She would have asked Victoria to come, but there wasn't time.

"We'll announce it to the press tomorrow morning, to give you a night of rest. Will that be all right, Your Highness?"

"Absolutely. Thank you," she said, trying to sound gracious rather than terrified. She remembered that Parker had said to fake it for a while, and no one would know. And she realized as she hung up, after thanking the prime minister again, that after eight o'clock that night, from now on everyone would address her as "Your Royal Highness." Everything in her life had changed in the blink of an eye . . . with the explosion of a car . . . It was impossible to absorb all that was hap-pening. The Family Court had voted unanimously to let her reign. All she could do now was pray that she didn't let them down, and work as hard as she could for the rest of her life to make sure that was the case. But her father's shoes seemed too big to fill, especially with feet as small as hers.

"We have to go to the chapel at eight o'clock," she said to Sylvie as she hung up. "And I need Sam and Max."

"Is there a mass?" She looked puzzled. She hadn't planned it or notified anyone. Christianna looked ravaged and vague.

"Sort of," she said. "It's just the members of Parliament and us." Sylvie nodded and went to notify Sam and Max. It was seven by the time she found them. At a few minutes before eight, Christianna and the others left her father's office for the chapel. And as they did, she couldn't help thinking that twenty-four hours before, her father and brother had been alive.

She had had a call from Victoria that afternoon, offering her condolences, and telling Christianna that when it was all over, she should come and stay with her in London. Christianna realized that from now on she couldn't do any of those things again. From today on, when she went anywhere, it was a state visit. Her life would be even more complicated than it had been before. And in much greater danger, given what had happened.

When they got to the chapel, the ministers and the archbishop were waiting for them. The ministers looked solemn, and the archbishop kissed her on both cheeks. He said it was both a happy occasion and a sad one. He spoke about her father for a few minutes, and as Sylvie, Sam, and Max realized what was happening, all three of them began to cry. It had never even occurred to them that this could happen.

The prime minister had had the foresight to get Christianna's mother's crown out of the vault, and her father's sword for the archbishop to use for the investiture. The prime minister gently set the crown on her head, and she knelt before the archbishop in the simple black dress she'd worn all day, as he touched her on each shoulder, after reciting the traditional rites in Latin, and declared her Her Royal Highness Christianna, reigning princess of Liechtenstein, as rivers of tears ran down her face. Other than her mother's crown, which was heavy with diamonds and dated back to the fourteenth century, the only piece of jewelry she was wearing was the narrow band of heart-shaped emeralds that Parker had given her in Venice, which had never left her finger since then.

She turned to face her ministers and her three faithful employees, still crying, as the archbishop blessed them all. She looked at her new subjects, and seemed like a very young girl, in the heavy crown and her plain black dress, that she had been wearing since that morning, as she planned her father's and brother's funeral. She looked like a child playing dress-up in the crown, but however young or frightened she was, she was now Her Royal Highness Christianna, reigning princess of Liechtenstein.

# Chapter 21

The state funeral at St. Stephen's Cathedral in Vienna for her father and Freddy was a ceremony of great pomp and circumstance. The cardinal of Vienna, two archbishops, four bishops, and a dozen priests stood on the altar. Christianna herself sat alone in the front pew, with armed guards all around her. The announcement of her investiture had been made three days before. And she walked behind the empty caskets both coming in and going out of the cathedral, with guards carrying machine guns following her closely.

The service itself took two hours, with the Vienna Boys' Choir singing. She had them play all the music that she knew her father loved. It was a somber, heart-rending service, and Christianna cried as she sat alone, with no one to comfort her or hold her, or even hold her hand. From where they stood near her, Max's and Sam's hearts went out to her, but there was nothing they could do for her. As the reigning princess, she had to stand alone now, no matter how hard the moment or agonizing the task. Her life as Her Royal Highness, reigning princess of Liechtenstein, had officially begun.

When they sang the Ave Maria, tears poured down her cheeks, as she stood with her eyes closed in a black dress and coat and a big black hat with a heavy veil.

And then, when it was over, she walked slowly down the aisle of the cathedral, behind the two empty caskets, thinking of her father and Freddy. People in the church whispered about how beautiful she was, and so agonizingly young to have to face so much.

There were two thousand mourners, all by invitation. Heads of state and royals from all over Europe had come. And afterward they entertained them all at Palace Liechtenstein in Vienna. It was the longest day of her life. Victoria was there, but she barely saw her. Victoria still couldn't get over the astounding fact that her cousin was now the reigning princess of Liechtenstein. Christianna couldn't get over it herself. She was still in shock.

She talked to Parker before and after the funeral, and she sounded utterly exhausted. And at nine o'clock that night, they began the drive from Vienna, to arrive at the Vaduz palace shortly after three A.M. They traveled in convoy, with lead and chase cars ahead and behind them. No group had as yet claimed responsibility for the car bombing that had killed her brother and father. And the security they were surrounding her with was immense. She was already sad and lonely, and she had only been reigning princess for three days. She knew that once she truly began the job of reigning, it would be even worse. She remembered now all too clearly how exhausted and discouraged her father used to get on some days. Now that fate was hers.

Sam and Max were in the car with her as they drove back to Vaduz from Vienna, and asked her several times if she was all right. She nodded yes. She was too tired to even speak.

She went straight to bed when they reached Vaduz. She had to be up at seven. The funeral in Vaduz was scheduled for ten the next day. And this one was even sadder, because it was the home she knew he had loved, the place where he had been born, and where he and his son had died. Christianna felt the weight of the world on her shoulders as she walked down the aisle with the empty caskets again, and the music was even more mournful, or seemed it to her, than it had been the day before. And she felt even more alone, in the home of her own childhood, now that they were gone.

The funeral in Vaduz was open to the public, and they opened part of the palace for a reception afterward. Security was so intense that it looked like an armed camp. And there were news cameras from all around the world taking pictures of her.

Parker sat watching it at home in Boston. It was four o'clock in the morning for him, as he saw it on CNN, and he had never seen Christianna look more beautiful. She looked absolutely regal as she walked down the aisle in her hat and veil. The day before, he had watched the funeral in Vienna as well. As best he could, he had been with her every step of the way. And when she called him late that night, afterward, she sounded absolutely drained. He told her how magnificent it had been, what an exquisite job she'd done, and within minutes, she was crying again. It had been the most awful week of her life.

"Do you want me to come over and see you, Cricky?" he offered quietly, but she knew there was no way she could see him now.

"I can't." The eyes of the world were on her. They both knew she would be under close scrutiny for a long time. She could do nothing scandalous, she had to run her country responsibly. Her life belonged to her people now. She had sworn to uphold Honor, Courage, and Welfare, just as her father had before her, and all those who had come before. They had given up their lives just as she had. She had to follow in their footsteps now, as best she could. And more than ever, she had no idea when she would see Parker again. There would be no more stolen weekends in Paris or Venice, where she could disappear for a few days. She had to live the job she had taken on every minute and hour of the day, for the rest of her life.

She was wearing formal mourning, and the day after the funeral, her life as reigning princess began. They barely gave her time to mourn. She had meetings with ministers, with heads of state who came to offer condolences, she had economic policy meetings, had to visit banks in Geneva. She had briefings and conferences and meetings of every possible kind. Within four weeks her head was spinning, and she felt as though she were drowning, but the prime minister told her she was doing a fine job. In his opinion, her father had been right. She was the best man for the job.

She canceled her plans for Gstaad that year. There would be no Christmas for her of any kind. She didn't have the heart for it, and she and the ministers had agreed that there was to be no formal state entertaining for six months, out of respect for her father. Whatever dignitaries she met with, she would invite for lunch. They had already shortened the official period of mourning from a year to six months.

She met with the foundation, and had quiet dinners at the palace with the prime minister, who was trying to teach her everything she needed to know about her new job. She wanted to learn everything as fast as possible, and soaked it all up like a sponge. She and her father had often spoken in depth about his policies and the intricacies of government, so it was not entirely unfamiliar to her. But the job and the decisions were now hers, with her ministers' guidance, of course.

Sylvie was with her night and day. Max and Sam were glued to her. The heavy security had not yet changed, and when Victoria called and said it would be fun to visit her, Christianna told her bluntly she couldn't come. Her childhood days were over now, she had serious things to do. She began her day in her father's old office at seven, and went straight through until late at night, just as he had.

The only thing that had changed was that Parker was able to call her now. But there was no way she could see him, even for a friendly visit between two old friends. She was single and a reigning princess, and every breath of scandal had to be kept as far away from her as possible. She told him that he couldn't come to visit her, not even for an informal dinner as an old friend she had worked with in Africa, for at least six months.

He wasn't pressing her, in fact he was a constant source of support for her. She called him every night when she finished work, sometimes at midnight for her, which was only six o'clock at night for him. He made her laugh sometimes, and she shared no state secrets with him. As much as the man she loved, he had become her best friend.

The press was also fascinated with her, and took photographs of her every time she left the palace. She found it wearing, but also realized it was part of the landscape for her now. Everything in her life had changed. The only thing that hadn't changed in the past month was the presence of her ever-faithful dog. Charles had become an office fixture now, and the staff jokingly referred to him as the royal dog. He was every bit as mischievous, boisterous, and sometimes badly behaved as he had been before. It was only his mistress who had changed. She worked endless hours, missed her father constantly, and had no time to play or relax. All she could think of now was representing her country and its citizens in the eyes of the world. She began to understand more and more the overwhelming sense of duty her father had felt, and each day she thought of him with ever greater respect and love.

And when she wasn't performing tasks of state, in the weeks after her father's and brother's awful deaths, she had to face painful tasks like going through their personal effects. Her brother's cars were quietly sold. All her father's personal things were stored. She hated walking past his empty rooms, and still felt like an interloper in his office, but she was deeply grateful to his staff for their invaluable support and assistance.

Two days before Christmas she was talking to Parker on the phone, and he had never heard her sound so tired.

"Aren't you going to do something for Christmas, sweetheart? You can't just sit there all alone." Just hearing the loneliness and exhaustion in her voice made him sad. She had become the lonely princess in the palace in Vaduz. She had no one to spend Christmas with, no family left to be with her. And when he asked her about it, she said that all she was going to do was attend midnight mass. Other than that, even on Christmas Day, she was going to work. She had so much to learn, so much to do, so many things she needed to understand, in order to do an ever better job. She was driving herself too hard, but there was absolutely nothing he could do to help, other than talk to her every night. Their time together in Venice seemed a million years away. The only reminder of it was the little emerald band she always wore.

Parker was spending Christmas with his brother in New York that year. He was too busy with his research project to go to California over the holidays to see his father. And on Christmas Eve, she hadn't had time to speak to him that day. She was planning to call him after midnight mass that night.

She ate a quiet dinner alone, with the dog next to her. Thinking of her father and brother, and the happy times they'd shared, she had a heavy heart and had never felt as alone in her entire life.

Max and Sam went to mass with her, they were always with her now. They had become her personal bodyguards. They were with her in the car as she drove to St. Florin's. In Vaduz that year, it was an icy-cold night. There was snow on the ground, but it had been crystal clear all day, and the air was like needles in her lungs as she got out of the car and walked to the church, wearing somber black and a heavy black hooded coat. Only her beautiful face peeked out.

It was a beautiful mass. The choir sang "Silent Night" in German, and as she listened, tears rolled slowly down her cheeks. It was impossible not to think of the overwhelming losses she had sustained, and the shocking changes in her life in the past month. Even Parker was almost a distant memory now, his existence unreal, a disembodied voice on the phone. He was still the man she loved, but she had no idea when they would meet again, and lying in bed at night, she still longed for his touch.

She walked slowly to the communion rail, following the townspeople of Vaduz, who were all her subjects now. And as they passed her in the aisle, even as sad as she was that night, she smiled at them, as though thanking them for the faith they had in her. They had all been so kind to her, and so welcoming, ever since her father's death. She wanted to earn their confidence and trust, and felt she hadn't yet. Honor, Courage, Welfare. She had finally come to understand the meaning of those words.

She was almost at the altar rail, as a man in a pew just in front of her stood up, turned, and she saw his face. She stopped in her tracks and stared at him. She couldn't understand what he was doing there. He had said he would be in New York. He stood there, smiling at her, and very gently took her hand. He pressed something into her palm, and not wanting to draw attention to them, she continued to move toward the altar rail with her head bowed and a smile on her face. It was Parker.

She took communion, still holding tightly to the tiny package he had slipped into her hand, and then she saw Max watching her. He had seen him, and he was smiling, too. And so was Sam. She went back to her own pew then, bowed her head, and prayed, for her father and brother, the people she owed so much to, and finally for Parker. She lifted her face finally, and with the longing of ages, she was looking at his back, and loving him more than she ever had.

When mass ended, she waited in her pew until he was nearly in front of her, and then he stopped to let her get out. She looked up into his face, thanked him, as people smiled at her, and he quietly followed her out. She shook hands with many of her subjects that night outside the church. Parker stood among them, and she looked into his face with unbridled love as he approached.

"I just came to say Merry Christmas," he said, smiling at her. "I hated the thought of your being alone."

"I don't understand," she said, not wanting to give anything away.

"I'm staying in Zurich, and I'm going back in the morning, to spend Christmas with my brother and his kids."

"When did you arrive?" She still looked confused. Had he been there for days? But she had talked to him in Boston the day before.

"Tonight. I just came for midnight mass." The thought of what he had done touched her heart. He had come for hours just so she wouldn't feel alone. She wanted to tell him she loved him, but she couldn't with so many people around. Max and Sam came closer and said hello to him. It was obvious that the foursome were old friends. She had slipped his little package into her pocket, and she had nothing to give him but her love.

"I can't take you home with me," she whispered, and he laughed.

"I know," he whispered back. "I'll come to visit some other time. In five or six months. I just wanted to give you that," he pointed to her pocket, and as they walked away from the church together, with Max and Sam on either side of her, she reached for Parker's hand again and held it tight.

As they walked, she was surrounded by people who wanted to see her and touch her. She wished them Merry Christmas and thanked them, and then turned to Parker with an aching heart. "How can I thank you?"

"We'll talk about it. I'll call you when I get back to the hotel." And then with a little bow to her, just like the bows all of her subjects made, he smiled at her, walked back to the car he had rented, glanced at her one more time, and drove off. He had been like a vision who had appeared to her, and disappeared into the night. It was the most amazing thing anyone had ever done. She reached into her pocket and felt the little package as she got into her own car with Sam and Max. Parker had done it perfectly. No one had suspected anything. He had been there when she needed him, just as he always was, and then he was gone. He had cost her nothing, and given much.

She waited until she was alone in her bedroom to open the little package he had left with her. It felt like it was wrapped in cotton, and it was so small she couldn't guess what it was. She wished she had been able to give him something in return.

She unwrapped it carefully, first taking the paper off, and then pulling the cotton off, and when she saw it, she gasped. It was a beautiful little diamond ring, in an old setting, and she knew instantly what it meant. But how could she accept this from him? Her father was no longer there to stand between them, but now she had a country to run, and a nation of people to represent. It was no more possible than it had been three months ago, if anything it was even less. The only difference was that now she was the reigning princess, and she made the rules and proposed the laws. She could in fact propose a law allowing her to marry a commoner, and ask for the approval of the Family Court. They would give him a title probably, if they decided to honor her request. But after all they had already given her in the past month, it was a lot to ask. She sat staring at the ring in her hand, and feeling like a young girl again, she slipped it on. It fit perfectly, as though made for her. The small diamond was beautiful, and meant more to her than her crown.

She was still looking at it in wonder when he called.

"How can you do this?" she asked him in amazement.

"I wish I could have put it on," he said, with a voice full of love. He had just gotten back to his hotel.

"So do I." But he had done it perfectly. He had slipped it to her so discreetly that no one could possibly have known.

"Does it fit?" he asked cautiously.

"Perfectly."

He took a sharp breath, frightened himself this time, before he asked the next question. "So, Your Royal Highness, what do you think?" She knew exactly what he meant, but she had no idea what to say to him. The answer to that question was no longer hers to give.

"I think you're the most remarkable man I've ever known, and I love you with all my heart." He had actually flown all the way from Boston for one night, to wish her Merry Christmas and give her the ring. And if she accepted it, he was hers, and she his.

"Well?" he asked nervously. "Is it no or yes?"

"It would have to be decided by the Family Court and Parliament. And out of respect for my father, I don't think I could ask them for a year."

"I can wait, Cricky," he said quietly. They already had since he left Africa at the end of July. It seemed like an eternity, but it had only been five months.

"I might be able to announce an engagement in six months," she said cautiously. "But we couldn't marry till the end of the year."

"Maybe by next Christmas," he said, sounding hopeful. "What do you think the Family Court would say?"

"I could ask them to make you a Count, or something equally suitable, in order to make you eligible. To be honest, I don't know what they'd say. What about your work?" She looked worried suddenly. She couldn't ask him to give up everything for her. It wouldn't be fair.

"I'll have finished my project by then." He had already thought about it long and hard for months, and again on the flight here. He was sure. "There's AIDS work I can do here. There's an excellent AIDS research clinic in Zurich." He had thought of everything long before tonight.

"I don't know what they'd say. I could ask. But if they say no . . ." Tears sprang to her eyes at the thought. She couldn't lose him now. But nor could she abandon the people she had promised her life to only a month before. "When are you leaving?" she asked him suddenly. She was dying to see him, but there was no way she could. And he couldn't come back to visit her for months. When he did, they would have to do it right. There was no way she could ever sneak away now. He would have to visit her at the palace and come to court her. It all had to be entirely aboveboard. She had to act with honor and courage, and think of the welfare of others before herself, no matter what it cost, even love.

"My plane is at ten tomorrow morning. I'm leaving the hotel at seven, and I have to check in by eight."

"I have to make some calls. I love you, Parker. I'll let you know before you leave. Just know how much I love you and always will."

"The ring was my grandmother's," he said, as though it made a difference. He had gotten it from his father on Thanksgiving. But it wasn't the ring Cricky wanted, it was him.

"I love it. But I love you more."

She made a single phone call, but he was out. And then she lay on her bed, thinking of Parker all night. He did the same at the hotel. And heard nothing from her before he left. His heart sank as he checked out of the hotel in the morning.

The prime minister called her back at eight the next morning. She swore him to secrecy but asked him the vital questions. He said it had been done in other countries, and he didn't see why it couldn't be in theirs, if she felt it was the right thing. In fact, she had the right now to overrule the Family Court and even the parliament. She had the power, just as her father had before, but wouldn't use it on her behalf.

"It is," she said, sounding jubilant for the first time in months. It was awful to say, and she wouldn't have to him, but even her investiture as reigning princess hadn't meant as much to her as this.

"It would have to be kept quiet for the next five or six months. You can get everyone used to the idea after that. I'll do what I can to help," he said, sounding more like a benevolent uncle than a prime minister. She wished him a Merry Christmas then and got off the phone.

She looked at her watch. It was eight-fifteen. And he hadn't called her before he left the hotel. She had said she would call him. She picked up the phone to call security, and asked them to send Max to her room. Sounding worried, they asked if she had a problem, and she said not at all. She grabbed a piece of paper then, and scribbled a few words. Max was at her door in five minutes.

"How fast can you get to Zurich? The airport," she asked, as she slipped the piece of paper into an envelope and handed it to him.

"An hour. Maybe a little more. Is it rushed?" He could read in her eyes how important it was to her. He smiled, knowing who he was going to see. It was easy to guess.

"It's very rushed. His flight leaves at ten for New York. It's Parker."

"Yes, Your Royal Highness. I'll find him."

"Thank you, Max," she said, remembering fondly the days in Senafe when he and Sam called her Cricky. Those days were gone forever, like so many other things in her life. But others had come in their place, and more were coming still. She hoped Max would reach him in time. If not, she would call him in New York. But she wanted him to know before he left. He deserved at least that after all he'd done.

Max flew from Vaduz to the Zurich airport. He took one of the palace security cars and kept his foot on the gas. He checked for the flights leaving for New York, found the right one, and headed for the gate to wait for him. The flight hadn't boarded yet. And then five minutes later he saw him, looking tired and walking slowly toward the gate, lost in thought. Parker gave a start when he saw Max, who gave him a broad smile and wished him a Merry Christmas, then handed him the envelope Christianna had given him. It was small and white, with her crown and initial on it. C with a crown overhead. He saw Parker's hands shake as he opened it, and read it carefully, as a broad smile spread slowly across his face.

She had written, "Yes. I love you, C.," on the piece of paper. He folded it and slipped it into his pocket, and then slapped Max on the shoulder with a huge grin.

"Can I talk to her?" Parker asked as they called his flight. He was laughing to himself. He had proposed, and she had accepted, and they hadn't even kissed. But they were engaged anyway. Things were certainly different with a princess! He hadn't even slipped the ring on her finger, but had flown all the way from Boston to bring it to her, and only see her for a few minutes at midnight mass.

Max called security at the palace on his cell phone, and asked them to connect him to Her Royal Highness. He smiled at Parker as he said it. They both remembered other days when she was a Serene Highness, but only Cricky to them in Senafe. She was on the phone two minutes later, and he handed it to Parker.

"Did you get my note?" She sounded anxious but happy.

"Yes." He beamed. "What happened?"

"I called the prime minister, and he doesn't see why it couldn't happen. As he put it, they do it in other countries, why not ours? We're getting very modern around here these days. And the truth is, I could overrule them anyway, but we have the prime minister's full support," which would make it easier for them. And she could no longer honor her father's promise to her mother. She smiled as she looked at the ring on her finger. It was the most beautiful sight she'd ever seen. She was wearing it with the emerald band.

"Does this mean we're engaged?" Parker asked, turning away from Max and lowering his voice.

"Yes." She was beaming, too. "Finally," she said with a victorious tone. They had worked hard for this, both of them, and had been patient. Destiny had taken a hand in it, a hard one, but in the end the prize they both wanted so badly was theirs. "He said we need to keep it quiet for five or six months. And I agree. I don't want to be disrespectful to my father or Freddy."

"That's fine with me." He had never been so happy in his life.

They called his flight for the last time, and Max tapped his shoulder, as Parker nodded frantically to him.

"I have to run. I'm going to miss my flight. I'll call you from New York."

"I love you . . . thank you for the ring . . . thank you for coming here . . . thank you for you," she said, rushing to get it all in before he hung up.

"Thank you, Your Royal Highness," he said, as he closed the cell phone and handed it to Max with a smile.

"Have a good flight," Max said, shaking hands with him. "Will we see you again soon, sir?" he asked with a wry smile.

"Don't call me 'sir,' and you bet you will . . . in June, and a lot more after that . . . Merry Christmas!" He waved as he ran for the plane. He was the last one in, and they closed the door behind him immediately.

He found his seat and sat down, smiling blindly out the window, thinking about her. She had looked beautiful the night before, when he saw her in church. He sat there thinking of everything that had happened in a few hours, as the plane circled the airport and headed toward New York. Not long after that they flew over Vaduz, as the pilot pointed out the castle and said that a real live princess lived there. As he said it, Parker smiled to himself. It was hard to believe. It still seemed like a fairy tale to him. He had fallen in love with a girl in braids and hiking boots in Africa. She had turned out to be a princess who lived in a castle, and now the princess was his, and always would be. The story even had a fairy-tale ending. *And they lived happily ever after,* he thought to himself, and grinned. And in the castle, the princess was smiling, too.